CARRIER

*These are the stories of the Carrier Battle Group Fourteen—
a force including a supercarrier, amphibious unit, guided missile cruiser, and destroyer. And these are the novels that capture the blistering reality of international combat. Exciting. Authentic. Explosive.*

CARRIER . . . The smash debut thriller about the ultimate military nightmare: the takeover of a U.S. Intelligence ship.

VIPER STRIKE . . . A renegade Chinese fighter group penetrates Thai airspace—and launches a full-scale invasion.

ARMAGEDDON MODE . . . With India and Pakistan on the verge of nuclear destruction, the Carrier Battle Group Fourteen must prevent a final showdown.

FLAME-OUT . . . The Soviet Union is reborn in a military takeover—and their strike force shows no mercy.

MAELSTROM . . . The Soviet occupation of Scandinavia leads the Carrier Battle Group Fourteen into conventional weapons combat—and possible all-out war.

COUNTDOWN . . . Carrier Battle Group Fourteen must prevent the deployment of Russian submarines. The problem is: They have nukes.

continued on next page . . .

AFTERBURN . . . Carrier Battle Group Fourteen receives orders to enter the Black Sea—in the middle of a Russian civil war.

ALPHA STRIKE . . . When American and Chinese interests collide in the South China Sea, the superpowers risk waging a Third World War.

ARCTIC FIRE . . . A Russian splinter group have occupied the Aleutian Islands off the coast of Alaska—in the ultimate invasion of U.S. soil.

ARSENAL . . . Magruder and his crew are trapped between Cuban revolutionaries . . . and a U.S. power play that's spun wildly out of control.

NUKE ZONE . . . When a nuclear missile is launched against the U.S. Sixth Fleet, Magruder must face a frightening question: In an age of computer warfare, how do you tell friends from enemies?

CHAIN OF COMMAND . . . Magruder enters the jungles of Vietnam, looking for answers about his missing father. Little does he know that another bloody war is about to be unleashed—with his fleet caught in the crosshairs!

BRINK OF WAR . . . Friendly war games with the Russians take a deadly turn, and Carrier Battle Group Fourteen must prevent war from erupting in the skies. Little do they know— that's just what someone wants!

book fourteen

CARRIER
Typhoon Season

KEITH DOUGLASS

J
JOVE BOOKS, NEW YORK

This is a work of fiction. Names, characters, places, and incidents are either the product of the author's imagination or are used fictitiously, and any resemblance to actual persons, living or dead, business establishments, events, or locales is entirely coincidental.

CARRIER: TYPHOON SEASON

A Jove Book / published by arrangement with
the author

PRINTING HISTORY
Jove edition / February 2000

The Penguin Putnam Inc. World Wide Web site address is
http://www.penguinputnam.com

ISBN: 0-515-12736-1

A JOVE BOOK®
Jove Books are published by The Berkley Publishing Group,
a division of Penguin Putnam Inc.,
375 Hudson Street, New York, New York 10014.
JOVE and the "J" design
are trademarks belonging to Penguin Putnam Inc.

PRINTED IN THE UNITED STATES OF AMERICA

10 9 8 7 6 5 4 3 2 1

My thanks to all of you who've written and sent e-mail. Some of you I've gotten to know well, and I'm honored that you've made me a part of your lives.

A couple of you are thinking about trying for one of the service academies. Remember, good grades in tough courses count. Take science, math, anything that will challenge you as much as getting on board the carrier at night will later on. Give me a shout when you pin those butter bars on.

To Joe, who lost his lovely wife earlier this year—peace, brother. All our best to you and your beautiful new baby.

And Slats, fighting the good fight—keep the faith.

For all of you who've asked about the earlier books and how to get them: Sometimes they go out of print for a while, but the publisher assures me that they're still kicking around in the system. I'm letting them know every time I get a question about them.

Just a note before you start the book—we're crossing the international dateline a couple of times, and the time ticks in the book reflect that. Easy way to remember it: If time is getting earlier when you cross the dateline, you add a day. In Hong Kong, it's a day later than it is in D.C., except at 1200 GMT. Hope that prevents some confusion.

1830 local (−8 GMT)
Flanker 84
South China Sea

At times, Colonel Hua Shih of the People's Liberation Army
Air Force thought of himself as a dragon. Not *himself*, exactly—he and his SU-37 together, man and aircraft joined
into a single spirit.

Mythology aside, he had the right to feel this way. The fact
was that the Chinese had invented manned flight in the first
place—no matter what the Americans said. Had not the Chinese been building kites while Europeans were still living in
mud huts and America was nothing but a wilderness populated by stone-age savages? Had not Hua's ancestors lofted
children into the sky on wings of bamboo and silk during
times of war, to spy upon the enemy beyond the city walls?

They had.

Yet today, there were those who considered the People's
Republic to be a fifth-rate air power. They pointed out that
the planes flown by the People's Liberation Army Air Force
were either Soviet exports or copies of obsolete Soviet designs.

As if that mattered. China had been first. Besides, where
was the Soviet Union now, in the scheme of world power?
Where was China?

Hua felt power suffuse him through the control stick, the

throttle quadrant, the rudder pedals. The SU-37 was the very latest variant of the SU family, and by far the finest aircraft in the world. With the sky above, the South China Sea below, and a Lyul'ka AL-31FM turbofan on either side, jointly generating almost 60,000 pounds of thrust, Hua was the master of the eternal forces of air and fire, water and earth.

Glancing over his shoulder, he peered through the fighter's bubble canopy to make certain his wingman, Tai Ling, was in proper position. He was, of course. Like the aircraft they flew, PLA pilots were the best in the world.

Not that they had an enemy they were allowed to prove it against. It was bitter medicine to think that at this very moment an American nuclear-powered aircraft carrier steamed along just three hundred miles to the east. Between there and here, the air and water swarmed with its fighter planes, attack planes, helicopters, cruisers, submarines. The Americans claimed that their assets in the South China Sea represented a peacekeeping force on ordinary maneuvers in international waters.

Ha. As if anyone other than a peasant would believe that. The alien forces infesting the South China Sea were a challenge to China's sovereignty, a warmongering collection of mongrels spoiling for a fight.

But he had his orders: Never approach any foreign aircraft flying outside what the Americans called the "twelve-mile limit"—as if the United States had the right to define a more ancient nation's territorial border.

Things were different in other parts of China, of course. It was only here, in the vicinity of the so-called "Special Administrative Region"—or SAR—of Hong Kong, that pilots were so unreasonably restrained. Hong Kong, he was repeatedly reminded, was a "unique case."

No question of that. In any other part of China, a fighter pilot was revered; in the city of Rolls-Royces and silk suits, he was just an underpaid government lackey.

Hua sighed and looked to the right, toward the coast of mainland China, where the sun was sinking behind the eternal mountains. The ragged peaks cast a long apron of shadow over the sea, creating an indigo haze broken only by small rocky islands here and there. The waters outside the SAR were studded with more than two hundred of these stone teeth. Most were waterless and uninhabited, while others supported entire villages or the estates of the especially wealthy.

His gaze shifted to the island dead ahead, which was of decent size, perhaps as long as three city blocks and half as wide. The central crag was surrounded by vegetation. Hua had flown over this island often enough to know that there was a long pier extending into the water on the lee side. Once he'd seen a small amphibious airplane tied up to the pier. No doubt a millionaire's mansion nestled beneath the trees. Such a luxury of space and possessions, when the most densely populated place on earth, reflecting both filthy wealth and filthy poverty, lay just a few kilometers away. And the most bitter irony of all: If the island were located only a few hundred yards farther north, it would lie outside the SAR and officially within the bosom of the People's Republic of China—as it should.

Hua always imagined diving down and giving the trees a high-speed, low-level pass. That would shake the millionaire up a bit. But Hua's standing orders prohibited him from "harassing" the locals, too.

Sighing, he made his regular scan of his instruments. The radar screen showed the usual clutter of air traffic from Hong Kong's Kai Tak Airport; nothing unusual there. Then his gaze snapped back to the upper left sector of the screen. He flicked on his radio. "Tai, do you register a radar return, low altitude, bearing one three two?"

There was a pause, then his wingman said, "Negative, Colonel."

"I thought I saw movement. Something moving fast, very close to the water."

"Perhaps it was surface clutter?"

Hua frowned and adjusted the SU-37's pulse-Doppler radar. The system was extremely powerful, capable of tracking multiple targets more than forty kilometers to the front and a hundred kilometers to the rear, not to mention straight down. Yet it was true that under the right conditions, even the most advanced radar in the world could confuse moving waves with a moving aircraft.

Still . . . if there *were* a plane down there, it was flying lower than even a cruise missile's preferred altitude. Certainly no jet pilot would fly so close to the surface unless he was determined to avoid radar. And of course, this *was* Chinese territorial airspace by anyone's definition. Which meant that if a plane was down there, it was up to no good: drug running, contraband smuggling . . . or . . .

Hua's heartbeat quickened. Perhaps an American fighter jet had decided to cross the twelve-mile limit.

He flicked his transmitter back to the tactical circuit. "Tai, we're going down to investigate for VID, visual identification."

"But Colonel . . . we're very close to the SAR . . . "

"I'm aware of that, Major. But this is our duty. If you're reluctant to fulfill your duty, I'm sure Major-General Wei will be interested to know why, when we return to base.

There was a pause, then, "I'm right behind you, sir."

Without responding, Hua nosed the SU-37 downward and tried to see what was happening near the water. Unfortunately, visibility was poor at this altitude because golden sunlight hazed the canopy, while the ocean below hid in shadow. On radar, there was no repeat of the fast-moving blip.

He had pretty much given up hope when, at about a thousand meters, he dropped into the shadows. Visibility instantly cleared, and Hua scanned the sea for activity. He immediately spotted a pale, ghostly flicker just above the water, not two miles ahead. It didn't register on radar, but when a flock of seagulls scattered before it, Hua knew he'd found his aircraft. He flipped on his radio again.

"Tai. There is an unidentified jet aircraft flying at wave level. Do you see it? I'm closing in."

"Colonel . . . is this Headquarters' order?"

Hua was surprised. His wingman was usually not much interested in what Headquarters said; Tai was fond of quoting the historic general Sun Tzu's famous edict: "No evil is greater than commands of the sovereign from the court."

"There is no need to report to Headquarters," Hua said.

"Not until I'm sure the situation warrants it." *In other words, until after I have the opportunity to shoot someone down.* "Now, do what you were trained to do and take high station. Remember, the Americans usually fly in pairs, too, so watch for—"

"*Americans?* What makes you think—"

"I feel lucky." Hua was closing in on the intruder now; he eased the SU-37's throttles back to reduce speed slightly as he descended along the fighter pilot's favorite attack vector—behind and above.

He was frustrated that he couldn't immediately discern the intruder's exact shape or size; like any fighter pilot, he was trained to recognize enemy airframes. All he could see was a dim, rakish shape so vague it actually seemed to *ripple*. Then he realized that he wasn't seeing the aircraft itself, but only its pale belly paint reflecting in the smooth surface of the South China Sea. Its upper surface was painted in eerily effective camouflage patterns and colors, and displayed no other markings or identification of any kind.

Hua moved in slowly, a tiger stalking its prey. The intruder still didn't seem to realize it was being shadowed; it kept zipping along at wave-top level without any deviation in course, heading straight toward the big island. Hua frowned. Perhaps the intruder's radar was faulty. Or . . .

Perhaps this whole thing was a trap, and Hua had jumped right into it. He quickly scanned his radar. There was the faintest trace of an image dead ahead—the kind of return a seagull might create.

Stealth, he thought, and his heartbeat increased. Only one country in the world possessed full stealth technology. He moved his weapons selector switch to guns, telling himself he was too close to the target to use missiles, even a heat-seeker. But the truth was he wanted a *real* kill, something personal—not a shoot-down observed from miles away.

He eased closer, closer. Finally, at a distance of only two hundred meters, his heart began to pound faster. Now he could really see the intruder. In size it was considerably smaller than his own SU-37. In shape it was a kind of boomerang, thickened in the middle, and with no tail surfaces at all. Each wing ended in an upright, inward-canted winglet. It reminded him of both the American F-117 and the B-2 Bomber, yet the actual shape was distinctly different from both.

"Tai," he said over tactical, almost whispering. "Do you see this?"

"Yes, sir." His wingman's voice sounded a bit thin.

Hua eased forward a bit more, then held position, thinking. Who was to say this was not some super-secret, experimental Chinese aircraft, something so secret not even the PLA Air Force had been notified that it would be overflying the area? That was possible. And if it were true, and he shot the plane down . . .

He should call this in, but he was loathe to surrender control of the situation. Finally, he settled on a compromise. He switched his radar into targeting mode and his microphone to the international air distress frequency monitored by every aircraft in the civilized world and said, in Cantonese, "Unidentified aircraft, this is SU-37 221 of the People's Liberation Army Air Force. You are in the national airspace of the People's Republic of China. I have you in my gun sights. Please state your nationality and intentions. Over."

There was no response. He repeated the challenge in English. Still no response. The intruder just kept flying along, low and level, with the big island rising out of the water in front of it.

In a minute or two the plane would enter SAR airspace, which would complicate matters considerably.

Hua banked to the left and pushed his throttles forward, drawing up parallel with the intruder, but at a wary distance. Still, he was close enough to notice stealthy details like top-mounted air intakes and a slit-shaped exhaust. He couldn't quite make out the shape of the canopy. It must be tinted to match the camouflage paint; an interesting idea. Regardless, the pilot had to have seen him by now.

Yet there was no deviation in course or speed.

Growing angry, Hua keyed the radio on and issued his challenge again.

No response.

"Excellent," Hua said, and pulled back up into killing position. He switched the radio to tactical. "Tai, you are my witness that I repeatedly challenged this aircraft and received no acknowledgment. It is time to end this."

"You still haven't checked with Headquarters?"

"When an unidentified military aircraft invades PRC territory and refuses to acknowledge official contact, I have to assume its intentions are hostile. There is no need to contact Headquarters. Now, prepare to fire."

"As you wish."

The blurry roar of a high-speed cannon caught him by surprise. Had he pushed the trigger? Then his control stick began pounding against his gloved palm, and he heard the scream of alarm sirens and saw warning lights flashing all over his panel. The plane yawed violently to the left. Hua immediately kicked the right rudder pedal to the floor but the SU-37 kept rotating the wrong way, the intruder vanishing from sight.

A horrible ratcheting sound came from the left engine, and blistering heat washed over Hua's shoulder and back. A moment later the canopy imploded in a shower of Plexiglas shards. Hua's left knee turned into red mist. The instrument panel disintegrated. As Hua threw his head back in anguish, he saw his wingman's plane flash overhead, completely intact, cannon blazing. Through his agony, Hua was briefly confused: At this angle Tai couldn't possibly be shooting at the intruder—so what *was* he shooting at?

The answer must be important. But while he tried to figure it out, the sky vanished, replaced by the glassy indigo surface of the South China Sea. The water was so smooth and dark he could clearly see the reflection of his beloved plane in it, blazing like a meteorite, growing larger and larger and—

Not a meteorite. A dragon.

Falling from heaven.

1900 local (−8 GMT)
Hawkeye 623
South China Sea

The E-2C Hawkeye cut lazy circles in the sky, cruising at its most economical speed of 269 knots. Deployed from the USS *Jefferson* as an airborne early warning aircraft, it carried a crew of five: two pilots, a combat information center officer, an air traffic controller and a radar operator.

"Now, what do you guess that was all about?" Fingers asked in her down-east accent as she stared at the her radar scope.

"Define 'that', Fingers," the pilot, Rabbit, asked.

"Those two Flankers we were watching dropped down to the deck, and now only one of them is coming back up."

"The other one must be lost in surface clutter." Rabbit's yawn was clear over the ICS, the internal communication system.

"I don't know, but the one I see is really hightailing it home." Fingers worked the radar controls with the deft touch of a violinist playing an arpeggio. She tweaked the resolution, added a filter to clear up the surface clutter, then swore softly. Still only one Flanker—where the hell was the other one? "Makes me nervous when our PLA friends play hide-and-seek."

"Relax, Fingers. This is Hong Kong, not the Spratleys. The PLA isn't going to do anything stupid this close to its main cash cow."

"Like you have any idea what the PLA will do," Fingers snorted. But he'd put his finger squarely on her fear—memories of the Spratley Island conflict a few years ago. Back then, the PLA had proven it was willing to do damned near anything to score a victory against the United States.

"Still no sign of Flanker Number Two," she said, tweaking the radar. "Nada."

"Maybe it splashed," Rabbit said. "Piece of duct tape holding the wing on came loose; something like that."

Fingers grunted.

"Come on, Fingers. Russian planes are like Italian cars—

great ideas, lousy execution. You go really fast for ten miles, then the wheels fall off. So just relax; no bogeymen are after us."

"I feel ever so much better now," Fingers drawled, still diddling with the radar, trying to coax out a reassuring image. She'd like to think Rabbit was right, but something told her not to bet on it.

With the Chinese, you just couldn't be certain.

Tai Ling placed his call from a public telephone booth outside the busy tourist attraction known as Ocean Park. Even this late in the evening, the place was overrun with tourists from America, Germany, England, Japan. Tai preferred the view he had of Hong Kong from his SU-37. He couldn't get used to seeing so many foreign faces up close at one time, especially in a city that should be exclusively Chinese.

"What happened?" the voice on the other end of the phone demanded after a single ring. Tai was surprised by the lack of protocol, which before now had always called for the exchange of inane passwords. The sound filter was working, though, imbuing the voice at the other end a constantly-shifting variety of tone, depth and even accent. Tai knew the owner of the voice only by his code name: "Mr. Blossom."

But the big shock was that Mr. Blossom already knew that something had gone wrong during Tai's patrol flight today. Tai had left his commander's office not a half hour ago. Just how far, and how deep, did Mr. Blossom's connections run?

Never mind. So long as Mr. Blossom believed he had a sound investment in the pilot Tai Ling, that was all that mattered. "My lead saw something he shouldn't have," Tai said. "I had to shoot him down. I reported it as an accident; I said he had a flame-out at low altitude and went into the water before he could eject. The incident will not be investigated; Hua was known for occasionally flying recklessly."

There was a long pause, filled with the strange clicks and hums of a scrambler or random line-routing device. Not far away, a fat blond-haired child was squalling furiously as he was led away from the park. Tai visualized the child roasting on a spit.

Finally Mr. Blossom said, "Your lead did not report this sighting?"

"No. He wanted to destroy the aircraft before reporting it."

"Then what you did . . . was the right thing to do. Congratulations."

Tai did not respond. He didn't feel that he had done the right thing, only that which *had* to be done. "The project remains on schedule, then?" he asked.

"Yes," Mr. Blossom replied, and the line went dead.

0505 local (−8 GMT)
Lady of Leisure
South China Sea

"How does it feel to help finance your own biggest enemy, eh, McIntyre?" blared Myron Carstairs, waving a cut-crystal tumbler of Scotch through the air.

Martin Lee winced and glanced at his boss, Phillip McIntyre. But, as always, Mr. McIntyre remained unruffled. He just smiled, his hands folded in front of him, his feet spread slightly on the polished wooden deck of *Lady of Leisure*. A waiter offered him a tray of canapés; McIntyre shook his head politely.

"I don't know what you mean, Mr. Carstairs," McIntyre said. "Financing my biggest enemy?"

"Well, your *country's* biggest enemy. I'm talking about CITIC, right? The bloody China International Trust and Investment Corporation, right? We both know who owns it: the State Council of the People's Republic of China. Now, why would the United States want to be letting the Red Chinese government invest in American securities, eh?"

A few other guests on the fantail of the yacht looked a bit uncomfortable, but McIntyre just continued to smile. He was very erect and trim in his tuxedo, and looked much younger than his sixty-odd years. "I guess they need the security," he said. "Like anyone else."

"Security for what? To finance food shipments to starving peasants out in the countryside?" Carstairs let out an extravagant snort and staggered slightly, his diminutive Filipino wife clinging ineffectually to his arm. Lee frowned. Carstairs had *arrived* drunk, lumbering up the gangplank like a great red bear, his wife staggering behind him. She'd been drunk, too. Still, the Carstairs were among the one hundred fifty wealthiest people in Hong Kong, which made them one of the wealthiest couples in the world. Their invitation to the annual McIntyre Electronics International Victoria Harbor Cruise was a given.

"I run an engineering company, Mr. Carstairs," McIntyre said. "PRC national politics aren't my business."

"You 'run an engineering company?' Phillip, that's like saying Bill Gates runs a software company." Carstairs gulped half his Scotch. "It also means you sell to Poly, right?"

"Poly Technologies is among McIntyre Industries Limited's customers, yes," McIntyre said mildly.

"Never mind that they're owned by the PLA and sell weapons to bloody Libyan terrorists, right?"

"What's the matter, Myron?" a voice called derisively from near the stern rail. "Did someone outbid your firm on a Poly job?"

Yet another guest, Pablo Cheung, stepped forward. "I did read that Poly sold several thousand AK-47 rifles to American street gangs, didn't I?"

"That's right!" Carstair's voice foghorned over the bright tones of Hayden being played by the string quartet on the upper deck. By now, Martin noticed, most of the guests were staring at Carstairs. "Bloody cheap Chinese knockoffs, at that. But gunrunning isn't the big problem, not by a long shot. No, it's what's going to happen when the People's Republic decides it has built its military up enough, and suddenly defaults on—what—eight hundred million dollars' worth of American bonds and securities? What are you Yanks going to do then, eh, Phillip?"

McIntyre raised his hands, palms up. "I'm an American by birth but a Hong Kong resident by choice. This is where my future lies, and where my decisions must be made."

"That's pretty damned evasive."

"There's a proper time for everything, Myron; that's a fundamental rule of both business and war. To quote a popular Chinese sage, 'Make timely and proper change of tactics, according to the conditions of the units and of the terrain— both on the enemy's side and on our own.' "

"Oh, hell, is that Sun Tzu? I might have known you'd be one of those blokes who uses *The Art of War* as a business primer."

"Actually, the quote is from Mao Zedong. Of course, he was a great aficionado of Sun Tzu."

"Mao? You're quoting *Mao*?"

"Even Mao didn't dare take on Hong Kong!" Cheung cried, and raised his glass high. "Here's to the *real* eternal city!"

Several guests on the fantail cheered and raised their glasses in return.

Carstairs snorted. "Where's that bloody waiter? I need a drink."

The Englishman wandered away, wife in tow, and Lee relaxed a bit. As McIntyre's personal assistant, he had been responsible for organizing the yacht cruise this year, and he wanted everything to go perfectly. For most of Hong Kong society, the McIntyre Systems annual harbor cruise was a must-do outdoor event prior to the beginning of typhoon season.

Not that *Lady of Leisure*, with her sumptuous private cabins, multiple wet bars, lounges and saloons, exactly represented "roughing it."

Two hundred feet long, *Lady of Leisure* was a floating mansion under ordinary circumstances; tonight, she was a palace: draped bow to stern with twinkling golden bulbs and silk banners, dotted with buffet tables holding prawns, raw vegetables, hundred-year eggs. And everywhere you turned, you saw another movie star, industrialist, banker, pop musician.

The view from the decks was just as spectacular: glittering Hong Kong to port; dazzling Kowloon to starboard, the cities like fountains of light sliding slowly past *Lady of Leisure*. It would be four A.M. before the yacht returned to her enormous slip.

"Martin," McIntyre said. "Would you come with me for a moment?" Lee followed his boss to an empty spot at the stern raid. "Martin," McIntyre said, "do you feel comfortable keeping an eye on things back here for a while? I want to make the rounds, make sure everyone's happy."

"Of course, Mr. McIntyre," Lee said. He would have said "Of course, Mr. McIntyre" if the man had asked him to jump in the water and push *Lady of Leisure* for the rest of her sedate journey. But in truth, he thought he'd rather push the boat than try to keep Carstairs in line.

Sure enough, not five minutes after McIntyre vanished, Carstairs was at it again. This time, for some reason, he'd cornered Lisa Austin, a world-famous clothing designer.

"So the PRC is getting rich," Carstairs bellowed, "and meanwhile Hong Kong is getting buggered. But we're supposed to think it's a coincidence, eh? Right! The People's Republic takes control of Hong Kong, and within the year the bloody stock market crashes and the rest of the Asian economy goes down the loo? No connection? Bollocks."

"Now, Myron," Lisa Austin purred. She was slim and diaphanous in one of her own creations. "You have to admit, the People's Republic has been very hands-off with Hong Kong so far."

Carstairs snorted. " 'One country, two systems,' right? Well, dear, the only problem with that philosophy is that nobody bloody buys it. Investors are taking their money elsewhere because they know that sooner or later the Reds will nationalize the whole mess, and nobody wants his willie caught in the door when it slams shut."

His wife giggled in the Asian way, with her mouth hidden behind her fingers.

Ms. Austin rolled her eyes. Other guests were discreetly moving away. Time, Lee thought, for polite intervention. "Mr. Carstairs, the New Rule absolutely forbids the PRC from interfering in Hong Kong's internal affairs. And really, why should they? What's good for Hong Kong is good for Beijing, isn't that so?"

"Good God, am I the only one around here with my eyes open? Tell me, Mr. Lee—what was the first thing the PRC did after the Handoff? Eh? They marched that bloody PLA garrison into the city, that's what. Tanks, planes, ships—and *five* generals! To defend us from whom? Indonesia?"

At that moment, as if on cue, a fierce white glare swept over *Lady of Leisure*. Lee looked around, startled. The yacht was crossing the broad reach of West Lamma Channel at the place where it opened into the South China Sea. Captain Chin had, as always, timed the turn to avoid any passing ship that might produce an uncomfortable wake—no easy task in one of the busiest harbors in the world. Lee would have sworn there were no other vessels within a mile of *Lady of Leisure*.

But the searchlight was real enough, its beam growing fiercer by the second, and now Lee could hear the thunder of diesel engines accompanying it.

"What the hell?" Carstairs raised a hand to shield his eyes. "Oh, Christ, speak of the devil."

Lee squinted, and then saw it: the legend COASTAL DEFENSE FORCE HONG KONG in both Chinese and English on the bow of a fifty-foot vessel painted maritime gray. From a radar mast flew the Hong Kong flag—the new one, of course; a red bahinia flower on a white background—as well as the flag of the People's Republic of China.

An amplified voice crackled across the water: "Attention. Attention. This is the Coastal Defense Force of the People's Liberation Army." The words were crisply English, the accent Cantonese. All members of the Hong Kong PLA garrison were required to have at least a high school education, and to be familiar with both Cantonese and English, the two official languages of Hong Kong. "Do not be alarmed. We are boarding your vessel. Everyone remain where you are. Repeat. Remain where you are. . . ."

The throb of *Lady of Leisure*'s engines abruptly dropped off to a burble. There was a slight braking sensation, and Carstairs staggered into his wife, cursing.

"Martin, may I have a word with you?" Lee jumped slightly; he hadn't noticed Mr. McIntyre approach. They moved to the rail, McIntrye smiling blandly. With his silver hair, his sun-bronzed face, his casual silk suit, he looked perfectly relaxed. But his words were as clipped as if he were in the boardroom: "Martin, I don't like the looks of this. I'm going up to the pilothouse to make a couple of calls. Please stay here and keep everyone calm."

"Of course," Martin said. He glanced at the patrol boat, which was slowing as it pulled up to the starboard side. "But . . . what do you think this is about?"

"I have no idea." McIntyre's smile remained in place. "That's what bother—"

The yacht jolted as the patrol boat cut in hard, crunching her metal plating against the fiberglass gunwale just forward of the stern plate. McIntyre gasped. "Bloody hell!" Carstairs shouted, doing a clumsy dance to keep from spilling the rest of his drink.

"Everyone remain where they are," the amplified voice repeated from the patrol boat. At the same moment, grappling hooks and ropes wound around *Lady of Leisure*'s railing, followed by a swarm of uniformed men. There were at least a dozen of them, all armed with pistols in side-holsters and some kind of large, ugly rifles. Staring at them, Martin wondered if they were AK-47s, like Pablo Cheung had been talking about. There was no mistaking the uniforms the men wore: The special cut and color, and the bahinia blossom shoulder blaze were reserved for members of the Hong Kong garrison of the PLA.

The guests backed away from them like a herd of cattle. Three of the soldiers took up positions on the fantail; the rest ran forward.

McIntyre's voice rose above the confusion: "Calm, everyone, please. We'll get this sorted out."

Another man vaulted from the patrol boat onto *Lady of Leisure* and stood quietly, looking around. He was small and agile, with fiercely slitted eyes, and although he wore the same CDF uniform as the other men, he carried no rifle.

After a moment his gaze lit on McIntyre and he strode across the width of the fantail. As he drew close, Lee read the nameplate on his uniform: Cpt. Wang I. He halted in front of McIntyre. "You are Phillip McIntyre?" he demanded in the same voice that had come over the patrol boat's loud-hailer. Lee was amazed the man could speak in anything but an adenoidal whine; his nose had been flattened completely, as if by a cricket bat. "You own this vessel?"

"I own *Lady of Leisure*," McIntyre said calmly. "What can I do for you . . . gentlemen?"

Something dangerous shone in Wang's eyes. "We have learned that this boat is being used to transport opium. The People's Republic of China does not tolerate drug activity of any kind."

"Commendable," McIntyre said. "But I thought drug smuggling control fell under local police jurisdiction."

Wang stiffened. There was a pistol in a holster at his side; he rested one hand on the butt. "Not in a vessel known to travel internationally. Opium is the curse of Hong Kong. It gave the British an excuse to enslave our ancestors and rob them of their heritage, and it continues to do the same today."

"Possibly so, Captain Wang. However, *Lady of Leisure* does not carry opium, internationally or locally. And I'm an American, by the way—not British."

"I know that," Wang said sharply. "I am not stupid. But the Americans are the worst of all; you think you are exempt from any law, including Chinese."

McIntyre smiled. "You're referring to Hong Kong common law, I'm sure."

"China is China. Now, you will move all these people into the main cabin. When we have completed our search of the vessel, you—"

"Oh, bugger this!" The shout came, unmistakably, from

Myron Carstairs. The burly Englishman shoved forward, planting himself in front of Wang. The back of his neck was the color of a pomegranate. "Look here, you bloody sod, I'm not about to moon around in some bloody saloon like a bloody sheep while you perform an illegal search, you understand? And neither is anybody else. This is *Hong Kong*, not Tibet, you wanker. You people can't—"

Wang's hand rose smoothly from his side. The sound of his pistol was startling, not much louder than a New Year's firecracker. As Lee watched, the back of Carstair's head opened like a flower—red and white; a bahinia blossom. A thick, warm spray hit Lee's face, and something like a fragment of ivory ticked off his forehead and bounced across the deck.

Carstairs dropped straight down and lay still. The Scotch glass was somehow still clutched in his hand, extended forward.

Lee heard screams, very loud in his ears. . . .

Then came one blur leading into another. Wang marched toward the bow, shouting orders. The guests were herded briskly into the main saloon and forced to sit on the floor. *Lady of Leisure* eased into motion, slowly at first, then faster until her diesels thrummed. Soon Lee felt the earnest rocking motion of the open sea beneath the yacht.

Some time later, Wang reappeared and said they were free to move about the upper decks, so long as they remained quiet and orderly. As people rushed out of the saloon, McIntyre touched Lee's shoulder. "I'm going to have a word with our host," he said. "Wait for me at the stern rail. Wait for me right there, you understand? No matter what."

So Lee planted himself at the stern rail of the upper deck and stared aft to where the lights of Hong Kong receded in the distance. They looked very far away. The city burned white-hot against mainland China's black hulk.

Down on the fantail stood a guard, his stance relaxed, his rifle held across his chest like a lover. His gaze never left the upper deck.

"So, Mr. Lee," a voice said, "where do you think they're taking us?"

Lee glanced over and saw that Pablo Cheung had joined him. The rest of the guests—more than a hundred of them—clustered near the darkened windows of the main cabin, murmuring nervously amongst themselves. Cheung alone seemed perfectly relaxed. Of course, he was from Macau, and it was rumored that all successful Macau businessmen were members of Chinese triads. Perhaps Cheung was used to having another man's brains splattered all over his tuxedo.

Lee made an effort to concentrate on Cheung's question. "I haven't seen another boat since they let us back on deck. We've left the regular shipping lanes."

Cheung lit a cigarette. "Perhaps they intend to motor all the way to Hawaii. Perhaps they're defecting."

Lee barely heard him. He kept thinking about his wife, Lila, too pregnant to come along on this year's company harbor cruise. She'd been so sad to miss it. . . .

Cheung was looking at him. "Relax, Mr. Lee. Whatever this is about, your boss will fix it. Phillip McIntyre fixes everything, isn't that right?"

Lee was silent. Two hours ago he would have said, yes, of course, without hesitation. But now . . .

Where *was* Mr. McIntyre?

At that exact moment, a distinct sound came out of the main cabin: slightly muffled, but unquestionably the same sound as the one that had burst Myron Carstair's head. Lee spun, but there was no movement, no light behind the curtains.

The crowd murmured uncertainly.

There was sudden, complete silence as *Lady of Leisure*'s engines cut off. Then the patrol boat reappeared from somewhere ahead of the yacht, cutting a wide circle aft, then moving up on the stern again.

Uniformed men began appearing down on the fantail, gathering in a silent group. Lee searched for the gleam of silver hair, but was not rewarded. All he saw were the CDF uniforms, dark hair, gleaming rifles. His stomach tightened. Where was Mr. McIntyre?

"Look," Cheung said. Far to stern, a searchlight beam winked on. It was too high off the water, and moving much

too fast, to come from a boat. Then Lee heard the beating rhythm of helicopter blades.

"This could be interesting," Cheung said, and lit another cigarette.

Guests surged to the rail, staring hopefully toward the light.

Below, the patrol boat banged into *Lady of Leisure* again. The PLA sailors swarmed back across the rail, and the instant the last one was clear, the patrol boat heeled away and roared off across the South China Sea, all lights off.

A cheer rose from *Lady of Leisure*. Clearly, no one cared that the helicopter didn't seem to notice the departing patrol boat. It descended toward the yacht, its rotor noise escalating into a painful thunder, its searchlight beam snapping back and forth. The guests at the rail waved, jewelry and sequins flashing. The helicopter slowed, moved to the starboard side of the boat, then hovered at a distance of fifty or sixty feet. Its rotor wash flattened the sea. Through the glare of its spotlight, Lee glimpsed a sleek silhouette not unlike that of the French-built helicopter Mr. McIntyre used for business trips. He looked closer. This helicopter was painted in irregular gray stripes, with a red star on the side.

And mounted in its open rear hatch was a machine gun with a man behind it. As Lee watched, the barrel pivoted.

Cheung said something sharp in Cantonese, but his words were eradicated by a sudden, pounding roar. Flames leaped from the helicopter, and a column of water exploded up from the sea and marched toward *Lady of Leisure*.

The guests stood staring silently.

Then the screaming began.

0510 Hours (−8 GMT)
Tomcat 302
South China Sea

"Oh give me a home . . . where the buffalo roam . . ." Lieutenant Commander Chris Hanson, call sign "Lobo," held each note as long as she could, until she heard her Radar Intercept Officer's groan through the Internal Communication System: "Please, God, make it stop."

Lobo grinned, even though she knew Handyman couldn't see her face from the backseat, least of all at night. "Honey," she said, "before you start praying, remember that there's only one God up here . . . and that's *me*." She yanked back on the yoke and slammed the throttles forward to full afterburner. As raw jet fuel spewed into the twin exhausts of the General Electric F-100 turbofans, the F-14D stood on its tail and shot up as if yanked by the Milky Way. Lobo felt her weight double, then triple, trying to shove her backward through her seat. She breathed in harsh grunts, tightening the muscles of her torso to force the blood to back into her head and extremities. Nothing better than flying an F-14 to keep the old abs in shape. Even so, gray haze crept in at the edges of her vision. She loved that. It never ceased to amaze her: A Tomcat was so powerful it could leave consciousness itself behind. . . .

Through the ICS came a loud yawn. Handyman always made a show of being unaffected by even her most violent maneuvering. A great backseater, Handyman; not a compulsive whiner like so many RIOs.

She eased the yoke forward with leaden arms, rounding out of the climb. Now the reverse occurred: She grew light in her seat, shoulders squeezing against the shoulder restraints of her ejection harness, breasts trying to rise beneath her tight flight suit.

She started as a comet shot past the canopy, whacking Tomcat 302 with an enormous fist of displaced air.

"Jesus, Hot Rock!" Lobo shouted over the tactical circuit. "You want to give us a little clearance here?"

Lieutenant Commander Reginald Stone's voice was calm. "You want to warn your wingman before you go ballistic like that? How am I supposed to know what's going on?"

"What were you doing so close in the first place? You're supposed to be flying loose deuce on me, not sitting on my . . . tailpipe. Get back where you belong."

"Rah-jah." Hot Rock's F-14, a collection of strobe lights

and twin exhaust flames in the darkness, drifted backward and higher, receding to the high position favored by American fighter pilots. Lobo didn't believe for a minute that Hot Rock had buzzed her by accident. Although he hadn't been her wingman for long, she'd already seen hints of the outstanding flying skills that had earned him his call sign. Still, he was young and clearly had a few things to learn about working as a team.

"Don't sweat it, Lobo, babe," Handyman said over the ICS. "Personally, I love it when you pull high 'g's and start panting that way. Puts me in the mood."

"Ah, you're too easy, sweetheart." Lobo grinned again. That was another thing about Handyman. He knew about her experience in Russia, what had happened to her there, but didn't tiptoe around certain subjects the way most people did.

Above, stars filled the canopy. A beautiful night, a tanked-up Tomcat, and a righteous backseater . . . what a life. She wasn't even concerned about trapping onto *Jefferson* later, although night carrier landings were amongst the most stressful activities in the world. Tonight, the South China Sea was smooth as a linoleum floor.

She rocked the F-14 to the left a bit and looked down. The water was purest black, dotted with the small clusters of jewelry that were ships, which grew very dense dead ahead, indicating the merging of shipping lanes into and out of Hong Kong. To the east and north were the scattered glints comprising Carrier Battle Group 14. The glow of USS *Thomas Jefferson*, the carrier itself, was lost in haze almost three hundred miles away.

Tonight, Lobo and Hot Rock were flying BARCAP, Barrier Combat Air Patrol, acting as the sharp point of the enormous knife that was CVBG-14. Strictly routine activity, of course, since there had been no overt conflict between the United States and the People's Republic of China in several years. Just an enjoyable evening cruise.

As if disapproving of this, the voice of the carrier Tactical Action Officer, or TAO, came over her headset: "Viper Leader, be advised we're picking up an SOS on IAD, to the north. There's no response to hailing, so it's probably an automatic repeater. Should be right in your area. Keep your eyes peeled, okay?"

Lobo clicked her mike. "Homeplate, Viper Leader; copy that. Peeling our eyes." Well, this was interesting. When an SOS came over the International Air Distress frequency, maritime law—and hundreds of years of seafaring tradition— bound all naval vessels, including Navy fighter jets, to respond. Not that an F-14 at altitude had much chance of spotting a single boat in the blackness below, but still . . . she whipped the Tomcat upside down to offer an unobstructed view of the ocean.

"I knew you were going to do that," Handyman said.

"Well, do you see anything?" she asked. "Flares? Smoke signals? People waving their arms?"

"What about that fire right below us?" Handyman asked.

"Huh?" Even as she spoke, she saw it—a tiny, unsteady flicker. "Well, I'll be damned." Still inverted, she keyed the mike. "Homeplate, we've spotted what might be a fire; we're going to investigate." She switched to the tactical circuit. "Hot Rock, you get all that?"

"Roger, Lobo. I'm with you."

Suddenly something occurred to Lobo. Considering the political orientation of the nearest nation, the SOS could be a ruse of some kind, designed to lure a couple of Tomcats down to killing position. "Hang on, Hot Rock," she said, and switched circuits again to call the E-2C she knew was airborne. "Spook One, Spook One, this is Viper Leader."

"Spook One," came the voice from the E-2C Hawkeye buzzing along a hundred miles to the east. "Go ahead, Viper Leader."

"You guys see any bogey activity at all in our area?"

"Negative, Viper," came the voice from the Hawkeye. "Commercial traffic only. A couple of Flankers were playing footsie with each other last night, but that was on their own side of the limit. Skies are friendly."

"Copy, Seven-Niner. Be advised I'm heading down to investigate a surface vessel SOS."

"Copy, Viper Leader. But speaking of the limit, remember you're right on the edge of it, so be careful."

"Roger." She switched back to tactical. "Hot Rock, follow me down to angels fifteen, then hold. Watch my back, and make sure you don't wander over the twelve-mile limit."

The sigh that came over the circuit was unmistakable: the grumpy whine of the guy forced to sit the game out on the bench. Hot Rock was young, unblooded. She wondered if he'd be so eager to fight after his first real battle. "Sure, Lobo," he said. "I'll make sure not to color outside the lines."

Lobo grinned, rolled the Tomcat upright, then punched it over into a near-vertical dive. "Oh, give me a home . . ."

"I knew you were going to do that, too," Handyman sighed.

By the time Lobo finished the first stanza of the song, the F-14 had devoured almost twenty-five thousand feet of altitude. She eased back on both stick and throttle, letting the plane's momentum carry it down under five hundred feet on a steadily flattening trajectory. The flicker of light now lay dead ahead. The Tomcat's nose would soon blot it from view, so Lobo flipped upside down again and ticked the throttles back as far as she dared. With a slight, rumbling buffet, the Tomcat's onboard computers automatically swept the wings forward to increase lift at the lower speed.

Still, even at its slowest pace, an F-14 was not exactly a hovercraft. In a heartbeat, the flicker of light flashed across the canopy.

Plenty of time.

"Holy shit," Handyman said breathlessly.

Mouth dry, Lobo rolled the Tomcat right side up and switched the radio to tactical. "Homeplate, Homeplate, this is Viper Leader. That SOS is coming from a civilian vessel taking heavy fire from a military helicopter. Repeat, a civilian vessel is under attack." She cranked the F-14 into a savage 180-degree turn.

"Whoa, watch it, Lobo," Handyman said. She knew he wasn't troubled by the G-forces so much as the fact that the Tomcat's extended wings expanded its wingspan from thirty-eight feet to almost sixty-four. The inboard tip had to be reaching for the water. But she didn't bother to reply; she knew where her goddamned wingtips were.

"Viper Leader, Viper Leader, this is Homeplate—are you sure it's a civilian vessel?"

As she leveled out, the sea below her was black and smooth, a waxed floor in which she could see the reflections of stars. She knew that to the rear, matters would be different. There, the horizontal vortex of air uncoiling from each wing-tip would be lashing the surface into a froth.

But all her attention was focused dead ahead, where the flame leapt into life once more.

"Yes," she said. "I'm sure." Her finger had gone to the weapons selector switch. But ... did she *really* have cause for action? Maybe this was target practice on some dere-lict boat. Or a legitimate shoot-out of some kind. Through her mind flashed the mantra of the few female Navy fighter pilots: *Don't fuck up; they're watching you soooooo closely.* . . .

Then she saw the American flag dangling, shredded, from a pole on the remnants of the sinking boat's fantail—and the red star painted on the side of the helicopter. Below her, the water was suddenly full of floating lumps. Lobo's finger jumped back to the weapons selector switch. Too close for missiles, but the Tomcat's M61A1 Vulcan cannon could shred that helo into a pile of tin cans . . .

. . . And drop it right on top of any possible survivors in the water.

Don't fuck up . . . .

Snarling, she slammed the throttles forward, turning the Tomcat into an arrowhead sixty-one feet nine inches long, and leaping toward the speed of sound.

0515 local (GMT −8)
South China Sea
Lady of Leisure

Martin Lee clung to the rail of what had once been the star-board side of *Lady of Leisure*, but now substituted for her slanted deck. He had moved to the starboard rail from the stern only when the yacht began to roll over, yet even then he had stayed as close as possible to the stern. *Wait for me right there, no matter what.* What a fool he was; what a brainless, unthinking lackey. Now, with one arm wrapped around an upright and his body sprawled across the yacht's slick fiberglass flank, he pretended to be dead. It was the only thing he could think of to do.

They had already shot most of the others. First they'd blasted *Lady of Leisure* herself, hammering rounds into her fragile body at the waterline, until she toppled over far enough to dump most of her passengers into the sea. Then the helicopter turned its attention to *them.* Circling slowly behind the bright eye of its searchlight, it picked out the passengers one by one and shot them, until the water turned scarlet-and-blue.

Lee watched all this from beneath his arm as he dangled against the side of the boat. He didn't *want* to watch, but closing his eyes was much worse; the noise, the screaming . . .

He saw Pablo Cheung diving under the water, pursued by silver spears where slugs yanked bubbles after them. Cheung stopped diving and turned into a red rug drifting just below the surface. Lee saw Lisa Austin, the clothing designer, raise her hands toward the flames, and disintegrate. He saw the helicopter hesitate, its searchlight beam probing the water, scanning back and forth, then sliding back toward the yacht.

He closed his eyes. Tried not to scream as the light blazed over him, turning his eyelids red, prickling his skin like the heat of the sun . . .

Then he *did* scream as something crushed down on him, driving the wreckage of *Lady of Leisure* deeper into the water, boring into Lee's ears, then releasing them so hard they popped. Water sprayed up around him, so dense he could not breathe. He jerked erect, gasping, his blood pounding in his ears. When he opened his eyes he saw the water falling back, and beyond that the helicopter's searchlight beam jumping erratically between the sea and the sky. The helicopter was bobbling in the air like a toy on a rubber band, the silvery disk of its rotor nearly touching the water on one side, then the other, its machine gun blessedly silent. Finally it steadied again, hovered for a moment, then pivoted, lifted its tail high and raced away to the west.

A few moments later, the air thundered again and something flashed overhead; enormous, silvery, pursued by two long cones of flame.

Even before the burnt-kerosene aroma of jet exhaust reached him, Lee knew what had passed over. Clinging to the remnants of the *Lady of Leisure* with one arm, he waved frantically at the sky.

0515 local (−8 GMT)
Tomcat 306
South China Sea

"What's going on, TT?" Hot Rock demanded over the ICS. He banked his Tomcat slightly, maintaining his altitude at the prescribed fifteen thousand feet, searching the ocean below. He couldn't believe this was happening. According to Lobo's last radio transmission to Homeplate, the boat under attack was carrying an American flag. An American boat, clear out here—what were the odds? "Come on, what's happening down there?"

"Hang on, hang on, I'm checkin'." Hot Rock had long ago noticed that the more intense the situation, the more the accent of his RIO, Tony "Two Tone" Cappelli, reverted to its Brooklyn roots. "Getting nothing but surface clutter; looking straight down ain't what AWG-9 is made for, you know?"

"Do you pick up the chopper at all? I see Lobo; she's going around again. She didn't take a shot, did she? Is the chopper still there? *Talk to me, Two Tone!*" Sweat slicked the space between his palm and the yoke. Blood sang in his ears.

"Lookin' for your first kill, youngster? Well, I'm getting a little signal here, something maybe runnin' west."

"Should I chase it or not?"

"Hey, you're the pilot. Or you could call Mommy and ask her permission if you like."

Hot Rock felt as if cold water had been dumped over his head. He could hear his father's voice: *What's the matter, Reginald? You scared to take the horse over that jump? Scared of a little fall? Your brother was clearing that jump before he was six years old.*

He flicked the radio to tactical. "Viper Leader, Viper Two. I'm in pursuit of the helicopter. Repeat, in pursuit of the helo, departing on a heading of two three zero."

"We're right on the edge of the twelve-mile limit," came Lobo's clipped tones. "Watch your position."

"Copy." He was proud of how dry and sarcastic that came out. Just the way his father would have said it if someone had challenged *his* expertise.

Nosing the Tomcat over, he started searching the dark water ahead. Of course, odds were he wouldn't spot the helicopter at all; the Tomcat wasn't equipped with infrared targeting, and for that matter Two Tone could have just been picking up random surface clutter, the bane of airborne radar.

Then he saw something. "Tally ho!" he cried, the words for "target sighted" leaping automatically to his lips. That pleased him. He'd said exactly what he had been trained to say, without thinking about it. Perhaps everything else would work that way, too. "I see his rotor disk, TT. Right on the deck." He licked his lips. "Um, he's heading for the twelve-mile limit. Better call Homeplate for orders before we do anything; this is a weird situa—"

Just then the voice from the Hawkeye interrupted. "Viper, Viper, you have incoming bogeys, bearing zero niner zero. Four bogeys, repeat, four bogeys inbound on your position. From their radars, they're Flankers."

The carrier TAO's voice cut in sharp and hard. "Vipers, remain on station. Keep bogeys away from that site; backup is on the way. Repeat, maintain control of that site if at all possible. You're over international waters. Backup and SAR on the way."

"Roger," Lobo's voice said. "Hot Rock, Hot Rock, break off and beat feet back to your previous position. I'm going to stay down here and make it real clear nobody gets near this mess but us—especially a helicopter. You copy?"

"Copy, Viper Leader." Hot Rock heard the slight tremor in his voice, but that was nothing to be ashamed of. He knew from experience that other aviators would interpret it as springing from anger and disappointment. Because *they'd* be feeling anger and disappointment at being called off potential target to play watchdog. "*Damn* it!" he cried, cranking the F-14 into a hard right turn and headed back and up.

"Tough luck, man," Two Tone said from the backseat. "Unless the bogeys will want to play."

Hot Rock said nothing. His climbing turn was smooth, powerful, and perfectly balanced, and the higher he got, the better he felt. Nobody could take this away from him; nobody could say there was a finer stickman in the entire U.S. Navy. When it came to carving up the sky, Hot Rock Stone was unsurpassed. He should be in the Blue Angels.

He should be flying in air shows. . . .

0520 local (−8 GMT)
USS **Jefferson**
South China Sea

As Rear Admiral Edward Everett "Batman" Wayne yanked on a fresh flight suit, he tried to clear his head. Before being awakened by the hard buzz of his direct line to the Tactical Flag Command Center TAO, he'd been dreaming about the last time he was in the South China Sea, about the Spratley Island campaign. Of course, back then he hadn't been a Rear Admiral, in charge of an entire Carrier Battle Group. Back then he'd been assigned to the Pentagon, helping test the new JAST Tomcats with their advanced Doppler look-down, shoot-down radar. When the Spratleys problem heated up, he'd helped ferry a pair of the new birds to *Jefferson*, and even piloted one in combat, going head-to-head against the finest Chinese pilots above the oil-rich chunks of rock they were trying to claim as their own.

What he *hadn't* had to do back then was worry about the "whys" of it. He hadn't had to concern himself with the deployment or tactics of the hundreds of assets that made up a carrier battle group. Back then, that responsibility had fallen on the shoulders of his friend and onetime lead, Rear Admiral Matthew "Tombstone" Magruder.

And Tombstone had risen to the occasion . . . well, admirably. He'd orchestrated the battle group in such a way that it not only fended off the Chinese, but kept the South China Sea open to all naval traffic . . . while managing not to start a full-scale war with the People's Republic in the meantime. An amazing job.

Now, ironically, it was Stony who was back in Washington, fighting the very different war that was life in the Pentagon while Batman was left to deal with the latest Chinese mess . . . whatever it turned out to be.

He mentally reviewed the brief summary the TFCC TAO had given him that had yanked him out of sleep: A Tomcat on routine patrol had engaged a Chinese helicopter it caught firing upon an unarmed American pleasure boat. Chinese bogeys were now en route to the site. Batman wasn't sure yet what "engaged" meant, or any other details concerning the episode, but he was about to find out.

0538 local (−8 GMT)
SH-60 Seahawk
South China Sea

Petty Officer Third Class Dwayne Pitcock leaned out the yawning side hatch of the helo and peered down. Although the eastern sky was beginning to brighten, the water below remained black except where the helo's searchlight created a lens of brilliant blue. The lens slipped this way and that, revealing chunks of fiberglass and foam rubber, a coffee table, a couple of ottomans, a glass coffeepot bobbing along. Tons of junk everywhere.

And then it passed over a human body, a woman in a

sequined gown, floating facedown over a brown-red cloud of blood. Her back had been ripped open like the doors of a cabinet, displaying muscle and bone.

"Jesus," Pitcock said. Since he was going to be hitting the water pretty soon, he didn't have a headset or helmet on, and he couldn't hear himself over the hammering blast of the Seahawk's engine and rotor noise.

The searchlight moved on, finding more bodies, one after the other, all floating with the distinctive liquid movement of the dead, all trailing slicks of blood behind them. The bodies turned slowly as the helo's downwash shoved at them. "Jesus," Pitcock said again.

Then the light found the largest piece of wreckage he had yet seen—a sleek white expanse like the lip of a dying iceberg, with more of it slanting down into the water below, vanishing into indigo depths. A man's body sprawled across the exposed section As the light hit him he stirred, turned, and raised an arm to wave.

The Seahawk immediately swooped over. Leery of the bloody water, Pitcock popped the seals on a couple of anti-shark packets and tossed them down beside the hull. They stained the water bright yellow as they emitted a chemical that supposedly drove sharks away. Pitcock, who had known sharks to swim *toward* the stuff, figured pissing into the water would do just as much good, but he was in the Navy, and sailors had a long tradition of superstitious behavior.

The crew boss manned the winch, spinning out a length of cable with the rescue collar attached. Before the collar hit the water, Pitcock jumped.

Still thinking of sharks, he practically bounced off the surface of the water and scooted up the tilted hull of the half-sunken yacht. He snagged an upright on the chrome guardrail a few feet away from where the man clung, then squinted up against the salt spray and pounding air and signaled the helo. It drifted forward until Pitcock was able to grab the rescue collar.

The man was staring at him now. He was Chinese—well, some kind of Asian—and maybe thirty, thirty-five years old. He was wearing a tuxedo. His expression was more vacant than grateful or even comprehending. But at least he was alive.

"I gotcha!" Pitcock shouted. "You're okay now, sir."

The man didn't respond. Pitcock slid toward him across the slippery fiberglass, dragging the collar behind. The man barely reacted as Pitcock maneuvered one of his arms through the collar, then his head. His other arm was locked around the guardrail. When Pitcock tried to pry it loose, the guy started flailing around and shouting in some shrill, staccato language.

"Easy, easy," Pitcock said as soothingly as he could, considering he had to bellow. He signaled "raise" at the chopper, and "slowly," and waited until the cable began to pull before trying again to pry the man's arm loose of the rail. Apparently calmed by the firm grip of the cable, the man finally relaxed his arm, and it slipped free. Pitcock whirled his arm, signaling for a faster winch.

There was a moment when the man in the tuxedo seemed to be standing on the canted hull of his own volition. His black eyes met Pitcock's. "Thank you very much," he said in clear English.

Pitcock grinned and gave him a thumbs-up, and he sailed into the sky.

0540 local (−8 GMT)
TFCC, USS Jefferson
South China Sea

"COS, what's the situation?" Batman asked as he stepped into the small compartment located within a few feet of his cabin.

William "Coyote" Grant, *Jefferson*'s Chief of Staff, looked away from the blue screen in the front of the room. The blue screen was the focal point of this information, distilling input from all over the battle group down to a series of icons representing friendly, unfriendly and neutral assets in the area.

"Good morning, Admiral," Coyote said. "Thirty minutes

ago we got a report from one of our BARCAP Tomcats. Lobo. She spotted a PLA helicopter firing on an American civilian vessel and its passengers. Her wingman pursued the helicopter to the edge of the twelve-mile limit, then turned back when a flight of four SU-27s scrambled." He gestured at the screen. "I made the decision to claim the wreck site as our own until all the bodies have been picked up."

Batman nodded as he examined the display, noted the positions of icons representing the Chinese assets, including a couple of surface vessels. "Looks like the bogeys are hanging back."

"For now. I vectored two more flights of Tomcats to the area to establish a perimeter, and so far there's been no challenge. The bogeys just keep cruising their side of the twelve-mile limit."

"Have we heard from the PRC yet?"

"Oh, sure; they're claiming rights over the entire area. Of course. Demanding we back off. Naturally. We keep reminding them the wreckage is in international waters, and they keep ignoring us—but like I said, so far they're not pushing it."

Batman frowned. His first thought after being awakened had been that he would be facing another Spratleys-type situation. There, the PLA had committed carefully planned atrocities designed to look like the work of the United States . . . and publicized, immediately and loudly, as such.

"This doesn't make sense," he said, mostly to himself. He knew that the Chinese military was willing to murder its own people, as well as those of its allies, in order to lure the U.S. Navy into a self-defeating combat situation. But killing American civilians could only damage their own international human rights reputation, which had never been exactly laudable. Why would they do that when there was apparently nothing to gain?

"How sure is Lobo of what she saw?" he asked.

"Absolutely sure, sir." To Batman's surprise, Coyote half smiled. "Evidently she gave the helo a low enough pass to scare the bejeezus out of it; that's why it took off. But Lobo was cool; she never even switched on her targeting radar."

The smile vanished. "She reports bodies in the water, sir. A lot of them."

"SAR?" Batman asked. In warm waters like these, the sooner Sea Air Rescue got under way, the better the chances for survival of anyone who had been on that boat. Hypothermia wasn't the problem—sharks were.

"Two Seahawks are already on station," Coyote said.

Batman weighed the situation. "I want everything picked up, COS," he said. "The bodies, the survivors, whatever's left of the boat, everything. Clear space in *Jefferson*'s hangar bay if necessary. Understand?"

"Yes, sir."

Batman looked back at the tactical display, all the assets arrayed there, and again found himself wishing for the relative simplicity of the combat pilot's role. Then he thought about Lobo, and the kind of near-instant decisions she'd been forced to make out there in the darkness, and decided maybe there were no simple answers for anyone anymore.

God, he wished Tombstone were here.

Friday, 1 August
1900 locall (+5 GMT)
Pitts Special
Two miles off the coast of Maryland

If there was one thing Tombstone Magruder hated, it was admitting that he enjoyed flying something other than a Tomcat.

He'd earned his call sign because of the lugubrious cast of his face and the fact that he was supposedly devoid of emotion. Yet here he was, grinning like a fool as he cranked the toy-like Pitts Special through its sixth barrel roll in a row, spinning the biplane so fast the ocean and sky turned into one mottled blur. Six rolls, seven, eight—it could go on forever, or at least as long as his stomach could take the abuse.

He eased the stick to the right to end the last roll, being

careful not to overdo it: The Pitts was a sensitive beast, with
a damned impressive power-to-weight ratio . . . for a prop-
plane, anyway.

Hell, why deny it? Flying this thing was fun as hell. No,
the Pitts wasn't capable of crushing you into your seat hard
enough to make you black out; couldn't rip a hole in the
fabric of the sound barrier; couldn't fly with impunity in
clouds or fog. On the other hand, it didn't make you concentrate on a Heads-Up Display instead of the sky and
ground; didn't feed your hands and feet synthetic control
surface pressures because a set of computers stood between
you and the ailerons, rudder and elevator; didn't have an E-2
Hawkeye peering over its shoulder all the time. There was
just you, the pilot, all alone with a single propeller, a pair of
wire-braced wings, and a solid blast of wind in the face.

Wonderful.

And there was no denying that this little bird could do
things a Tomcat couldn't. Rolling . . . hell, the Tomcat's roll
rate was terrific given the plane's size and mass, but the Pitts
could whip around twice in the time it took an F-14 to make
it through one full revolution. And landing a Pitts was as
easy as stepping off a curb; nothing like the sweaty-palm
work of dropping 72,000 pounds of Tomcat onto the heaving
deck of an aircraft carrier.

Time to be meandering back to the field, though. His wife,
Joyce—although he still thought of her as "Tomboy," her
call sign from her days as his RIO—would probably be waiting for him, and none too patiently. They were supposed to
have dinner with his uncle, Admiral Thomas Magruder.

He sighed. Not that he didn't enjoy his uncle's company,
but the conversation was certain to turn to politics and Pentagon infighting. God, he missed the straightforward banter
of Tomcat drivers: clean traps, aerial maneuvers, missiles
launched, bogeys splashed.

Thank God for the Pitts Special, and for a wife who knew
her husband well enough to insist that he buy it. If it weren't
for those two things—and the stick time he still occasionally
got in an F-14, of course—he didn't think life would be
bearable. During what the media called the Second Cuban

Missile Crisis, he'd flown his last combat mission. He knew that. He'd never go up against a MIG again. For that matter, he'd even given up the command of Carrier Battle Group 14 for a billet in Washington. A promotion, supposedly.

But now . . . he was at loose ends. An advisor here, a consultant there. A guy standing around in the hallways of the Pentagon, looking for something to do. Waiting, he supposed, for a war.

It didn't help that Tomboy's assignment took her down to Pax River all the time, where she got to test fly the latest Navy aircraft while he sat around in stuffy meeting rooms.

Life just wasn't fair.

But a smart man could make it fairer. Grinning again, he put the biplane's nose down hard and listened to the wind's shriek rise in the rigging as the surface of the ocean swooped up at him. Turned a couple of barrel rolls in the meantime. Too bad there was nobody to watch except the herons and ducks in the nature preserve a mile or so to the west.

Although he tried to resist, he pulled out of the dive too soon—another holdover from flying Tomcats, with their infinitely greater inertia. He'd have to pract—

He cringed as something shot underneath the Pitts with a whistling shriek. What the *hell*? That had sounded for all the world like a jet engine. The Pitts jolted through a disrupted airstream, then steadied. Looking down, Tombstone glimpsed a dark arrowhead shape racing just above the waves, then shooting upward. It rose vertically, trailing a faint string of vapor behind it. Against the pale glow of the eastern sky, it was shaped not like one arrowhead but two, joined in tandem. The impression he'd gotten during its close pass was that it was only a little longer than the Pitts—but far faster. As he watched, it arched over in the sky, then seemed to disappear. Finally he spotted it—a tiny dot, growing larger by the second. Coming straight at him.

In his career, Tombstone had flown against a wide variety of aerial weapons, including fighter planes, air-to-air missiles, surface-to-air missiles, and, once, an UAV—an Unmanned Aerial Vehicle that he'd pursued and shot down before it could deliver a nuclear warhead on Cuba. This thing didn't resemble any of them.

Its intent, however, was unmistakable.

From this angle Tombstone couldn't begin to judge its speed or trajectory. He had no RIO to feed him radar data, and no countermeasures to dazzle its radar or confuse its heat-seeking head—whatever it was using to track him.

So he used instinct instead, jamming the stick forward and firewalling the throttle. The Pitts dove as if fired straight down out of a cannon, jolting Tombstone into his shoulder harness.

The bogey missed again, but it seemed to Tombstone that it adjusted at the last second, almost clipping the Pitts' tail. Whatever it was, if it carried a warhead the explosive wasn't detonated by proximity; that was something. Tombstone hauled back on the stick, pulling the biplane out of its screaming dive. This time he was afraid he'd let it go *too* long, that he was going to strike the surface of the ocean at a speed that made water every bit as unyielding as concrete.

Then the crests of the waves were whipping past so close he was sure the biplane's bulbous tires were getting wet. Tombstone kept the stick pulled back, but easier now, lest he lose all his airspeed. Now he *really* wished he was back in his Tomcat, with enough thrust to yank him quickly up where he could maneuver. The Tomcat might even be able to flat outrun this little bogey, whatever it was.

He swiveled his head back and forth, squinting against the setting sun, wishing he had Tomboy in the backseat to help. If there were a backseat. Meanwhile, the coolest part of his mind debated his options. Found them to be limited. He had no idea what he was up against. He was flying in an unarmed plane. A propeller-driven plane. An *unfamiliar* propeller-driven plane.

But he was a pilot, damn it—not just a pilot, a naval aviator. No one, and no *thing*, was better in the air.

He spotted the bogey again, zipping in from the rear, and he executed a left turn so sudden and violent it stalled the inside wings. As he dropped the nose to restore airspeed and circumvent a spin, he heard the whistle of an oncoming jet turbine growing shriller, and pulled his head down into his shoulders instinctively . . . then the sound faded again. He straightened the Pitts out and let it dive slightly, building up airspeed.

Meanwhile, the cold part of his mind was steadily examining impressions and making decisions. The bogey was obviously not manned; it was much too small and made turns that would black out any human pilot. On the other hand, it was not an ordinary missile. Which left only two choices: a Remotely-Piloted Vehicle, or a UAV like the one he'd shot down over Cuba. If the former, then someone was flying it by joystick from a distant location, using an onboard video or infrared camera for guidance. If the latter, then the bogey was a fire-and-forget weapon, with an onboard navigation computer guiding it to its destination.

He immediately discounted that option; all the UAVs he'd ever heard of, including the one he'd shot down, found their destinations through a combination of ground-mapping radar and Global Positioning Satellite navigation. They were programmed to locate and strike at stationary targets; they couldn't dogfight. So: This was an RPV.

Not that the information helped him much right now. All it meant was that the pilot of this bogey could turn, accelerate and climb his vehicle at the limits of the plane's capabilities, not his own.

Limits . . .

Tombstone suddenly remembered the BD5-J, a stubby homebuilt jet even shorter than the bogey. He'd watched them fly at air shows, and spoken to their pilots. Although fast and agile as hummingbirds, the little jets had strictly limited ranges due to greedy engines and minute fuel tanks. The bogey that was chasing him around had to be subject to the same restrictions. Given enough time, it would simply die of starvation.

But how much time was enough? Trying to drain the bogey meant juking and jiving for as long as it took. But every maneuver would have to be a miracle of timing. Too slow, and the bogey wouldn't be fooled. Too fast, and the bogey would simply reacquire. Either way, the result would be the same.

All this went through his head in the time it took the bogey to complete a quick half circle and come back at him again. This time Tombstone noticed the round maw of an air intake, mounted in a depression atop the vehicle. If it weren't for that black circle, the damned thing wouldn't be visible at all from this angle.

He kept his eyes on the circle, timing its approach, making himself wait . . . wait . . .

Too long! He knew it even as he slammed the Pitts through an ugly maneuver that was half barrel roll, half loop. Holding his breath, he thought about Tomboy and waited for the impact.

But then the bogey was past him, slanting off toward the shore. Too startled to recover from his maneuver, he stared through the tunnel formed by his spinning windscreen. The bogey began to turn again, but this time without the relentless certainty he'd come to fear. In seemed to settle into a lazy arc. Perhaps it was running out of fuel.

Tombstone leveled out.

Instantly, the bogey jinked toward him, accelerating.

Without thinking about it, Tombstone put the Pitts into a fresh series of barrel rolls. The bogey flashed past, thirty feet to the rear, as if he'd vanished from its sensors. It didn't make sense. Snap rolls were hardly an evasive maneuver for missiles, especially one approaching from the side.

The moment he leveled out again, dizzy and ready to retch, the bogey made an abrupt turn back toward him. He glanced around. He was almost to shore, but there was no hope there: nothing but low marshland, without a hill or stand of trees to hide behind.

The bogey grew larger in the corner of his eye. Tombstone held his breath and started another series of rolls, meanwhile letting the Pitts plummet toward the ocean.

The bogey flashed through the space he'd occupied a moment earlier. It kept going, then entered into another of its broad, lazy turns.

"Okay, you," Tombstone said, still spinning, blood pounding in his head. "I've got you now."

The beach passed by, no more than a hundred yards below. *Feet dry*, Tombstone thought automatically, trying to keep his stomach from erupting through his teeth. He'd lost track of the bogey. Hoped it had really run out of gas this time. Hoped it had dropped into the water like a shotgunned mallard.

But if not . . .

Leveling out, he pulled the Pitts into as steep a sustained climb as it would endure. He looked back and forth, up and down, searching the sky, trying to blink the dizziness away. In a moment he knew that the bogey hadn't run out of gas after all. He saw a triangular flash of red light to the north, then the air intake racing toward him. He watched it, watched it . . . and jammed the stick forward, diving back toward the marsh as hard as he could. Although he didn't look back, he sensed the bogey swinging onto his tail.

"Now!" he shouted, and yanked the stick hard right. The swamp began to whirl around the cockpit. Timing it carefully, Tombstone stomped on the left rudder pedal, then hauled back on the stick. The vertical spin abruptly hooked into a flat-out climb. Looking over his shoulder, Tombstone saw a geyser of water shoot out of the marsh and rise so high its tip glowed orange in the last light of the sun.

Whooping, he rolled the Pitts Special one more time . . . for joy.

THREE
Saturday, 2 August

0700 local (−8 GMT)
Tomcat 306
South China Sea

"Well," Two Tone said dryly from the backseat, "that was a real waste of fuel."

Hot Rock knew his RIO was talking about the extra hours they had pulled circling around and around the site of the sunken sailboat, including an aerial refueling so they could stay on station until the SAR and salvage ops were finished. All that without so much as a glimpse of a Chinese fighter.

He made his voice sound rough and disappointed. "Who knows? We might get another chance."

"We already had a chance with that helo," Two Tone said.

"We were too close to the twelve-mile limit. You heard our orders." Hot Rock eased the Tomcat into a left bank, maintaining his position in the Marshal pattern until it was his turn to trap back onto *Jefferson*.

"Well, let's just hope that helo doesn't decide to take out some other poor civilian boat," Two Tone said. "Or if it does, that we don't let it get away again."

Hot Rock didn't respond. He wasn't sure if there was a reprimand behind those words, or not. He had to remember that not everyone was his father. Not everyone could peer into his heart and see that, deep inside, Reginald Stone knew he wasn't good enough.

Besides, Two Tone was almost a stranger. Apart from the absolute synchronicity imposed by life in a Tomcat, they shared no common interests and rarely hung out together.

Fifteen minutes later it was his turn at last to land, and he angled the big bird down toward what looked pretty much like a post card-sized deck. But his hands remained steady on the controls, his breath flowed smooth and easy, he was perfectly relaxed. He loved this part.

A moment later the Tomcat's tailhook snagged the three wire and the Tomcat jolted to a halt. Hot Rock smiled. Another perfect trap. His father could never have done such a thing. His brother, either.

"I'll say one thing," Two Tone said in his honking accent. "Nobody knows how to get a bird home as safely as you do, man."

Friday, 1 August
1945 local (+5 GMT)
Meadowlark Air Field
Maryland

Although Tombstone was a member of the flying club at the Naval Air Station, he preferred to keep his Pitts Special at a small private strip in the middle of the Maryland countryside. Somehow, the biplane looked more at home amongst the motley collection of Supercubs, Cessna 150s and Stearmans that lodged there than it did surrounded by sleek Bonanzas and Sky Kings, not to mention F-14s and F/A-18s. Besides, Tombstone liked the laid-back atmosphere. He liked the grass strip adjacent to the paved one, and he liked how a pot of bad coffee was always percolating in the office building.

By the time he eased the Pitts down onto the grass, the sun was squatting on the horizon, pushing long shadows across the field. Tombstone taxied to his tie-down area, the Pitts bumping over the sod, and killed the engine. Climbed out of the cramped cockpit and dropped onto the grass—and almost all the way to his knees.

His legs were shaking like Slinkys.

He should be dead. That was the thing. He should be dead right now. He'd had close calls before, sure; but this was different. This time he was alive for only one reason: luck. Not because he was such a damned fine pilot, but because he didn't know how to handle the Pitts properly. The truth was, that bogey should have nailed him on its first pass. And it would have, if he hadn't pulled out of his dive too soon. Luck had saved him. Pure luck. That was all.

He heard the crunch of gravel under car tires, and demanded that his legs stiffen. He couldn't endure being seen like this. As he stood, he had to reach up and grab the Pitts' cockpit coaming to maintain his balance.

"You got back just in time," said a familiar voice, and Tomboy appeared before him, short and buxom and beautiful in the shadows. Instinctively, he reached out and pulled her to him, and hung on to her rather than the biplane. Her red hair smelled of violet, as if the twilight had gotten caught in it.

"Hey, big guy!" she said, sounding both surprised and pleased. She hugged him back. "That must have been some flight."

Tombstone began to laugh. "Oh, yeah," he said. "Yeah, that was some flight."

Tomboy pulled away from him. Her face was serious. "Before you tell me about it, I've got something to tell *you*." Within a couple of minutes, she gave him an encapsulated version of a terrible event in the South China Sea. CBG-14, his old command, was involved.

Atop the airport building, a beacon began to flash at the first stars.

"The Chinese again," Tombstone said, thinking of his longtime wingman and best friend, Batman. "What the hell are they up to this time?"

Tomboy put her hand on his arm. "There's something else, sweetheart. The man who owned the yacht was someone you know. Phillip McIntyre."

"Phillip . . . you mean . . . Uncle Phil?" His knees weakened again. Phillip McIntyre wasn't really an uncle, but an old friend of Tombstone's *real* uncle, Admiral Thomas Magruder. The two older men went way back together. They'd been regular blood brothers all during grade school and high school, and remained close after that even though their careers had taken them in opposite directions from college on. Phillip McIntyre had gone into engineering, focusing on the development of computer circuitry long before it was trendy, then cashing in on the sudden bonanza. From there he'd diversified into other forms of manufacturing and high-tech development.

Tombstone remembered his uncle Phil as a kind of jetsetter, always sending cards and gifts from exotic corners of the world. When Tombstone graduated from Annapolis, a brand-new Japanese motorcycle was waiting for him, courtesy of Uncle Phil. More recently, while Tombstone and Tomboy were in Vegas for their quick, supposedly secret wedding, a complete set of hand-carved rosewood bedroom furniture was en route from the Philippines, on one of Uncle Phil's commercial ships.

"Is he . . ." Tombstone said. "Did he . . ."

"They don't know yet. They're still searching. Anyway, your uncle called and told me he won't be having dinner with us tonight."

"I understand." Tombstone shook his head. "That's okay. Frankly, I don't think I'm up for it myself."

She rested a hand on his forearm. "Phillip might not be dead, Tombstone. We don't know yet."

"It's not that. I mean, that's a shock, but there's something else."

"Don't tell me: Your new toy scared the piss out of you. Go on, admit it."

He gulped down another mad surge of laughter. "Not exactly."

Then he told her what *had* happened, and watched her eyes widen in the darkness.

Saturday, 2 August
0732 local (−8 GMT)
Central District
Hong Kong

"Very bad thing. Very bad. Is why I left Vietnam. Now same thing here!"

Dr. George wished the cabbie would shut up. The horrendous midmorning Hong Kong traffic was distracting enough without this man jabbering on about something or other. Dr. George was on his way to make a crucial presentation, and he wanted to rehearse it in his mind. He wanted it to be just right. Absolutely convincing. Hundreds of thousands of lives were at stake.

No, millions of dollars. That's the angle. This is Hong Kong, remember. Millions of dollars are at stake, that's what I've got to tell them. Billions *of dollars.*

It was a shame he had to behave like a door-to-door salesman to seek financing for his work. Unfortunately, for political and economic reasons, the United States government had cut back drastically on direct research into Dr. George's specialty: Pacific Basin tropical storms. The logic was that typhoons were a Pacific phenomenon, and the National Oceanographic and Atmospheric Administration had reason to concentrate its resources on Atlantic Basin storms. It was hurricanes, after all, that endangered American homes and American businesses. With the exception of Hawaii and a few pissant military enclaves, only faraway Asian lands were threatened by typhoons.

The cabbie shouted something in Vietnamese, his voice high and throbbing. Arms waving, he switched to English. "Where are police? Need order! Need order now!"

George tried to close out the racket and concentrate on his speech. *Mr. Chairman, members of the Board . . . you operate a major shipping company here. How much income does your business lose annually to storm damage, time lost to bad weather, and high insurance premiums?*

The irony was, studying typhoons was a *perfect* way to increase knowledge of hurricanes. Both phenomena had the same causes, but typhoons tended to be larger in size and scope, and to live longer as well. This made them the ideal subjects for detailed study.

If NOAA would only give him a bit more time . . . a year, two years . . . he could hand them the Holy Grail of meteorological research: a truly reliable method of predicting unborn storms. But no, they—

The cabbie shouted again, slamming down simultaneously on brakes and horn. "Traffic very bad today!" he cried. "Very bad! See all people? See signs? Is protess today. You know protess? Is to complain to Chinese about boat sink. Hong Kong people always protess!"

My system, Dr. George recited in his head, *once it's finalized, will allow your business to operate throughout typhoon season with complete confidence. This will give you considerable advantage over your competitors, who will continue to be subject to the vagaries of . . .*

His own government hadn't been the only one to turn him down. After NOAA informed him they would be shifting the majority of his personnel and all of the Guam station's research aircraft to the Atlantic, he'd immediately started contacting other Pacific Rim nations for possible funding.

He'd started with Japan, but they'd bowed out on him. Literally. Ditto the Filipinos, South Koreans, Taiwanese, Indonesians . . . all citing Asia's economic woes.

Which left only Hong Kong. If George failed here, Project Valkyrie would also fail. He had seven meetings arranged over the next two days—far and away the most critical two days of his career.

And that cabdriver just wouldn't shut up.

"Is no good!" the cabbie shouted. "Protess cause big trouble! No good! You see!"

After being rebuffed by governments, George had had what he'd believed to be a stroke of genius: going straight to large, private businesses for financing.

Gentlemen, for an initial investment of only 1.6 million

dollars, you will reap savings of tens of millions annually. . . .

Unfortunately, so far every corporation, conglomerate and guild he'd contacted had been just as shortsighted as their governmental counterparts. Money was tight these days, they pointed out with elaborate regret. As for George's promise to come up with a nearly-flawless storm prediction system, well, they'd heard that before. . . .

"Chinese get angry!" the cabbie shouted. "They say, 'You want trouble? Okay, we give trouble! Sink more than American yacht.' Never trust Chinese!"

George gave up. For the first time he realized that the traffic around them really *had* congealed, even by Hong Kong standards. Young people on foot streamed amongst the stationary cars, heading in the direction of Victoria Square. Many of them carried banners or signs marked in both Chinese characters and in English: YOU WERE WARNED! KEEP HONG KONG FREE! NO TIENANMEN SQUARE! They waved the signs and chanted as they marched.

Dr. George sat back and sighed. Whatever it was they were protesting, in a few days it wouldn't matter. They didn't know what *he* knew: Somewhere out in the Pacific Ocean, the first typhoon of the season was brewing. Not just a typhoon. A super typhoon, king of storms. Winds in excess of two hundred miles per hour. Rain like a barrage of cannon fire. Surf capable of flattening buildings and sweeping cars into the ocean.

George knew, because Valkyrie had told him. Although the program wasn't perfect yet, it was good enough to recognize the approach of a true monster . . . like the one coming to life, right now, in the Pacific not far to the west. Coming to life and turning its attention toward China.

When it arrived . . . well, that would end any protest.

1650 local (−8 GMT)
Carrier Intelligence Center (CVIC)
USS **Jefferson**
South China Sea

Lieutenant Commander Curt "Bird Dog" Robinson strode
down the corridor toward the CVIC, hopping briskly over
each knee-knocker he encountered. He was a little late for
the special briefing, but he'd wanted to make sure his notes
were in order before he arrived. He knew the meeting had
to do with the scuttling of the civilian yacht just before dawn;
all morning he'd watched CH-46E Sea Knights, the twin-
rotored helicopters normally used to ferry Marines into
combat, unloading body bags and a few blasted chunks of
fiberglass onto the apron of the flight deck. As he understood
it, *Jefferson*'s morgue and pathology lab had quickly over-
flowed, and now some of the body bags had joined pieces
of wrecked sailboat in the hangar bay.

He'd heard a wide variety of other rumors, too: The Chinese had fired a torpedo at the yacht; American fighter jets
had tangled with Red Chinese fighters over the site of the
sinking; CBG-14 was about to go on full alert.

The last bit was probably nonsense; as for the rest, he
wasn't so sure. So he wanted to be prepared for any even-
tuality during this meeting. It was important for a lot of reasons. God knew that so far, he hadn't exactly wowed his
superiors with the strategic acumen he'd picked up in his
studies at the Naval War College. In fact, during his first
combat situation after graduation—the Second Cuban Missile Crisis—he'd not only done a lousy job of helping direct
Navy tactics, he'd gotten his butt shot out of the sky.

To make matters worse, at the time, he wasn't even supposed to be in the air. He was lucky to still have his wings,
far less be called in to provide analysis during an emergency
meeting off the coast of the last major Communist power in
the world. He most sincerely did *not* want to screw up again.

Admiral Wayne was already at the table when Bird Dog
walked into the CVIC. So was Chief of Staff William Grant,

call sign Coyote. Bird Dog knew that Batman and the COS went way back together; they'd flown Tomcats during the retrieval of American hostages held in North Korea.

The table was also occupied by four pilots in rumpled flight suits, and an enlisted man in khakis. Bird Dog barely glanced at them, because the Admiral was giving him the cold eye. "Commander, glad you could join us. We're waiting on Commander Busby; please have a seat."

Bird Dog took a chair, silently thanking Lab Rat for being even later than he was.

No one in the room seemed disposed to chitchat, so Bird Dog began organizing his papers on the table. Not that there was a lot to organize . . . his notes about recent military encounters in the South China Sea and adjacent North Pacific; the current political situation in the People's Republic, Indonesia, and Hong Kong. Finally, he sat back and raised his eyes—and found himself looking directly at Lobo, sitting across the table from him.

Oh, shit. He immediately looked away. From experience he knew that if he hesitated, he wouldn't be able to turn away from her at all. Ever since they'd met last year, he'd had this stupid problem. She wasn't *that* goddamned beautiful.

Fortunately, at that moment the door that connected CVIC with the adjacent Tactical Flag Command Center opened, and Commander Hillman "Lab Rat" Busby, *Jefferson*'s Intelligence Officer, stepped through. "Sorry I'm late, Admiral," he said. "Wanted to check the latest Chinese radio traffic."

"And?"

"On the diplomatic end, they're still demanding we turn the wreckage and bodies over to them. On the military end, we're just picking up a lot of 'What's going on?' and 'Stand off for now.' "

Batman frowned. "Very well. Now that we're all here, let me bring everyone up to speed. This morning, Lieutenant Commander Hanson, on routine patrol, spotted a PLA helicopter firing on an unarmed American pleasure boat in international waters. She and her wingman, Lieutenant

Commander Stone, drove the helicopter off. We then established a defensive perimeter and began recovering what we could from the wreckage. So far only one survivor of the attack has been found; he's currently in sick bay here on *Jefferson*. The bodies of the other passengers, as well as whatever pieces of hull can be recovered, are being ferried in. Does that pretty much sum it up?" He looked around the table.

Bird Dog had been taking notes, his thoughts streaking ahead on full afterburner. War College had stressed the ancient precept that war was politics by other means—national policy expressed in violence. In the twentieth century, certain Communist nations had been especially fond of mixing the two. But a massacre of civilians on the open sea? What political aim could China possibly expect to serve by *that*?

He looked up as Batman turned toward the rescue swimmer. "Petty Officer Pitcock, you recovered several of the bodies yourself, as well as the survivor, is that correct?"

The swimmer was a young, freckled guy with hair so blonde and short he looked almost bald. His eyes were the fierce red color that proved he'd spent a lot of time blinking against the salty spray blasted up by a hovering helicopter. "Yes, sir," he said. "We found the survivor, Martin Lee, hanging on to what was left of the boat. Spotted him pretty quick."

"And there were no other survivors, is that correct?"

"Not yet. SAR is still ongoing, but . . . no, it doesn't look good."

"Tell me, how many bodies would you say you counted out there?"

The swimmer cleared his throat. "I'd say close to a hundred. Maybe more. Some of them were just shot to pieces, plus the sharks had been at them. . . ." He dragged a palm over his scalp.

Sharks. Bird Dog suppressed a shudder. He knew everyone else in the room was doing the same; sharks were the great nightmare of everyone who sailed on, or flew above, the sea. But he knew from personal experience that you didn't even know what that fear was all about until you got dumped into the drink and had to float around awhile, watching for a triangular dorsal fin to break the surface of the water. . . .

And this kid had jumped in on *purpose*.

He brought his attention back to the room. "I understand Mr. Lee spoke to you," Batman was saying.

The swimmer licked chapped lips. "Yes, sir, on the way back. He said the yacht was American, and it got hijacked and sunk by the PLA for no reason. Mr. Lee's Chinese, but his English is real good, and—"

"But you saw nothing, personally, to indicate why that particular boat might have been attacked," Batman said. "I'm only asking because you were in the water, closer to the wreck than anybody, before it sank."

"No, sir, I didn't see anything at all. Just a real nice boat shot to pieces."

"Thank you." Batman turned to Coyote. "COS, any questions?"

"I believe you covered everything."

"Commander Busby?"

Lab Rat seemed to blink out of a reverie. "Um, no, sir. I'm going to want to talk to Mr. Lee as soon as possible, of course, but that's it."

"We're waiting for Doc's okay on that. Bird Dog, anything for Petty Officer Pitcock?"

Bird Dog was startled by the use of his call sign, and immediately wondered if this was a good or bad indicator. He'd been paranoid that way, lately; second-guessing everything. He was pretty sure it had started with his being dumped by his fiancée. "Not right now, sir," he said.

"Very well. Petty Officer Pitcock, thank you."

After the swimmer was gone, Batman turned his attention to the pilots and RIOs. "Lobo, you were first on the scene. Describe exactly what you saw."

There was no avoiding it now. Bird Dog looked across the table at Lobo. Her eyes were socketed with exhaustion and her flight suit was all wrinkled and creased. No doubt about it: She was absolutely the most enticing thing Lieutenant Commander Curt Robinson had seen in his life.

And she flew F-14s. Flew them like an angel.

He'd met her in a bar, not long after Callie notified him that she'd changed her mind about marrying him. Pretty cliché for a fighter jock to catch the eye of a beautiful woman in a bar, except that Bird Dog hadn't intended to even be there. His regular RIO, Gator Cummings, had introduced him to Lobo because, he confessed later, he was pretty sure Lobo had balls at least the size of Bird Dog's. He wanted to see who swung first.

Nobody had swung. In fact, Bird Dog hadn't exactly caught Lobo's eyes. In *fact*, when he'd asked her for her number, she had grinned and said, "One."

Fine, he'd thought as he and Gator left the bar. Who needed to deal with an uppity—if beautiful—female Tomcat pilot? Probably some kind of radical feminist, if not a lesbian.

Last thing he'd expected was to be sent on WestPac with her. To see her almost every day, in the corridors and on the flight deck of *Jefferson*. To hear other male pilots talk about her the way male pilots do, albeit more privately than in years gone by. To see her absorb their more public teasing and fire it right back. He hadn't expected to . . . to . . .

He watched Lobo as she spoke, even jotting down an occasional note so he'd appear to be paying attention to her words instead of just the shape of her lips. He picked up enough of what she said to return his attention sharply to the matter at hand. Now was no time to let his mind wander.

Lobo's RIO—the lucky bastard—spoke next, seconding everything Lobo had said—not that that meant anything. Any backseater worthy of the name backed his pilot up, no matter what. Hell, the RIO would swear he'd seen Elvis on a flying carpet, if that was what Lobo reported.

The second Tomcat pilot, Hot Rock, and his RIO were next. They recited what they'd observed from their higher altitude, and the brief tale of the helicopter chase. Although he was just a pup, Hot Rock looked more exhausted than anyone else, Bird Dog noticed.

"Could you identify the type of helo?" Lab Rat asked the young pilot.

"No, sir. It was dark, and I was above it. I can only say it was single-rotor. I was just about to go down for a closer look when—"

"We got called back," his RIO filled in. Just as Bird Dog's RIO, Gator, often finished his sentences for him. Annoying as hell.

COS leaned forward. "What about missiles?"

"Missiles?" Hot Rock said.

"Yes, was the helo carrying missiles?"

The men looked at one another. The pilot shrugged. "I couldn't tell, sir; not from my angle."

"Lobo? You certainly had the angle."

"But no time." She paused, bit her lip, then shook her head. "No, sir, I only took one pass; I can't say for sure if the helo was carrying missiles."

COS nodded, made a note and leaned back.

"I have a question for Lobo," Batman said. "What convinced you that you were justified in making a low-altitude, high-speed pass at another nation's helicopter with an American fighter plane?"

She started. Her face hardened. "That helo was *mincing* those people in the water, Admiral. You heard Pitcock; it was a massacre. At the time, politics seemed . . . irrelevant."

Batman held her gaze for a long time, then nodded. "Be sure to stress that in your report. I'll back you up a hundred percent, but I'm warning you all, if the Chinese know something we don't, this whole affair could turn around and bite us in the butt."

"Yes, sir." Lobo stared right at him, uncowed. Bird Dog's heart stumbled with pride. *Go, girl.*

"Very well," Batman said. "If none of you have anything else to add, you pilots and RIOs are dismissed. Get some rest. You've earned it."

As the pilots and RIOs filed toward the door, Bird Dog took the opportunity to glance up, as if by accident, and meet Lobo's eyes. He nodded at her, very cool and professional. To his horror, she gave him a broad, theatrical wink.

After the door closed, Batman said, "All right, I want ideas and I want them now. At the moment I'm not interested in whether or not you think our response was appropriate; I'm only interested in what you think the Chinese might be up to, and what they might try next."

Lab Rat said, "Their next move is bound to be political. They'll spin some kind of yarn for public consumption."

"I agree," Bird Dog said.

The earned him a quick, unnervingly searching glance from Batman. Bird Dog forced himself to meet it. "While I was at War College, there was a lot of talk about a war game they conducted there a year or two earlier. It was intended to be a complete assessment of the probable outcome of an all-out war with the PRC." He paused. "We lost."

Batman frowned. "Lost?"

"Yes, sir. The Chinese ended up controlling all of the Far East, including Japan. It created quite a flap—well, in an underground sort of way—about cuts in American military spending. Because the gap is widening."

"And you think the Chinese have chosen to start World War Three by blowing the hell out of an American yacht?"

Bird Dog blinked. "I'm just saying—"

"Coyote?" Batman turned to the COS. "Your assessment?"

"I'm not sure what the PRC's overall motivation is, but when they started things in the Spratleys, manipulating public opinion was their next trick—so I'd expect that next."

"Okay, they're going to make a public stink. Agreed. But what's their next step *here* likely to be?"

"The Chinese study their ancient sages," Lab Rat said. He took a slim book out of his pocket and tossed it on the table. Looking at the title, Bird Dog felt a thrill of recognition. It was Sun Tzu's *The Art of War*—the oldest known treatise on organized warfare. They'd studied it in War College. Lab Rat said, "This is what helped me guess what they were up to in the Spratleys. They believe the best general wins without fighting at all. He uses deception, infiltration, undermines his enemy's alliances—"

"Political warfare," Bird Dog blurted. He couldn't help himself. "They'll complain about the way *we* handled this. Try to shift the blame to us."

"That's all fine," Batman said impatiently, "but it doesn't

answer my question. What can we expect them to do next *here*?"

Since Lab Rät didn't seem to have anything to say, Bird Dog spoke again. This time he tried to keep his voice mild. "Down in the Spratleys," he said, "the Chinese blew up their own assets and tried to make it look like *we* did it. Their goal was to make us look like aggressors so they'd be justified in driving us out of the South China Sea. This time, they're doing the opposite: They attacked American *civilians* . . . so the only possible reason is that they want to make sure we *stay* in the area."

A thudding silence ensued.

"Commander," Batman said, his voice as slow and cold as a glacier, "what have you been taking notes on all night?"

"Sir?" Bird Dog felt the tips of his ears burning.

"The Chinese might be obtuse, but they're not stupid. First of all—especially if you're correct about their long-term goals—what possible reason would they have to keep a Carrier Battle Group near their coast?"

"I don't know," Bird Dog said. "But—"

"Good answer," Batman said. "Now, assuming that *was* their goal for some reason, wouldn't they want to do something really *public* to ensure our attention? Wouldn't they launch a few missiles our way, or at least attack an American yacht in Victoria Harbor at high noon, rather than in the South China Sea, outside the shipping lanes, at five o'clock in the morning?"

The heat swarmed across Bird Dog's face and neck. "Not if they *intended* to leave survivors," he said—knowing it was a mistake even as he spoke, but once again unable to trap the words. "The automatic SOS signal from the boat was triggered, which suggests—"

" 'Automatic' means just that, Commander. And the Chinese plainly did *not* intend to leave any survivors—or even evidence. You heard Pitcock. Only Lobo's quick action kept anyone alive out there."

Bird Dog closed his mouth. Why couldn't he ever seem to do that *before* he started flossing with his shoelaces?

To his relief, Lab Rat spoke up as if none of the previous

discussion had occurred. "Admiral, I hate to sound like Mr. Spock, but we need more information before we can reach any conclusions at all, far less try to predict the next move the Chinese might make. Meanwhile, I suggest we convey as many facts as possible to Seventh Fleet so they can get our version out there before the Chinese make up some kind of PR story."

"A preemptive publicity strike," Batman said dryly.

"It's a media-driven world, Admiral."

"So it is. I'll expect a draft of your recommended wording of such a public statement in an hour. Get together with the staff PAO on it."

Lab Rat sighed. "Yes, sir."

Batman glanced around the table. "Anything else? COS?"

Coyote shook his head. Bird Dog started to speak, but when he saw the sharp, assessing look in the admiral's eye, he changed his mind.

"Thank you, gentlemen." Batman got to his feet. "I'm going to go see how the recovery operation is going." He strode out of the room, COS on his heels.

Bird Dog stood up and began gather his notes. His knees were a little wobbly, but he wasn't sure whether that was from anger or shame. As he turned toward the door, he heard Lab Rat say, "Bird Dog?" Bird Dog turned.

"With the Chinese," Lab Rat said, "it's probably best to keep all lines of thinking open . . . even those that seem ridiculous. Don't tell the admiral I said that." He held something across the table. "Why don't you keep this awhile?"

Bird Dog accepted the gift. It was the slim copy of Sun Tzu's *The Art of War*.

1950 local (−8 GMT)
Pri-Fly
USS **Jefferson**

Batman stood in the tower next to the Air Boss, looking out beyond the flight deck to the silhouette of an oncoming CH-

46E Sea Knight. There were two silhouettes, actually: the helicopter's and that of its cargo, dangling beneath. Behind them glared the red furnace of the setting sun; beneath spread a blood-colored river of light. Blood-colored, Batman thought grimly. How appropriate.

"That's the last trip, Admiral," the Air Boss said. "Got the biggest piece of the boat. Had a hell of a time hooking it up." He paused. "I understand most of it broke off and sank anyway."

"Will it fit in the hangar bay?" Batman asked.

The Air Boss scanned the double silhouette with a practiced eye. "I think so. Barely. I'm having them set it down by the aft elevator; we'll see from there."

Batman nodded.

"I heard the legal eagles are disturbed about us bringing any of the boat aboard," the Air Boss said. "Something about salvage laws."

Batman set his jaw. "I'd say that taking control of evidence of international piracy and mass murder is a bit more important than salvage law."

"I don't mind telling you, Admiral—I'm glad it's your headache and not mine."

"You've got enough to worry about, Chad. Let me take care of the bullshit."

The Sea Knight circled aft, gradually changing from a blunt silhouette to a long, sun-smeared loaf of French bread with enormous rotors fore and aft. Beneath it, suspended by cables and netting, hung a slab of fiberglass bursting with aluminum rails, foam insulation, wires, miscellaneous pieces of upholstery and carpeting.

"Used to be part of the upper deck and main cabin, I guess," the Air Boss said. "We could get lucky; maybe there's a logbook or something in it."

Batman, not trusting to luck, just nodded.

The Sea Knight positioned itself off the stern and began easing toward the deck. Like any other aircraft, helos benefited from using prevailing wind conditions to increase lift—especially when heavily loaded.

On deck, the landing signals officer, or LSO, signaled the helo toward the aft elevator.

The helo drifted over the stern, rotors beating heavily, cargo just clearing the non-skid. As usual, the skill required to maneuver the big helo stirred a grudging respect in Batman, who generally shared the jet jockey's ingrained disdain for "eggbeaters."

The LSO backed up step by step, drawing the helo in. When the cargo was finally hovering just above the elevator, the signals changed and the Sea Knight eased to a halt. The cargo began to descend, cables trembling as the winch played out. Flight deck personnel eased in toward it, ready to wrestle the massive hulk into position.

The smashed piece of yacht hull touched the deck, and the cables began to slacken. Suddenly Batman felt a chill flash through him, so powerful it shook him to his heels. "Get those men—!" he began.

A flash of light blotted out the sunset, ripping into the sky and across the deck, pursued by a roiling black cloud and a bellow that rattled the Plexiglas in Pri-Fly. Batman instinctively ducked, and found the Air Boss crouching right beside him. "What the *hell*?" the Air Boss shouted.

Then both were back on their feet. "Fire on the flight deck!" the Air Boss shouted. He slammed the General Quarters alarm on and jabbed at the bitch box. "Officer of the Deck, Boss. Did you see that?"

Batman stared at the flight deck, unmoving, as the alarm went off. Where the wreckage of the yacht had been was now nothing but a blackened, cratered section of the elevator pad. Inboard from that, a ring of flames leaped across the deck. Four parked Hornets were on fire. So were two prostrate bodies. There was no sign of the LSO. How many other—

Then the Sea Knight appeared, dropping from the sky on a comet of flame. It barely cleared the flight deck, vanishing over the side.

A moment later, an enormous plume of water rose in a bursting fountain. It spread and collapsed down again, and not one drop reached the blazing deck.

1955 local (−8 GMT)
USS Jefferson

If the army is confused and suspicious, neighboring rulers
will cause trouble. This is what is meant by the saying, "A
confused army leads to another's victory."

Bird Dog lowered the book and stared at the ceiling above
his bunk. Even back at War College, he had found *The Art*
of War an interesting but frustrating read. It was one thing
to pass a test on it, and another to actually understand it.
Despite its brevity, Sun Tzu's book was more difficult to get
your brain around than the dense and detailed Clausewitz'
treatment of the same subject. Sun Tzu was so . . . so *Chi-*
nese. Allegorical, poetic, as suggestive as a pen and ink
sketch.

And about as practical.

Bird Dog cringed when he thought about his attempt, at
the special briefing, to explain China's motivation for sinking
the *Lady of Leisure*. As if he had a clue; as if Sun Tzu
provided one. *The Art of War* might be hailed as a classic,
but as far as Bird Dog was concerned, its obtuseness explained why the Chinese hadn't won a major military campaign in years.

Closing the book, he sighed and tried to concentrate on
something more predictable: the flow of activity on the flight
deck, its music transmitted to him in the muffled roar of
spooled-up jet engines and the thump of the catapult shuttle
hitting its stops. Just by listening to that symphony overhead,
he could tell what was going on. Today, the rhythm had
alternated between the launching and landing of fixed-wing
aircraft and the arrival of helos bearing bloody presents from
the South China Sea. Currently, the quiet heralded a helo
period.

God, he wished he was scheduled to fly tonight. Or better,
the next time Lobo was scheduled. He frowned. What *was*
it about that woman? Maybe he was just on the rebound.
After all, not long ago he'd had a very hot thing going with
a Navy woman—he'd even proposed to her, idiot that he
was—but she'd dumped him for a fellow surface officer, of

all things. So it was only natural he'd be attracted to a good-looking female pilot. Somebody who shared his passions, problems and dreams. Of course. That made perfect sense.

Okay, that took care of that. He opened the book again, arbitrarily, and started reading.

He who knows the art of both the direct and indirect approach will be victorious. This is the art of maneuvering.

Well, now, *there* was a solid piece of military advice. "The direct and indirect approach." Very informative. Very—

He dropped the book onto his stomach as the ship transmitted an unfamiliar sensation to him: a sharp jolt, followed by a deep, buzzing vibration. A moment later came the sound of thunder.

Bird Dog's feet hit the deck before general quarters began to sound.

FOUR

Saturday, 2 August

The sky above Hong Kong was a shimmer of purple silk as General Ming Wen Hsien strode toward the administrative wing of the Hong Kong garrison of the People's Liberation Army. At the door, he paused to take in the view of Hong Kong's lights soaring up against the twilight. The scene looked like one of the postcards sold in the lobbies of the fancy Central District hotels.

With his aide just behind him, Ming entered the building and saluted a surprised-looking desk sergeant. "Remain where you are," he said, as the guard started to stand. "Do not notify the commanders I am here."

"Y-yes, sir," the sergeant stuttered.

Ming moved through the reception area and down a long corridor. At the closed door of the main conference room, he signaled his aide to wait, then opened the door and strode in.

He scanned the changes to the room since his last visit— April 21, 1997. That had been the greatest day of his life— the day the British Crown had, at last, turned the military garrison over to its rightful owners. On that day, this room had been bare of furniture; the English had taken theirs away, of course. Now it contained a circular conference table and matching chairs, sideboard and audio-visual equipment cabinet, all made of teak hand-carved in dragons and the fishes of good fortune.

The furnishings had clearly been chosen not for utility so much as the way they complimented the room's original walnut paneling and plush wall-to-wall carpeting.

Ming kept the disapproval off his face. He knew that Major General Wei Ao was responsible for the decor in this room.

Three men sat at the conference table, staring at him first in anger, then surprise. Then they were on their feet and bowing respectfully. And so they should. Ming represented the ultimate authority—not just the PLA, but the entire Chinese Communist Party. In the People's Republic, all members of the State Central Military Commission also served on the Communist Party's Central Military Commission—"Two organs with one leading body." For the PLA, military and politico-social goals were the same.

At least, this was the belief and the goal, especially in the so-called Special Administrative Region. Ming let his gaze scan the group standing around the long table. The men had, he noted, positioned themselves equidistantly around the table, as if to illustrate their separation: Political Commissar nearest the door at eight o'clock, Coastal Patrol at four, and the Major General of the Army firmly enthroned at the twelve o'clock position. They all wore the special Hong Kong uniforms of their departments—dark green for the Army, white for the Coastal Defense Force, khaki for the Political Commissar. The only consistent feature was the shoulder blaze shared by all: the scarlet bahinia blossom of the Hong Kong SAR.

On the day the garrison became Chinese once again, there had been five Major Generals in this room. Unfortunately two of them—the commanders of the Air Force and Navy contingents—had recently died. Filling their positions would be no easy task; it took a special kind of officer to work in the SAR.

Ming fixed his gaze on Wei. Fortunately, the old Army leader was not one of the newly deceased. He had been in command of the entire Hong Kong garrison since the Handover, and got dubbed "First Among Equals" by local newspapers, in sardonic commentary on what the Hong Kongese considered a top-heavy command structure.

Ming marched directly around the table toward the old soldier, who immediately shifted his squat body to his left. The other two moved as well, rearranging themselves to maintain at least one empty chair between them.

Then they all sat, with Ming now at twelve o'clock.

Yeh Lien, the Political Commissar, cleared his throat. "Comrade General Ming, this is an honor. Perhaps we missed the message that you were coming."

"There was no time for niceties. The Central Council is concerned about the incident with the American yacht. None of your reports on the incident are acceptable. How is it possible the perpetrators of this crime were not apprehended?"

Old Wei, First Among Equals, shook his head. "This incident occurred in international waters and airspace—the provinces of the Navy and Air Force. Unfortunately, both these forces are currently under the command of inexperienced officers. They were not certain how to respond. Until new commanding officers arrive—"

"Until that time, *you* will be held responsible," Ming said coldly. "You are commander of the entire SAR garrison, are you not?"

Wei drew himself up. "I am. But remember, General, we must all operate under standing orders which forbid us from initiating a 'potentially hostile encounter' with foreign military forces—especially the Americans. It happens that several U.S. Navy jets reached the SOS area before we did, and since they were in international airspace, our commanders elected to stand off. As per orders."

Ming stared at him flatly. "The Americans claim otherwise. In fact, they claim that the People's Liberation Army was responsible for the attack on the yacht itself."

"That's *ridiculous!*" Wei shouted, to a chorus of agreement from the other two officers.

Ming raised a hand, creating instant silence. "You all deny any involvement, then?"

Now came a barrage of angry affirmation. Ming watched their faces closely. "The Americans say they have both evidence and witnesses," he said.

"Then let them present this evidence," Yeh, the Political Commissar, said.

"Yes, let them present it," echoed Chin of the Coastal Defense Force.

Ming eyed Chin. He was by far the youngest of the garrison commanders, only fifty, but that did not excuse the man's helpless incompetence. His having a cousin in a position of power on the State Council was a different matter. Ming felt fortunate that he'd managed to limit Chin's command assignment to the CDF, the least glamorous of all China's military branches. And the least likely to get the fool into serious trouble.

Ming addressed the table at large. "Let me explain our difficulty. Since even before the Revolution, Hong Kong has been the government's connection to the foreign world. For now, sustaining it is a necessary evil. The People's Republic ohas long-term projects under way here; their progress must not be interrupted. This means that to the rest of the world, the image of the SAR must remain one of stability and safety. You will all be approached by the Hong Kong media concerning what happened to the *Lady of Leisure*. Since the State does not currently control the news media here, we must all agree on a correct version of events, to balance whatever lies the Americans intend to tell the world."

"What correct version?" Wei asked. "How can we know what to say to the Americans if we don't even know what evidence they have?"

Ming looked at the staring faces around the table and squelched a surge of anger. Wei was a soldier of the old school, tough but lacking in personal vision; Yeh was a blind idealogue; Chin a cretinous lump. In losing Hsu and Po, the SAR garrison had lost its best military—and political—minds.

"Comrade Major General Wei," Ming said, "I'm sure you have studied your Sun Tzu."

"Of course."

"Then you know that Sun Tzu taught this: The wise general conquers because he has foreknowledge. He employs spies in the enemy camp."

"You're saying we have spies?" Wei said. "In America?"

Ming offered a small smile. "And closer to home as well. It is not even necessary to infiltrate our own people. It is only necessary to provide the proper incentive to Americans already in place."

"Money," Yeh said.

"What else? Money is Hong Kong's national product. And thanks to it, we have already learned the broad outlines of what the Americans claim happened to that yacht. Now we need only to create our own story to fit the same circumstances. . . ."

2100 local (−8 GMT)
CVIC
USS **Jefferson**

"Semtex," Lieutenant Jim "Bomber" Marsh said. "There's no question about that."

Batman nodded grimly. If anyone would know, it would be the SEAL officer assigned as Special Forces Advisor to the carrier's staff. Although the explosion had disintegrated the chunk of *Lady of Leisure*'s hull in which it had been contained, in doing so it inevitably left behind a particular signature: a distinctive blast pattern, particular chemical deposits, certain bits of debris, all of which were like fingerprints to an expert. Even without specialized demolition training, Batman knew that Semtex was a very popular form of plastic explosive, equivalent to America's C-4 but much more widely available. Terrorists had made it the favored clay of their bloody art.

Batman realized that against all odds, he had been clinging to the macabre hope that the explosion had been some kind of accident—the spontaneous combustion of a fuel tank on board the salvaged hull, perhaps. That would be better than the thought that someone had succeeded in sneaking a massive bomb on board *Jefferson*. No—in getting the U.S. Navy to place the bomb there themselves. My God, if they'd had time to lower the wreckage onto the hangar deck, as they'd planned . . . with all those parked planes and jet fuel . . .

"What about the fuse?" he asked. "How was this damned thing set off?"

"Can't be sure," Bomber said. "What didn't go up in smoke went over the side. But judging by the sequence of events, it was probably a pressure-sensitive trigger. When the weight of the wreckage settled on deck—boom."

"What, you mean the Chinese *guessed* we'd be putting that particular chunk of wreckage on board *Jefferson*? That doesn't seem credible."

There was a moment of silence. Then Lab Rat said, "Maybe the bomb wasn't meant for us at all."

Batman frowned at him. "Explain yourself."

"Maybe its real purpose was to finish off the *Lady of Leisure*; it wasn't supposed to go any further than that. Not pressure detonated, but it had a bad time—a dud. We just got . . . unlucky."

Batman closed his eyes briefly. "Unlucky." He looked at Bird Dog, who had yet to say a word. Batman was ambivalent about this particular officer. At one time he'd described Bird Dog as a "good man"—but that had been before Cuba and all the childish nonsense Bird Dog had pulled down there. Add to that the man's seeming inability to transpose all his book learning to real-life situations . . . and you had to wonder, what was the use of including him in these meetings?

On the other hand, where would Rear Admiral Batman Wayne be if nobody had ever given *him* a break? And Bird Dog could fly, there was no doubt about that. Lately, he'd even shown some signs of gaining a little maturity.

"Commander Robinson?" Batman said.

Bird Dog raised his head, and his hands slid over the tabletop—he seemed at a loss without his usual notebooks and charts. Then he took a deep breath and squared his shoulders. "I'm inclined to agree with Commander Busby. This seems like an awfully complicated way to get a booby trap on board *Jefferson*. Especially since if damaging us was their goal, why didn't they do a better job?"

"A *better job*?" Batman said. "We lost ten sailors in that blast, Commander. Six aircraft are in the shop, and one Sea Knight is on the bottom of the South China Sea."

Bird Dog placed his hands in his lap, but his jaw was set. The guy had moxie, you had to give him that. "I know all that, sir. But it seems to me the damage could have been much worse. They could have loaded more explosives on the wreck, or used a shaped charge or some kind of incendiary chemical. They could have holed the flight deck, blown the parked planes away, taken out the antenna array . . . they could have tried to *really* hurt us. But they didn't. So that tells me they didn't intend to."

Batman stared at him a moment longer, then turned toward Bomber. Bomber cocked his head and raised one eyebrow. "It's true, they could have rigged something with a lot more muscle behind it."

"Here's another piece of evidence in that direction," Lab Rat said. "At the time of the explosion, we detected no increased Chinese military activity in the area. If they'd intended to soften us up with a booby trap, wouldn't they have taken advantage?"

"Answering that kind of question is your department, Commander." Batman caught himself, sighed. "Damn it, it goes against my instincts to think we got damaged by an explosion and it was just a . . . fluke. You can't strike back at a damned accident."

There were grim nods all around the table.

"All right. We'll report that this was an accident of sorts. No retaliation."

"Sir . . ." Bird Dog said. "If I may make one more suggestion."

"Go ahead."

"It might be best if the Chinese don't even learn about the explosion. Even if it was an accident . . . well, us being hurt by that bomb . . . it makes us look stupid."

Batman noticed that Lab Rat was nodding. "You mean we lose face."

"Face is important to the Chinese," Bird Dog said. "No point in giving them ammunition against us."

Batman nodded. "I'll make sure to note your suggestion in my report, Bird Dog. It's a good one."

Bird Dog smiled and visibly relaxed.

But not Batman. Although the "accident" theory should make him feel less threatened, the opposite was true. Because he'd just realized what that theory meant, strategically speaking: They were right back where they'd started. Nowhere.

The only people who knew what was going on around here were the Chinese.

Friday, 1 August
1300 local (+5 GMT)
United Nations

As Ambassador Sarah Wexler rose to her feet at the long table, she managed not to glance over at her counterpart from the People's Republic of China, Ambassador T'ing. Controlling her expression took a much greater effort.

It was hard to believe that the Spratley Islands affair had occurred only four years ago. On that occasion, the results for China had been so devastating that the U.S. had deemed it necessary to provide Beijing with a face-saving cover story: that the downed Chinese aircraft had been caught in a freak typhoon.

Privately, of course, insiders in both countries knew that the "typhoon" had taken the form of Carrier Battle Group 14 of the U.S. Navy. You would think that the Spratley Islands affair would have taught China the grave dangers of throwing its weight around, even in Asia.

But now . . . this.

"I'm sure," Ambassador Wexler said to the assembled dignitaries, "you're all aware of recent, horrible events in the South China Sea. Two days ago, an unarmed, private yacht owned by an American businessman was attacked and sunk by a military helicopter of the People's Republic of China. The result was the deaths of more than sixty people of a half-dozen nationalities."

She paused to scan the table. So far, no face had assumed the shape of its owner's political inclination. She went on in the same voice of controlled outrage, describing the assault on *Lady of Leisure* by quoting almost verbatim from the transcript of the sole survivor of the attack. She left out only such details as the name of the man who had commanded the attacking vessel, such tidbits being more useful in behind-closed-doors negotiations.

As she spoke, she glanced around the table. Sure enough, delegates from nations friendly to the United States looked outraged; those from unfriendly countries appeared scornful or, at best, impassive.

T'ing seemed barely interested.

She bit back her anger and went on. "If it weren't for the timely intervention of a United States Navy fighter plane on routine patrol from the aircraft carrier USS *Jefferson*, it's safe to say there would have been no survivors of this tragedy at all. No one to have brought this story before the public. As it is, we have such a survivor, as well as the eyewitness testimony of four American aviators—including the heroic pilot who drove the attacking helicopter off without firing a single shot of her own. We also have physical evidence of the most conclusive and terrible kind—pieces of wreckage and the corpses of one hundred and sixteen men and women, all riddled with twenty-two millimeters bullet holes—the same caliber as the cannons mounted on PLA Navy Z-9 helicopters."

She looked around again, matching everyone eye for eye. T'ing's face remained impassive, his eyes half-closed as if he were listening politely to a folktale recited by a child. Again, she reined in her anger.

"This murderous assault," she went on, "would, of course, be unconscionable no matter where it occurred. However, it's all the more disturbing because the site is Hong Kong, which is of crucial importance to the economic well-being of the entire Southeast Asia region. The wanton massacre of the *Lady of Leisure* is certain to rekindle the doubts felt by many nations regarding the trustworthiness of China's pledge to honor the provisions of the Sino-British Agreement of 1985. The massacre of the passengers on *Lady of Leisure* represents an unprovoked act of aggression so extreme it eclipses even the student killings in Tienanmen Square. It . . ."

She realized T'ing was coming to his feet, rising as slowly and inexorably as the mercury in a thermometer. She fell silent, surprised by an act of rudeness she'd come to expect of the Cuban and Libyan representatives, but never of the Chinese.

When he had everyone's attention, T'ing said, "Your passion about this matter is understandable, Madame Ambassador. However, the fact that an atrocity occurred in the vicinity of the People's Republic of China does not automatically mean we are responsible."

Wexler remained silent.

"The People's Republic of China denies any knowledge of, or involvement in, the act of piracy and murder you describe. We remain completely committed to the agreement under which the illegally annexed Hong Kong territories were returned to our control.

"Ladies and Gentlemen, the attack upon the American yacht was not, in fact, carried out by personnel or equipment from the People's Liberation Army. Major General Wei Ao, the officer in charge of the Hong Kong garrison, assures us that all PLA personnel and equipment were accounted for on the evening in question; the records supporting this claim are available for anyone's review."

Wexler knew that the value of such documents was equal to the ash they would make when burned. "What of the witnesses, Mr. T'ing?" she asked coldly, refusing to sit.

T'ing's eyes shifted her way briefly, then back to the table at large. "We believe that this incident was the result of an illegal narcotics transaction. We know that one of the guests aboard the yacht, Pablo Cheung, was a notorious racketeer and drug dealer in Macau; Macau itself, yet another illegally sequestered fragment of Chinese territory, is a haunt of gangs and gangsters as terrible as America's own Chicago or New York. As for your witnesses, Madame Ambassador, by your own admission one of them is a very frightened and no doubt shocked young man, who might or might not have himself been involved in the narcotics activities aboard the yacht. Perhaps he really thought the attackers were in military equipment, perhaps he can't tell the difference—or perhaps he fabricated that detail. How would we know? He has been questioned only by representatives of the United States, who can hardly be considered neutral in this matter. And this, despite the fact that this man is a citizen of China, not the United States, and the People's Republic has repeatedly asked for his return.

"As for your other so-called witnesses, they are fighter pilots of the United States Navy . . . and I doubt I need to remind anyone at this table that no one is quicker to look for an excuse to involve her military in situations where they do not belong than is the United States."

Wexler drew herself to her full height. "If you're accusing the United States government of trying to take advantage of this tragedy to—"

"There is a word for what you are showing now, Ambassador," T'ing said. " 'Paranoia.' I have accused no one of anything; I merely recite historical fact. I'm sure the governments of Iran, Iraq, Libya, Korea and many other nations will agree."

T'ing bowed and sat.

Wexler did not. She continued to recite the official United States position on the massacre, but in the back of her mind, she wondered.

T'ing had interrupted her. Stood up and cut her off. For him, that was the equivalent of hysterics. Either that, or he *wanted* her to think he was hysterical.

No. After all these years as an ambassador, she'd learned to trust her instincts. Something was very wrong here, beyond even the murder of one hundred and sixteen innocent people. As awful as the massacre had been, there was some deeper work going on. Of course, the disguise of one motive behind another was business as usual for the Chinese, who

were steeped in the teachings of the semi-mythical Chinese
military philosopher Sun Tzu: "All war is deception." But
the *Lady of Leisure* massacre seemed to be more than mere
sleight-of-hand to mislead an international audience. If even
T'ing was out of the loop . . .

What was going on in China?

Saturday, 2 August
2200 local (−8 GMT)
Hangar Bay
USS Jefferson

"Looks like war to me."

Petty Officer Jackson Ord waited a moment, then pulled
his head out of the small compartment set into the side of
Tomcat 304 and saw that one of the tow tractors used to haul
planes around the hangar had pulled up next to him. Behind
the wheel sat Petty Officer Orell Blessing, a Vipers ball cap
perched on his red head. Jackson didn't want to talk to Orell,
far less listen to him, but what could he do? He longed for
the last few days, when Orell had been gone on leave to
Hong Kong.

You didn't ignore Orell Blessing. Didn't kid him about
his name, either. Orell was six and a half feet tall, no matter
which way you turned him. Barely made it through the passageway doors. Rumor was he could carry five tie-down
chains in each hand, one hooked over each finger . . . and
those chains weighed twenty-five pounds *apiece*.

There were a lot of terrific things about the Navy—good,
regular food; clean rooms; good work; more money than he
could spend—but Orell Blessing was not one of them. He
was one of those white-on-white dudes who, under all
the grinning and back-slapping, really didn't believe that the
Confederate Army got its ass whupped in the Civil War.
Suspected the blacks would all come creeping back to their
slave cribs any time now. Navy was full of dudes like that,

but most of them you could ignore. Not Orell.

The only time Jackson felt belittled by having greasy hands, by being a junior petty officer in the U.S. Navy, was when Orell chugged up on his tow tractor.

But right now, Orell wasn't looking at him; he was staring across the hangar bay at the three rows of body bags and chunks of blasted, burned fiberglass lined up there. What was left of yesterday's "incident." People said the morgue couldn't hold all the bodies and shit; it had reached its limit. So they put that stuff in here, the way they used to lay the dead out in the parlor back home, for people to pay their last respects. Except these bodies were in black bags, and had no relatives on the ship. Seemed like bad luck, having them there.

Not that he'd say any of that to Orell. He glanced around to see if his shift supervisor, Petty Officer Rinaldo, was in sight. Wasn't. That figured; guys who outranked you weren't ever around when you needed them. And Orell never came around when Jackson was with any brothers, either. Wiping his hands on a rag, Jackson said in a carefully neutral voice, "I don't got time to talk to you right now, man. Busy with this hydraulics line."

"Don't got time to talk to me, eh?" Orell said, grinning, and winked. Guy came from West Virginia white trash, got dumped out of his division for shit details all the time, couldn't even qualify as a Plane Captain, but acted like he had some degree from Harvard. "Got lots of time to fix that baby gonna drop bombs on your yellow brothers though, right?"

"What you talkin', man?"

"What I talkin'? I talkin' look around you. I talkin' pay attention. We got us lots of airplanes and bombs here. And now we're gonna use 'em, and guess what? Not one of 'em's gonna land on whoever shot up that yacht. We don't even know who those people *were*."

Now Jackson couldn't resist looking toward the bow, at the rows of bodies. Two officers stood amongst the bags, heads close together in discussion. One officer was short and blond-haired, with glasses; Jackson didn't know who he was.

The other was Bird Dog Robinson, the pilot who usually flew this bird. Jackson hadn't had much personal contact with Bird Dog, although the other plane crew members either loved him or hated his guts. Right now, both he and the blond-haired officer looked grim as hell.

He looked back at Orell. "Somebody kills Americans, we gotta do something."

Orell grinned. "I agree. Absolutely. What we should do is load this here bird up and send it off to drop ordnance on a bunch of poor people didn't do anything but go fishing last night. Know who lives in Hong Kong, Jackson? A few dozen billionaires, and about fifty million people living in shit, just like your family does back home. Nice, huh? Think about it. Who's gonna die when we go deliver our payback for what happened to that yacht? The billionaires? Not likely." Orell bobbed his head toward the corner, then turned and bobbed it in the other direction, toward the crew of technicians working on the bomb-damaged aft elevator. "A whole bunch of colored people gonna die for this. But there's too many of 'em anyway, so that's okay. You just make this plane work real nice, son."

Orell winked, draped his massive, freckled hands over the wheel of the tow tractor, and hit the gas. As he pulled away, he had to turn abruptly to avoid three more men walking across the hanger floor. When Jackson saw who one of those men was, he almost crammed his head right back into the service bay, because it was Rear Admiral Wayne walking along right there. With him was some little Chinese guy in an oversized T-shirt and khaki pants, and a corpsman from the ship's hospital.

But the Admiral didn't glance his way, or even seem to be aware he existed. No doubt Orell would point out that was typical of officers. Wouldn't mention—wouldn't need to mention—that most of the officers were white, too.

"Excuse me, Petty Officer Ord." Beaman's voice came from between two parked planes. Jackson whirled, almost rapping his head on the corner of the open service hatch. Beaman was as black as the F-14 was silvery-gray, and would have been swallowed up by Orell Blessing's shadow, but the Plane Captain was nobody to screw around with. "Maybe you'd like me to have Lieutenant Commander Robinson come over here and tell you what it's like to fly a Tomcat when an improperly tightened hydraulic line gives way, and all the fluid leaks out of the control surface system. Would you like that, sailor?"

"Sorry." Then he waved his wrench at the figures in the corner. "I was just wondering what's going on."

Beaman barely glanced across the hangar. "The brass have their work to do, Ord, and we've got ours."

"But what do *you* think's going to happen? Think we're going to mix it up with the Chinese?"

"I don't get paid to have opinions outside this hangar bay. I get paid for the same thing you do: making sure these birds are ready to fly when and if they *do* have to fight. And it so happens this bird has to be ready to fly tomorrow."

"Already?"

"Yep. We're going to be cycling planes pretty fast for the next few days."

Jackson glanced toward the corner with the body bags. The Admiral was there now, bending over one of the bags, the Chinese man bending down with him. "Why?" Jackson said.

"Because they tell us to, Ord. Because they tell us to."

"I don't see him, Admiral," Martin Lee said in a voice as thin as the gauze bandage taped over one of his ears. "Mr. McIntyre is not here, and he was not in the morgue. He is . . . his body is one of the missing."

Batman nodded. It was amazing, really; from memory alone, Lee had identified every single one of the corpses brought back from *Lady of Leisure*, often based on no more than a piece of jewelry on a severed hand or the color and length of hair on a crushed skull. Still, eight bodies were missing—including Phillip McIntyre's, it appeared. That wasn't a bad ratio, considering all that had happened. And as for McIntyre, his disappearance was no surprise at all. Lee himself had stated that McIntyre was shot to death inside the yacht well before the helicopter arrived. Which meant his corpse was now feeding crabs at the bottom of the South China Sea.

But Batman said none of that. Instead, he put a hand on Lee's shoulder. When the man turned, Batman held out his other hand and said, "Mr. Lee, thank you. I know this was difficult, but you were very brave."

Lee stared at his hand for a moment, as if afraid it would not be attached, then reached out and shook it. "May I go home now? My wife was very worried over the phone. She is pregnant."

"The doctor's given you a clean bill of health," Batman said. "As soon as arrangements are finalized, we'll fly you back." He didn't mention how difficult it had been to make those arrangements. For several hours the PLA had refused to allow any American military aircraft or surface vessels access to Hong Kong without prior "inspection." At the same time, they were demanding that *Jefferson* immediately release the wreckage and corpses they'd recovered from *Lady of Leisure*. Catch-22.

Fortunately, the civilian aeronautical authorities in Hong Kong had quoted certain provisions of the Sino-British agreement, pointed out that American warships docked in Hong Kong all the time, and insisted that the return of Hong Kong citizens, living and dead, did not fall under the purview of national security. Rather to Batman's surprise, the PLA had backed down.

Batman signaled the corpsman to take Lee back to sick bay. As the young man was led off, he hardly seemed to be aware of his surroundings, far less who he was with.

"Tough," Bird Dog said, watching him go.

Batman nodded. "I wouldn't want to have his nightmares for the next few nights."

"Admiral," Lab Rat said, "what were the autopsy results?"

Batman sighed and looked down at the body bags. "Officially, a couple of these people drowned. Of course, that was after they took a cannon hit or two. The rest were simply shot to pieces."

"Except Mr. Lee."

"Yes. He got lucky; he was hanging onto the section of

boat that had all those explosives inside. Would *you* fire a cannon into that at close range?"

"And the Chinese are still claiming they had nothing to do with this," Bird Dog said. It was not a question.

Lab Rat snorted, a rare display of disbelief from a man who had seen almost every form of misdirection and chicanery. "They just presented a theory at the U.N. claiming the whole massacre was part of a Hong Kong drug war. We're talking a story as thin as my father's hair, but some people have grabbed hold of it anyway. For some people, believing any old lie is a better than fighting China."

Batman stared down at the body bags, thinking of the terror and agony they represented. "It's my fault. I should have pushed for an immediate retaliatory strike before the Chinese got their bullshit on the table."

"The Joint Chiefs would almost certainly have vetoed it," Lab Rat said.

"I still should have made the request." Batman shook himself. "Never mind. Okay, the explosion yesterday might have been a fluke, but we're still in agreement that this whole thing isn't over, right?"

"I'd say it's just begun," Lab Rat said.

"So would I," Bird Dog said.

"Then from now on, we're going to behave accordingly. There are thousands of American citizens in Hong Kong, with more flying in every day. We're going to do our damnedest to make them feel safe here."

Lab Rat nodded. "Good."

"Admiral?" Bird Dog said.

Batman looked at him.

"If you're increasing Combat Air Patrol, I'd like to request some air time. I'm getting rusty, if you know what I mean."

"Do I ever," Batman said. Then he remembered something. "No offense, Bird Dog, but I understand you've had a little trouble finding an RIO who wants to fly with you."

Bird Dog's eyes widened. "That's not true at all, sir. Hell, before this trip I had the same RIO for longer than anyone else in the Navy. Gator Cummings. And my RIO, Catwoman—she loves to fly with me."

Batman debated calling the young aviator on his rather freeform interpretation of events. Surely the aviator knew that everyone on *Jefferson* was aware of the circumstances of his split with "the same RIO" he'd had for so long. According to scuttlebutt, the RIO, Gator, had finally demanded transfer—not just to another pilot, but to an entirely different ship. "Back in Cuba, he put me into the water," Gator had said. "Then I turned around and flew with him again in Turkey. After that, I started wondering if maybe I had a death wish. I decided to get as far away from that maniac as I possibly can."

Gator was now flying with VF-91 off the USS *Eisenhower*.

Maybe Bird Dog had learned something from that whole experience—certainly, the youngster was trying hard to do well in his new position as advisor. Finally, Batman nodded. "Talk to CAG. Tell him I said it was all right."

Bird Dog grinned with the palpable relief of any Naval aviator who hadn't been in the air for a while. It made Batman long, more than ever, for the feel of a Tomcat strapped around his own body.

Across the hangar bay, in the entrance to the aft elevator, sparks showered down from welding arcs.

FIVE

Sunday, 3 August

0800 local (−8 GMT)
PLA Destroyer Juhai
Victoria Harbor

The *Juhai*, a Luda III class destroyer, steamed slowly into the West Lamma Channel and turned toward the open sea. Her orders were to join her PLA Navy sister ships in the area where the American aircraft carrier battle group was currently operating, and take up a flanking position. With her four twin C801 missile launchers, new twin 37mm guns and brand-new electronics, *Juhai* was more than formidable enough to cause the Americans concern.

Of course, these days a "flanking position" did not imply close proximity. *Juhai*'s commander, Kung Choug, had been warned to exhibit special care not to appear hostile in any way. It had something to do with an American yacht that sank in the South China Sea a couple of days earlier. The Americans had apparently accused the PLA of involvement.

Standing on the bridge, Kung surveyed the busy waters ahead of his ship. Navigation was no problem; despite the 200-plus small islands that made the Hong Kong vicinity a spiders's web of channels and tributaries, the routes in and out had been charted for centuries. However, these waters perpetually swarmed with boats: fishing craft, pleasure boats, sailboats, commercial steamers, cruise ships, and visiting military craft from innumerable nations. They made maneuvering a headache. Despite his recent pleasant leave in Hong Kong, Kung looked forward to seeing the open sea once more. Weather predictions warned of scattered squalls over the next week, but nothing too heavy.

One good thing about moving a large ship in and out of Hong Kong: Here was one of the greatest deep-water harbors in the world, so there was little danger of going aground. Which was ironic, really, considering that the South China Sea was itself comparatively shallow.

In the distance, he saw a small military vessel chugging slowly across the channel. Even before he focused his glasses on it, he had a feeling he knew what kind of boat it was: a CDF patrol boat.

He scowled. Say what you wished about the British, they had known how to control the harbor. But Major General Chin, commander of the Coastal Defense Force, was a fool. His boats were always tangling with the wrong vessels, halting and searching steamers loaded with New Zealand wool while tankers full of opium sailed right past. And so far, there had been at least three reported collisions between CDF craft and civilian vessels cruising in the bay. Such incompetence could only be the product of leadership selected for political clout rather than military competence.

So Kung kept his gaze warily on the craft dead ahead. It was stern-on to him, and too far away for him to read any of its markings, but sure enough, he recognized the CDF uniforms of the men scurrying over her fantail. Kung sighed. Probably the boat had fouled her screws on a piece of flotsam in the water, a nylon rope or a wayward fish pot. It was an embarrassment.

He was about to direct the destroyer's radioman to contact the patrol boat when he saw the small craft's stern dig into the water, foam billowing out behind her. The patrol boat tore off across the Channel at high speed. Kung was startled. Her skipper might be incompetent, but that was one well-maintained boat.

He returned his gaze to the water ahead, searching for other obstacles.

• • •

The one obstacle he couldn't see, and wasn't even thinking about, lay dead ahead at a depth of eight meters. It was an American-made MK65 Quickstrike mine, essentially a 2,390 pound bomb sheathed in a thin-walled casing, tethered to the bottom of the channel by a long cable.

As the *Juhai* approached, her 3,700 ton bulk pushed before her a pressure wave that registered on the preset triggering device of the mine. Acoustic sensors analyzed the sound saturating the seawater, broke the signal into its component parts, and arrived at a decision. Critical arming circuits clicked shut.

Kung felt a sharp jolt through the bottoms of his feet. His immediate thought was that his ship had, somehow, impossibly, run aground. Then—even worse—that she had struck some unseen civilian or commercial vessel. After what had happened to that yacht the other night, no one—least of all Major General Po Yu Li—would believe there had been an accident.

But even as these thoughts raced through his mind, a huge column of water and foam shot up from the port bow. Kung felt the deck rear up under his feet, and the next thing he knew he had stumbled back into the wall. Then he was stumbling forward again, catching himself on the console. Through the windshield he saw metal plates buckled back on the weatherdeck, which was almost underwater. Then it reared up again, even as the column of water crashed back down, much of it exploding across *Juhai*'s bridge windscreen, making Kung blind.

Even so, he knew instantly that his ship had been severely holed. Its movement was abruptly all wrong, a heavy corkscrewing as the bow settled deeper into the water, pushed there by the still-churning screws.

Kung began shouting orders to reduce speed and get damage-control crews to the bow. Then he let the Officer of the Deck take command of the immediate emergency while he got on the radio to contact Hong Kong.

Saturday, 2 August
0900 local (+5 GMT)
Briefing Room
The Pentagon, Washington, D.C.

There were advantages to being the nephew of the chief of naval operations. For one, you got to sit in a plush chair in a nice meeting room while being grilled. For another, they served better-than-average coffee.

That was about it.

Besides Tombstone, four men sat around the conference table. They must have been chosen from Pentagon Central Casting: There was the Air Force rep, perhaps forty years old, with a cleft chin punctuating a square, Dudley Doright jaw. There was the Navy rep, older, appropriately bright of eye and ruddy of complexion, with clipped white hair and steely gaze. There was the colorless guy in the gray suit, who had introduced himself as "a consultant on advanced aviation technology." And finally there was the kid representing DARPA, the Defense Advanced Research Projects Administration. He couldn't be more than twenty-five years old and was not actually in the military himself, a fact he emphasized by wearing a Hawaiian shirt over baggy chinos and tennis shoes.

Tombstone wished he were on the *Jefferson*. Things were escalating out there; the latest word was that a PLA destroyer had been damaged by an explosion in Victoria Harbor, and the Chinese immediately accused the United States of planting a mine. It was a messy situation, and getting messier.

But at least you knew who your enemies were.

Tombstone had been grilled for a half hour now—or, rather, been warmed up for grilling by being asked to clarify a few points from his preliminary report.

There was a moment of silence, then the man in the suit leaned across the table. "Tell me, Admiral," he said. "Who do you think might want to shoot you down that way? Not in combat, but over American soil?"

"Shoot me down?" Tombstone raised one eyebrow. "Well,

let's see. The North Koreans, the Chinese, the Russians, the Ukrainians, the Indians, the Cubans, the—"

The man in the suit held up a hand and smiled blandly. Everything about him was bland. "You miss my point. This wasn't a normal terrorist-style attack, or even a military assault. There are conventional surface-to-air missiles that could have done the job."

"Not to mention car bombs," the DARPA kid said. He had his tennis shoes propped on the armrest of a vacant seat. "Or a bullet in the back of the head while you're asleep in your bed."

Tombstone looked at him, then back at the suit. "Maybe the wreckage from the bogey will tell you something. There must be something left. I assume you've found it."

"That's being taken care of," the Air Force rep said.

The Navy rep scowled. "Don't be coy, Foster. He'll figure it out soon enough on his own; plus we owe him as much information as we can spare. It was *his* ass on the line yesterday. Could happen again tomorrow." He transferred his blue gaze to Tombstone. "We found the impact site, yes. We're in the process of recovering the wreckage now, but it's a hell of a job working in that muck. Especially with environmental groups screaming to high heaven in the background. Could take a while."

Tombstone nodded. "Thank you." He looked back at the suit. "Surely there aren't that many governments capable of building an RPV like that. Maybe the CIA could narrow down our list of suspects for us."

The suit shrugged. "I wouldn't know. Now, what about markings? Did this vehicle have any kind of national or manufacturer emblems on it? Words? Symbols?"

"It was moving a little fast to be sure, but no, I didn't notice anything like that. Just marine camo paint."

"And it didn't resemble any aircraft or missile you're familiar with, is that right? You're sure of that?"

"Absolutely. It not only didn't look like anything I'm familiar with, it didn't fly like anything I'm familiar with. You've got a drawing of it right in front of you; what's it look like to you?"

"A paper airplane with another paper airplane stuck up its ass," the DARPA kid said. He poked at his copy of the drawing. "My question is, what makes you so sure this was a Remotely Piloted Vehicle in the first place?"

Tombstone frowned. "Do you see a cockpit there? Or any room for one? Also, I repeat: This bogey's flight characteristics were well outside the envelope of survivability for a human pilot."

"Unless the pilot were prone," the Air Force rep said. "The human body can take a lot of extra g's that way. Jack Northrop once developed a flying wing fighter like that."

"Which crashed during a test flight," the DARPA kid said, still poking at his drawing.

Tombstone shook his head. "This aircraft was unmanned, gentlemen. Based on the way it was flying, I assume it was remotely piloted as well."

"Piloted from where?" the kid asked. "An RPV isn't like a radio-controlled model, you know; you'd have to have some kind of command post, a power supply . . ."

Tombstone frowned at him. Two years ago this kid was probably building plastic model airplanes; now he worked for DARPA, the government agency responsible for dreaming up the military's most exotic hardware: the SR-71 spy plane, the F-117 Stealth Fighter and the B-2 Bomber, not to mention fiascos like Star Wars. And who knew what else? A vast slurry of DARPA's funding came out of the "black budget," money protected from Congressional oversight.

"Maybe the command post was on a boat," he said. "How's that? There were plenty of large pleasure and fishing craft around. Or didn't you read my report?"

"Not really. Not enough pictures."

Tombstone leaned forward. "Tell me something, young man. Do you fly airplanes?"

"Not the kind I have to actually get into."

"Then I suggest you keep your smart-ass comments to yourself, you little twerp."

"Whoa." The kid sat up. "Whoa. *Whoa.*"

"You want to be flippant," Tombstone said coldly, "that's fine. *After* you've flown against an unidentified aircraft that's trying to knock you out of the sky, shoot off your mouth all you want. Until then, if you don't have something constructive to say, shut up."

The kid looked around the table. No one came to his defense. He sat there blinking behind his glasses, then slumped deeper in his chair and picked up his pencil. Started doodling on the bogey drawing. "Whatever," he muttered.

"This brings us back to what's supposed to be the main point of this briefing," the Navy rep said. "Admiral Magruder, even if we're able to reconstruct something useful from the vehicle's wreckage, we'll still need your impressions about how the thing actually *flew*."

"And how you got away from it." The Air Force rep picked up his copy of Tombstone's report. "It says here you started turning snap rolls. Are you sure you don't mean *barrel* rolls?"

"I know the difference, Colonel. No, it was snap rolls. They seemed to disorient it."

"*Disorient* it?" the Air Force rep said.

"That's right. It would be tracking me, I'd start snap-rolling, and the bogey would miss. Then it would start circling and come back at me again."

The Air Force rep glanced at the DARPA kid, who just kept doodling on his drawing of the bogey without looking up.

"Perhaps I should be asking these questions," the Navy rep said. "The Admiral and I are both Naval aviators. We speak the same language."

"I'm sure you do," the Air Force rep said. "But since the Navy doesn't have an RPV program, I think I'm better qualified to determine the flight characteristics of—"

"Nothing!" the DARPA kid shouted. He raised his face, lips curled in scorn. "Remember the Mig-29? Remember how American military intelligence, that famous oxymoron, didn't believe the Soviets could possibly produce a truly competitive all-weather fighter? Oops! What a big surprise." He fixed his gaze on Tombstone's face. "Admiral, you want some advice? Here's some advice: Don't go flying again until I examine what's left of your bogey. And one other thing."

"What's that?" Tombstone asked in a flat voice.

The kid smiled. "I'd carry a gun if I were you. Somebody's got it out for you real bad."

Sunday, 3 August
0110 local (−8 GMT)
Mongkok District
Kowloon

Sung Fei was watching CNN when the phone rang. His tiny flat in the Mongkok District of Kowloon was far from overfurnished, but by local standards he lived in luxury: He had no roommates, and his television was the latest Japanese model, with a satellite dish that picked up over two hundred stations from all over the world. In the last two days nearly half those stations had been broadcasting continuous "updates" on the so-called "*Lady of Leisure* attack."

How symptomatic. In a world where millions starved to death every year, and hundreds of thousands more were ground into poverty by wealthy industrialists, what story was deemed worthy of round-the-clock dissection? Only the one where a handful of wealthy, worthless socialites and megacapitalists died at sea in the middle of one of their debauched, high-profile soirees. Even the retaliatory attack on a PLA military ship in Victoria Harbor was referred to in the briefest of sidebars.

Another staple part of most broadcasts was an appearance by a so-called "expert" who dissected events in the South China Sea and speculated as to motivations and possible outcomes. While admitting that solid evidence about exactly what had occurred in the South China Sea was scanty, these experts seemed remarkably certain about what the events meant, what had caused them, and what would happen next. None of them seemed to question the U.S. Navy's policy of keeping all shipping and aircraft out of the area of the supposed "attack."

So much for experts. The truth was, not one of those talking heads knew as much about what was happening in the Hong Kong area as did Sung Fei. Not nearly as much.

He had been waiting for the phone to ring all day and night, so when it happened, he was not startled. Instead, a shimmer of excitement played down his backbone.

He picked up the receiver. "Sung," he said calmly.

As always, Mr. Blossom's voice was weird, changeable, obviously run through a distorter. "You've been watching the news?" the voice asked in Cantonese.

"I always watch the news," Sung said, reciting the words he'd memorized, knowing his voice and its point of origin were also being scrambled. "But I've never seen anything like this before."

That concluded the password exchange. The voice said, "It is time."

"I thought it might be, Comrade. I regret the loss of life aboard *Suhai*, but my heart is full of joy that the moment of freedom has arrived at last. I am honored to be participating."

"You did an excellent job of filling Victoria Square with anti-China protestors this morning."

"Students are easy to convince of anything. After what the Americans did in the harbor, I can guarantee hundreds more."

"Both pro- and anti-American? This is very important."

"I understand, but trust me. The Hong Kongese love a demonstration."

"Not for long," the voice on the other end said.

0300 local (+3 GMT)
Bethesda, Maryland

Tombstone was awakened by the ringing of the phone. He sat up groggily, only to find the soft pressure of his wife's breasts on his naked chest as she slid over him to reach the receiver first. She muttered a few words into it, listened, then sighed and held it out to him.

She remained sprawled across him as he put the receiver to his ear. "Magruder."

"Admiral, this is John Palmer."

It took Tombstone a moment to remember that was the name of the man in the suit from the previous night's meeting. The spook. Of course, Tombstone thought, his concentration wasn't helped by the things Tomboy was doing to him. "How can I help you, Mr. Palmer?" he asked, struggling to keep his voice even.

"We were wondering if you'd come to Andrews as soon as possible. We've got something you might be interested in seeing."

Instantly Tombstone's concentration was on the phone. He sat halfway up, almost tumbling Tomboy off him. "I'll be there right away."

He hung up the phone and found Tomboy kneeling beside him on the mattress, her naked body as pale and beautiful as a marble statue in the darkness. "I take it this is important."

"Very." He reached out and touched her cheek, then slipped his fingertips down the front of her body. "I'm off to Andrews. I think it has something to do with my little encounter the other day."

"Ah." Her eyebrows rose. She knew about the bogey, but nothing about the content of his meeting the previous night. Nor had she asked about it. Her own job had made secrecy second nature to her. She waved a hand at him. "Go. Go."

He looked her up and down, and sighed. "Damn the Navy."

"Not to mention the Air Force," she said.

Monday, 4 August
1900 local (−8 GMT)
Dirty Shirt Officers' Mess
USS Jefferson

"I see you're on the flight schedule for CAP tomorrow," Bird Dog said in his most casual voice.

Lobo looked over her shoulder at him. She was pouring coffee, not spilling a drop despite the fact she wasn't watching what she was doing. "Gee, you're capable of reading a flight schedule. That's very impressive."

"I went to college and everything," Bird Dog said. "It's just that I'm surprised they're putting you in the air again so soon."

"Part of the job. I don't write the flight schedule." She stared at him over the rim of her cup. God, she had killer eyes. "Besides, Bird Dog, I *want* to be up there. In case the Chinese try something else. And especially after the lies they told the U.N."

Bird Dog moved up to the coffeepot. "So, who's your backseater again?"

"Handyman."

"Like him?"

"He's the best."

"And who's flying wing for you?"

"Hot Rock."

"Hm. He's pretty raw, isn't he?"

That maddening smirk climbed into her eye. He felt the stream of scalding coffee dribble over his thumb, and suppressed a wince. "Why?" she said. "You worried about me? Think I might get into *trouble*? Need a big strong man to help me out?"

"I just wish I could be your wingman, that's all. We'd make a good team."

"I'm sure whoever you *are* flying wing with wishes you could be my wingman, too." She gave him a wicked grin. "Who's *your* backseater these days, anyway?"

"Catwoman."

"Good RIO. What did you do to deserve her?"

"I don't make the assignments. But yeah, she is good. We'll be up there tomorrow, too. So if you run into trouble . . ."

"Well, that's nice, because Handyman and I will be up there if *you* run into trouble."

Sunday, 3 August
0800 local (+5 GMT)
Andrews Air Force Base, Maryland

There were a couple of fundamental differences between Naval Air Stations and Air Force bases, apart from the obvious fact that the majority of Naval bases were situated near water. For one thing, Air Force bases served better coffee while making you wait for the meeting that had dragged you out of your bed. For another, the base commander's office had photos of F-15s and B-2s on the walls.

Other things were exactly the same. The murmur of voices in the corridor, the distant ringing of phones, the whistling shriek of jet engines outside.

Tombstone stood at the window, staring at what little of the airstrip he could see from this angle. Every now and then an F-15 Eagle, the Air Force's answer to the Tomcat, would come in to land. Like any naval aviator, Tombstone was mildly contemptuous of Air Force weenies and their birds. However impressive an Eagle might be in the air, in the end it only had to land on a motionless, fifteen-hundred foot long strip of asphalt. Nothing to it. Now, try putting one down on top of a boat in the open sea.

There was a knock, the door opened and an enlisted man stuck his head in. "They're ready for you now, sir. Please follow me."

Tombstone followed the crisply laundered back out of the building and across a tie-down area toward an enormous, windowless hangar where his pass was carefully examined by another, better armed and altogether meaner-looking weenie. Finally the guard saluted and opened the door.

Tombstone stepped into a vast, echoing hangar. At first it appeared to be empty. Then he saw a small collection of metal objects scattered across a tarp in the center of the concrete floor. Three men were bending over the tarp: the Air Force rep from the meeting; John Palmer the spook; and the young DARPA nerd. The Air Force rep looked up and waved him over.

As Tombstone approached, he stared at the garbage on the tarp. Immediately he recognized pieces of the bogey that had pursued him all over the Maryland sky, laid out in roughly correct configuration. Part of the rear half appeared to be intact, if scorched and bent; one of the forward fins had been laid out in more or less correct position; of the nose section there were only tiny fragments, unrecognizable to Tombstone. Other pieces sat in trays to either side. Tombstone was reminded of an archaeological dig, with a half-exposed fossil.

Still, the general shape of the bogey was recognizable enough to give him a chill. "I'm surprised there's this much of it left," he said.

"It wasn't easy to find," said the Air Force rep. "Fortunately, the vehicle buried itself in six feet of mud before the warhead went off. A lot of the aft section was simply fired right back out like a cannon shell."

Tombstone released a breath. "So, what is it, who built it, and why was it following me?"

The DARPA kid looked up, eyes shining with excitement behind his glasses; Tombstone was reminded of a twelve-year-old kid staring at the Milky Way. "It's a UAV," he said.

"A UAV? But—that can't be right. Didn't you read my report? It was *dogfighting* me."

The kid grinned. "No it wasn't; it was just following you around, like a Sidewinder, and trying to take you out."

"You mean it was a heat-seeker?"

The kid glanced at Palmer, then back. "Not exactly. You ever hear of Predator?"

"You mean the Air Force drone?"

"Predator's a lot more than a drone, Admiral," Palmer said. "It's a completely automated surveillance aircraft. It takes off, flies to a defined location, performs its mission, then returns to base and lands . . . all without a bit of human intervention. It's the future of aerial reconnaissance."

Tombstone frowned. "That's all very interesting, but a surveillance aircraft—unmanned or not—does its thing over stationary ground. I'm sure it's fairly simple to write a mission program for that, but I'm telling you, this thing was *dog-*

fighting me. Somebody had to be flying it, like a radio-controlled plane."

"Wrong-Oh, Admiral," the kid said. He pointed into one of the bins. "Wrong kind of antennas for radio control. It used GPS—geosynchronous positioning satellite—data to get into position, but after that something else took over, and that's when things got hairy for you."

" 'Hairy?' " Tombstone said. He leaned forward. "You might call it that. I'd say it was a little more serious than 'hairy'."

The kid grinned. "Not tweaking you, Admiral. Here's the deal: This thing carried enough fuel to cruise for maybe an hour or so. It could be launched from a meadow or a country road, or even a boat if some kind of catapult was used. Once it reached its assigned territory, it would start to circle around while its video camera—actually, four of them—scanned everything that entered that airspace. Its onboard computer would match each image against images stored on its internal hard drive. When it got a match, boom—it went in for the kill."

"Wait. You mean this thing was set up to recognize my *aircraft*?"

"Looks that way. Somebody programmed it to fly around until it spotted a Pitts Special—maybe even a *specific* Pitts Special—and then go after it. That's another major difference from Predator. Predator is slow, a prop-plane with long wings, basically a motorized glider. This sucker used a nifty little turbofan a lot like a Tomahawk's. There are some of the fan blades."

Tombstone stared at the debris again. "I can't believe you can tell so much from *this*."

"Well, only part of what I know is based on the wreckage itself. See, DARPA has been doing research along these same lines, so—"

"Mr. Williams," Palmer said quietly.

The kid glanced over at him with a glint of humor in his eye. "Sorry, 007." Then, to Tombstone, "Guess this is where your need-to-know stops. Anyway, the main reason I know what kind of guidance system this thing used is because of how you avoided getting shot down. It finally hit me: You said that whenever you snap-rolled the Pitts, the vehicle seemed to lose track of you. Right?"

"So it seemed."

"That's because it wasn't programmed as well as it could have been. I'm betting it was taught what a Pitts Special looks like from all kinds of angles, so it could always recognize your plane in the sky, regardless of your attitude or position. Right? But somebody forgot that when a plane rolls fast enough, it takes on a whole new profile, visually. It could be interpreted as a sort of big cylinder. The vehicle couldn't recognize that shape, so it went back into search mode until you stopped rolling."

"That's it," Tombstone said. "That's exactly what happened."

The kid shrugged. "Elementary."

"So where did it come from? Who built it?"

The kid started to respond, glanced at Palmer. The spook nodded. Picking up a curved piece of the fuselage, the kid tilted it so Tombstone could see a character painted inside.

"Made in China," the kid said.

Tombstone glanced from the kid to the spook, then back at the wreckage on the floor. "*China* built this?" he said.

"That's what these symbols tell us," Palmer said. "They say something like 'Gift of the Eastern Wind.' There are other indicators, too, like some of the construction methods and materials. China was involved."

Tombstone shook his head. "I knew the PLA was developing cruise missiles, but this . . ."

"We thought the United States had a lead time of years, if not decades, in UAV technology," Palmer said. "As you can imagine, this came as quite a shock to us as well."

"Especially since this puppy was really well-designed," the kid said. "I mean, most of China's aeronautics is based on old Soviet stuff, right? And until real recently, the Russians were still building fighters using rinky-dink 1950s technology. Sheet steel, big clunky aluminum fittings; they even used vacuum tubes in their instruments long after we'd switched to solid-state circuitry."

Tombstone nodded. He'd heard all that before; he also knew that the tune had changed dramatically with the advent of the Mig-29 and its successors.

"Okay," the kid said. "So China has been just as bad, or worse. But *this* thing . . ." He picked up the piece of fuselage again, put it back. "It's a masterpiece of minimalism. The fuselage and moving parts are sophisticated stuff—graphite composites, bonded aluminum, titanium alloy . . . but the electronics, what's left of them, are pretty much off-the-shelf. In fact . . ."

Tombstone looked at the kid for a moment, then at Palmer. "What?"

For the first time, Palmer appeared a bit uncertain. "Well, despite the mess you see here, we were able to determine that more than seventy percent of the control and navigation components on this UAV came from the same manufacturer."

"And?"

"It was MyTronic Corporation—the electronics division of a company you might have heard of: McIntyre Engineering International."

1034 local (−8 GMT)
Main Conference Room
PLA Headquarters, Hong Kong SAR

Ming sat alone at the conference table, sipping a cup of tea. When the door opened, he spoke without looking up. "Major General Yeh. Please have a seat."

Only after he heard the creak of a chair did he raise his head. He noted that the Political Commissar was looking around nervously, clearly disturbed to find himself alone with the Party's representative. Good.

"You sent for me?" Yeh said.

"Yes. We need to discuss the situation here in Hong Kong. Things are not going well."

"If you're referring to the American attack on our destroyer, I can assure you that—"

"No, that is not what I'm talking about. That, or something like it, was to be expected. What I'm talking about is this." And he held up a piece of paper. "This is a message from Beijing. Our spies in Washington tell us that the survivor of the *Lady of Leisure* gave the Americans the exact name of the man responsible for attacking the yacht."

Yeh sat up. "His *name?*"

"Yes. Captain Wang I of the Coastal Defense Force."

"The CDF? But . . . that's not possible."

"I agree. For one thing, Major General Chin is much too

dim to even conceive of so brazen an act, far less disguise it afterward. For another, we have already learned that Wang I was absent from Hong Kong at the time of the attack, visiting his mother in Pok Lo. So it would appear that someone assumed Wang's identity in order to commandeer the *Lady of Leisure*."

"Who?"

"I don't know. That's why I want to talk to you. As Political Commissar, it's your job to know the moral strength of our fighting men. Do *you* know of any who might be responsible for this disaster?"

"Of course not. Only the most politically reliable men were selected for service in the Hong Kong garrison."

Ming waved his hand. "I'm not interested in speeches, only reality. Perhaps I'm speaking to the wrong man. Allow me to test you: If all four of your fellow major generals were still living, which would you consider most likely to have organized the attack on the yacht?"

Yeh's eyes flicked from side to side as if seeking escape from the man's narrow face. "If you really think . . . well, I suppose Hsu Pi would have been the most likely candidate. The PLA Air Force was humiliated by its last major conflict with the United States, in the Spratley Islands. Revenge ran very hot in Hsu."

"An excellent analysis," Ming said, "assuming Hsu could have gotten access to a patrol boat and a full complement of sailors. However, it would appear you aren't aware that when Hsu had a fatal heart attack, the only thing running hot in him was his lust. He was in a Hong Kong brothel. Evidently you can't buy six beautiful Filipino women at the same time in Beijing."

Yeh's mouth sagged open.

"Or what about our other deceased commander, Po Yu Li of the PLA Navy? Officially, he died in the line of duty, shot by a drug smuggler he was attempting to arrest. This is somewhat true; he was shot by a drug smuggler. Of course, at the time, our major general was attempting to raise his standard bribe for allowing the smuggler to pass unmolested."

Blood crept up in Yeh's cheeks. "I cannot believe it."

"Perhaps you're wondering about our current commanders, eh? The venerable Wei Ao, First Among Equals? It appears he has a passion for collecting antiquities smuggled out of temples during the Cultural Revolution. He has a warehouse full in the New Territories; you really should see it."

Yeh stared at him. "You *know* about these crimes?"

"Of course. These 'crimes,' as you put it, are why I selected those men for their jobs in the first place."

"But—"

"Major General, your outrage does you credit. But remember, this is Hong Kong, city of temptation. I must be practical. In my opinion, it is easier to watch over and control men whose weaknesses are known than those whose vices are secret. Especially when the men in question believe their personal activities *are* secret."

Yeh's face had grown stiffer with every word that reached him. Ming almost smiled. "What about Chin?" the Commissar asked. "You have something against him as well?"

"Only his worthlessness."

"But if he has no vices to protect," Yeh said, "then he's the only one of us who might be responsible for attacking the yacht, true?"

Ming nodded approvingly. "You're learning. But in this case you're wrong. Major general or not, Chin has not a shred of martial wisdom or courage. He could never mount a surprise attack against any boat—even an unarmed American yacht."

Yeh shook his head. "You have a very cynical attitude, Comrade General. Does the State Council know about it?"

"Of course. Their attitude is the same when it comes to leaders in Hong Kong. Later there will be time for ideological reconstruction, but for now, a decadent place must be dealt with on its own terms." Ming looked at Yeh sidelong. "You're wondering what my own vices might be?"

"Actually, I was wondering what you thought mine to be."

"Ah. Your vice, Comrade Major General, is your stubborn belief that people can be redeemed by devotion to high ideals. And that vice, my dear Political Commissar, is exactly why I recommended you for *your* job."

1100 local (−8 GMT)
Kai Tak Airport
Kowloon

Dr. George hurried across the tarmac of the private jet section of Kai Tak airport, his briefcase bumping rhythmically against his thigh. Today he'd gotten stuck in traffic trying to *leave* downtown Hong Kong. Those damned protestors again, except this time the signs read NO WAR IN HONG KONG and KEEP THE PEACE, AMERICA and, an apparent favorite, HONG KONG IS NOT BAGDHAD. People were marching in the streets, waving their signs and chanting. Armed soldiers in green uniforms had been standing around, looking grave.

But not as grave as George felt. This whole trip had been a waste of time. One corporation after another, and every time the same result. During his last meeting at a huge conglomerate called MIL, several of the Board members had turned and glanced through the windows that faced toward the South China Sea. George knew they were examining the clear blue sky, the handful of puffy white clouds, the limp flags on surrounding skyscrapers, the lack of whitecaps on Victoria Harbor. They were thinking about the television weather reports, which predicted only normal spring squalls on the open sea. In other words, the executives were observing that there was no hint at all a Super Typhoon was imminent. Or even remote.

Naturally they'd been unconvinced, and now it was too late. George's time was up. Not far away was the converted Gulfstream IV business jet that was the last NOAA aircraft in all the Pacific—and after today it, too, would be heading East. After today, Dr. Alonzo George would be grounded in Guam, in his little office with its earthbound instruments. No more soaring into the stupendous gray world of the typhoon. No more ferreting out its most intimate secrets, including what exactly made it decide to rise out of its saltwater bottle like an evil genie in the first place.

He already knew so much. As he'd told the Board, with Valkyrie he could predict the size and location of developing tropical storms four to seven days in advance. Well, okay, he could predict with reasonable accuracy one time out of four. But that wasn't bad, and given another season or two of intensive reasearch, he'd improve on both the hit-to-miss ratio and the precision of qualitative data. He'd make them damned near perfect.

The Gulfstream's pilot appeared in the doorway and raised a hand to his mouth. "Better hurry, Dr. George!" he shouted. "Look at the sky! Looks like a big storm's coming!" He laughed.

George scowled and climbed the steps, which were formed by the lowered door itself, and squeezed into what used to be the passenger compartment of the jet. This space, intended to contain a few comfortable lounge chairs and perhaps a wet bar, was stuffed with meteorological equipment: dropsonde console, anemometer, barometer, gradient thermometer, three separate radar screens, and real-time satellite monitoring gear.

George squeezed into the seat by the dropsonde console.

The pilot was buckling himself into his seat up front. "I don't know, Dr. George," the co-pilot said, turning and grinning. "You sure you want to take off in all this wind?"

"Enough, already; just fly the plane."

Ingrates. George longed for the heyday of NOAA, when there would have been seven scientists on the crew, and the plane itself would have been supplied by the U.S. Navy. A large, roomy military aircraft, built to take a beating. But the Navy had pulled out of the storm-chasing business in 1975—Dr. George still wasn't sure why, since who should be more concerned about oceanic storm systems?—leaving only the Air Force to provide transport. And the Air Force was reverting more and more to using converted civilian craft like this Gulfstream.

Still, right now he'd sell his soul to keep this little plane, even if he had to operate every piece of equipment himself.

Outside, the plane's twin turbines began to whine.

"You all strapped in back there now, Doc?" the pilot asked. "Don't want you to get tossed around by any severe turbulence."

George sighed.

The jet eased into motion and taxied briskly toward the runway. Through the window appeared the blue expanse of Kowloon Bay with the skyscrapers of central Hong Kong on the far side. George gazed at the skyline glumly, wondering how much damage the oncoming typhoon would do to those glittering structures. Then the plane was on the runway and accelerating, wheels thumping, engines squealing. Next came a soft floating sensation, followed by the clunk of the landing gear retracting. Out the window, downtown Hong Kong reappeared, foreshortened as the plane banked.

The intercom clicked on. "Your hostess will be back shortly to serve the beverage of your choice."

Again, Dr. George lamented the end of Navy involvement in NOAA research. Forget the larger, more comfortable planes—at least the damned pilots showed some respect.

Swiveling the chair, he gazed out the left-side windows, toward mainland China. Blade-shaped mountains receded into haze as the plane headed out toward international airspace. Wistfully, Dr. George wondered if the People's Republic might be interested in investing in typhoon research. Probably not; they were—

"Holy shit!" The voice of the pilot carried above the whistle of air and turbines. "Look at that. What the hell is *that*?"

Up front, the co-pilot was leaning across the aisle, almost in the pilot's lap, staring out the left-side window. George turned to the same direction and squinted into the sunlight. After a moment he spotted another aircraft out there, moving along on a roughly parallel course at a distance of a half mile or so. That was a bit close, but Hong Kong was a major hub of Asian air traffic; the sky was always full of planes coming and . . .

Wait. George looked closer. He had spent a lot of time in and around aircraft, but he had never seen anything like this. First of all, the plane had no distinct fuselage, but rather a sort of thickened area in the center. Nor was there a tail. The overall shape reminded him of a manta ray with its wingtips upturned, or perhaps a pregnant boomerang. But one thing was unmistakable: The nearest winglet was emblazoned with the red star of the People's Republic of China.

The Gulfstream's co-pilot began speaking in the kind of low, cadenced voice that George had come to associate with a radio transmission. At about the same time, the strange plane fell back. As it did so, George glimpsed a narrow door or hatch sliding open on its belly. Then the plane banked behind the Gulfstream, out of sight. George swiveled around and peered out the window, waiting for the plane to reappear on that side. It didn't.

On the eastern horizon pearly-white castles of a child's imagination loomed into the sky. Cumulonimbus clouds; thunderheads. Ranks and ranks of them hovering over the South China Sea and the Pacific Ocean, thirstily sucking moisture out of the lower atmosphere and vaulting it to cooler heights. Exchanging hot for cold and cold for hot, firing up the engine of a typhoon.

Only a matter of time. Two days at most; typhoons were capable of leaping up almost overnight. Why couldn't anyone but he seem to understand—

There was a shout from the cockpit, this one as loud as a trumpet blast: *"Incoming!"* At the same moment, the Gulfstream dipped violently to the left. George's head banged against the dropsonde console. There was a brilliant flash of light. A concussion slapped his ears. Grabbing the sides of the chair, he tried to pull himself upright. Lightning strike? He'd been in planes hit by lightning before . . . but the sky was clear . . . wasn't it?

He shook his head, then glanced at the window. The dark of the sea swung across it, as if the whole world had tilted. A moment later the sky reappeared. Then the water. Then the sky, now divided by a garland of black smoke. Shouts and curses echoed back from the cockpit, accompanied by an electronic shrieking.

The ocean reappeared. It was closer now; he could see the mottled ranks of waves rolling shoreward. The plane bucked, shivered. Dr. George realized he could see sunlight coming through the wall near the tail. As he watched, the crack widened.

"What's going on?" he shouted blearily. He tried to stand, but his seat belt yanked him back.

Now he could finally understand the co-pilot's words, a high-pitched chant: "Mayday, Mayday, Mayday . . ."

Through the window, water swung into view again. Now it was close enough to show white birds racing across the waves.

"Oh, my," Dr. Alonzo George said. "Oh my, oh my." Pivoting his seat toward the front of the plane, he bowed forward as far as his belly would let him, and placed his hands over his head.

1130 local (−8 GMT)
Office of the Commander
People's Liberation Army Air Force
Hong Kong SAR

Wei Ao lowered the telephone receiver from his ear and looked over at the man sitting across the desk from him. Until the interruption of the emergency call, Wei and Yeh Lien, the Political Commissar, had been having a very dry discussion about restructuring political training sessions for off-duty PLA soldiers. At least, that was what the discussion *seemed* to be about, but Wei had his doubts. Yeh seemed overly eager to increase the number of warnings about the dabbling in the black market. He kept stressing the importance of "clean spirit, Communist spirit."

Now, however, Wei was very glad to have the commissar present. Replacing the receiver in its cradle, he said, "Comrade, I have just been informed that an American military jet departing Kai Tak Airport has been shot down."

"Shot down?" Yeh Lien straightened in his seat. "An American military jet? What do you mean?"

"Just what I say. It was a NOAA aircraft—which is to say, an American Air Force jet supposedly used to study weather. Its pilot reported being paced by an unknown aircraft with a red star on the wing. He then reported missiles being fired, and began to go down. He has since vanished off radar and is presumed to have crashed."

Yeh closed his eyes. "This American plane—it was not armed?"

"No. Many times these kinds of planes are used for spying, so they are not armed. It would ruin the illusion."

"I assume you can identify who fired at it?"

"No. It was not one of ours."

Yeh's eyes opened. "But you said—"

"Anyone can paint a red star on a wing. Comrade, the American pilot reported that his attacker resembled a 'stealth fighter.' To the best of my knowledge, the PLA Air Force possesses no such aircraft. Also, our own radar detected only the smallest return, other than that of the business jet, in that area. They would have taken it to be a bird or temperature anomaly if it weren't for what happened later. And finally, all PLA aircraft have reported in and been accounted for. None is, or was, in the vicinity of the attack."

"What exactly are you telling me, Comrade Major General?"

"I'm telling you we need to find out what really happened." Wei leaned forward. "There's only one way to do that. I want to route a squadron of fighters to the area to search for this mystery plane and the American jet. Immediately."

Yeh looked uncomfortable. "You say the American went down outside the twelve-mile limit?"

"That's the radar indication. We won't know for sure until we get someone out there."

"Perhaps . . . perhaps we should consult with General Ming before—"

"Ming is on his way back to Beijing. By the time we contact him, the enemy will be gone. We must act *now*." Wei was pleased. Here was the perfect opportunity for him to show Beijing how dedicated he was to his job, while at the same time sharing responsibility for the final decision with his own Political Commissar.

But Yeh just stared out the window.

"Comrade," Wei said. "Radar indicates there are currently

no conventional American aircraft in the vicinity of the crash—but that won't last. If we wish to get there before the Americans cordon off the site like they did last time, we must act *now*. I'm asking for your concurrence in this decision."

At last Yeh looked back at him. "Not an entire squadron; it would look . . . aggressive. Some smaller number, perhaps."

Wei carefully kept the sneer off his face. Evidently living in Hong Kong had taught the Political Commissar the finer points of a very Capitalistic practice: haggling.

"Very well," he said, and reached for the phone.

1200 local (−8 GMT)
CVIC
USS Jefferson

"No doubt about it," Lab Rat said. "A small USAF jet, departing north out of Hong Kong, was taken out with an air-to-air missile fired at close range. This was a unarmed transport plane, sir. Whatever fired the shot dropped to the deck and disappeared."

"What do you mean, 'whatever fired the shot'?"

"Well, Admiral, the contact was . . . odd."

"Don't dance around the question. Tell me."

"It was an extremely weak return; nothing like your average fighter plane—especially one carrying missiles. Also, it never switched on its *own* radar. Not *any* radar, passive or fire-control. Nothing. It came up, shot off a couple of heat-seekers, and disappeared again."

"But it *was* described as a PLA aircraft, correct?"

"Well . . . that's the other thing." The intelligence officer pointed at the icons shifting over the blue screen. "The American pilot did say the bogey had PLA markings, but as you can see, right now eight Flankers are converging on the site; half of those are the newest model. It's weird; if the PLA is responsible for taking out the Air Force plane, why all this activity *now*?"

"So everybody will ask exactly that question. Please tell me this shoot-down happened on our side of the property line."

"Yes, sir. Barely."

Batman turned to the flag TAO. "Get SAR and air cover out there *now*. I want that area sealed off."

"It might be too late for that, sir," Lab Rat said. "This site is quite a bit north of our present position. Our closest assets are a pair of Hornets and a pair of F-14s, but they're all at least ten minutes out. No way they can get there before the PLA."

"Then have them get there second and make it clear we won't be cut out of this. Launch the Alert Five and Alert Fifteen birds, too; we want to match the PLA plane for plane as soon as we can. We're not going to start anything, but we want it understood we're in this game."

Lab Rat stared at the blue screen. "No one could have lived through that."

Batman shook his head. "That's not how we do SAR. If they are, we're not going to make them wait around for a certain helicopter to show up."

1205 local (−8 GMT)
South China Sea

Dr. George awoke to the feel of warm water sweeping around his ankles. What was this—Monsoon rains leaking into his office again? He started to sit erect, but a twisting pain arced through his lower back and he cried out. After a moment's rest he tried again, more slowly.

My, his office was a mess. No, not his office . . . this looked more or less like the rear compartment of the NOAA Gulfstream that had been flying him back to Guam from Hong Kong.

Then he remembered: The strange-looking fighter plane, the explosion . . . and the rear of the Gulfstream breaking open like an eggshell.

The water was swirling around his calves now. He looked forward, into the cockpit. The windscreens were both opaque, shattered. He could see the right shoulder of the pilot, the left shoulder of the co-pilot, leaning together across the central aisle. Neither was moving.

"Hey!" George called, and winced at the pain in his back. "Hey! Hey, are you all right?"

No response. The water was now up to his knees. A small jellyfish floated past. The plane remained remarkably level, though, as if the sea were entering with equal speed from both ends. He looked out the nearest window just as a low swell rolled past, its crown sweeping along the bottom of the glass. Water surged into the plane, soaking his thighs.

"Oh God." He fumbled with the release catch on his seat belt. Saw fresh blood on his hands. He wasn't sure where it was coming from, and wasn't sure he really wanted to know. "Oh God, oh God . . ."

Finally, the catch popped and he yanked himself out of the tight seat, groaning at spasms in his back. Something was wrong with his right leg, too; it would barely support him. Bracing his weight against various pieces of equipment, he yanked himself toward the cockpit. "Hey! Hey, guys!" No response. The water was up to his knees now.

At the cockpit entrance he halted. The nose of the Gulfstream had been crushed; the instrument panel looked like it had slammed back like a horizontal guillotine blade, chopping deeply into the chests of both pilots. One glance was all George needed, and all he could stand. He turned, pushed himself back against the water.

The Gulfstream's door was designed to hinge outward along its bottom edge, creating a staircase. He reached for the handle that would break the seal, then thought of something and groped into one of the overhead compartments for a life vest. It looked pathetically small; how could he ever wrestle it on in these confined quarters?

And what would happen when he opened that door? He thought of the physics of it: The water would rush in, and its mounting weight would roll the plane in the direction of the flow, at least at first. The entire doorway opening might dip beneath the surface before George could swim out against the current. On the other hand, the plane's wings—assuming they were still attached—would resist the roll, perhaps buying him enough time to escape before the door was submerged. On the other hand—how many hands was that?—what if the incoming water was moving so fast he couldn't push against it anyway?

Water swirled around his crotch, leaching out his body heat. He started to shiver. No time to argue with himself; the plane was almost half sunk as it was. At any moment it might choose a direction to rock and start diving for the bottom of the South China Sea—and all his options would be gone.

He grabbed the door handle, braced himself, and put pressure on it. Screamed as his back let out an electric bolt of pain.

He'd forgotten one hand: The airframe was warped; the door jammed. It wouldn't budge.

The water was up to his waist, tendrils creeping up his shirt to his armpits.

He looked around for something to pry with, to gain leverage. Nothing, and no time to search. Setting his feet, locking his hands around the handle, he closed his eyes, said a silent prayer, and hauled as hard as he could.

His back felt like a missile had hit it. Still, he kept twisting. There was a grinding sound, a thump, and the top of the door eased out, then down. There was no ferocious flood of water, although the level immediately rose faster. Physics again: The air trapped in the fuselage was resisting the incoming flow.

But soon the plane would sink.

Clutching his life vest under one arm, George plunged like a walrus through the diminishing gap between the water and the top of the doorway.

1215 local (−8 GMT)
Tomcat 306
South China Sea

"Well, now, what are the odds?" Two Tone said, sounding pleased. "You, me, Lobo and Handyman . . . here we go again."

"Yeah." Following the lead of Lobo, a thousand feet below and as far ahead, Hot Rock banked the Tomcat onto the new heading sent to them by Homeplate. Much farther down, the South China Sea shone silver and blue. At ten o'clock, the mountainous coast of China shimmered in the haze like a fever dream. A few jagged-sided islands of various sizes thrust up from the water. Everything was so gorgeous from up here.

Hot Rock eased the throttles forward and felt the delicious shiver as the Tomcat opened the door to the sound barrier and stepped through. He loved that. Back when he'd started flight school, he'd thought the training jet, a T-45A Goshawk, had been powerful and intimidating; the F-14 had seemed an impossibility to handle. So large, so expensive and particular. When the time had come to strap one on he'd expected it to be the horses all over again, and him washing out with his tail between his legs. . . .

Instead—God. The Tomcat and the sky, and hurtling along faster than sound. If it could only be like this all the time. If only he could just fly and fly up here between the sky and the water. . . . "What the hell are the Chinese thinking?" he said. "Sinking our boats, shooting down our planes . . . do they really want to go to war with us?"

"Why not?" his RIO said. "Bound to happen sooner or later."

"You think so?"

"Sure. China's the last major Communist power in the world, unless you want to count Berkeley. Hard-core communists believe in world domination. It's part of the deal."

"Didn't work for Russia."

"Won't work for China, either, but they don't know that.

And they won't figure it out until they get their butts kicked a few times."

Hot Rock realized his palms were sweating, and his chest felt tight. "And you think this is the start?"

"Got your steel-toed boots on?"

1220 local (−8 GMT)
South China Sea

Dr. George raised his head when he heard the rippling roar of jet engines. He'd been floating along quietly, almost enjoying himself. Hadn't been this close to the water for quite a while, that was for sure. The South China Sea was a nice temperature, not too warm, kind of soothing on his twisted back. The only troublesome thing was the stream of blood that kept running down his face from a cut somewhere on his scalp. The blood dripped into the water, of course; he couldn't stop it. Which meant he couldn't stop thinking about sharks.

Overfishing, he kept telling himself. For decades the Asians had been decimating the shark population, netting the fish left and right, lopping off their dorsal fins for soup and tossing the maimed animal back into the water for its brethren to devour. Then catching the brethren. More recently, half-baked theories about the ability of shark cartilage to prevent cancer in humans had led American fishing boats to join in the massacre.

Still, sharks . . . it only took one. And these waters were the hunting grounds of one of the most notorious man-eating species in the world: the tiger shark.

That was why the sound of approaching jet engines brought feelings of relief to him, as well as dread. He wanted to be found and rescued. On the other hand, it had been a jet that shot down the Gulfstream.

To his relief, when he finally spotted the two aircraft that were making the racket, they didn't look like the one that had fired the missile. These had angular bodies, double vertical stabilizers, and wings that pointed in the right direction.

Then he spotted the red stars on their undersurfaces, and his fear doubled. Chinese fighters, not American.

But the jets were searching in the wrong place, a mile or two to the south. Without the Gulfstream itself to focus on, they seemed to be streaking around almost arbitrarily, close to the water, possibly trying to make sense of the debris that had fanned across the surface of the South China Sea.

George debated what to do. There were flares in one pocket of the life vest; he could draw attention in his way in an instant with those. But . . . one of these maniacs' friends had shot down the Gulfstream; what would they do to him if they picked him up?

The jets began to spread out, circling. Then he saw more jets moving in from the southeast, pair by pair, at a much higher altitude. At least eight planes up there. But this group didn't circle; it continued straight east, heading further out to sea.

Fighter planes, nothing but fighter planes. Where were the rescue helicopters, the slow search aircraft, the boats?

Maybe, George thought, he should just keep floating along here until a fishing vessel came along.

Down in the water, a brown shadow cruised past his dangling feet. It had a blunt, squared-off snout, and dark stripes on its flanks.

Dr. George groped wildly in the pocket of his life vest.

1230 local (+8 GMT)
Tomcat 302
South China Sea

"Well, here they come." Handyman's voice was dry over the ICS. Lobo thought he sounded like a bored suburbanite announcing the arrival of neighbors for the annual block party. "Six new bogeys, altitude thirty thousand feet, bearing zero one zero. Flankers, by their radar. And they aren't searching for anything but favorable position."

Hot Rock's voice came over tactical: "Lobo? Did you happen to notice we're getting a tad outnumbered here?" His words were flyboy-cool, but under them his voice was as tight as a spool of cable. Lobo reminded herself that her wingman hadn't tasted combat yet. Never knew how anyone would react to the real thing until it happened. She wondered if the tension in his voice was the product of eagerness, or of fear . . . and which would be better. "Backup's on the way," she said. "And remember, we're just here to hang around, not to fight. So stay cool."

"Tell them that."

Looking up through the canopy, Lobo spotted six double-wide vapor trails etching across the blue. Her skin tightened. For any fighter pilot, altitude almost always equaled power. But today she didn't have the option of seeking the high slot, not if she was going to perform her assigned duty of protecting the area where the jet had gone down. If what had happened to *Lady of Leisure* was any indication, the biggest danger to potential survivors would come not from a high-flying jet, but from a boat or helicopter. Still . . .

"I hate this," she said over ICS.

"Lobo," Handyman said, "high or low, you can out-fly anyone in the sky. You got that?"

She blinked. "Thanks, Handyman." Switching to tactical, she said, "Okay, Hot Rock, get ready to start searching."

"What a grand idea."

"Relax. Reinforcements are ten minutes out. Keep tight this time, Hot Rock. Welded wing unless somebody starts something."

"Welded wing, roger."

Lobo clicked off. Easy to tell her wingman to relax, but she was facing a bit of an inner chill herself; couldn't deny it. The last major air battle she'd been in . . . well, she'd ended up punching out of her plane. And then, of course, spending some quality time with a Russian militia.

And later still, spending a lot more time getting her head shrunk.

She hoped it was the right size for whatever came up now.

1240 local (−8 GMT)
Hornet 108
South China Sea

"I always thought Hornets were speedy," Major "Thor" Hammersmith growled, thumping the throttles of his F/A-18 with the heel of his hand. "Come on, you bitch."

"We're getting there," his wingman, Reedy, said in the voice that had earned him his call sign. "Besides, we were told to grab for altitude at the same time."

"Yeah, yeah." All Thor wanted to do was shoot down a bad guy. The last major military action he'd been involved in, down in Cuba, he'd gotten his ass blown out of the sky while he was refueling. Refueling! Spent the rest of that little affair tied to a chair while different Cubans pounded on him and used him to taunt the U.S. Navy. Not any Marine's idea of "participation."

Not that he was planning on starting a fight here. No way. But these assholes had blasted an innocent American yacht to pieces the other night, then actually ripped a chunk out of *Jefferson*—accidentally or otherwise, it didn't matter—and now they'd shot down a commair with a missile. How brave. How warrior-like. Well, Thor's Hornet was loaded down with air-to-air missiles, so if the Chinese were ready to try their luck against the big boys, Thor was ready for them.

He knew that more than half the planes awaiting them were the latest model Flanker. Rumor had it that although these Flankers were as big as F-14s—or "Turkeys," in Hornet driver parlance—the Russian fighters handled more like F/A-18s. In the case of the SU-35, they supposedly handled *better* than Hornets.

That's what he'd heard. But what you heard and what you *knew*, well, they were often two different things. And Thor Hammersmith knew that nothing could beat an F/A-18 in a close-in knife fight. Nothing.

He thumped the throttles again. Tried not to think about the rate at which his two F404-GE-402 turbofans were gulping down precious fuel. That was the Hornet's biggest disadvantage compared to the Turkey: Hornets had short legs.

It would be just his luck to get in a punch or two in an air battle, only to have to run away again to gas up.

Not that there was going to be any fight, mind you. . . .

1242 local (−8 GMT)
Tomcat 306
South China Sea

An axiom of dogfighting stated that all else being equal, a lone fighter plane was a victim, while a pair acting in concert was like a two-headed snake: It saw everything, and could bite in any direction.

As wingman in the so-called "welded wing" formation, Hot Rock's primary job was to be the rear head of the snake, keeping his lead safe. In the event of an actual battle, he would fly in tandem with Lobo, protecting her vulnerable back from attack so she could concentrate on her primary job: shooting down enemy aircraft. His own weapons load would serve mostly as a backup to hers.

That was why most fighter jocks preferred the "loose deuce" formation, developed by American pilots during the Vietnam war. In loose deuce configuration, the two fighters kept a great deal more space between them, and depending on circumstances, one or the other might become the primary attack plane, with the second flying in the support and backup role.

Although he'd never admit it, Hot Rock not only liked flying welded wing, he preferred the wingman slot. It was challenging from a piloting standpoint, because a wingman had to not only anticipate his lead's movements so as to maintain proper relative position on her, but do so while constantly scanning the surrounding sky for enemies.

This meant the wingman had to leave the most crucial battle decisions up to the lead.

And that was fine with Hot Rock, because such an arrangement almost eliminated the possibility that he might make a bad tactical error.

He followed Lobo as she flew a grid search pattern, drawing an invisible tic-tac-toe board over the approximate area where the business jet had gone down. Looking down at the water, Hot Rock glimpsed the occasional fleck that was a drifting cushion or other piece of flotsam. He was hoping to see a flare or spreading dye marker, or even a life raft. Nothing.

Of course, it was difficult to concentrate on searching the water, because he and Lobo were not alone in the air. Apart from the eight bogeys far overhead, two more were hurtling around at virtually this same altitude, probably conducting their own search. Twice already, Hot Rock had gotten a much closer look at them than he would have preferred as the Flankers cut across the Tomcats' path.

He toggled the radio to tactical. "Viper Leader, they're going to be just above us on the next pass," he said.

"I know that." Lobo's voice was curt. "Be ready, but ignore them."

Hot Rock started to reply, then toggled to ICS. " 'Be ready, but ignore them'? What's that supposed to mean?"

"It means to keep your finger over the weapons selector," Two Tone said. "I'll let you know when you need it."

"You mean 'if.' "

"Right."

Tomcat 302
South China Sea

"Here they come," Lobo said, eyes locked on the two Chinese aircraft crossing from her right. She felt sweat prickling her scalp as they closed in, everything moving too fast—

—and then the Flankers thundered overhead, so close the shock of their passing gave Lobo's Tomcat a savage yank. For once, she was glad for the tight fit of the cockpit.

"Assholes," Handyman said dryly.

"Looked like SU-27s," Lobo said, as if she'd had all day to study the Chinese plane going by. "Guess they left the top-of-the-line fighters in the high-altitude hairball."

"Yeah. Probably all the missiles these two are carrying are low-budget models, too," Handyman said. "Now I feel a lot better about having them playing chicken with us. It's—Lobo! Flare at two o'clock!"

She looked to her right and saw it, a red spark burning bright and hot even against the sunny sky. She immediately put in a call to the carrier. "Homeplate, Viper Leader. We've spotted an emergency flare. Repeat, an emergency flare; looks like it came from the area where the plane went down."

"Viper Leader, this is Admiral Wayne. Maintain overhead orbit until SAR arrives. Don't start anything, but make it clear we're involved, understood?"

"Roger." She rolled her eyes. *Involved?* What did that mean? "What's the ETA for SAR?"

"Fifteen minutes," Homeplate said. "Be advised a Luhu-class destroyer just pulled out of the harbor and is making flank speed to your datum. ETA twenty-five minutes."

Tomcat 306
South China Sea

"A destroyer?" Hot Rock said, switching to ICS. "Great." He knew that China's *Luhu*-class ships were new, fast, and armed with Crotale anti-aircraft missiles, among other treats. And the ship was already close enough to take part in any air battle. Of course, so were CVBG-14's destroyer and Aegis cruiser, with their over-the-horizon firing capabilities . . . but still, in a missile situation, a difference of seconds was all anyone needed. Any ship leaving Hong Kong would already have the drop on both American support ships.

"We got other problems at the moment," Two Tone said. "Like the fact that those two Flankers are coming back around on us."

"They're just doing the same thing we are," Hot Rock said, forcing his dry lips to move. "Circling the flare."

"And what about the six dudes overhead?" Two Tone

asked. "Why do you suppose they're there? Tour guides?"

"Doesn't matter." Hot Rock's hands weren't just sweaty inside his gloves now—they were slathered, and shaking a bit. Had been ever since those goddamned Chinese fighters galloped past, close enough to kiss. He sharpened his voice. "Our orders are to keep things clear for SAR, so we keep things clear for SAR."

"But what if the Chinese get their SAR here first? Because I'm picking up a low-level return, bearing?? . . . same bearing and distance as the destroyer. That's gotta mean the Chinese launched a helo. And guess what? It's going to get here before any of our eggbeaters do."

SEVEN

Monday, 4 August

1245 local (−8 GMT)
Flanker 67
South China Sea

Tai Ling gazed down through the golden haze of sun on water, searching for his prey. He couldn't visually pick out the four fighters circling far below. His look-down radar showed they were there, and their relative positions, but he wished he could see them with his own eyes. It would make it much easier to recognize the signal when it came. He didn't know what the signal would be, exactly, but he'd been told that it would be unmistakable.

He'd also been told that the Americans, unbeknownst to themselves, would be the ones to give it.

Speaking of Americans . . . Tai's radar also showed the approach of four more fighter aircraft from the direction of the aircraft carrier.

The sight of those blips filled him with a strange emotion: half eager anticipation, half sick hope. The anticipation was the natural sensibility of any trained fighter pilot facing his possible first real dogfight. The hope was inspired by the unremitting memory of Hua Shih's SU-37 exploding into a burning comet in front of him, its beautiful skin punched full of 20mm cannon holes. From Tai Ling's cannon.

Although Tai knew that what he had done was essential in the long run, that didn't make accepting the fact any easier: He had shot down one of his own men. His own section leader, in fact. And he'd done it from the trusted position of wingman.

The fact that he had himself been promoted to section leader following Hua's "flame-out and crash" only made the memory of that day more bitter.

Perhaps making a true, man-to-man kill on an American plane would clean the slate, would erase the shame of what he'd done. Had to do. Perhaps even Hua would understand and applaud.

Focused again, Tai returned his attention to the radar and willed the Americans to come closer.

1246 local (−8 GMT)
Tomcat 304

"Scimitar Leader to Viper Leader," Bird Dog said over tactical. "We're fifty mikes out. Copy?"

"Copy, Scimitar Leader. Don't hurry on our account. I've always wanted to get a nice, long, close-up look at a Flanker. Or two."

"We're buster, Lobo. Just hang in there."

"Copy." Her damned voice was all business. "By the way, the inbound PLA helo is going to get here in less than a mike. You're the War College brain; what do you advise if it makes a play for the survivor?"

"Just do what you did the other night," he said. "Those are our orders: Just let the helo know you're there. Make life uncomfortable for it. *Shiloh* advises two Seahawks are en route, ETA fifteen mikes."

"Um, Mr. Dog, it seems to me that if I run interference on this helo like you say, the Chinese could make a pretty good case that the USA is interfering in a benevolent SAR attempt."

"Not after what happened to *Lady of Leisure*," Bird Dog said.

Two sharp clicks indicated acknowledgment of the message. Then the ICS came on. "I don't think she liked your advice, boss," Catwoman said.

I didn't either, Bird Dog thought, but didn't say. How could anyone justify risking the lives of American pilots, not to mention a damned expensive aircraft costing, in order to guard a chunk of water in which a person might or might not be floating around alive?

But then he remembered how he'd felt as he drifted helplessly in the warm Atlantic, waiting to see who was going to pick him up first—the Cubans or his own people. Remembered that, and was glad he'd kept his lip zipped for a change.

But his imagination was a different matter. When he visualized Lobo flying around out there at suicidally low altitudes, doing a job better suited to prop planes or helos, his anger and frustration surged up again, and he thought, *Hang on, Lobo, just hang on. . . .*

1247 local (−8 GMT)
Tomcat 302

There was nothing worse than flying this low in a fighter plane. Lobo ached for altitude, for the superior speed and maneuverability that altitude conferred.

Right now the two SU-27s were living up to their NATO nickname, flanking her and Hot Rock throughout their long, constant turn, as if escorting the American planes. The Flankers were large craft, with twin vertical stabilizers and graceful, recurved fuselages . . . in fact, they looked disturbingly like Tomcats. She mentally reviewed what she knew about their capabilities: Twin afterburning Lyul'ka AL-21 turbofans each providing almost thirty thousand pounds of thrust—compared to the 27,000 pounds available to the Tomcats—which gave the Chinese planes a top speed of Mach 2.35 as compared to Mach 1.88 for the Tomcat. The SU-27 had a better ceiling, too.

According to the latest intel, the Flankers also turned

tighter than Tomcats, and had radar equipped with look-down, shoot-down capability.

And these were the *old* models. The SU-35s and SU-37 up above had, reportedly, even higher performance numbers.

In other words, for the first time since early in the Vietnam war, it was possible the American aircraft in any given air battle were not intrinsically superior. It was actually possible that the Tomcat was outmatched, not only in turn radius but in pure, brute power.

On top of that, Homeplate had warned them to be on the lookout for an "unidentified fighter aircraft of unknown abilities." Whatever that meant.

Not that Lobo was frightened by either the known statistics or the unknown variables of the situation. Regardless of how swell a pilot's hardware was, the plane was no better than the pilot. And that was where nobody could touch the United States Navy.

Still . . . there was no denying that this situation *sucked*.

She looked over her right shoulder, gazing down at the water on the inside of her steady turn. There was a small red-and-white dot floating on the water. The survivor, presumably, although there had been no more flares. She wondered what the poor schmuck thought about this private air show. Assuming he or she was still alive.

"Lobo," Handyman said, "I've got a visual on that Chinese helo. I hate to ask awkward questions, but what are we supposed to do if it ignores us? Shoot it down?"

"I wish," Lobo said.

Hornet 108

"Let's get horizontal," Thor said into his oxygen mask. Toggling the radio, he reported to Homeplate that he and Reedy had arrived on site, at an altitude of fifty-two thousand feet—all they could manage, but still below the ceiling of the Russian planes. He and Reedy started circling well outside the orbit of the six bogeys, trying to look innocent.

But Thor could see the enemy, the dying light of day flaring silver-gold off the lower surfaces of wings and canards as the Flankers circled. Six of them, not to mention the two older models far down below, dancing with Lobo and Hot Rock just above the water.

Bad position. And a bad fuel situation for him and Reedy. Who cares?

Thor ran his thumb over the weapons selector switch and waited for something to happen.

Tomcat 302

"Viper 304, Viper 302," Lobo said. "Hot Rock, we'd better make things a little rough for that helo before it gets any closer. We're going to need to spread out some."

"What?"

"If we're going to keep that chopper off the survivor, we've got to put up a wall. I go past it, then you go past it, then I go, like that. Constant circles. Rip up the air. No gap big enough for him to slip through. You're such a hot stick, you think you can handle that?"

A pause, then, "You're the boss."

"Then let's do it."

Tomcat 304

"How much farther?" Bird Dog snapped over ICS. "How much farther?"

"You sound like a little kid in the back of a station wagon," Catwoman said. "Five mikes. Keep your shirt on— sir. What can happen in the next five minutes?"

Tomcat 306

"They didn't teach this in flight school," Hot Rock muttered as he eased back on the throttles, letting the distance between his Tomcat and Lobo's lengthen. At the same time, both planes were descending. Hot Rock rarely saw the ocean this close except during launches and landings—the two most dangerous times to be a Naval aviator.

But he wasn't worried about the water; he was too busy keeping an eye on the two escorting Flankers. For a few moments they seemed uncertain what to do; then they both rose up and took up new position, one behind each of the Tomcats. Overall, the formation was odd. Hot Rock had a clear belly-shot at the Flanker following Lobo, but at the same time he was dead in the sights of the Flanker on his own six o'clock. A Mexican standoff.

"No need to hit the deck." Lobo's voice was flat but intense in his hears. "Use your wingtip vortices. Got that?"

Hot Rock clicked his mike twice. Lobo was talking about taking advantage of what was usually an annoying feature of fixed-wing aerodynamics—the tilted hurricanes of air that formed at the outer ends of a wing, where compressed air from the underside met low-pressure air from above. The resulting braids of turbulence were a major source of drag, as well as a potential hazard to other air traffic because they could linger for minutes in the air, invisible and tenacious, like horizontal tornadoes.

In this case, though, Lobo was advocating using the vortices as blunt instruments to make the Chinese helo think twice about approaching the survivor in the water. Painting the air with turbulence that way would require some fine flying, and Hot Rock felt himself relaxing just thinking about it.

Ahead of him, Lobo was making her first turn toward the helo, which was a slick-looking Z-9 with retractable landing gear and a shark-fin fairing around its tail rotor. The helo was flying low enough to create a gray shimmer on the water.

Lobo increased her angle of bank, slipping down as she crossed the path of the helo. Her Chinese escort, Hot Rock noted, remained at his own higher altitude. Lobo roared past the helo, well above and in front of it, but plainly within the pilot's sight. This was obvious because the helo immediately raised its nose in a hard braking action and swiveled partly to its left as it halted.

Hot Rock felt an electrical prickle on the back of his neck. What Lobo had just done could, arguably, be interpreted as a highly aggressive act. He waited to hear the sharp warbling tone in his helmet that would indicate a fire-control radar lock on his aircraft . . . but it didn't happen. So far, everything was still cool.

Hot Rock increased his own angle of bank and let the Tomcat slip down along the same path Lobo had taken. He felt the slight bumping of disrupted air where her plane had been, although the harsher turbulence of its wingtip vortices were well below him, hammering down on the water.

He was beginning to level out for his close pass on the helo when he heard Two Tone shout: "Hot Rock! He's going guns! Going guns! Gunfire in the water!"

Later, Hot Rock would review that moment over and over again in his mind. The helo was dead ahead, its tail pivoted somewhat toward him, but not at such an oblique angle that Hot Rock couldn't see the open side hatch and the machine gun mounted there. He was sure, later, that he'd seen those things. He also plainly saw gouts of orange flame ripping into the air. That wasn't just his imagination, or an illusion caused by sunlight flaring off passing swells. No way.

In fact, the sight of the flames was so startling he hesitated a moment, as if he wanted to convince *himself* it wasn't real.

"Hot Rock!" Two Tone's voice, sharp, so much like an older man's voice. Disappointed, commanding. "Get on it!"

Hot Rock flicked his weapons selector switch to the Sidewinder position. "Fox Three," he said.

South China Sea

From water level, everything that had been happening so dreadfully slowly suddenly accelerated to unbelievable speed. For what seemed like hours, Dr. George had been switching his attention between the circling jets, the approaching Chinese helicopter—and the water beneath his feet. The tiger shark kept disappearing and then coming back again, moving with increasing speed on each pass, as if making up its mind about something. Once it came so close George actually kicked it, after which it became more wary. But it was still around, or maybe there were more than one of them. It was hard to tell. The setting sun no longer cut its light into the water, showing him what lurked below. Soon he wouldn't be able to see his legs at all.

The sharks would be under no such restrictions.

So, let the Chinese pick him up. He didn't care anymore. He just wanted to be warm and dry and safe.

The helicopter was perhaps a hundred yards away when it halted. The jets continued to circle overhead, so low now that George could see the shapes of the pilots' heads through the canopies. Two American jets, and two Chinese, cruising around together in a big, roaring circle. What the hell was going on?

Just then there was a brilliant flash from one of the American jets, and a sound like high-pressure water shooting from a hose. A rope of white smoke abruptly connected the American jet to the helicopter. The helicopter exploded. It broke in half like an egg, but the bright-yellow yolk rose up and up instead of falling. The shells of the fuselage dropped. Spinning rotor blades hit the water and broke free, skipping across the surface for some distance before vanishing in sheets of spray.

Where the fuselage vanished into the water, a roiling dome of bubbles and smoke boiled up, hissing and crackling.

Dr. George felt something nudge his foot, and started to kick.

Flanker 67

Tai Ling saw the fireball light up the dark waters below, and heard the radio chatter erupt from the two SU-27 pilots down at sea level. Their message was shocked and furious: One of the Americans had just taken an unprovoked missile shot at the PLA helicopter arriving to rescue the person in the water. The helo was down.

If that wasn't the signal Tai had been waiting for, nothing was.

"Weapons free!" he cried over the tactical circuit, and reached for his own weapons selector switch. "All aircraft, weapons free!"

Tomcat 302

"Holy shit!" Handyman yelled, a vast expression of emotion for him. "What the hell—"

Lobo had her back to the helo and Hot Rock, but she heard him signal the firing of a Sidewinder, and simultaneously saw the fiery reflection of an explosion reflecting from the inside of her canopy. Her response came long before thought: She slammed the throttle quadrant full forward, and as the afterburners gave their mule kick, she hauled back hard on the stick. In a heartbeat of time, the Tomcat went from cruise mode into a neck-snapping climb out.

Lobo cranked her head around, searching for the Flanker that had been roofing her. Gasped as it flashed past to the left, showing its belly in a hard bank that had to have been initiated simply to avoid a collision.

"Well," Handyman drawled, his voice back to normal, "that worked."

Lobo eased the stick forward an inch, putting the Tomcat into a marginally more relaxed, sustainable angle of climb. "Where is he?" she demanded. "Where did he go?"

"Coming up behind us, babe."

On her radar, Lobo saw the lozenge-shaped return of the Flanker coming around hard on her tail. A moment after that, she heard the warbling signal that indicated she was being painted with fire-control radar.

Radar or not, at this range the bogey was inside missile range; he'd be going to guns. Leaving the stick where it was, Lobo kicked the Tomcat over on one wingtip, rotated over like a gymnast doing a one-handed cartwheel, then dove back toward the deck. At the same time, the white-hot flare of tracers swept past her inboard wing.

The Flanker was right below her, from this angle nothing but a round fuselage, a couple of rectangular air intakes and the blazing flower of its cannon.

"Recommend guns," Handyman said even as Lobo hit the trigger.

Her tracers ripped beneath the Flanker, a miss of only a few feet—but there was no room for a pull-up to bring the shells on target, not unless she wanted a certain head-on collision.

She jammed the stick forward instead, initiating the start of an inverted loop.

As her head filled with pressurized blood, she held her breath and grunted loudly, holding off unconsciousness as she mentally tracked the Flanker's likely behavior. He should be rounding out of his vertical climb right about now, gleefully expecting to be right above her, in perfect position for a kill. Lobo snapped the stick to the right, then back, flipping the Tomcat right side up and simultaneously reversing its direction. Now the blood drained out of her head and she was struggling for consciousness against a different enemy. At the same time she found herself staring directly at the boiling patch of water where the helo had gone down ... staring as it grew larger and larger, the Tomcat's weight fighting her attempt to pull out, its engines fighting gravity and momentum, Lobo's will fighting the same things ... fighting ...

And then she felt the wings grab air with authority and the surface of the South China Sea was blurring by beneath her.

"You just love this low-altitude shit, don't you?" Handyman grunted.

Hornet 108

"Man, did you ever screw up," Thor said as he put his Hornet into a tight left turn. His scorn was not directed at the two Flankers left up here to fight him and Reedy; rather, it was aimed at whoever had ordered them to do so. Could anyone really be dipshitty enough to believe that a one-on-one ratio represented good odds for the Chinese pilots?

Not that things started out so hot for him and Reedy. The Flankers were a few thousand feet higher than the Hornets when the shooting started, and immediately came hurtling down, missiles streaking off their wings. That took some fancy flying to get out of. And Thor had to admit that at least some of the grim intel on these new birds was true; big as they were, the Flankers turned like plastic models tugged on a wire.

But Thor and Reedy flew in perfect harmony, using the high-low loose deuce formation, and the damned Chinese were overconfident; when they took the bait and converged on Reedy, Thor swooped over and in, crying "break right!" on his radio. Instantly Reedy's Hornet showed the Flankers its belly. At the same moment Thor triggered a Sidewinder. Since the Flankers were displaying the most tailpipe, real sex to a Sidewinder, the missile selected the brighter of the two and drove itself home. Thor grinned to see a pillow-shaped eruption of smoke and flame. An ejection seat rocketed out of the mess, which pleased him even more. Personally, he loved to shoot down hardware, not software. "Splash one Flanker!" he cried.

Then he gasped as Reedy's Hornet dissolved into fire and smoke.

He immediately compartmentalized his fury and did what he'd been trained to do: broke into a hard evasive turn and scanned his radar screen. Instantly, he knew what had happened. The descending Flankers had pulled a fast one. One of them split off from its fellows and returned to the high-altitude battle. The bastard had killed Reedy.

And at the same time, reversed the odds.

Tomcat 304

Bird Dog didn't need to hear the radio signals from the Vipers to know that the dogfight had started in earnest. He could see it all over his radar screen as the various blobs and blips began to move in fast, devious directions. And one Marine had been splashed already.

He forced himself to relax. One advantage of coming in from a distance was that he'd already had the time to tag each bogey's radar image with a targeting marker.

But that didn't make his fellow aviators any less outnumbered. For a moment he felt unreasoning anger at the admiral and all the other boneheads who'd failed to be prepared for something like this . . . then he remembered that he was one of those boneheads.

He assessed the situation playing out over his radar screen. One Marine F/A-18s was still up high, tangling with a pair of bogeys. Down low, Lobo and Hot Rock were engaged with two Flankers—and in between, descending fast, were three more Flankers exchanging the high-altitude furball for the lower one. They were going to bounce Lobo and Hot Rock.

Not if Bird Dog Robinson could help it. "Phoenix," he snapped, setting his weapons control switch accordingly. The Phoenix had the longest range of any missile in the American inventory. The downside was that as a radar-guided weapon, it required a nice steady course from the targeting plane to maintain radar lock. Also, it was rather easy to shake and had therefore earned a mediocre rep for successful kills; still, there was nothing like seeing a one-ton missile coming at you from over the horizon to make you rethink your attack strategy.

But before Bird Dog could hit the trigger, Catwoman said, "Uh, Birdy-boy, you might want to remember how close we are to one of the most populous city in the world."

Bird Dog started to make a sharp retort, then realized what she was saying: The Phoenix had a range of over one hundred miles, and if it missed its target, it would simply fly until it ran out of fuel . . . or struck something else. Like a skyscraper. At this angle, that was likely.

"Oh, hell," Bird Dog said. He considered the range. "Okay, Sparrows." Although the current distance was at the outer limit for the Sparrow, at least the missile wouldn't free-fly into Hong Kong if it got dodged.

He had two Sparrows on his wings. He assigned one of them a target blip, then triggered it off and felt the pleasant upward bump as their weight left the Tomcat. He watched the Sparrow depart on a strand of white smoke, and felt, as always, a strange sense of empathetic fear for the pilots on the other end. Missiles moved so quickly, they were like a bad dream. Especially if they were sniffing for you.

"Come on, baby," he said. "Come on . . ."

Flanker 67

Tai heard the warning alarm in his helmet, and saw the return image of the incoming missile on his Heads-Up Display. Cursed. Took his focus off the battle raging below, and turned it to the radar. Waited. Waited . . .

He released a bundle of chaff and juked hard to one side without breaking out of his dive. The chaff expanded in the air behind him, creating a metallic cloud designed to fool radar signals. An instant later, the shock wave of an explosion rocked his plane. The missile had taken the bait.

"Status?" he cried over tactical. All three of Sukhois reported back. Tai smiled.

So far, the score was one kill for the PLA fighters, and zero for the Americans. That was about to change—but not in the Americans' favor. As Tai's plane shot through the spot where sunset turned to twilight, he was at last able to visually select a target from the possibilities below.

Tomcat 302

As Lobo bottomed out of her dive, she pulled the stick back and then sideways again, once more reversing both the Tomcat's direction and its orientation, so now she was following the top curve of an outside loop back toward the bogey. If what she'd pictured in her head was accurate, the Flanker should now be above and in front of her, still climbing, clawing for precious altitude.

And so it was. Better still, the reach between them was just about broad enough to—

"Clear," Handyman said.

"Fox three!" Lobo triggered a Sidewinder.

Given enough room, a Sidewinder would attain supersonic velocity in a matter of seconds. In this case, it didn't have the chance. Nor did the Flanker. Lobo saw a flare pop out of the enemy fighter and start to ignite as a lure to the Sidewinder's infrared seeker head, but the move was much too late.

"Splash one!" Handyman cried as the Flanker turned into a fireball with wings. A moment later the wings were alone, fluttering down toward the water like falling leaves, flipping this way and that, preceded by a shower of miscellaneous smoking debris.

"Oooh," Handyman said, "that has *got* to hurt."

"Where the hell is my wingman?" Lobo said.

Tomcat 306

"Come on, Rock, shake him," Two Tone said from the backseat.

Hot Rock didn't bother telling him to shut up. If he did that, it would look like he had time to chat.

The Flanker pilot was good, he'd give him that. No sooner had Hot Rock taken out the helo than the Chinese plane was dropping in on his tail, cannon blazing. Ever since, the Flanker had been right there, trying to get a clean shot. An occasional burst ripped past, tracers stitching the air first on one side, then the other. Not one hit, though.

The Chinese pilot was good, but Hot Rock was better. He felt it instantly in his heart, and in the seat of his pants. He knew he could take this guy. He could get on his tail and take him whenever he wanted.

It would be the first real kill for Hot Rock Stone. You couldn't count the helo, that sitting duck.

And yet . . . what if he missed, after all? What if he reversed positions on the Flanker, took the offensive and then, for whatever reason, blew it? Everyone would know. Everyone would know that Hot Rock wasn't good enough.

This way, only he knew.

"We got all these weapons here," Two Tone growled, "and no one to shoot them at."

Again Hot Rock said nothing. He was giving the Flanker pilot all he could handle just keeping within killing range. Not quite throwing the Chinese plane, but not allowing the Flanker a clear shot, either. Hot Rock knew he could do this all day long, or at least until he ran out of fuel. Or the Flanker did. Or the fighting ended and they could all go home.

"Heads up, boy," Two Tone said. "Three bogeys straight up; one's picked us out to bounce."

Hot Rock glanced up, and saw three flashes of light that winked out abruptly at the place where sunlight gave way to shadow.

"Sparrows," Two Tone said. "They'll go where we want no matter what direction they start out in."

"Can't keep radar lock like this," Hot Rock grunted, half-rolling to the right, then abruptly left again.

"Never mind; bogey's too close now, anyway," Two Tone snapped. "Hotshot, I suggest you get us off the killing floor here."

Flanker 67

Too late, Tai thought in fury as he watched one of the SU-27s erupt into flame. The fire ignited Tai's heart as well, but he coldly shifted his attention to his target: the Tomcat that had fired the killing missile. He snapped directions over the radio, and he and his wingman sheered off and headed in for the kill.

Tomcat 302

"Lobo, my love," Handyman said, "we got two Flankers who love the looks of your ass—not that I blame them."

"It's *our* ass, sweetheart," Lobo said, watching the radar, then looking over her shoulder and pulling the Tomcat into a hard climb. She spared a glance at the fuel indicator as well. Still okay, although that wouldn't last long if she didn't get off the afterburners.

"They got lock," Handyman said, businesslike, although the alarm in Lobo's helmet told her all she needed to know.

"Chaff," she said, and felt the small bump as the foil bounced out of the Tomcat, hopefully to confuse the seeker head on the incoming missile. To increase the odds of that happening, Lobo changed the trajectory of her climb as well. A moment later, she felt the violent jolt of the shock wave coming after her.

"Nice job, but they're closing," Handyman said. "Good position, too."

Meaning they were diving in on the Tomcat. "I don't give a damn, I'm not going fishing anymore," Lobo snarled.

"Okay by me."

"Where the *hell* is my wingman?"

Hot Rock's voice came over the radio, calm as the surface of the South China Sea. "I'm just a little busy at the moment, ma'am."

Tomcat 306

Two Chinese fighters above him and on his tail, water less than a thousand feet below, no place to go, nowhere to run.

This was great.

They couldn't get him. They scissored him, they bounced him, they tried to herd him into a pincher. He slipped out of everything. Wing-sweep control set to manual, he took precise command of his airframe, adjusting speed and balance with exquisite finesse. Cannon shells whipped all around him, but none touched.

The only problem, the only niggling uncertainty, came from the knowledge that his lead, Lobo, was also confronting multiple bogeys. She was a terrific pilot, of course, but she was also trying to get in a kill of her own. Generations of experience, not to mention the instructors in flight school, taught that the best defense was a good offense. Lobo flew that way.

And she expected her wingman to help, if he could.

But I can't, he thought. *I'm overloaded with bogeys, anybody can see that. I can't help her at all.*

Hornet 108

"Thor, break left," a voice snapped over the headset.

Thor didn't even think about it. He slammed the aircraft into a hard left turn. A moment later, he glimpsed a fierce explosion from the corner of his eye.

"Splash one Flanker," Bird Dog said coldly. "You okay for the other, Thor?"

Thor looked back at the Flanker still hanging onto his ass. It was the same plane that had taken Reedy out. "You bet I am," he said.

Tomcat 304

Bird Dog turned his attention away from Thor and focused it on the ACM farther down. He knew that his taking a Sparrow shot at one of the bogeys harassing Thor had been chancy from five miles out, but it had been the only assistance he could render from that distance. Fortunately the missile had functioned exactly as intended, and so had Thor.

Now for the real thing.

Bird Dog switched his attention to the low-altitude dogfights, and his weapons selector to "guns."

Tomcat 302

Lobo kept trying to climb out, but the Flankers were faster than she was in the vertical mode. When flying one-against-two, the main goal of any fighter pilot was to keep both bogeys on the same side of your plane. To never get caught in the middle.

Easier said than done.

The intel was right about that, dammit. In fact, as she recalled, an SU-30—cousin to the bogeys on her tail—had been the first jet aircraft to break the sound barrier in a *vertical climb*.

Still, she found this situation unbelievable. She was used to having the upper hand in any altitude battle; although the Tomcat wasn't king of the sky in an angles fight, it had always ruled in the vertical plane. Always.

Until now.

Unfortunately, in the horizontal field things were even worse. The Flankers really were as nimble as Falcons. She had all she could do to keep them from boxing her in.

Looking to the left, she saw Hot Rock below her level, a pair of Flankers trying to get position on him. Still no help there.

After what happened the last time she was shot down, Lobo hadn't been sure she'd be able to strap a Tomcat on again, far less fight. Time and hard work had put that fear to rest. In fact, she'd once again become convinced that she was invulnerable, too damned hot a pilot to be shot out of the sky again, ever.

Now she was beginning to wonder if that was true.

Flanker 67

Tai heard the radar-lock alarm in his helmet, but ignored it. Just one second more. One second more and his targeting pipper would close on the American jet. Just—

There was a terrific concussion, the rear of his plane leaping up, making him fight the stick. Hit? Had he been hit? Pivoting his head wildly, he saw the fireball behind him, and the F-14 behind *that*, and knew his wingman had been destroyed. The Tomcat was stooping on him at tremendous speed, taking full advantage of gravity and momentum.

From hunter to hunted in half a second. Tai jerked the stick left, then hard right, rolling out of the line of fire as tracers flickered past him, deceptively beautiful in the twilight.

Tomcat 302

"It's Bird Dog!" Handyman cried. "He splashed one of our bogeys, Lobo!"

"Peachy," Lobo said, hearing the anger in her voice and wondering at it. So someone had saved her butt, and that someone happened to be the ever-cocky Bird Dog. Was she so petty she'd begrudge him her thanks? Hell, her eternal gratitude?

Looking over her shoulder, she saw that the second Flanker that had been pursuing her was now busy evading Bird Dog. Good luck to him.

She turned her attention to her wingman, who had problems of his own.

Hornet 108

"Got you," Thor said as his targeting pip centered between the Flanker's vertical stabilizers. He triggered the cannon, and watched the metal spine of the Flanker split open as if torn by a can opener. Flames and debris gouted from the wound, and Thor banked away hard to avoid sucking any of it into his engines. At the same time, he saw the Flanker's ejection seat shoot up.

"Long way down, bozo," Thor said, and turned his own jet in that direction. Below, he could see the flicker and flash of jet exhausts against the dark water. Then he glanced at his fuel indicator, and cursed. He had no juice for more fighting. Not even close. Hell, he'd be lucky to reach the Texaco in time to keep from ditching the plane.

He radioed Homeplate, and was reassured by one bit of news: Four more good guys were bustering in, due in as many minutes.

"Godspeed," he said to the fires below, and turned his tail to the setting sun.

Tomcat 304

The Flanker was a terrific airplane, no doubt about it. But it was dead meat, and Bird Dog Robinson was going to be the butcher. He had the speed, the trajectory, the weapons, and the experience. The Flanker was racing away at low altitude, undoubtedly fearing to take advantage of a marginal speed advantage for fear of simply moving out of gun range and into the grasp of a Sidewinder. Out of the frying pan, so to speak.

Of course, Bird Dog was more than happy to use the cannon on this guy. That would be just fine, and he matched the Flanker swoop for swoop, not allowing him to pop up, not allowing him to jink free. Cut left. Bird Dog followed. Cut right. Bird dog moved the stick that direction . . .

. . . and for once, his Tomcat didn't turn. No, it turned, but much too slowly. The Flanker vanished off the targeting ring.

What the *hell?*

A sense of foreboding drenched Bird Dog like ice water. Even as he pulled back to regain altitude, he twitched the stick to the left and got quick response. Back to the right. Very slowly, the plane started to roll in that direction.

"Catwoman?" he said over ICS. "We got systems trouble here or what?"

There was a brief pause, then a cool-voiced response: "Losing hydraulics in the left wing, Bird Dog. Down to forty percent, and falling."

"Why?"

"How the hell would I know? Maybe the warranty ran out."

Oh, Christ, mechanical failure. If the plane weren't fly-by-wire, if the controls were linked directly to the flying surfaces, right now the left rudder pedal would be flapping like the tongue of an untied shoe.

"By the way," Catwoman said, "that Flanker? I think he's in love with us, because he's coming back for more."

Flanker 67

Tai didn't bother wondering why the American had failed to press his earlier advantage to its conclusion. All that mattered was he'd made a mistake, and it would be his last.

Pulling the SU-37 up and around as hard as he could, squeezing his belly muscles against brown-out, Tai used the Sukhoi's swiveling exhausts to full advantage. In an instant he was on the F-14's tail, bringing his cannon to bear.

The Tomcat cut left. Tai cut left. The Tomcat straightened

slightly, then cut left again. Tai followed it, patiently trying to join the enemy plane and the gun pipper in the firing ring on his HUD.

Again, the Tomcat cut left; he was practically in a spiraling dive now. No wonder the American had bounced Tai and his wingman from high altitude. Take away that advantage and the man was not much of a pilot. He just kept turning left, turning left, turning left. . . .

Turning into the sights of a better pilot flying a better aircraft.

Tomcat 304

"We got—!" Catwoman's voice cut off as the Tomcat began to shake and bounce. A strange whistling roar filled the cockpit, and the few loose parts of Bird Dog's flight suit began to flap wildly. Bird Dog was filled with fury. Getting taken out by a missile was bad enough, but he wasn't going to go down to guns. No way was he going to be shot down like some World War One-era biplane pilot; give some PRC hotshot bragging rights for years to come. No *way*.

He pulled the shuddering Tomcat even farther to the left, skating it on the edge of a spin from which he knew he would never recover, not without right rudder.

"Catwoman?" he cried over ICS. "Catwoman—?"

Flanker 67

Tai's glee turned to shock when he saw a piece of the Tomcat, a service panel or chunk of wing, come hurtling back at him. It looked as big as a hangar door, and if it got sucked into the greedy intake of one of his AL-35s . . .

He broke off hard, cursing the fates, yet certain that it didn't matter, the Tomcat was dead anyway. . . .

Tomcat 302

Lobo was ten seconds from closing on Hot Rock and his pursuers when she glanced over her shoulder and saw something stunning: Somehow, in only the last half minute, circumstances there had reversed themselves. The bogey was hurtling past Bird Dog's F-14, which was itself dropping in a messy half turn, its aspect loose and wobbly. Pieces of metal were floating up off it.

"Shit!" Lobo cried, making her decision instantly. Hot Rock was still being hunted by the other two bogeys, but at least his goddamned plane was intact. She knew where her services were required.

Yanking her Tomcat into a hard left turn, she reversed direction and started to climb out. To her relief, Bird Dog's plane had steadied and was now flying along straight and level, about five hundred feet above her. To her left, the Flanker was also turning, but for some reason he didn't appear to be in much of a hurry. Perhaps his plane was also damaged.

"Bird Dog!" she cried over the radio. "You okay?"

"Hydraulic damage; can't turn right. Took some hits. Think Catwoman's hurt. Am I in one piece here?"

"I'll know in a second. Coming up on your six."

She glanced to her left again. The bogey had completed its turn, far out over the ocean. Lobo realized why and shouted, "Bird Dog! Break! Break!"

He did so instantly, dipping hard left, evidently the only direction he could go, the perfect direction. Lobo blasted straight over his Tomcat, holding steady on course.

"Incoming!" Handyman cried. Lobo glanced back just long enough to see an incandescent white dot swooping toward her.

Then she did the only thing left to do.

Flanker 67

Tai was shocked to see his missile take out the wrong air-craft—then he was delighted, because the victim was the Tomcat he'd intended to destroy in the first place. The fool had flown right into the line of fire, and presented the heat-seeker with a better home in which to nest.

Afterimages of the explosion floated in his vision. Evening was deepening toward night. A night he would remember for a long—

His gaze, automatically conducting its scan of instruments, halted on the radar screen. Four new returns had appeared, approaching from the east. Four *more* American fighters, fresh and fully loaded with fuel and weapons, versus his SU-37 and the two planes wasting their energy on the other Tomcat. Even if the odds were evened up, the Americans had more fuel and weapons.

The radar showed nothing coming in from his own country. Anger swelled up inside him, darkening his vision before he pushed it back. Some of his officers were weaklings and cowards, no doubt about that. But there were others who had vision, and will. They would prevail.

Tai spoke briskly into his radio. The time had come to break off and return home, wait until they had numerical superiority. Return, rest, and prepare to fight another day. Prepare to push the arrogant Americans back out of Asia, and destroy their ill-gotten power. It was inevitable.

For as Sun Tzu taught, *Of the four seasons, none lasts forever. . . .*

1700 local (+3 GMT)
Bethesda, Maryland

When Tombstone walked into his house, he was greeted by a sharp-planed face not unlike his own. "Uncle Thomas," he said, pleased.

His uncle held out his hand, and they shook. "This isn't a social visit, Matthew, sorry to say. Joyce and I were just discussing some business. It involves you, too."

Tombstone peered around the corner into the sitting room. Tomboy looked back at him, her expression grim, yet there was something else shining in her eyes. The kind of fierce excitement he recognized from any number of combat sorties.

"Uh-oh," Tombstone said. "What is this?"

"They're sending me to China," she said. "To *Jefferson*."

Tombstone turned toward his uncle. "What for?"

"Better sit down, Matthew." Thomas Magruder led him into the room and sat him next to his wife, then took a chair opposite. The admiral, the most powerful man in the navy, was wearing civilian clothes. All at once Tombstone realized he hadn't seen his uncle's car in the driveway, or even on the street. This visit was incognito.

"What *is* it?" he demanded.

"Things are heating up over in Hong Kong," his uncle said. "Early this morning our time, an American Air Force jet used for NOAA research was shot down outside Hong Kong. *Jefferson* got involved again; this time there was a real tangle. We lost some, Matthew."

"Who?" Tombstone asked.

"Chris Hanson, Randall Carpenter, Benjamin Rogers."

Tombstone had steeled himself, and was surprised—and guiltily relieved—that only one name was familiar. Still, that one name rocked him. "God, not Lobo."

"She's MIA. Carpenter is KIA; Rogers is presumed KIA. One Tomcat down, and one Hornet. That's all I have right now."

Tombstone was faintly aware of Tomboy sliding her arm through his. "What's our response? From Washington?"

His uncle hesitated. "As you know, dealing with the PRC requires exceptional delicacy. Nobody wants to start a world war."

Tombstone snorted.

"Nobody *here* wants to start a world war," his uncle amended, face hard. "And the Chinese absolutely deny responsibility for the shoot-down, just as they did for the *Lady of Leisure* massacre. Frankly, that's got me a little puzzled. It's not like them to deny the things they do; they typically just make transparent excuses or refuse to discuss it at all."

Tombstone shook his head. "Batman must be livid."

"Of course. But he'll do what's right, just as you would if you were in his place. And right now, that means waiting. When the North Koreans shot down a civilian airliner, it didn't lead to war, and this shouldn't either."

"What's the Air Force's position on it?"

"What else? They wish they'd had the chance to tangle with the Flankers, instead of us. But their wings are tied in that part of the world." His uncle paused. "Speaking of the Air Force, what else have they found out about your little UAV?"

Tombstone's eyebrows rose. He looked from his uncle to Tomboy, then back. "You know?"

"I was fully briefed on the background before I came up here. Just finished briefing your wife. We're all on the same page now."

"Not exactly," Tombstone said, and described what the DARPA kid had discovered about the bogey's nation of origin. Then he took a deep breath and added, "But here's the trick: It was loaded with electronics from one of Uncle Phil's companies."

His uncle blinked, then shook his head. "Don't be thinking 'treason,' Tombstone. The PRC has been buying up technology for years. American, Japanese, you name it; if they want it, they simply buy it. It's perfectly legitimate."

"Legitimate?"

"Good for business," his uncle said expressionlessly. "Good for international relations. It's not like anyone's letting them buy *weapons*, after all."

"Just the means to make them."

Thomas Magruder sighed. "As far as Phil's concerned, the odds are he didn't even know who the end buyer was, far less what the components were going to be used for. No man in the world was more committed to democracy and free enterprise than he was."

"Maybe that's why he was killed," Tombstone said, suddenly both relieved and excited. "Maybe he figured out where the technology was going, and what for, so they murdered him."

"That occurred to us," his uncle said somberly. "We're checking out the possibility."

Tombstone suddenly sobered, too. "But . . . from what the DARPA kid told me, this bogey was years ahead of what we thought anyone else was capable of, never mind China. So even with the right parts, how could they . . ." He noticed that his uncle's face looked grimmer than ever. "What?"

Tomboy spoke up. "Your bogey isn't the only surprise the Chinese had for us. The aircraft that downed the Air Force jet was a completely unknown design, from all descriptions a flying wing with stealth characteristics. It's got JCS worried."

"A *stealth* plane?" Tombstone said numbly. "The Chinese have *stealth*, too?"

As he listened to Tomboy describe what little was currently known about the mystery bogey in Hong Kong, Tombstone felt himself tensing. Although stealth technology was largely an Air Force game, Tombstone had a good understanding of it. Most people, including some in the military and most in politics, had the right idea about stealth. To them, it seemed like a clever but otherwise innocuous idea, and prohibitively expensive. But that wasn't the case at all. From a military standpoint, stealth was at once the most important and most extraordinarily successful technological development in decades.

The original goal of stealth was simple and realistic. It wasn't to make an invisible airplane, or even one completely transparent to radar; no one expected that. The problem was that radar installations were relatively cheap to build, upgrade and maintain, while bombers were expensive to make, more expensive to improve upon, and most of all, expensive to lose. Imagine a bomber with the radar cross-section of a goose or an eagle. Imagine how deeply such an aircraft could infiltrate before AA noticed it.

This was the Pentagon's dream when, in 1975, they funded Project Harvey—named after the invisible rabbit—to fund research into the problem. In the end, Northrop and Lockheed each presented DARPA with a wooden mock-up of its design, to be tested head-to-head at the Gray Butte radar cross-section test site. The Northrup model created quite a stir: To radar, it was no bigger than a pigeon, DARPA's dreams exceeded. Then came the Lockheed entry, nicknamed "Hopeless Diamond," which didn't even look like it could fly. It was bathed in radar waves ... and nothing happened. Nothing at all. In fact, according to legend, the model produced its first return only when a crow landed on it.

The battle for technological advantage in military applications is usually measured in tiny evolutionary steps. Relatively speaking, with the creation of what would become known as the F/A-117 Stealth Fighter, the United States had just stepped from the Stone Age directly into the Space Age. A stealth plane could fly over your headquarters and release a precision-guided bomb before you even knew you were in trouble. No other country was close to finding a way to combat this menace, far less produce a counter-menace of their own.

At least, that had been the belief. Until now.

Tombstone was so busy contemplating the ramifications of this information that he almost missed Tomboy's next words: "That's why I'm going to China. They want to see if I can get more information on this plane, maybe even get a glimpse of it. We've got to know more about it."

Tombstone scowled. "This doesn't make any sense. Okay, the Chinese could have stolen stealth technology; everybody knows it's bound to leak out sooner or later. But UAVs? I got the impression from DARPA that the best the U.S. has come up with so far are nice little recon drones."

His uncle was shaking his head. Tombstone had never seen the man look so grim. "That's what I thought, too, until my briefing today. The truth is, the UAV program in this country has been struggling uphill for all the wrong reasons. It's not because the technology's really that hard to develop, especially if you're satisfied with only partial stealth capability. The guidance system used to be tough, but hell, one of today's ordinary laptop computers has more processing power than the computer that runs the guidance system of the entire space shuttle. The UAV program lags for one reason only: money."

"Well, I understand new technology is expensive to develop, but—"

"Virtually all of China's GNP gets squeezed through a single pipeline," his uncle went on, as if he hadn't spoken. "That's the Communist way, of course. No matter where the money comes from or who generates it, it gets divvied up by the government, no arguments allowed.

"In the U.S., it's obviously a different matter. Here, *everybody* argues. You've been in the Pentagon long enough to know what I mean about bickering. The Army fights for funding with the Navy, who fights with the Air Force. The technology guys fight with the grunts-in-the-mud types, and taxpayers fight with Washington over the whole thing. And underneath it all you've got politics. Remember what happened with *Arsenal*."

Tombstone grimaced. "Don't remind me." *Arsenal* had been the Navy's newest creation, essentially a floating weapons barge stuck inside a Navy hull and capable of doing battle almost entirely by remote control. When things flared up with Cuba, the president of the United States himself had tried to utilize the ship in just that way, with predictably disastrous results.

"The *Arsenal* mess wasn't just about Washington micromanaging a battle," his uncle said, as if reading his mind. Maybe he *was* reading his mind. After all, they were both Magruders. "Remember, a senator from the state where *Arsenal* was built played a big part in the whole fiasco."

Tombstone nodded. "He figured his state would get rich building ships like *Arsenal* for the navy, if the prototype proved herself in battle."

"Exactly."

"But I don't see how that applies here. You just said China doesn't have the same financial entanglements."

"Which is why they could be building UAVs," his uncle said.

"Whoa. I hate to sound stupid, but—"

"Look at it this way, sweetheart," Tomboy said. "A brand-new Tomcat ain't cheap and B-2s are over two *billion* each. A UAV? Maybe a quarter-mil; you get three for the price of a single Tomahawk. Sounds good, right? Nice and cost-effective. Now think about it from the perspective of a senator lobbying for defense contracting dollars for his state. You've got thousands of voters on welfare, on unemployment. Are you going to grab for the B-2 contract, or the UAVs?"

"Wait." Tombstone held up a hand. "You mean to tell me we'd be developing and using more UAVs ourselves . . . except they don't cost *enough*?"

His uncle gave him a grim smile. "And you always thought it was because you and your fellow aviators were irreplacable, didn't you?"

Tombstone sat silently for a moment, trying to reconstruct his whole image of his life, and what it was all about. Finally he tightened his jaw. "Look, if you're going to send Tomboy out there as an expert, you ought to send me, too. I'm *the* expert on Chinese UAVs."

His uncle shook his head. "Sorry. We don't need you on the carrier. We need you somewhere else. But this is a volunteer job, Matthew. Not up your normal alley at all."

"Pardon?"

"Earlier, you mentioned that Phillip McIntyre's death might have been related in some way to his business, and from there to the UAV. Since Phil's not around to talk to, we need to ask someone else about that. Unfortunately his headquarters is in Hong Kong, so we have no authority to go in and simply start demanding information. But one of his top executives survived the *Lady of Leisure* massacre. He's in Hong Kong right now, and evidently he's frightened for his life, and a bit difficult to reach. We need someone he might trust to go speak with him. You're the closest thing Phillip's got to a son, so the employee should trust you. I wish I could go instead, but I can't, not with the way things are over there right now. I'm needed in Washington."

Tombstone folded his wife's small hand between his. "If it would get me out from behind a desk, I'd go to Antarctica."

Tuesday, 5 August
2100 local (−8 GMT)
South China Sea

Lobo awoke with a sense of terrible pressure in her lungs, and darkness burning in her eyes. Immediately she knew where she was, and why, and she struggled not to panic. Instead she kicked steadily, patiently holding her breath.

She burst through the surface of the sea and coughed up seawater for so long she thought she would turn inside out.

The sea was smooth and warm. This was not the Aleutians. She was not going to be picked up and gang raped here. Not with her own people ruling the air, and SAR already on the way.

Don't even think about what happened in the Aleutians. One thing at a time. She checked to see that her saltwater-activated beacon was flashing. Yes. Presumably the radio beacon was, too.

She looked around for her RIO, or for his chute. Far to the east she saw a fiercely flashing strobe, the wrong color, though—but beneath it was the darting beam of a search-light. A helo! Perhaps SAR had already found Handyman and was even now plucking him from the water.

Between her and the helo moved a surprising number of lights, cruising slowly. Boats. Of course—she'd seen them from the air. All kinds of boats; trawlers, pleasure craft, junks. Should she signal one of them? Or just wait?

At that moment, not fifty yards away and very low to the water, a bright strobe appeared. Her heart leaped with joy. Handyman! He must have been turned away from her until now. She tried to call his name, but her throat was caked with salt, and all she could do was croak. She paddled toward him instead, moving clumsily through the piss-warm water. Tears flowed down her cheeks. His strobe swayed back and forth, vanished, then reappeared. Handyman must be swim-ming, too.

Then she saw his helmet, his splayed arms. She thrashed closer, reached out and grabbed his harness. "Handyman!" she rasped. "Handy, are you—"

His head rolled back, eyes open, staring over her shoulder. Blood stained his lips. Yet his body moved with jerking, trembling vitality in her grasp. A seizure? He—

With a violent shudder, he pulled away from her hands and sank a couple of feet beneath the surface. Rose again, eyes still wide open.

That was when Lobo realized the water beneath him was full of sharks.

She had no way of knowing how much time passed before she realized she was screaming, thrashing, doing all the things you weren't supposed to do around sharks. Handyman was twenty yards away now, still marked by his strobe as it swayed and dipped. Lobo made herself stop kicking, stop slapping the water, and grab for her shark repellent instead. She popped it into the water and stared at the sky. Where was that SAR helo? Where was—

She heard the soft throb of a diesel engine, smelled its fumes. Spinning in the water, she saw the black bulk of a boat creeping toward her. Then a fierce spotlight beam struck her in the face.

"Help!" she croaked, squinting, waving her arms. Would a spotlight attract sharks? Were sharks moving in on her at this very moment? "Help! Please, hurry!"

The tone of the engine rose a third, and beneath it she heard the hiss of a curling bow wave. She raised a hand to block the glare of the spotlight. Now, as the boat came closer, she could read the printing on its bow:

COASTAL DEFENSE FORCE HONG KONG.

2130 local (−8 GMT)
Tomcat 306

Jefferson at night was a chaotic Christmas tree of lights suspended in darkness. But right now Hot Rock was interested in only two clusters of lights. The first was the meatball, the stack of big, colored lenses that indicated when he was deviating from his preferred glide path to the deck. The second was the strip of lamps that descended vertically over the stern. The so-called "landing area line-up lights" provided an essential third dimension of visibility at night; before they had been created, aviators coming in for night traps faced the appalling illusion that the landing deck was not coming closer, but rising straight *up*, like an elevator. The results had frequently been fatal.

As Hot Rock came in on final, he listened to the murmured comments of the Landing Signals Officer, or LSO, standing on his platform adjacent to the meatball and coaching the Tomcat's approach. Listened, but didn't really pay attention. He knew his approach was perfect; he could feel it.

The ass end of the carrier slipped under his wing, and he

brought the Tomcat down decisively, simultaneously shoving
the throttles to full military power in case of a bolter, but
knowing it was pointless. He'd snagged the three-wire; he
always snagged the three-wire. How many perfect traps in a
row was that for him? If the navy had an Olympics for aviators, this would be his gold-medal event.

"Nice trap, slick," his RIO said as the Tomcat jolted to a
halt and Hot Rock killed the engines. "Especially since we
came back with such a heavy load under the wing."

2130 local (−8 GMT)
Tomcat 304
South China Sea

"Bird Dog, what's your situation?" the air boss said over the
radio. Hot Rock had just landed. Bird Dog was still limping
toward the carrier.

"Good to go," Bird Dog said. "Get me a green deck and
I'll get onboard."

"I understand you've lost some control function," the air
boss said in a careful voice.

"Just enough to take me out of the dogfight," Bird Dog
snarled. "Not enough to keep me from putting this bird on
the carrier."

"Commander, don't make me order you to eject." Now
the air boss sounded almost kind, although there was steel
behind the tone. He was in absolute control of everything
that happened on the flight deck, and responsible for it all as
well. "I can't let you jeopardize this boat just to keep from
dumping that Tomcat in the drink. Is that understood?"

Bird Dog forced his voice to stay calm. "Listen, my RIO
is unconscious. I don't know . . . she might be hit, might have
a broken neck . . . I don't know. I can't fire her out of this
bird, not if I've got a chance of landing on the carrier. Which
I do. So with your permission I'm coming in."

There was a long pause. Ahead and to his left, *Jefferson*
was a glowing blur in the darkness. Amazing how huge a

carrier seemed when you were on it . . . and how tiny it looked from here.

"Roger that," the air boss said. "Green deck. Tell me what you need."

Bird Dog let out a breath. "You might have *Jeff* brought a few degrees to port. That's the only way my Tomcat wants to turn, so I'd feel better having a little push on that side."

"You got it. Stay in the stack until I let you know it's time."

Bird Dog clicked his mike twice, then concentrated on keeping the Tomcat wings-level as he flew in the marshall stack. In a way, the difficulty of handling his crippled bird, the effort required to keep it airborne at all—never mind trying to land it on a moving postage stamp—was good for him. It kept him from thinking about other things.

Like what might be happening to Lobo.

2130 local (−8 GMT)
TFCC
USS **Jefferson**

"Missing?" Batman said. "You mean, *completely*? But I understood her chute was sighted."

Coyote looked haggard. "Here's the situation, Admiral. Her plane was struck by a PLA heat-seeker and downed. Her chute *was* seen, fully deployed; so was her backseater's. But it was getting dark at the time. The backseater was located and picked up by the SAR helo from *Shiloh* . . . but he was dead. And . . . the sharks had been at him."

"Oh, Christ. Lobo—"

"Her situation is a different matter, Batman. SAR hasn't found any sign of her at all. *No* sign, you understand? Not even a shred of cloth."

Batman looked up. "You're saying she might have been picked up by somebody."

"It's a possibility, sir. SAR reports there was a lot of surface traffic in the area: Commercial boats, cabin cruisers, fishing boats . . . Could easily be one of those grabbed her."

"Until we know for sure, keep SAR going out there." Batman clenched his jaw so hard he felt two molars grind. "Lobo got shot down before . . . and it went very badly for her."

"I'm aware of her story," COS said softly.

"Of course." Batman sighed. "All right. So now I suppose we just wait until we get some kind of word."

"On the positive side," Coyote said, "our pilots shot down three Flankers, and ran the rest off. And we also picked up a civilian survivor."

Batman made a shamed grimace. The survivor. Somehow, in the last few hours the object of this entire disastrous episode had been relegated to the status of "Oh, yes, by the way . . ."

"His condition?" Batman asked.

"Strained back, cuts and bruises, dehydration. Shock. He was out there for hours, and I guess he spent some time fending off sharks himself. We know his name's Alonzo George, and he's with the National Oceanic and Atmospheric Administration. He's out of it for now; Doc says we can visit him in medical tomorrow."

"Tomorrow." Batman wondered if tomorrow would be soon enough, then pushed the thought out of his mind and turned toward the hatch. "I'm going to watch Bird Dog's landing."

2143 local (−8 GMT)
Headquarters, PLA Air Force
Hong Kong Garrison

Major General Wei Ao, supreme commander of the Hong Kong PLA, had obviously expected this phone call. It was equally obvious to Political Commissar Yeh that Wei had called him into the room specifically so he would be involved in the conversation.

As soon as Yeh was seated, Wei flicked on the speakerphone. "Yes, Comrade General Ming," he said. "We did consider your orders, of course. But the situation was unique. We not only needed to provide aid and assistance, but to try to find and identify the attacking aircraft."

Ming's voice crackled slightly over the speakerphone. "And who authorized an air battle with U.S. Navy aircraft not a hundred miles from Hong Kong? Do you realize that this was seen *live* on television all over the world?"

Yeh watched the garrison commander's throat pulse with his swallow. What had Ming said about this man's vices? He collected imperial Chinese antiquities. . . . "I'm aware of it, yes," Wei said.

"The American jet's last transmission has been played on the media as well, over and over: 'It's Chinese; it's got a red star.' This is your interpretation of my orders *not* to provoke the United States?"

Wei drew himself up defiantly, something Yeh suspected he'd never dare do if the general were physically in the room. "The media broadcasts should work to our advantage, General. As you know, the attacker was described as a stealth-type aircraft, a flying wing. Obviously it could not have been a PLA fighter. The American pilot was obviously mistaken. That's why I considered it in the interests of national security to send aircraft out to investigate what actually—"

"And once again," Ming said, "the only direct witness of the event ended up in the hands of the Americans. How is that possible? I consider this a very poor job on your part, Major General. Very disappointing."

Wei slumped back in his chair. "But—"

"Gather your co-commanders at eight o'clock tomorrow morning," Ming said. "I'm flying down to talk with all of you and get this straightened out once and for all."

2145 local (−8 GMT)
Tomcat 304
USS Jefferson

As Bird Dog turned on final, he was annoyed to see that the
crash barricade, that giant badminton net designed to catch
wounded aircraft that missed the cables, had been raised
across the deck. Well, of *course* they would raise it, under
these circumstances, but he still found it infuriating. What,
they didn't think he could hit a three wire with half an airplane?

"You hang in there, Catwoman," he said over ICS. "You
just hang in there, okay?"

There was no answer. She was resting, he told himself.

Watching the meatball, listening to the patter from the
LSO, he brought the Tomcat in toward her home. Many pilots referred to carrier landings as "controlled crashes," but
Bird Dog had a higher standard than that. And he was going
to live up to it now, too—not because of his pride, but because he didn't want to jar the precious cargo in his back
seat any more than he had to.

And he was *not* going to need that damned net.

2142 local (−8 GMT)
Dirty Shirt Officers' Mess
USS Jefferson

As Hot Rock entered the dirty-shirt mess, he was greeted
with subdued applause and slaps on the back. With pilots
dead and missing, the usual after-battle banter was subdued,
but Hot Rock was still congratulated for making his first
kill—even if it was only a helicopter, at least it was probably
the same helicopter that blew up the *Lady of Leisure*, right?
He was congratulated for his flying skills, outmaneuvering
multiple bogeys even if he didn't have the chance to take
any of them out.

Only his RIO, Two Tone, stayed out of the group, Beaman said. "She's a sorry sight, isn't she?"

Franklin couldn't look at him. Tomcat 304 was now a hangar queen. Fist-sized holes punched all over it, the metal blackened and splintered around the edges. The back half of the canopy just *gone*. How Bird Dog had managed to bring the plane in, Franklin had no idea.

Franklin felt sick and angry. He wasn't sure who he was angry with, but it was a strong feeling.

"The RIO," he said. "Is she . . ."

"In sick bay. Alive. Bad. And you know what? She's lucky at that. I just had a little talk with Lieutenant Commander Robinson. He says that about the time things got hot, he lost hydraulic pressure in the left wing control surfaces. That was *before* he took any hits. Now, how do we explain a loss of hydraulic fluid?"

Franklin felt a frightful chill clatter down his spine. "I tightened that fitting," he said. "I tightened it right down. I *know* I did."

Beaman nodded gravely at the plane. "We'll see."

Tuesday, 5 August
0700 local (+5 GMT)
The Beltway
Maryland

As always when they were going to the car to drive somewhere together, Tombstone and Tomboy both strode straight for the left front door. "I'm more current than you are," Tomboy joked.

Tombstone handed her his duffel bag. "Exactly why I need some stick time. Besides, this is my car."

"Sexist pig."

They tossed their luggage in the back of the GTO and climbed in. Tombstone fired up the Goat's engine and hit the street with a bit more velocity than necessary. He said,

"Sorry. But I'm going to be spending the next fourteen hours letting somebody else fly us to Singapore, and then I have to switch to a *civilian* airliner. A *Third World* civilian airliner."

Tomboy reached across the console and squeezed his thigh. "The way things are over there right now, it's either that or swim."

Only an hour ago, as a consequence of the air battle that had taken place following the downing of an Air Force plane, the Pentagon had curtailed all military flights into Hong Kong. Most American airlines had immediately canceled service to Hong Kong as well. Other nations were picking up the slack; Tombstone had been booked on a Thai Airlines flight out of Singapore.

"God, I wish I were going to *Jefferson* with you," Tombstone said. "Not that Batman can't handle the heat, but . . . hell, that's where I *feel* like I should be."

"Your talking to Martin Lee could make a big difference," Tomboy said, her gaze on the road. "If you can help figure out how the Chinese got their UAV program up and running so well, it could make all the difference in the world—to *Jefferson* and to the United States."

"According to you and Uncle Thomas, it's not really an issue. According to you, UAVs are the Volkswagens of the aerospace world. Anybody can make one."

"No, anybody can *afford* one. That's not the same thing." She paused. "Especially when you're talking about *combat* UAVs."

"Like the one that attacked me."

"Yes. The Air Force supposedly has a CUAV program under way, but like Uncle Thomas said . . ." She shrugged. "The financial and political support is minimal. Of course, that might change now."

"Because the Chinese are ahead of us. I can't believe the politicians have gotten us into the position of playing catch-up."

"It's strange when you think about it," she said. "I mean, from the Chinese perspective. UAVs have two big advantages over conventional aircraft: low unit cost, and zero pilot mortality. But let's face it: The PRC has always been known for throwing human bodies at the enemy; after all, they've got more of them than anyone else in the world. So why this sudden interest from them in cost-effective, user-friendly UAVs?"

"Maybe they're *not* really interested. Maybe it's like during the Cold War, when the Soviets used to park fake bombers on runways for our spy satellites to photograph. We spent billions developing countermeasures to a threat that never existed."

"That's possible . . ." Tomboy said. "I know there are people in the Pentagon who would consider it a blessing if more effort went into CUAV programs. Some people say CUAVs are the wave of the future—a natural extension of the success of cruise missiles and smart bombs."

Tombstone shook his head. "People have been predicting for years that future wars would be fought by machine. At the beginning of the Vietnam war, American fighter jets didn't even have guns because it was believed that missiles made dogfighting unnecessary. All it took was a bad kill ratio to bring things around. This is just another instance of that. There will always be the need for human beings on the front lines—including inside aircraft."

"The Chinese seem to agree with you," Tomboy said. "At least, judging by the fact they've got this other new aircraft out there, the flying wing."

"That's the one that scares me," Tombstone said.

Wednesday, 6 August
1000 local (−8 GMT)
PLA transport
10 miles north of SAR

The officer in charge of the radar station on the mountain just outside of Hong Kong picked up the phone and dialed the number given to him the previous night by Major General

Wei Ao, First Among Equals. *I want to know the moment General Ming's flight appears on your screen*, Wei had said.

So now, after identifying himself, the officer in charge said, "General Ming's transport is two hundred kilometers out, sir. He's vectoring in to Kai Tak Airport rather than the Air Force base."

"The quicker to arrive at garrison headquarters," Wei grunted, as if to himself. "Very well."

After hanging up, the officer in charge went back and stared at the radar screen, watching the incoming blip. General Ming had left Hong Kong for Beijing only a couple of days ago, and now he was back. This did not bode well for certain military people in Hong Kong. The officer was determined to keep his installation running in top form, lest he be caught unawares in some sort of snap inspection.

He was about to turn to other duties when he noticed something strange on the screen—a tiny, brief return registering perhaps twenty kilometers to the rear of General Ming's plane. It brought his full attention immediately back. Only after he stared at the screen for several sweeps without seeing anything else did he start to relax. Suddenly a strong, clear return appeared out of nowhere behind Ming's plane. A moment after that, two more blips appeared, close together, racing toward Ming's plane.

Even as the station officer reached for the radio, he wondered how quickly he could disappear, as so many others had, into the teeming hive of Hong Kong.

1030 local (−8 GMT)
Aft elevator
USS Jefferson

Under the pretext of inspecting the repair work being done on the aft elevator, Bird Dog walked out onto the platform and took in the afternoon air. Odd, when you thought about it: Here they were in the open ocean, yet for those who worked and lived in the carrier, fresh air was an uncommon

gift. When you were on deck you were stepping lively, concentrating on things, trying not to get killed by any of the
myriad heavy, sharp, fast-moving objects around you. When
you were belowdecks, the air was filtered, air-conditioned,
flattened. And of course when you were in a Tomcat, you
flew through the air but didn't feel it on your skin.

He inhaled deeply and looked out across the South China
Sea. The water surged past below, appearing to move faster
than it really was. Whitecaps were beginning to appear on
it, he saw. On the horizon, thunderheads rose like white cliffs
crowned in rubble. The wind yanked at Bird Dog's khakis,
and he heard the sizzle and crackle of an arc welder at work
behind him, but he didn't react, didn't turn.

He was miserable.

It was a terrible thing to lose pilots in a battle. Even worse
when one of them had been shot down saving your ass. And
worst of all when that pilot was . . . well, one of the best
damned sticks in the U.S. Navy.

He thought again about the hydraulic failure in his wing.
Beaman, his plane captain, had been checking the Tomcat
out ever since Bird Dog thumped it back onto the carrier.
"I'm still looking," he said every time Bird Dog asked him
what he'd found. Plane captains were fanatically—and blessedly—devoted to their aircraft, and so to the pilots who were
allowed to borrow the machines from time to time.

After climbing out of the aircraft last night, Bird Dog had
looked at the rear cockpit and surrounding area and felt suddenly nauseous. It wasn't the blood, because there wasn't
any. It wasn't even the sight of the motionless Catwoman,
who was already being checked out by corpsmen. It was the
realization that his plane had been destroyed. Half the canopy
was gone, and the right wing looked like a colander. There
was more air than metal left in that wing. Bird Dog had
landed a pile of scrap on the carrier, and he had no idea how
he had done it, or what had made him think he could.

In retrospect, he wondered how anyone could hope to figure out what had gone wrong with the control-surface hydraulics on the mangled wing. But Beaman, aided by damned
near every hydraulics tech onboard the carrier, refused to

give up. If the Tomcat had had a mechanical seizure in the air, the plane captain wanted to know why, and where, and how. And as soon as he figured it out . . .

Last night, Bird Dog had been ready to kill whoever was responsible for the hydraulic failure. There had been a time— it seemed a lifetime ago, somehow—when he would have ripped into anyone who might even be remotely involved. Now, he found himself hoping the cause turned out to be something purely mechanical, a failed part no one could have anticipated or prepared for. Because if it was human error, God help the poor kid responsible.

And it was easy to forget that these *were* kids, most of the technicians and mechanics. Eighteen-, nineteen-year-olds responsible for millions of dollars of equipment, and dozens— or thousands, indirectly—of lives.

If one of the kids had screwed up, he'd have more than the plane captain to contend with. More than an official inquiry. That kid would have to think about dead aviators for the rest of his life.

Dead pilots.

Stop that. You don't know she's dead.

Bird Dog stared across the sea, and on the eastern horizon, under the flat bottoms of the thunderheads, lightning drubbed the ocean with white, skeletal fingers.

1300 local (−8 GMT)
Conference Room, PLA Headquarters
Hong Kong

Major General Yeh Lien, Political Commissar of the Hong Kong SAR, thought that the meeting room seemed much too empty these days. Only two months ago there had been five major generals here at every conference. Then, two nights ago, Ming's presence had filled the room all by itself. But now . . .

Now there was just Wei Ao of the army, Chin Tsu of the Coastal Defense Force, and he, Yeh Lien, representing the heart and soul of Chinese Communism.

No, there was someone else as well. Someone invisible. The person responsible for the death of General Ming Wen Hsien.

Or was that guilty man actually here in the flesh? Yeh couldn't help thinking about the secrets Ming had hoarded about the commanders in the SAR. Perhaps one of those commanders had become aware of this knowledge. Perhaps he had decided to free himself.

Yeh watched the other two men, shifting his gaze back and forth as Wei Ao described the latest reports about Ming's death. Evidence indicated that the general's plane had been shot down by a missile or missiles of relatively small size; they could have been either air-to-air or ground-to-air. Yeh stared at the Army commander's blocky, self-satisfied face. Who would have more access to weapons than the First Among Equals? Wei, collector of decadent antiquities, and now sole and supreme commander of the Hong Kong SAR . . .

"Now," Wei said, his voice grave but his eyes glittering. "You've all seen our new orders. Until a replacement for Ming is officially assigned from Beijing, I alone dictate military actions within and around the Hong Kong SAR. I answer directly to the State Council, and you answer to me, and that is all."

"What are we going to do about the Americans?" Chin demanded in his impetuous way, as if he hadn't heard a word Wei had just said.

Wei fixed the younger man with a heavy-lidded gaze. "What are *we* going to do? *We* are going to do nothing. More to the point, *you* are going to do nothing. These matters don't concern the Coastal Defense Force one way or the other. Besides, who said anything about Americans?"

"But it had to be Americans who shot down the plane!"

"Consider the area where the shoot-down occurred, Comrade. A hundred miles inland, in rough terrain. The missiles were of the short-range variety, not something the Americans could have launched from over the horizon. Therefore, they were almost certainly fired from the ground. Are you claiming that the Americans placed troops that far inland without our being aware of it?"

"But—you'll do nothing in retaliation, then?"

To Yeh's surprise, the old major general smiled. "It's not necessary to retaliate, Major General Chin. Even if the Americans are guilty. Remember, as Sun Tzu said, 'The way to be certain to hold what you defend . . . is to defend a place the enemy does not attack.' "

Chin looked baffled. Yeh *felt* baffled, but he gave a sage nod. As Political Commissar, he must not allow himself to look slow or foolish.

Certainly Major General Wei Ao was neither of these things. From the words of his own mouth, the old commander was up to something, some unspecified activity. An activity he did not care to share.

Which meant that Yeh must find out what it was.

1320 local (−8 GMT)
USS Jefferson

"I wish Tomboy were here," Batman said as he strode down the passageway toward sick bay. "She should hear this."

"When's her COD due?" Lab Rat asked, from behind him.

"Zero eight hundred tomorrow."

"Well, we can't wait that long," Lab Rat said. "Memory's a fickle thing. The sooner we get Dr. George's story about what happened, the better." He paused. "Tombstone's not coming, too?"

Batman answered in clipped tones: "Admiral Magruder and his wife happen to be two professional officers with different duties and assignments. They aren't joined at the hip, you know."

"I realize that, sir. I didn't intend any offense. But Tombstone's experience in—"

"Oh, hell, Lab Rat, forget it. The truth is, I've been thinking the same thing. I wish Stoney were coming, too. But he's not on the passenger list." Batman stepped over a knee-knocker, made sure no one else was in the corridor, then said over his shoulder, "Do you think I should have asked Bird Dog to come along with us to talk to Dr. George?"

"No, I don't think so. Not so soon after what happened yesterday."

"But maybe that's why he *should* be with us. To keep him from dwelling on things he couldn't help."

He heard the wryness in Lab Rat's response: "If there's one thing nobody's ever accused Bird Dog of before, it's thinking too much. But that seems to be changing, and I think you should let him work it out for himself. I believe you made the right move."

Batman nodded, relieved. "Got your recorder ready?"

They had arrived at the main entrance to Sick Bay. Batman shoved open the double doors and headed aft toward the Critical Care Unit.

In the bed nearest to the CCU entrance, lay a man somewhat beyond middle age, with white hair, badly sunburned pale skin, and a belly that produced a swell in the sheet like the bow of a nuclear submarine about to breach. He was sucking juice from a plastic cup, using a bent straw. A hospital corpsman stood on the far side of the bed, saying, "Plenty of fluids, doctor, that's the ticket. Keep them going."

As Batman entered the room, he glanced at the closed curtain that divided off the beds inside the CCU. He'd already visited Catwoman, stared at her and willed her to get well. She had a fractured neck and skull, and had lost a lot of blood. Once she was stable, she would be medevaced to the base hospital in Singapore.

But now he had to concentrate on this civilian with the bright blue eyes and the straw in his mouth. He and Lab Rat waited patiently until, with a wild slurping sound, Dr. George finished his drink and handed the cup to the doctor. "Thanks," he said. "That's better than the juice I remember from my days flying with the navy."

"You were in the navy, sir?" Batman asked from the side of the bed.

Dr. George looked at him, taking in the uniform and its two stars without any evident reaction. "Oh, no, not me. I work for NOAA, which is part of the Department of Commerce, actually. But we used to fly in Navy hurricane hunters back before 1975—when you people pulled out of the program." He managed to make it sound like a personal affront, and Batman fought off a smile.

Batman held out his hand. "I'm Rear Admiral Wayne. This is my intelligence officer, Commander Busby. How are you feeling, sir?"

"Like I never want to go swimming again," George said with feeling, and this time Batman couldn't stop the smile. Hell, why try? He felt some of the tension slide off his back.

"I can imagine," he said. "Mind if we sit down and ask you a few questions about yesterday?"

"Yesterday? Oh, yesterday." A shadow flitted over the man's face. He sighed. "Was it only yesterday? Those poor pilots. They never had a chance."

The corpsman brought in three metal chairs, which the three officers situated in the scant space around George's bed.

"We'd like to ask about the aircraft that shot you down, sir," Batman said. "We need as precise a description of it as you can give us, your impressions of its flying characteristics—everything."

George nodded, and for a half hour he talked about his harrowing, truncated voyage of the day before. Lab Rat and Bird Dog took notes, plus each of them had a microcassette tape recorder running. When George got to the part about the flying wing, they both asked questions that would help paint a technical picture of the bogey. George answered the questions with the immediacy of a good memory, and the accuracy of someone with at least a passing knowledge of aircraft. That was good, in that it made his information somewhat reliable. It was bad for the same reason.

From the sound of things, the Chinese possessed a working airframe not dissimilar to America's F-117 Stealth Fighter, but possibly even more advanced. This mystery carried its missiles in internal bays to prevent them from providing radar signatures.

All of this raised a number of important questions, but from an immediate standpoint, the one that interested Batman was: Why use such an exotic asset to shoot down a helpless business jet in a very public manner, only to keep it out of combat during the subsequent air battle? There had to be a reason.

"Dr. George," Batman said. "The plane you were in—did it carry NOAA markings, or U.S. Air Force?"

"Air Force." George's eyes teared up. "It was the last dedicated storm-chasing plane in the Pacific basin. It was going to leave for the Caribbean tomorrow. Would never have even been in Hong Kong if I hadn't—"

Batman spoke quickly, decisively, cutting off that line of thought. "Now, are you *sure* it was only carrying meteorological equipment? It couldn't possibly have been used for anything else?" He was thinking about the navy's spy ships, which, disguised as trawlers, crept up and down the Asian coast day and night. Back when Batman was still just a Tomcat pilot, the North Koreans had attacked and captured one of those spy vessels in an attempt to trigger a war with America.

Dr. George looked confused by the question. "Of course I'm sure. It was *loaded* with weather gear. When you fly into a hurricane, you want to gather all the data you can, on the spot."

Batman nodded, but exchanged glances with Lab Rat. Just because the little Air Force jet truly was a scientific platform, that didn't mean the Chinese *believed* it. The question of motive for the shoot-down was still open.

"Excuse me," Dr. George said. "But where exactly is this ship positioned right now?"

"We're about two hundred miles east-southeast of Hong Kong," Batman said. "Once we get you thoroughly debriefed and the doctor okays it, we can have you back to the city in a couple of—"

George shook his head. "That's not why I'm asking. How seaworthy is this ship in a typhoon?"

"We've weathered our share," Batman said. "If you position yourself properly on the edge of one, the relative wind across the deck makes it very easy to launch aircraft. They take off almost by themselves."

"And if you're *not* positioned properly?"

"It can get a little rough. But *Jefferson* can take almost anything. . . . Why?"

"Because you're about to get caught in the biggest typhoon to hit the South China Sea in the last ten years."

Batman looked at his fellow officers. Bird Dog seemed oblivious, but Lab Rat's eyebrows were elevated. He said, "We haven't received any severe weather warnings from Metoc, have we?"

"That's because they don't know yet. Nobody knows but me. Because only I have Valkyrie."

"Valkyrie?" Lab Rat said.

"It's a program I developed that gives weighted values to more than a hundred factors affecting tropical weather. It lets me predict the time and place where a typhoon is likely to begin, its probable direction, and its probable strength. My accuracy is very impressive. Valkyrie is what I was trying to peddle in Hong Kong before . . ." His voice trailed off. "Those poor young pilots. I'll bet they have wives and children. I'll bet their wives and children are crying. . . ."

Again, Batman interrupted quickly. "And this program of yours, Valkyrie, it tells you a typhoon is going to strike *here*?"

" 'Told,' not 'tells'; my laptop went down with the plane. And not just a typhoon, a *super* typhoon. That means sustained wind speeds in excess of 150 miles per hour. For this storm, I'm predicting a minimum velocity of 200 miles per hour in the eyewall. Perhaps as high as 250, not that I'll be able to measure it anymore." His blue eyes sharpened. "So, how would you like to launch your aircraft *straight up*, Admiral? Without even starting their engines?"

"It's a bit early in the season for typhoons, isn't it?" Lab Rat asked in a painfully polite voice.

Now the sharp eyes fixed on him. "Yes, it is, Commander. But typhoons don't give a damn about statistics. All they care about is warm water, minimal wind shear, and plenty of moisture in the atmosphere. And a few other odds and ends I've managed to figure out over the years."

Batman decided to give the man some credit. Turning to Lab Rat, he said, "What's the satellite data been like recently?"

"Well . . . we can certainly expect increased thunderstorm activity, but—"

"No, no, no," George said irritably. "Satellites only provide *part* of the picture, that's the whole point. They don't factor in certain events, like seismic activity. Tremors in the sea floor can shift deep currents and bring scalding water up from thermal vents. That contributes to the heating, and can really accelerate a storm along. That's a theory of mine that I factored into Valkyrie. I'm telling you, the surface layer in the Pacific just east of here is a good four degrees warmer and a hundred feet thicker than usual for this time of year. It's pumping incredible amounts of energy into a weather engine that's about to switch on and grind right over this place."

"You're suggesting we move the battle group somewhere else, then?" Batman said. He sounded only vaguely interested.

"Young man, I know naval vessels are very seaworthy, and that they can move fast when they have to. But this storm I'm talking about is going to develop in less than a two-day period, and it's going to be *huge*. You don't want to be anywhere near it when it gets going."

Again Batman exchanged glances with Lab Rat, and caught the intelligence officer's suppressed amusement. It reflected his own. Few civilians understood the capabilities of modern naval vessels; every ship in the battle group could be sealed up so tightly that virtually nothing shy of capsizing could flood or sink them.

"We appreciate your warning, Doctor," Batman said. "I promise we'll keep an eye out for conditions to change."

George shook his head. "That's what they all say. But by the time you notice anything, it's already too late."

1400 local (−8 GMT)
Victoria Square
Hong Kong

"Free Hong Kong!" Sung Fei shouted through his loudhailer. He strove to make his voice sound sincere. *"No more PLA atrocities!"* He stood on a makeshift platform in Victoria Square, with the glass cliffs of international banks and brokerage houses looming on all sides. A crowd surged around him, waving signs that read CHINESE FOR DEMOCRACY and FREE HONG KONG and REMEMBER TIANANMEN SQUARE. *"Look what they've already done! Look at the boat they sank, the airplane they shot down! What's next? What do you think?"*

Most people within range of his voice cheered; a few booed. Personally, Sung would prefer to bite his lips off than to utter these reactionary, hollow words. But he was part of a larger plan. Could he do any less?

There was no denying the mounting frenzy of the mob, nor its increasing division into pro-Beijing and pro-Western factions. This schism had widened with the air battle that had taken place not a hundred miles off the main shipping lanes. People in Hong Kong felt threatened in a way only the older ones, those who had endured the Japanese invasion of Hong Kong in the 1940s, could recall. In the United Nations, the People's Republic and the United States were growing more and more vocal in accusing one another of aggression, with no end in sight.

Sung Fei glanced around at the sea of bodies, the spume of waving banners and signs. He never ceased to marvel at the incredible crush of bodies that characterized Hong Kong. In a nation as vast as China, this was unnatural. The small village, the community farm, the egalitarian life of fresh air, hard, honest work and simple food . . . that was the way things *should* be. That must be the future. Not these artificial canyons, these cliffs of money, these hives of screaming mouths.

Still talking, he raised his eyes to the periphery of the mob, where Hong Kong Police officers mingled uncomfortably with the green uniforms of the PLA. It was the PLA that Sung had been waiting for. Under the provisions of the so-called New Rule, the PLA could interfere in "civil affairs" only when activities were deemed to threaten national security. That was, of course, a very flexible term.

He lowered his gaze again, and nodded at a young woman standing not far from the foot of the platform. She nodded back, then pulled a red-and-white bundle of cloth from beneath her jacket. "Free Hong Kong!" she shouted. "Beijing out!" The people nearest her, all fellow students, took up the chant. "Free Hong Kong! Beijing out! Free Hong Kong! Beijing out!" The chant, in English, rolled across the square, lifting from voice to voice, growing louder and louder. Sung joined in the chant as well, adding his amplified voice until the crowd was in such an uproar he couldn't even hear himself.

Then he lowered the loudhailer, which was a signal. The girl raised her bundle of cloth over her head and let it unfurl—the bloodred flag of the People's Republic of China. Other hands grasped its edge, pulling it tight, holding it high. Cigarette lighters flared.

Flames rose on the sound of the chanting. At the edge of the crowd, the PLA soldiers began to push inward, using their AK-47s to clear the way. It was not legal to deface the PRC flag, even in liberal Hong Kong. Even under the New Rule.

The flag was now a sheet of flame, which was released. It sailed into the air, billowing, dropping hot ashes back onto the crowd, onto their pumping fists as they chanted, *"Free Hong Kong! Beijing out! Free Hong Kong! Beijing out!"* Someone threw a crushed soda can at Sung.

The soldiers were having trouble moving through the sheer bulk of the crowd. Yet one soldier had miraculousy arrived, appearing suddenly from behind the platform. He was a small, wiry man with the flattened nose of a gorilla. Actually, he'd been waiting underneath the platform all day. Sung knew that whether he was a real PLA soldier or not, his true commander was Mr. Blossom. Other men like him were scattered through the crowd, all wearing PLA uniforms and carrying standard-issue AK-47 assault rifles.

Sung didn't know exactly what was going to happen next, only that it was something Mr. Blossom had orchestrated carefully; something that, along with the pro-democracy chanting, would work to end the ridiculous idea of "Hong Kong self-rule" and bring the SAR back into the arms of the PRC, the real China.

The soldier with the flattened nose continued to shove toward the students who had burned the flag. So did the real PLA soldiers. Meanwhile the students themselves jumped up and down, chanting, pumping their fists. No doubt they hoped that the television cameras all around the square were catching the action. Other students scrambled onto the platform with Sung, shouting incoherently, waving their arms in the air. Sung was irritated. This was not in the plan. These idiots were not even politically motivated; to them, this was a party.

The flat-nosed soldier and three of the PLA soldiers were about to converge on the students below. As Sung watched, there was a sudden, deafening *crack*, a noise so loud Sung staggered sideways. At the same moment one of the real soldiers fell, the center of his face abruptly as red as the flag that had burned. Instantly, the mob fell silent, as if collectively holding its breath. The PLA soldiers halted. Everything halted. All the faces turned toward Sung.

Sung felt hands close hard around his right hand and arm. Something cold and heavy slapped into his hand, and his fingers closed around it reflexively. His arm was dragged up. He stared in amazement at what was in his hand: a large black pistol, smoke wafting from its barrel. "Here!" the student beside him shouted, waving Sung's arm wildly, as if fighting with it. "He did it! Help me!"

Sung wanted to say something, wanted to point out that he didn't even know what was going on, but his attention was caught by the flat-nosed soldier. Flat-nose was turning toward him, raising his AK-47. The small black eye of the assault rifle's barrel was staring at Sung. Farther back, so was the non-soldier's cold eye. Sung started to say, "You don't understand."

The first round caught him in his open mouth.

1500 local (−8 GMT)
Singapore

"So far, the death toll stands at seventeen." Navy Captain Joe Tacstrom, Singapore's U.S. Naval base commander, held out the latest sitrep, or situation report. "Some reports have the PLA starting the shooting; others claim it was one of the pro-democracy students. Either way, both civilians and PLA soldiers ended up dead. If this happened anywhere but Hong

Kong, the PRC would have already declared martial law and parked tanks in the streets."

"Are you sure I'll even be able to fly into Hong Kong?" Tombstone asked. He and Tomboy were sitting in Tacstrom's office. Tomboy was wearing her khakis preparatory to flying out to *Jefferson*, Tombstone was dressed in a business suit someone from the base had rushed into town to buy for him. Originally he'd intended to enter Hong Kong as a tourist, but that had all changed. Considering the most recent turn of events, the only Americans likely to run the gauntlet into that part of the world would be those with financial interests to protect.

He felt ridiculous.

"So far, most non-American airlines are still flying into Kai Tak," Tacstrom said. "Remember, Hong Kong fuels the economies of most of the countries on this side of the Pacific Rim. None of their neighbors can afford to slam the door on them if they can help it."

Tombstone nodded. "What about my American passport? Is that going to be a problem?"

"No. There's still no official restriction on Americans entering or leaving Hong Kong. It's just that it's an at-your-own-risk sort of thing. When you think about it, it's probably better that you're going into the civilian airport, anyway. Less chance of anyone noticing who you are that way."

Tombstone nodded again. This amateur 007 stuff drove him crazy. It fed into his mounting conviction that he was on a snipe hunt, while the real action was happening out at sea, with the carrier group.

But orders were orders. In his wallet he carried a piece of paper with Martin Lee's telephone number and address written on it in both English and Chinese, courtesy of someone at the Pentagon. Not that Lee had agreed to speak with Tombstone, or anyone else. Evidently he had even stopped answering his telephone.

Joe checked his watch. "We'll have someone drive you to the airport, Admiral. Your flight leaves at thirteen hundred. Commander Flynn, we've got a Tomcat on the deck waiting to get you out to *Jefferson*." He rose to his feet. "If you'll excuse me a moment, I'll double-check its status."

After he left, Tombstone turned to Tomboy. "Decent of him. Give me a kiss. It might be a while before we have another chance."

"Why, Admiral . . . what if someone were to walk in?"

"I'd accuse you of attacking me."

"And you'd be right."

Still, they kept the kiss short.

Tuesday, 5 August
1800 local (−8 GMT)
Hilton Hotel
Washington, D.C.

It had been a hectic day in Washington, an endless string of meetings with various cabinet members and think tank groups, and Ambassador Wexler was about to slide into a hot bath when the phone rang.

She scowled at it, debating letting the hotel's answering service pick it up. Any really critical calls would have come in on her cell phone.

But in the end, she went and grabbed up the receiver anyway. Sometimes she lamented her own compulsiveness.

The first thing she heard was the unmistakable background cacophony of a kitchen in full swing. *What's this, room service?* "Hello?" she said loudly.

A clipped, formal voice said, "Madame Ambassador, this is Ambassador T'ing from the People's Republic of China."

"Right, and I'm Little Orphan Annie from the planet Zondar." She was about to hang up when the voice said, "Please."

Something about the tone of that word . . . well, it wasn't a word you often heard expressed with sincerity in her line of work . . . something about it made her bring the receiver back to her ear. "What is this?"

"Please, Madame Ambassador. It is very difficult for me

to make this call at all. I ask you not to make it any more difficult."

By God, the voice *did* sound like T'ing's. Still, Sarah Wexler was nobody's patsy. "It's rare for the United Nations Ambassador from one major world power to call the United Nations ambassador from another major world power from the middle of a kitchen," she said.

"Not in my country." That did it. The voice was so dry, the words so ambiguous, their source *had* to be T'ing. He went on, "I must meet with you, Madame Ambassador. Privately."

"You mean—*privately* privately?"

"Just so. There are certain things I must discuss with you. Things for your ears only, you understand."

"Not entirely. There are channels for this. And how did you find out where I was staying, anyway?"

He didn't answer her question. "It is crucial for the futures of both our nations that we have this conversation, Ambassador. And that only you and I are involved at this point. Could you meet with me? Shall we say, at the Lincoln Memorial?"

She blinked. He *had* to be kidding. And yet, dry wit aside, intrigue aside, "joking" was not a characteristic one ordinarily associated with T'ing.

She surprised herself by saying, "When?"

Thursday, 7 August
0800 local (−8 GMT)
Vicinity USS Jefferson

"Bit bumpy, ma'am," the COD pilot said over ICS. "Sorry about that."

"I'm used to it," Tomboy said from the backseat. She tried to keep the irritation out of her voice. He was right about the turbulence, though. Serious-looking storm clouds crowded against one another all over the water surrounding *Jefferson*, turning the atmosphere into a roller coaster.

This particular Tomcat was on its way to the carrier to replace the one shot down during the previous day's air battle. There was something grim in hitching a ride on this particular bird . . . still, she found few places more comfortable than the backseat of an F-14. The sounds, the smells, the vibrations . . . they were all a part of her.

As the jet banked onto final, she felt the usual mixture of exhilaration and fear leap up in her gut. It was a sensation familiar to all RIOs. After all, short of opting to punch out, backseaters had absolutely no control over what the Tomcat did with them in the air other than the ultimate veto option—the ejection seat handle. On the other hand, RIOs also didn't have to worry about actually landing the big bird on the deck of a pitching aircraft carrier . . . so they could, at some fatalistic level, simply relax and enjoy the ride.

After the jolt and the stomach-compressing deceleration that told her the wire had been successfully snagged, she let out a long breath and grinned. "Nice trap," she said over ICS.

"Thank you, ma'am," the pilot replied.

Batman was waiting for her when she climbed out of the plane. As always, she had to suppress the urge to hug him. His smile, tired but genuine, told her he was thinking the same thing. "Good to see you, Tomboy," he said.

"You too, Admiral."

"How's Stoney?"

"I'll fill you in on him real soon, Batman," she said as they ducked in out of the wind and noise of the flight deck. "But first, let me go talk to our witness."

"You bet," he said. "Just do me one favor: Don't mention all these thunderheads, okay?"

0900 local (−8 GMT)
The Walled City
Kowloon

The boy scurried past the rows of illegal dentist offices and into the Walled City. Immediately, he left behind the light and clamor of Kowloon for an older, darker city.

The Walled City had been a curiosity, an embarrassment, and a dangerous pain for every ruler of the region ever since the British expanded their control from Hong Kong proper onto the mainland. At that time, due to a bureaucratic snafu, a section of Kowloon had remained, strictly speaking, an unleased section of the People's Republic. The British dealt with this anomaly by pretending it wasn't there. Squatters immediately moved into this lawless section of the city, erecting a shantytown devoid of electricity, fresh water or sanitation. Here was where criminals and drug runners fled and hid, knowing their foreign landlords would never dare pursue. The British responded by constructing a stone wall around the sector.

During World War Two the Japanese occupation government tore down the wall itself to supply raw materials for extending the runway of Kai Tak Airport, but the Walled City remained there in spirit. And it remained there still, demarcating the line between bright Kowloon and an intricate warren composed of narrow alleys and staircases descending to deathtraps. Even now, under PRC control, the Walled City remained a land apart, a shadow city where lived those who wished to avoid the attention of the authorities. Any authorities.

The boy ran down an alley barely a meter wide, his rubber sandals slapping through puddles of water that never went away. He glanced over his shoulder. No one behind him. Immediately he turned and darted down a steep set of steps. At the bottom he rapped on a door, then pushed through. "I have a message," he said in Cantonese to the hard-faced man standing there. The man, who appeared to be Japanese or Korean or some other foreign race, merely nodded.

The boy flapped on, down dark hallways, up rickety staircases, darting from one building to another. Finally he confronted a door with a peephole in it. He knocked. After a moment, the door opened. A small man stood there. Small even by Hong Kong standards, but filled with the taut energy of a fighting cock. His nose had been smashed enough times that it lay almost flat across his cheeks. His name was Chou Hu, or so he said. Probably he had lied; that was the way in the Walled City.

The boy respected Chou. Everyone in the Walled City respected Chou, and this was an accomplishment. Here, respect could be won only one way.

The boy could not tell if Chou was alone in the dark room. Up and down the corridor, other doors stood partly open. Were more quiet, watchful men behind those doors as well? Were guns pointing at him right now?

He bowed respectfully, then pulled an envelope out of his pocket and held it out. "A new message for you, sir."

"Open it," Chou said. "Then hand me the paper."

The boy swallowed. He knew why he was being asked to open the envelope: It might explode. He had heard of such things.

Hands sweating, he tore the end off the envelope. Nothing happened. Letting out a long breath, he pulled out a single slip of paper and handed it to Chou without even glancing at it. He didn't want any of these watchful people to think he had read the note. Especially since he didn't even know how to read.

Chou took the slip of paper and opened it. In the gloom, his eyes moved from side to side. He nodded. "Go back to Mr. Blossom," he said. "Tell him the location is ready for another visitor. And tell him something else as well: Tell him his money is welcome, but we'd prefer blood. Can you remember that?"

The boy nodded. Being without the written word, he had developed an excellent memory.

Perhaps too good. That night, Mr. Chou would pursue him through the Walled City of his dreams.

0900 local (−8 GMT)
Kai Tak Airport
Hong Kong

Tombstone hated civilian airports. He hated the crowds, hated waiting in lines, hated the smiles of the ticketing clerks, which managed somehow to be obsequious and surly at the same time.

Still, being in an airport meant one terrific thing, at least on the debarking end: It meant you'd survived yet another flight during which someone else controlled your fate.

His knees were still a bit wobbly from the landing. The pilot had bashed the Boeing 737 down like he was trying for the three-wire. Obviously this was a guy who believed the old saw, "Any landing you can walk away from is a good one." Or maybe he'd just been in a hurry to get out of the air, which had been far from smooth. The flight down from Singapore had meandered through cathedrals of billowing cloud.

Inside, Kai Tak Airport looked like all airports, from Germany to Iowa. There were even a lot of people from Germany and Iowa. You could tell the latter because they were leaving, and they looked nervous.

There were also a lot of armed guards around. They looked nervous, too, as well as grim.

Tombstone stood in line at Customs, trying not to let his impatience show. When he was asked his purpose in Hong Kong, he swallowed the urge to say, "I'm here to make sure the United States can beat the PLA's ass out of the sky for generations to come." Instead, he just said, "Business," and was promptly allowed through. Maybe the suit had been the right idea after all.

Shouldering his overnight bag, he followed the flood of humanity toward what the signs assured him was the exit. From there, he'd grab a taxi and head straight to Martin Lee's address. He'd already decided not to phone first, lest he warn his wary contact off.

He still had no idea exactly what he was going to say when and if he did meet Mr. Lee. What *could* he say to convince the poor young man that he, Tombstone Magruder, was someone to confide in? This whole enterprise really was ridiculous.

Then he remembered how he'd spent the last half hour of the flight: staring fixedly out the window. Not at the clouds, but at every passing airplane. Wondering if the next one would be manta-shaped and carrying air-to-air missiles. Wondering if he, Tombstone Magruder, was going to die in an aircraft with someone else at the controls.

No. He was here for a reason, and he'd do the best he could to complete his mission.

As he was making his way across the main lobby toward the doors, eyeing the taxis lined up outside, he heard a soft voice say, "Admiral Magruder?"

He halted and turned. A young Chinese man stood nearby, his hands folded in front of him. He wore an expensive-looking charcoal suit. Tombstone recognized him instantly, from the photographs he'd been shown. "Mr. Lee?"

The young man nodded, looked around nervously.

"How did you know I was coming in?" Tombstone asked.

"I . . . I am sorry I didn't answer your calls before, sir. I was frightened. For my wife, you understand. But now she is gone from Hong Kong. She is safe. So I . . . I wanted to talk to you. I called America. I spoke with your uncle; he told me you were coming."

"Well, it's good to meet you." Tombstone held out his hand. Lee shook it quickly, still looking around.

"It is not safe," he said. "Please come with me, quickly."

Tombstone followed the smaller man outside, where Lee gestured away a swarm of taxi drivers, then walked into a parking garage and up to the last thing Tombstone had expected to see: a large black American car, a Lincoln. Not quite a limousine, but close. It had a limo's black window glass and boomerang-shaped antenna on the back. "This is from the MEI fleet," Lee said, almost apologetically. "Always available for executive use." He pointed a remote control at the car and an alarm bleeped off. Tombstone heard locks pop open. Lee walked to the trunk and opened it. It was enormous inside; Tombstone's overnight bag looked like a Chicklet in there. Lee moved toward the passenger side, which Tombstone found to be an enormous relief. He couldn't imagine the nervous little man driving this boat.

But when he opened the left front door, he was confronted by an empty seat. Where the hell was the steering wheel? Then he remembered: Hong Kong had spent most of the last hundred and fifty years under British management, which meant people drove on the wrong side of the road around here. For the right amount of money, American car manufacturers were willing to take that idiosyncrasy into account.

Sighing, Tombstone slid into an atmosphere of leather and cigar smoke.

On the opposite side of the vast bench seat, Martin Lee perched like a tiny porcelain doll, the steering wheel rising almost to the level of his eyes. "Seat belt, please," he said gravely.

Tombstone had just clicked the buckle home when something hard and quite cold ground into his head just behind the bend of his jaw. "Please do not move," a voice said in his ear. The accent resembled Martin Lee's, but it was a man's voice. "Or you will die."

Tombstone glanced at Lee. He was staring at the dashboard, head lowered.

"What is this?" Tombstone asked.

"I am sorry," Lee told the dashboard. "They have my wife. I am very sorry, sir."

"No more talk," the man behind Tombstone said, and a moment later, Tombstone winced as a coarse bag was hauled over his head.

1300 local (+5 GMT)
Lincoln Memorial
Washington, D.C.

"This is very irregular, to say the least," Sarah Wexler said as she mounted the last step to the top of the Lincoln Memorial. T'ing was standing in the shadow of one of the columns. Wexler found herself glancing around for body-guards—or assassins—or something. She had no idea; she was functioning entirely on instinct.

"No one knows you came?" T'ing asked. He was wearing his usual charcoal suit and white shirt.

"No. You?"

He shook his head once. "As you say, this is very irreg-ular."

"It had better be good, Ambassador."

"We do not want war," T'ing said in a low voice.

"Ah." Wexler felt the tension leave her shoulders, and her stomach start to smolder. "You disappoint me. After all this cloak-and-dagger stuff, I at least expected to hear some new lie instead of the same one you keep repeating at the UN"

"It is not a lie. I am telling you the truth from Beijing."

"Really? Well, I'm afraid 'the truth from Beijing' pretty much equals a lie from my perspective." *God, it was liber-ating to speak openly for once.*

T'ing did not seem offended. "I am not here to bicker,

Ambassador. Bickering is for the United Nations. I am here to be blunt."

She raised an eyebrow. Blunt? An ambassador? A *Chinese* ambassador? That was like the Iranian representative claiming to extol freedom of religion.

Still, she was more intrigued every minute. "Be blunt, then," she said.

"Beijing believes America began the trouble in Hong Kong."

"Oh, please, not the drug war nonsense again. There's absolutely no evidence Phillip McIntyre was involved in—"

"I am not referring to the drug war story. No one in Beijing believes that. This is blunt speaking. However, they *do* in fact believe American began this trouble. That is also blunt speaking. You understand, Ambassador? They *truly* believe it."

"But . . . that's absurd. Sink a boat belonging to one of our own citizens? Shoot down our own airplane?"

T'ing shrugged. Wexler understood, and felt a little chill: He was telling her that his masters wouldn't think twice about doing such a thing; destroying Chinese citizens if it would further some strategic purpose. They expected it from other governments, as well.

She glanced to the foot of the steps outside the monument, where a family was gathering: three children scrambling around a pair of adults and an infant. With part of her mind, Wexler heard the kids' shouting voices, and thought, *Dutch*.

"Ambassador T'ing," she said, "you've lived in the United States long enough to know that even if our government was into murdering its citizens for political gain, they would never get away with it. It's not the way we do things here."

Again, T'ing shrugged. The Dutch family was coming up the steps, and T'ing moved farther behind the pillar. "Nevertheless, my government, like your own, bases its conclusions on the evidence at hand. They look at events in Hong Kong and think, 'America is doing this.' My point is simple: Until more evidence surfaces to explain what is happening in Hong Kong, the wise ruler exercises caution. And the rash ruler causes disaster."

"But meanwhile, of course, you're suggesting that the stupid United States just sit back and let the PLA kill its citizens in Hong Kong, right? I don't think that's going to work out, do you?"

"Many leaders in Beijing speak the same way about dealing with the American military near Hong Kong. This is the pity. And never forget, we have the largest army in the world." With that, T'ing gave a short bow, turned, and walked away down the steps.

Wexler stared after him, wondering if she'd just been given delicate inside information, or a red herring, or a dire warning . . . or nothing but an insult.

With the Chinese, it was impossible to tell.

Thursday, 7 August
1200 local (−8 GMT)
Mess Hall
USS Jefferson

"Heard Robinson's been bad-mouthing you, brother."

Jackson Ord looked up at his friend Skinny Washburn. "What?"

Skinny squeezed his 250 pounds behind the table and put his tray down. "Bird Dog Robinson, Mr. Hotshot. He's been bad-mouthing you all over the hangar bay. You ain't heard that?"

Franklin's stomach gave a sour lurch. He scowled. "He can't bad-mouth me. I didn't do nothin' wrong. I tightened that connector, and there ain't nobody can prove different."

Skinny raised one massive shoulder; his other arm was busy shoveling food into he mouth. "Don't matter if they can prove it; once you on an officer's shit list, you got nowhere to run."

Franklin's scowl deepened. "Who you hear talking about that pilot bad-mouthin' me?"

"I don't know. Everybody."

"Shit." Franklin threw down his fork. "This ain't fair."

This time Skinny raised both shoulders. "It's the navy."

1400 local (−8 GMT)
Headquarters, PLA Air Force
Hong Kong Garrison

In his dream, Tombstone could not escape from the UAV. It stayed glued to his tail, banking when he banked, rolling when he rolled, looping when he looped, refusing to be evaded or tricked. And yet it didn't come in and hit the Pitts, come and blow the little plane out of the sky, either. It just stayed there, not a foot behind the Pitts' rudder, as if connected with a tow bar. Showing him that it was a better flier than he was. That it could take him out whenever it wanted. That it was the wave of the future . . .

Tombstone opened his eyes, but the darkness remained. There was a sour odor in his nostrils. His head pounded, and he had to fight the desire to vomit. He remembered the hood being yanked over his head. After that, nothing . . . but judging by the smell and his symptoms, the bag must have been soaked in chloroform or some other knockout chemical.

He felt a sense of movement. He was stretched out on something, on his back, moving along at a fair clip. His wrists were tied together in front of him; his ankles were tightly bound. He breathed shallowly, and waited.

At last the rolling motion stopped. Someone spoke a few clipped words of Chinese, and Tombstone felt hands clutching his armpits and the backs of his knees. He was lifted, turned vertically so his feet touched the floor, and supported there. Try to fight now? No, not blind.

He heard the sound of a lock turning, followed by the squeal of rusty hinges. The same voice that had spoken before now shouted in English, "Back! Get back!"

Then, without warning, Tombstone found himself hurtling

forward. He threw his bound hands out just in time to catch his weight against a floor of hard, cold stone. He skidded and rolled to a stop, then brought his hands up and yanked the hood off his head.

He was in a small, gloomy room. The walls and floor were made of stone, the low ceiling of wooden planks. The only light leaked through a narrow slit window of pebbled glass, mounted up near the ceiling. The glass was translucent, and barricaded behind metal bars.

The heavy *thump* of a bolt sliding home echoed across the room. Tombstone rolled over. The door was narrow and solid-looking, made of riveted metal. There was no window in it.

Tombstone's wrists were tied with hemp rope. As he tugged the knots loose his teeth, he looked around more carefully. There wasn't much to see—a pair of buckets standing in one gloomy corner, a pile of blankets piled in another. No furniture, no cot, no nothing. The air smelled damp and salty.

Once his hands were free, Tombstone untied his ankles, then got unsteadily to his feet. The nausea rose with him, and he bent over and waited for it to either do its job or go away. He was relieved when it chose to fade without emptying his stomach first.

He was furious with himself. Okay, so he'd never been trained as a spy. That didn't excuse his climbing right into the trap of the enemy. So now he was a prisoner of the Red Chinese—and nobody on the outside knew it. At least, he assumed they didn't, unless his captors had chosen to reveal their hand. If not, then it would be at least a couple of days before any of his friends or contacts began to worry about him.

"Idiot," he wheezed at the floor. "Moron."

From the corner of his eye, he saw one of the blankets in the corner move. He whirled. "Admiral Magruder?" a voice said, and a figure rose up, pale in the gloom. The blankets fell away, and the figure staggered toward him.

Tombstone's eyes widened. *"Lobo?"*

1438 local (−8 GMT)
Admiral's Conference Room
USS Jefferson

"—so Washington would like me to get a look at this new bogey, if at all possible," Tomboy concluded. "Based on our radar data, the attacking unit could have been a Combat UAV with its own warhead, A Combat UAV, or CUAV, possibly carrying multiple missiles, has really got the Pentagon sweating. They want to know more about it, and they want to know *now*."

She looked around the table. Besides her, the meeting was attended by Batman, Coyote, Lab Rat and Bird Dog. She found comfort in their familiar faces. She also felt the slight buzz in her head that accompanies west-to-east jetlag, and struggled to remain focused.

Batman drummed his fingers once across the top of the table. "I take it you were impressed by Dr. George's story, then."

"I'd call him a credible witness."

"So would I. The question is, what do you want to do about it? What exactly is your plan?"

She took a seat and leaned across the top of the table. "I need to fly as near the coast as possible, in an unescorted Tomcat, to see if it's possible to lure this bogey out. If it engages, fine. If we get the chance to shoot it down, even better. But the main goal is to gather as much data on it as we can. If the Chinese have one of these things, they probably have more, and we need to know how to face them in the future."

"Oh, *that's* all you want to do?" Batman said sardonically, one eyebrow raised. "Fly around and play bait for a basically unknown enemy aircraft?" The eye beneath the peaked brow was socketed in bruised-looking flesh. Tomboy wondered when was the last time Batman had gotten more than a couple hours of sleep. "Plus," he said, "I assume you want to use one of my aircraft."

"Those are my orders," Tomboy said. She knew Batman

was already aware of this, but let him have his say. He deserved the opportunity to vent.

"Well, I don't like it," he snapped. "At best, it's likely to be a wild-goose chase, or should I say a wild Tomcat chase? At worst, it could cost me a pilot, and a certain RIO on loan from the Pentagon, not to mention a perfectly good F-14."

"The Pentagon considers this worth a try, Admiral," Tomboy said quietly.

"Well, what about the storm? There's no sign of the typhoon Dr. George keeps talking about, but the barometer *is* falling, and the weather definitely *is* picking up. Tell me, how do you expect to go bogey-baiting if visibility goes to hell?" ·

"That's what radar's for, Batman."

"Not with this thing; this thing is stealthy."

"The Pentagon considers this worth a try," Tomboy repeated, in exactly the same tone of voice as the previous time.

Batman sighed. "Wouldn't want to argue with them, would we?"

1740 local (−8 GMT)
PLA prison cell

Dinner was dried-out white rice with a few pieces of fatty pork in it, and water. This was passed into the cell by an unarmed PLA soldier while another PLA soldier, this one carrying an AK-47, stood guard behind him. Lobo understood the logic: Jumping the inner guard would do no good; he had no weapons to steal.

She glanced at Admiral Magruder. Tombstone. He stood in the middle of the room with his arms crossed and his scowling face as unyielding as a granite carving. Although she hated to admit it even to herself, especially since in the final analysis result he was just as powerless as she, nevertheless she felt almost desperately happy he was here. Before his arrival, every time the door opened she had pressed herself against the back wall or burrowed into the pile of musty blankets in a pathetic attempt to hide. She had expected, each time, to see a long file of PLA soldiers waiting outside while the first one came in, smiling, laughing, reaching for her in the darkness. . . .

She knew there would be nothing Tombstone could do if the soldiers came for her in that way—nothing any one person could do—but still, his presence was welcome.

At least she had someone to talk to.

He'd already told her how he ended up here, and she had described being picked up by the PLA boat after punching out of her Tomcat and floating around for a while. She'd told him about Handyman, and saw the pain cross the admiral's face.

Now, rice bowl in hand, she asked the one thing she hadn't dared bring up yet. "What do you think they're going to do with us, Admiral?"

"Tombstone," he said absently, squatting on his heels and eating the rice with his fingers. They had been given no utensils, not even chopsticks. "I have no idea. Most likely they'll questions us, then use us for propaganda or bargaining chips."

"And what are *we* supposed to do?"

"You know the drill from SERE school. We hold out as long as we can with name, rank and serial number. When it gets too bad, do as little damage as possible. Make them work for every bit of information. If they force you to read a confession, do it in a way that makes it clear you're reciting a speech someone else wrote for you."

She nodded, remembering the wooden, almost comically insincere "confessions" given by the few allied pilots who had been shot down over Baghdad and subsequently captured.

She ate some rice. Her throat was so tight she could barely swallow it, even with a chaser of water. She didn't want to ask the next question, but felt she had no choice: "Do you think they'll question us?"

He turned toward her, his eyes unexpectedly kind in the hard face. "I expect so. But if it's torture you're worried about, I can't say what they'll do. It's best not to dwell on it."

The dirty hands ripping at her flight suit, at her breasts, tearing away her underwear . . .

She swallowed, lowered her head. She would *not* give in to this fear. Not *ever*.

"They'll come get us, Lobo. You can count on it."

Lobo looked up at him, despair in her eyes. "Like they got your father out?"

Just then, the door clunked open, and a grinning Chinese soldier walked in. "All finish eating?" he asked. "Good, good. We have question for you. You first, lady. You come with us now."

1800 local (−8 GMT)
Sick Bay
USS Jefferson

Hot Rock sat on a chair beside Catwoman's bed and stared down at her. "How are you doing?" he asked.

"Okay." Her voice was soft and dopey, her face as purple and mottled as an overripe plum. "I'll be NPQ for a few days, then I'll be back on the flight schedule."

"Yeah, I know. Busting my ass again." He started to reach for her hand, then changed his mind. She looked like one huge wound, and that was only the parts not covered by sheets. The worst stuff was hidden. From what he'd heard, it was amazing she was alive at all. And fly again? Maybe. Probably not.

No thanks to you, a voice snorted in his mind.

He licked his lips. "Catwoman, I just wanted to tell you I'm sorry I wasn't more help out there. They had me boxed in. There was nothing I could do."

Her eyes rotated toward him. "I'm sure everybody did their best."

He nodded. "That's right. Bird Dog did a hell of a job flying back in. Half his wing was shot off, but he refused to dump the plane for fear of losing you. Did you know that?"

Her lips curved up briefly. "I always said he was too stupid to be a pilot."

"I just wish I could have done more to help, that's all," he said again. He sounded so sincere he startled himself.

She gave a brief nod. Her eyelids fluttered. "Maybe next time."

"Sure. Next time." He watched her eyes close, her breathing slow down and deepen. "Next time it will be different, you'll see."

There was no reaction. Hot Rock rose to his feet and walked quietly around the privacy curtain. As he was passing the only other occupied bed in the hospital, a voice cried cheerfully, "Excuse me, young man, but could you tell me what the weather's like this morning?"

2100 local (−8 GMT)
Tomcat 307
South China Sea

"Sorry about the rough air, Tomboy." Bird Dog's voice sounded soft and pensive over the ICS. If Tomboy hadn't seen him get into the front seat, she wouldn't have believed it was Bird Dog Robinson up there.

"I doubt—you had—anything to do with—the weather," she said from behind her radar hood, her voice cracking every few words as the Tomcat hit a particularly violent spot in the sky. Although no RIO could afford to be prone to motion sickness, she was definitely feeling greenish.

"Dr. George says this is just the start of the bad weather," Bird Dog said. "He predicts a super-typhoon. What do you think?"

"I'm no meteorologist geek."

"Me neither. According to Lab Rat, the National Weather Service is predicting no more than a mild tropical storm."

"Bird Dog, you—seem distracted today. Are you—keeping your eyes peeled—up there?"

"Yes. Sorry. Didn't mean to babble. Catwoman's going to make it. I saw her this morning."

"That's great news, Bird Dog." Which was true. Still, he *was* babbling; combined with the roller-coaster air, it made concentration difficult. Tomboy's fingers moved over the radar's controls, each bump and knob identifiable by its unique shape. One advantage of the rowdy atmosphere was that there was relatively little air traffic today. Unfortunately, so far none of it looked suspicious.

She was losing hope for a quick encounter with the bogey. Bird Dog had made innumerable passes up and down the coastline of the SAR, and had seen and passed both commercial and military aircraft, but so far nothing had challenged them. Not even one of the ubiquitous PLA fighters that periodically moved in disturbingly close, then peeled away again.

Tomboy was painfully aware of how helpless they were out here, without support and armed with nothing but a cannon. On the other hand, their wings-clean configuration probably explained why the PLA was not pressing them too hard.

She realized she'd lost all her concentration. She had the feeling Bird Dog wasn't adequately focused on doing his job today. She leaned back, extracting her face from the hood, and winced as the sunlight crashed in on her through the greenhouse bubble of the canopy. She flipped down the tinted visor of her helmet. "Bird Dog?" she said over ICS.

"Yes?"

"Want to talk about it?" It was easier to converse in a level voice when you could see around you, even if the bounces themselves remained unpredictable.

"Talk about what?" Bird Dog asked in an elaborately casual voice.

"What happened the other day, at the end of the ACM. You aren't feeling guilty about coming back when other people didn't make it, are you? Because—"

"It's not that. I know there was nothing I could do, the way my plane was acting."

"Then what's eating you? Your backseater's going to be okay."

"Yeah, but . . . I'm kind of worried about Lobo. She took that missile for *me*."

"She was just doing her job, Bird Dog. Besides, I understand she's still MIA, which means there's hope."

"Maybe. But it also means if somebody did pick her up, it must have been the wrong people." Then, in a fast, gruff voice, he added, "She saved my ass, man. I owe her."

Tomboy was silent, frowning. Then her eyes widened. Could it be . . . ?

But the idea that had occurred to her wasn't something she could say out loud, not on a mission, not even over the privacy of ICS. "Tell you what," she said. "When we get through with this gig, I want to talk to you about something."

"Okay," he said. "Speaking of finishing, we probably ought to head back, unless you want to call up a Texaco for refueling."

"I don't think so. But tell you what. When you make your turn, let it get you closer to the twelve-mile limit. Let's really push it on the way back, see if it stirs up any wasps."

"Roger."

The Tomcat leaned into a slow, smooth bank. Tomboy looked to the west, where the mountains of China winked in and out of sight between billowing piles of cloud clearly visible in the full moonlight. Then, instinctively doing her job as backseater, she turned and looked over her shoulder to check their tail. And suddenly she was shouting, "Bogey at five o'clock! Bogey at five o'clock! It's right on our ass, Bird Dog!"

"Countermeasures," he said in a steely voice.

"Right." She calmed herself and twisted in her seat as far as possible, trying to keep the thing behind them in view at all times. Meanwhile, her hands did their work unseen. She didn't bother glancing at the radar screen again, either; if it hadn't detected the bogey creeping up behind them, it undoubtedly didn't display it now.

In fact, she could barely see the aircraft even now. If the shadow of a passing cloud hadn't wrapped over it briefly as it banked behind the Tomcat, she wouldn't have noticed it in the first place.

But what she *could* see jibed exactly with Dr. George's description: a flattened, narrow manta ray of an aircraft, with angled winglets in place of conventional tail surfaces. Distances were difficult to judge, but the bogey couldn't be more than a quarter-mile behind the Tomcat.

"Hold your turn," she said to Bird Dog as she groped for her camera. "Don't let him know we've noticed him."

"Swell."

She got the camera out and started snapping. The bogey stayed exactly where it was relative to the Tomcat, as if both aircraft were sliding along on the same set of rails.

"This is sure fun," Bird Dog said, "but I'd be happy to go buster anytime you say."

"Another few seconds. Hold the turn, hold the turn; the bank gives me a better view of—"

Her words were sliced off by the insistent beeping of the ESM gear. "Fire control radar!" she cried, but even as she dropped the camera and reached for the chaff-release controls, she knew it was too late. A corona of flame appeared beneath the bogey as a missile's rocket booster ignited and hurled the warhead forward at speeds far greater than human reflex.

For a half heartbeat, Tomboy actually saw it: a white circle trailing flame and smoke, growing larger as if by magic.

Then she was staring only at the smoke trail, just below them. What—

She slammed back in her seat as Bird Dog hit the afterburners. "Missed!" he shouted over ICS, and the Tomcat cranked into a neck-snapping left turn. "Sucker missed us!"

With her helmet locked against the inside of the canopy by centrifugal force, Tomboy watched the missile's smoke trail billowing away into the distance, puncturing each cloud that stood in its way, lacing them together. Then she saw what lay beyond the clouds.

"My god," she said.

"What? What?"

"It's heading straight for Hong Kong."

2110 local (−8 GMT)
Hangar Bay
USS **Jefferson**

"Hey, Bubba."

Franklin smelled the stink of diesel fumes, and turned slowly. "I'm busy, Orell."

"Know who I saw down here earlier? Ol' Bird Dog."

Franklin wiped his hands on a rag. "So?"

"He was checkin' this bird out real careful. I mean *real* careful. Know what he told Beaman?"

Franklin just kept wiping his hands.

"He said he was glad he was takin' some other Tomcat up today. And he didn't want you touching his plane again."

"I didn't do nothin' wrong," Franklin said, jaw clenched. He was getting *sick* of saying that.

"Sure, of course," Orell said. "Lots of you techies work on these planes, right? Coulda been anybody, doin' anything. 'Course, they're not all the same color as you. Shit brown. Wonder why Bird Dog is so sure *you're* the one fucked up?" And with a wink, Orell released the tractor's brake and moved off across the hangar.

Friday, 8 August
1400 local (−8 GMT)
PLA compound

Tombstone was squatting on his heels next to the wall, face upturned to the intermittent sunlight, when he heard the blockhouse door open. He lowered his head and looked down. Two guards were escorting Lobo into the compound.

Her legs looked wobbly, but she stood in place when the guards released her.

Refusing to acknowledge the screaming pain in his own muscles, Tombstone rose to his feet and walked toward her. The guards eyed him disdainfully for a moment, then turned and walked back inside the blockhouse. They closed the door behind them. That left only the armed guards on top of the wall. Two of them. More than enough.

"How are you?" Tombstone asked when he got close enough for Lobo to hear him.

She raised her head. Her face was unmarked but very pale. He was pleased to see that her eyes smoldered from their bruised sockets. "They beat me with a rubber hose. I thought the Chinese were supposed to be masters of subtlety."

"Maybe that was back before the Revolution. Follow me." He turned and led her toward the center of the compound, which wasn't much larger than a good-sized patio. On one side was the blockhouse, a tall stone building with barred windows and a steeply-slanted roof of brown tiles. From either end of this extended the high stucco walls that formed the enclosure. Set in the wall opposite the blockhouse was a tall, arch-shaped doorway and a pair of solid wooden doors. Teak, Tombstone thought—one of the hardest woods in the world.

Above the walls, the occasional crown of a tree swept into view, tossed by a strong wind Tombstone could hear but not feel. Beyond that, the sky was crowded with towering thunderheads. Below, the ground was covered in crushed white limestone. There was no dirt, no trash. In fact, the surroundings were generally not all that grim. Throw around some lawn chairs, potted palms and maybe a Jacuzzi—and open the doors, of course—and this place could be almost pleasant.

Nothing like the underground rooms. Especially the one with the bolted-down chair fitted with leather restraints.

He halted in the middle of the compound and turned toward Lobo. "Turn your face up," he said. "Get some sun while it's still there."

She looked at him strangely. He tilted his head back and spoke from the corner of his mouth.

"Don't you remember your training? Make your face visible to spy satellites, just in case."

Although he couldn't see her now, he heard her speak softly: "I keep forgetting they can actually I.D. us that way."

"Only if the timing is right. But it's worth a try." He paused. "Lobo, you said they beat you. What about . . ."

"No. I kept waiting for them to . . . but . . . no." She sounded both relieved and surprised, but Tombstone detected no shakiness in her voice at all. This was one tough woman. Still, there was no point in dwelling on that aspect of her situation. It could always change.

"What questions did they ask you?" he asked.

"About the battle group's plans. I told them I didn't have a clue. That's the truth, but of course they didn't believe me."

"They didn't believe me, either. But I guess my being a rear admiral might have had something to do with it." He paused. "This is going to seem like a weird question, but when they were working you over, did they seem . . . sincere?"

"Sincere?"

"I'm no expert on torture, but . . . I don't know, I got the impression they were just going through the motions. Not really trying. I *know* things could have been a lot worse than what I got."

She was silent for a long time. Overhead, the thunderheads were beginning to crowd together, shutting out the sky. Solid cloud cover would make things much more difficult for any spy satellite that happened to be parked over Hong Kong. Assuming, of course, that this prison was located anywhere near Hong Kong. For all he knew, it was on the outskirts of Beijing.

Then Lobo said, "You're right. Things could have been worse. A *lot* worse. But maybe they're working up to it slowly. Psyching us out."

"Either that," Tombstone said, "or like I said before, they have some other use for us. Did they take your photograph?"

"Just before the rubber hoses came out."

"Mine, too. Yeah, I'm sure they're planning to use us as bargaining chips of some kind. The good news is, that means they won't torture us too badly."

"And the bad news?"

Tombstone stared at the last visible crack of open sky, watching it close up. The air smelled of electricity. "Frankly," he said, "the bad news is everything else."

1500 local (−8 GMT)
Admiral's Conference Room
USS **Jefferson**

"So you think it was a setup," Batman said. "You think the Chinese fired a missile at their own city in such a way it would look like *we* did it."

"Yes, sir," Bird Dog said in a level voice. "It was a radar-guided missile. It could have easily nailed us in the backside, but it didn't. Which means it had to have been intended for Hong Kong all along."

"How bad was the damage?" Tomboy asked. Her face, with its typically pale redhead's complexion, looked almost greenish in the conference room's subdued light.

"Bad," Batman said. "Hong Kong's the most densely populated piece of real estate in the world. Lab Rat's checking on the latest reports right now. But it was bad."

Tomboy compressed her lips so hard they almost disappeared. "I can't believe they did it," she said. "Killed their own people that way."

" 'To win one hundred victories in one hundred battles is not the acme of skill,' " Bird Dog said, as if to himself. " 'To subdue the enemy without fighting is the acme of skill.' "

"What?" Batman said.

For a moment Bird Dog didn't seem to have heard him. Then he blinked and looked up. "Sun Tzu, *The Art of War*. Offensive strategy."

"Win without fighting?" Batman said. "Excellent idea. Any idea how to implement it, Commander?"

Bird Dog shook his head.

So did Batman. "We need practical ideas. We need some idea what the Chinese are likely to do next. Where the hell is Lab Rat?"

"Right here." Lab Rat was just pushing open the door, holding a piece of paper by one corner, as if it had been used to wipe up something vile.

"I suppose that's a Chinese press release denouncing the latest American aggression," Batman said.

"No, sir." Lab Rat's glance shot toward Tomboy, then away.

"So what is it?" Batman demanded impatiently.

Lab Rat raised the sheet of paper with both hands this time. "We just received word that Admiral Magruder . . . Tombstone . . . is a prisoner in the People's Republic of China."

1530 local (−8 GMT)
PLA Headquarters
Hong Kong Garrison

Yeh Lien, Political Commissar of the Hong Kong SAR, watched the argument with a sinking feeling.

"We must declare martial law," Chin said. "Immediately."

Strong words from a junior officer, even though Yeh agreed with them. But Major General Wei stared at Chin down the length of the table. "We do not make such decisions, Comrade. That is up to Beijing. And Beijing has ordered us to keep Hong Kong in operation, as usual."

"As usual? How can Hong Kong operate 'as usual' when boats and ships are fleeing by the dozens?"

"These are minor vessels, not major shippers."

"But—"

The old PLA soldier raised his hand. "The Americans claim not to have fired the missile at Hong Kong, Chin. Whether they are lying or not, that statement allows us to keep this port open and running without loss of honor."

"But half of Kowloon is still burning!"

"An exaggeration. Besides, half of Kowloon can afford to burn, just as the harbor can afford to lose a handful of junks and fishing boats."

Yeh stared at the man in astonishment. Glanced at Chin and saw the same expression on the younger man's face, too.

"This is Hong Kong!" Wei shouted, pounding a fist on the table. "If we declare martial law here, the economies of every country in Asia immediately crashes! This is not acceptable, to Beijing or to me!"

"So the Americans are free to attack us with impunity," Chin said. "Whose economy does *that* help?"

Shocked, Yeh held his breath. Major General Wei sat silently for a long moment, his body as immobile as one of the rocky islands in the bay. Then, slowly, he reached for the telephone on the corner of the table, lifted the receiver and muttered a few words. Yeh could not hear what he said. He hung up.

"I have taken enough of your insubordination, Major General Chin," he said flatly. "Not even your connections in Beijing permit you to question my authority this way—remember, for the foreseeable future I represent both the PLA and the State Council itself."

"I realize that, but it is my job as a commander to question—"

"Major General Yeh," Wei said, turning slightly in his seat. "You are the political commissar. Is it permissible for a subordinate officer, however highly placed, to question the orders of a superior?"

Yeh swallowed. "Your orders came directly from Beijing?"

"That is correct."

"Then . . . there is no question. Comrade Major General Chin, you are required to follow these orders without hesitation." *And more's the pity*.

Chin stared at him. "Even if the man issuing them is a traitor to the State?"

"What?" Wei shot to his feet. His face was purple.

"Collector of forbidden antiquities. Briber of smugglers

and customs officials. Friend of thieves and corrupt capitalists of all kinds."

Again, Yeh was stunned. How had the Coastal Defense Force commander gotten this information? Perhaps the man wasn't quite the helpless dolt he appeared to be.

Wei's face slowly reversed its color trend, becoming pasty. "You—you—"

"First Po, then Hsu," Chin said, shaking his head. "They were also politically unreliable. Criminals. I thought that when they were eliminated, things would improve."

"Are you saying—"

"I thought that you, of all people, would remember our true purpose here. I hoped you might even recommend me to fill one of the vacant posts here in the SAR. Instead—"

The door opened. Three PLA guards stepped in. Wei nodded at them, and all three turned and aimed their AK-47s at Chin.

"Comrade Major General Chin," Wei said in his most formal voice, "you are under arrest for treason and, from your own mouth, the murders of two of our country's highest ranking and most distinguished military officers." He nodded again at the guards, who moved in close to Chin, rifles pointing steadily at his head.

Chin rose slowly to his feet. If he was frightened, he didn't show it. He pointed a long finger at Wei. "*You* are the traitor, not I," he said. "I accuse *you* of capital crimes against the People's Republic of China."

Wei shot straight up from his chair, face purple. "How dare you, you young—"

With a tremulous crash, half the room's windows burst inward. At the same moment Wei's head snapped to one side, and blood exploded against the wall. His stocky body collapsed forward onto the table, then to the floor. As if in sympathy, all three guards folded straight down, and as they toppled over one another, Yeh saw that their skulls had been caved in by high-energy ammunition.

There had been no sound of gunfire. But Yeh's old soldierly instincts, honed as an infantryman in Korea, reached out and yanked him to the floor beneath the enormous teak table. He waited there, head covered by his arms, for more gunfire.

Nothing happened. Then he heard the crunching sound of footsteps in broken glass. Turning his head, he saw a pair of military-issue boots. He looked up from under his arm.

Major General Chin loomed over him, fists on hips. Didn't the fool realize he was a potential target, too? How could he seem so totally unconcerned? Chin held a hand. "Up, Comrade Major General."

"But—"

"It is safe."

This was said with such conviction that Yeh allowed himself to be helped to his feet. He stared at the shattered windows, jagged openings into the darkness beyond. Through the gaps came the wail of sirens, voices shouting, running footsteps. And something else: the drumming rattle of rainfall.

"Comrade," Chin said. "You and I think alike, and feel alike about the future of your country. You and I both know Hong Kong is no place for politically unreliable leaders. Is this not true?"

Yeh glanced at Wei's collapsed body. He said nothing.

"Hong Kong is a cancer in the body of China," Chin went on. "A cancer that must be cut out. Men such as Wei are not the ones to do it, but you and I are. Work with me. With your support, Beijing must give me at least interim command of the Hong Kong garrison, and I can turn this territory into the kind of place the People's Republic can be proud of."

Yeh heard the words, but couldn't seem to take his gaze off Wei's corpse. It reminded him of the many lifeless bodies he'd seen lying at the foot of the wall where firing squads did their work. More than a few of those men had died for crimes far less severe than the theft of forbidden antiquities.

"The guards will be here any moment," he said to Chin. "How do you intend to explain what happened here?"

"The attack was carried out by an American SEAL team," Chin said promptly. "An assassination squad. And we'll have the videotape to prove it, you can be sure."

Yeh looked at Chin again, and saw the fires of determi-

nation glowing in the young man's eyes. It was hard to believe he had never noticed it before, even in the form of coals
awaiting a breeze. Hard to believe he'd ever considered Chin
a fool, a hapless political appointee.

He recalled one of Sun Tzu's precepts: *When capable,*
feign incapacity. He remembered what Ming had said about
Chin: His only vice was his incompetence.

"You've been planning this for some time," Yeh said.

" 'He will be victorious who is prudent and lies in wait
for an enemy who is not.' "

Yeh made a slow bow. "I am behind you one hundred
percent, Comrade Major General."

ELEVEN

Friday, 8 August

Tomboy spread the stack of freshly developed photographs across the table in the admiral's conference room. She was alone, and grateful to Batman for the offer of this room and the solitude it provided. She had the feeling that her terror might leap onto her face at any moment, and she refused to let anyone see that. Refused to see her dread reflected in the pitying faces of others.

Matthew, her husband, her love, was a prisoner of the Red Chinese. She still couldn't get her mind around that fact. How often had she heard him talk about his father, himself a navy pilot who had been shot down over North Vietnam? First a POW, then MIA . . . Never seen again.

And now Tombstone.

A piece of the shirt Tombstone had been wearing when he left for Hong Kong had been left at the American Embassy in Hong Kong, along with a photograph showing Tombstone in the grasp of two Chinese men in PLA uniforms. No one knew who had left the package. There had been no note, no further information.

In the hours since then, the PRC had not denied being involved in the kidnapping. They hadn't admitted it, either.

There was a disturbing lid of silence over the second-largest nation in the world.

"We'll find him," Batman had promised her. "We'll get him out." Fine words. But how?

For now, she was better off not thinking about it. Better off concentrating on something she might actually be able to do something about.

So she stared at the photos she'd snapped of the bogey.

They weren't very impressive. The damned plane was too skinny, too carefully camoflaged. All she had in her pictures was a discolored sliver in the sky, really. A shape like a staple with its flanges bent up slightly.

It was a radical shape; the kind of airframe that almost certainly depended on high-speed computers to maintain stability. All top-end fighter planes, including F-14s and the latest-generation Russian designs, were aerodynamically unstable. If it weren't for the dozens of tiny corrections automatically made each second by the onboard computers, the aircraft would not be able to fly at all. This natural tendency to diverge from level flight resulted in extraordinary combat agility. But shut the computer down, and all that expensive hardware would tumble out of the sky like an autumn leaf.

Such sophisticated technology wasn't developed overnight. Neither was a radical new airframe like this flying manta shape. How had the Chinese done it? Borrowed from the Russians? Unlikely. Like any technologically-advanced nation, the Russians kept their hottest new gear for themselves.

She went over the photos again and again. Many of them were enlarged. She picked up the last shot she'd made before being interrupted by the radar-lock alarm. She stared at it for a moment, then picked up its matching enlargement. Yes—there was a dark blob beneath the plane, almost like a fuel drop-tank, that wasn't there in the previous shot. Then she realized what it was: a head-on view of the missile, extended into firing position.

Unfortunately, no more detail was visible even in the blow-ups. Too grainy. All she could tell was that the missile had popped out of some kind of internal bay. Still, she kept staring at the photo. Something about it . . .

Wait. Wait. The missile itself. How big had the real thing been?

She thought back to what she'd seen as the missile flashed under the Tomcat, and compared that to how much damage had been done to Hong Kong. Not a small missile, but not a behemoth like a Phoenix, either. A mid-sized weapon, then; like a Sparrow. The diameter of a Sparrow was eight inches. Given that measurement to work with, she could compare the cross-section of the missile to the shape of the aircraft that carried it and estimate the latter's wingspan and overall thickness.

She did so, and frowned. It didn't make sense. The span would be only about twenty-five feet, and its center thickness . . . no more than two feet.

That was impossible. The pilot would have to be lying flat to fit in such a tiny airframe. Of course, such a pilot position had been tried before. There was that experimental Northrop flying wing of the 1940s, the Flying Ram, whose pilot lay prone inside the center section of the wing. . . .

But even the Flying Ram was significantly larger than this. If her estimate was correct, only a genuine midget could pilot the Chinese bogey, even assuming he was lying on his belly. And come to think of it, there was no clear view of a canopy in any of her photos. No variation in color or pattern that indicated a viewport or window of any kind.

It was as if . . .

"My God," she said, and reached for the phone.

When Batman walked into the conference room, his Gang of Four was gathered around a collage of photographs on the table. The intensity of their concentration made him decide to wait before relating the message he had just received from CVIC. "What is this?" he asked.

Tomboy looked up. Her eyes burned like blue-hot coals in pits of ash. "I was just explaining that I don't think the bogey that fired that missile at Hong Kong is a fighter at all."

"What?" Batman moved closer to the photos and stared at them. Frowned. "Then what is it?"

"A UAV."

Coyote shook his head. "But you said UAVs are single-warhead vehicles, sort of like ultra-smart cruise missiles. This thing was *carrying* missiles."

"There's no theoretical reason to bar that development from occurring."

"Terrific," Batman said, looking up at Tomboy. "So what made you so *sure* this was a UAV all of a sudden?"

"For starters, its size. Look at that photo right there. See the missile? Using that for comparison, I was able to determine that the aircraft itself is bigger than Tombstone's UAV, but still too small to carry a human pilot. Also, see if you can spot a canopy."

All the men examined the photos more closely. "These aren't very clear," Lab Rat said dubiously. He looked at Bird Dog. "When you were in the air with this thing, did you notice a canopy?"

"I didn't see the bogey at *all*. It was right behind us the whole time."

"It didn't have a canopy," Tomboy said firmly. "And it was too small to be piloted. I'm sure about this, Admiral. *Positive.*"

Batman straightened, although he felt his heart going the other direction. "So what you're talking about here is a low-cost, disposable fighter plane."

"Something like that."

"Is it supersonic?"

"Probably not. The platform doesn't look right, and I doubt the engines are large enough to do the job anyway."

"I agree," Lab Rat said.

"So what?" Batman said. "It carries supersonic missiles." No one responded.

"All right," Batman said. "Tell me what we should do if we have to go to war with these things."

He'd tried to keep his voice neutral, but Tomboy didn't miss a thing. "Is there something we should know?"

He gave a single nod. "The PLA just declared martial law

in Hong Kong. No one gets in, no one gets out. COS, you might want to get to the bridge. The battle group has been ordered to steam toward Hong Kong and take up a close support position, in case action is necessary to defend American interests."

"Yes, sir." Coyote turned without another word and strode out of the room.

Batman faced the others. Their expressions were uniformly grim. "I don't need to tell you what this could lead to. Washington is working for a diplomatic solution, but it's our job to assume, and prepare for, the worst." He pointed at the photos. "Which could include dealing with this thing—or things, if it's got relatives. So, Tomboy, I repeat: How do we kill them?"

She chewed on her lip. "Okay. We can expect UAVs in general to be much more agile than a Tomcat or even a Hornet because G forces aren't a problem for a pilot. They'll also be tough targets for missiles; they have diffusion exhausts to blur their heat signatures, and stealth profiles to throw off radar. . . ." She looked at Batman and must have caught something from his expression. "Sorry, sir. Our best strategy is to fly high and watch low. Stealth or no stealth, the Chinese seem to like hiding these bogeys in surface clutter, so that's the direction they'll come from. Also, make sure fighter teams stick close together. Solitary aircraft seem to be the preferred targets."

"Especially if they're unarmed," Lab Rat added.

Batman nodded. "All right, let's make sure the wings of all patrolling aircraft are as dirty as possible. We want everything we put in the air to look like a major threat."

Abruptly, Bird Dog spoke. "Wait. Wait . . ."

Everyone turned toward him. For the first time, Batman noticed that the young pilot was clutching a worn paperback book between his hands. *The Art of War*. Bird Dog stared into space for several seconds, then seemed to snap back into the room. "Has anyone wondered why we've seen this bogey *at all*?"

"What are you talking about?" Batman asked.

"Tomboy just reminded us about its stealth characteristics.

So I was thinking . . . this bogey could have shot down that Air Force jet before anyone knew it was there. Same thing with Tomboy and me. The bogey hung behind us for God knows how long before releasing its missile. In other words, both times it was spotted, it seemed *deliberate*."

Batman frowned. As rational explanations went, this one ranked right up there with Bird Dog's earlier claim that the Chinese must have attacked *Lady of Leisure* in order to keep the U.S. Navy in the vicinity.

"Why would the Chinese want us to see their stealthiest plane?" Batman asked. "Why tip their hand that way?"

Bird Dog riffled the pages of his paperback. He didn't seem to be aware he was doing it. "Politics," he said finally. "When one nation gains enough of a military technological advantage over another, the second country *has* to react. If the Chinese can convince us they've got highly advanced UAV capabilities, that will affect how Washington behaves in future negotiations. And if that can be accomplished without actually having to *produce* a working inventory of combat UAVs, all the better."

"You're suggesting this bogey was a red herring?" Batman asked, pointing at the photos.

"No. Obviously it's a viable weapons platform. I'm just suggesting it might not be as viable as we think it is; the Chinese might be using it so sparingly because it has weaknesses they don't want us to know about. I say we have to factor that into our planning, so we aren't too conservative out there."

Batman stared at Bird Dog for a long time, then at Lab Rat. Lab Rat's expression never changed, but Batman read his eyes and nodded. "All right. Bird Dog, I want you, Tomboy and Lab Rat to come up with a range of battle plans based on facing both UAVs and normal Chinese assets." He turned back toward the pictures. "Earlier you said the Chinese try to win wars without fighting. If that's so, I want us to be ready to give them a punch they'll never forget."

1300 local (−8 GMT)
Main cell
PLA prison compound

"Wonder why they didn't let us outside today?" Tombstone said. He was sitting on the floor, back leaning against the concrete wall of what he and Lobo had come to call "Grand Central," the large cell in which they were both usually kept. He'd folded one of the blankets that were the room's only furnishings into a thick cushion beneath him. Lobo sat on a second blanket. A third had been rigged as a privacy screen around the waste bucket.

"Guess they don't like the rain," Lobo said, nodding toward the single small window. Nothing was visible beyond it except darkness, but earlier in the day they had been able to see water droplets running down the glass.

"I don't think that's it," Tombstone said. "Now that I've had time to think about it, I'm bothered by the fact that they ever *did* let us outside."

"Because of the satellites?"

"The Chinese aren't stupid. They know we have spy satellites capable of picking out a particular face from orbit, and they're bound to assume we have one parked over Hong Kong right now. So, yeah, I have to wonder: Why did they let us wander around outside at all?"

Lobo turned toward him. Although it probably wasn't possible, her face looked thinner than yesterday, almost gaunt. But her eyes were fierce with calculation. "I've been wondering about that, too, and I can only think of two reasons: Either they want Washington to know where we are, for some reason, or else they're holding us someplace satellites aren't likely to be watching."

Tombstone nodded. "Neither one makes me optimistic about our chances of rescue. You?"

"No, but what can we do about it?"

"We can leave," Tombstone said.

1330 local (−8 GMT)
PLA Air Force Operations Room
Hong Kong

"What is your strategy?" Yeh asked. "Why are you sending so many fighters up in this weather?"

Chin didn't even turn from the tactical display screen on the wall of the Operations Room. He pointed at an icon. "The American aircraft carrier *Jefferson* is steaming toward Hong Kong."

Yeh stared at the display, and felt a shiver of dismay at how little of it he could decipher; how far he had fallen behind in matters of warfare. These days, his job was politics and enforcing philosophical rectitude. Still, he knew that Chin was in the process of launching nearly half the SAR's fighter aircraft into the thundering pre-dawn darkness. "Hong Kong weather warns that this storm could be developing into a typhoon," he said.

"Our aircraft are all-weather fighters, Comrade. The weather means nothing to them."

"But why so many?"

"Because the Americans are preparing to attack Hong Kong."

The skin on Yeh's back prickled. "You know this for a fact?"

"Yes."

"How?"

"They will have no choice."

"You've warned Beijing?"

"Not yet. 'He whose generals are able and not interfered with by the sovereign will be victorious.' "

"You are a very daring man, Major General Chin. Perhaps too daring for your own good."

Chin shook his head. "Beijing will question my actions only if we lose."

"You do realize that an American battle group carries more firepower than—"

Chin raised a hand. "I know the statistics. They don't concern me."

"Why not?"

"Because an aircraft carrier battle group is only as good as its carrier."

"What are you saying?"

"I'm saying I have some surprises in store for our American friends."

1400 local (−8 GMT)
CDF Patrol Boat
South China Sea

The Coastal Defense Force patrol boat had seemed large and capable enough in Victoria Harbor, but in the open sea its limitations became obvious. Still, it had been modified for that environment with an extra-heavy keel, sealed doors on all hatches and ports, and a snorkel intake for the engine that helped keep water out. It could be completely submerged without any danger of shipping water and sinking.

That didn't mean that riding in it in these conditions was a pleasure. But that was all right. Chou and his men were not being paid to have fun.

"Distance?" Chou asked the radar operator.

"One hundred and fifty kilometers."

"And our ducks?"

"Unless the aircraft carrier alters course, the ducks will converge on the intercept location just before dawn."

"Not too much before. They'll need light to see what they're doing."

The radar man nodded. "I'll keep an eye on it. But these conditions make predicting anything very difficult."

"The ducks have been well paid already, and know they'll receive double that amount when they return—if they do what they're supposed to do. It's more money than any of them expected to see in ten lifetimes. I think that's plenty of incentive to get them where they're supposed to be *when* they're supposed to be there."

"This storm is turning into a typhoon. Many of the ducks

will never make it back to Hong Kong at all."

"Then they won't be paid." Chou turned to the radio operator. "You're still in touch with all the ducks?"

"Yes, sir."

"And they understand the importance of coordination? Everything must happen exactly on our signal. They understand that?"

"They understand."

Chou nodded. "Carry on."

1450 local (−8 GMT)
Bridge
USS **Jefferson**

Coyote was swaying on his feet from exhaustion, although he was trying to pretend that it was just the unpredictable motion of the ship. Despite all odds, Dr. George had been right; during the night, the weather conditions had graduated to "tropical storm," and were moving rapidly onward. Satellite data showed the clear cloud patterns of a typhoon developing to the southeast.

Outside, the horizon line was smudged from existence by wind-whipped spray, pounding rain and streamers of cloud. Everything was shades and tints of gray. This was weather only fools and Navy sailors—assuming there was a difference—would be out in.

Then he saw the first junk.

Later, there would be questions asked of the officer of the deck and the junior officer of the deck who was responsible for watching the SPA-25G radar repeater on the bridge, and of the lookouts, and of the boatswain's mate of the watch, who was supposed to be keeping an eye out for obstacles in the water, but no blame would be laid. Not in conditions like these, where curtains of visibility were opened and closed at random.

The junk looked ridiculous out here, a silly toy with its elevated stern house and stubby bow. The sails were furled, of course, leaving the job of propulsion to some kind of rinky-dink engine that had to fight winds currently peaking at over eighty mph, not to mention seas that must look like mountains from the deck of the junk.

Before Coyote could say anything, he heard one of the lookouts say, "Holy shit" in a wondering voice.

Coyote turned back toward the windows. His eyes widened.

The junk was not alone. The ocean was full of boats. Not ships but *boats*, none more than forty feet long. Junks, sampans, rectangular houseboats, sportfishing cruisers. At a glance, they were all in pretty sorry shape; not one looked like the kind of vessel you'd want to take out of protected waters even during mild weather—never mind *this*.

But there they were, bobbing around like rubber ducks in a bathtub while 97,000 tons of nuclear-powered aircraft carrier ploughed through them.

"Oh, lord," Coyote said. "OOD, back off to bare steerageway. Just pray nobody's right in front of us." But he wasn't going to call for evasive action. For one thing, an aircraft carrier was not a cigarette boat; a carrier turned as nimbly as a skyscraper with a keel. For another, in this weather the visibility in any direction, including straight ahead, was so intermittent and limited that attempting to set any kind of avoidance course was pointless.

He grabbed for the phone.

1455 local (−8 GMT)
CDF Patrol Boat
South China Sea

"All ducks reporting in," the radio operator said. "They are in position, and the carrier is in sight."

Chou nodded, although he doubted all the ducks were truly in position. Not in this wind and these seas. Many of the ducks were almost certainly far off the mark, and simply denying it. But that was all right. There were a lot of ducks

out there; only a handful had to have reached their positions
on time.

"Begin the countdown," he told the radioman.

"Countdown begins," the radioman said into his headset,
broadcasting to all the ducks in the South China Sea.

"On my mark," Chou said. He raised a hand. "Ten—"

"Ten," the radio operator repeated into his headset.

"Nine—"

"Nine," the radio operator repeated.

"Eight . . ."

1500 local (−8 GMT)
Bridge
USS Jefferson

Refugees, Coyote thought. It was the only possible expla-
nation for this haphazard flotilla—Hong Kong citizens making a truly desperate attempt to escape the abrupt iron hand
of the People's Republic. Fools, but brave fools. Imagine
deliberately sailing out into this weather, with a typhoon
roaring into existence just over the horizon. You had to ad-
mire—

His thought was cut off by a small but intense flare of
light in the distance, down near the water. This was followed
by another, then another, and another, originating from points
all over the compass. The flares turned into long streamers
unwinding toward *Jefferson*.

Before Coyote had quite registered what the streamers
meant, the carrier's Phalanx Close-In Weapons System began
to roar.

1510 local (−8 GMT)
Main holding cell
PLA prison

Tombstone was beginning to fear the guards would never arrive with lunch. His butt was going numb from sitting in one spot, waiting.

But finally he heard the heavy thud of the bolt sliding back. The door swung open, revealing the usual arrangement: one guard standing at the ready, AK-47 raised, with another guard behind him holding two bowls of rice and a jug of fresh water.

The armed guard looked at Tombstone sitting against the wall, a coarse blanket pulled halfway up his chest. His *naked* chest. Tombstone saw the man's eyes register the nakedness, then move to the tufts of short brown hair exposed above the top edge of the blanket. Move down to the unmistakably feminine shape the blanket made under Tombstone's curled arm.

The guard grinned and said something over his shoulder to the guard with the food, who laughed. Both men walked into the room. The armed guard kept grinning, but never lowered the muzzle of his automatic rifle.

Neither man saw or heard Lobo step out from behind the privacy curtain. Her feet were bare. Tombstone was careful not to let his gaze even flicker in her direction, but his view of her was clear nonetheless as she set her feet, then charged straight at the guard with the food. She slammed into his back with all her weight, driving him into the back of the armed guard.

Tombstone was already moving, rolling to one side in case the guard reflexively triggered the AK-47. At the same time, he tightened his grip on the handle of the empty waste bucket he'd been holding under the blanket.

There was no gunfire. Tombstone stumbled to his feet, cursing the numbness of his legs, as the two guards stumbled toward him. He swung the bucket over his head and down like a sledgehammer, smashing it with all his strength and fury against the back of the armed guard's skull. The wooden slats of the bucket exploded in all direction. Without hesitation, Tombstone took a step and drove the point of his elbow into the second guard's throat. Both guards crashed to the floor, one unconscious and bleeding, the other coughing and gagging. Tombstone raised a foot and stomped down on the latter man's head once, twice. Felt the surrendering snap of bone. The gagging sounds stopped.

Tombstone looked at Lobo. "Guess I'll have to report you for a grooming violation," he said, trying to keep the quiver out of his voice. "That haircut's awful."

Lobo bent down and unholstered the second guard's sidearm. "Are you kidding? People in Paris pay a fortune to have their hair look like this."

"Then maybe Parisian barbers should start cutting with wood slivers." Tombstone gathered up a couple of the blankets and threw one to her. Then he grabbed the AK-47 off the floor. "Let's get the hell out of here."

1511 local (−8 GMT)
USS **Jefferson**

The Phalanx CIWS was a carrier's last-ditch line of defense. There were two Phalanx installations on *Jefferson*; one mounted on the port bow, the other on the starboard stern. At a glance, they looked like giant water heaters mounted on top of M-61A1 Gatling guns. The water heaters were actually housings for the systems' automatic search-and-track radars, along with 1,550 rounds of ammunition. The Gatlings were, in turn, mounted on balanced, motorized carriages that could rotate, pivot and rock through all three axis.

A Phalanx system was designed to detect an incoming airborne threat with its radar and pass this data on to the carriage's motors, which immediately swung the Gatling gun toward the threat. The gun then spewed ammo at the rate of 4,500 rounds per minute, creating a curtain of metal through which virtually nothing could pass intact. Everything happened with breathtaking speed, the 13,600-pound Phalanx unit bobbing and twisting as nimbly as a flyweight boxer.

At least, it sounded good on paper. But even though the Phalanx system had surpassed its performance specifications in all tests, it was still not much trusted by sailors. How could you really put your faith in something almost untested in actual combat? Especially since to activate the system, an incoming missile or enemy aircraft had to first make it safely through the other defenses of the fleet, including the cruisers and frigates with their ship-to-air missiles, Hawkeyes and their radar net, and numerous fighters flying BARCAP. This was something that simply did not happen.

Until now.

A total of fifteen missiles raced toward *Jefferson* from various boats in the Hong Kong flotilla. Eleven of the bogeys were FIM-92 Stingers, American-made hand-launchable heat-seeking missiles designed for foot soldiers to use against low-flying helicopters and aircraft. The Stinger had a dual-thrust rocket motor capable of pushing its 2.2 pound armor-penetrating warhead to Mach one in a couple of seconds. From there, a heat-seeking head equipped with a reprogrammable microprocessor would guide the missile to its target over a maximum range of approximately three miles.

The other missiles in the salvo were AT-4 anti-tank missiles, also fired from hand-held, expendable launchers. But the AT-4 was designed for one purpose only: to destroy armored land vehicles. It had a range of only a thousand yards, which it reached in less two seconds; then, at the moment of impact, an 84mm HEAT shaped-charge warhead would go off, flash-melting a hole in even rolled homogenous armor plating of up to 400mm thickness. The rest of the warhead's energy would turn the interior of the vehicle into a fiery cauldron.

Even an AT-40's guidance system was optimized for striking at large, slow-moving targets: It had none. AT-4s were aimed by eye, like a gun; and their missiles, like bullets, could not be redirected after being sent on their way.

The fifteen missiles came at *Jefferson* from all sides, and all within a few seconds of one another. Two of the Stingers fizzled out well short of the carrier, having been fired from almost five miles away. A third Stinger and one AT-4 veered off into the storm, the Stingers' infrared seeker heads confused by the cold spray, the AT-4's trajectory thrown off by a last-moment tilt of the boat from which it was fired. All these missiles disappeared into the raging rain.

Of the remaining eleven missiles, seven were met by the the Phalanx weapons, which detected them, targeted them, then spewed masses of slugs out at them. When the missiles met the barrage they exploded, sending sparkling debris streaking through the gloom. For a few seconds, *Jefferson* was surrounded by a garden of bright, short-lived flowers.

But the Phalanx system was subject to the same physical laws as any other piece of machinery. Nimble as they were, neither unit could aim at two simultaneously, nor reverse direction faster than momentum would allow.

Two missiles got untouched through the barrage. One was a Stinger, fired late but from almost dead astern; the other, an AT-4 aimed from the deckhouse of a junk on *Jefferson's* port side.

The moment the Stinger lofted out of its fiberglass launching tube, its infrared-sensing head sought a heat signature. Although no aircraft were currently launching from *Jefferson*, the carrier's stern was crowded with parked aircraft that had recently trapped. To the Stinger, their steaming exhausts stood out like beacons against the cold steel of the ship. The missile whipped toward this feast, and from the embarrassment of riches, selected an F-14 carrying a full complement of ordnance. It sang right up inside the left exhaust.

The Tomcat's fuel tank was almost empty—but fumes, not fuel itself, is what burns. The rear half of the Tomcat disintegrated in a blinding flare, instantly killing three nearby brown shirts and blowing their blazing corpses into the ocean. Simultaneously, the front half of the jet obeyed Newton's Third Law of Motion by lunging away from the impact like a giant piston, crashing into the adjacent nose-tail-nose mosaic of parked aircraft. There was a rapid propagation of crumpling metal as wheels broke loose from tie-down chains, landing gear struts collapsed, knife-edged wings swung wildly. Aluminum skins ruptured. Jet fuel poured out onto the non-skid. Flames raised a roaring, yellow-and-black wall. In an instant, seven aircraft sat cooking wildly in the rain.

The missile fired from the junk, the AT-4, had been intended to strike the "island," the heart of the carrier that included Pri-Fly, the bridge, and all the major communication and tracking equipment of the ship—and therefore the entire battle group. But even at point-blank range, *Jefferson* was a difficult target to hit from the lunging deck of a small wooden boat. The AT-4, flying straight and true, did not strike the island.

Instead, it struck the underside of the protruding flight deck, just above the closed door to the aft elevator. Its conical warhead, a shaped charge designed to concentrate virtually all its explosive energy on a single spot, liquified the steel plate of *Jefferson*'s hull and passed straight through, spraying molten metal and chunks of shattered steel before it at high velocity. The majority of the shock wave slammed up into the deck over the hangar bay, buckling it and sending a wave-shaped ripple through the flight deck above. There, sailors were flung off their feet as if someone had jumped on a trampoline beside them. Aircraft yanked and shuddered against their tie-downs, and deck plates sprang free from their rivets. Within seconds, what had been a flat surface the length of three football fields became a warped, rippled mess.

In the hangar bay itself, the results were even worse. Flaming debris rained down on the parked aircraft and the hundreds of men and women working on the planes. Sections of catwalk scaffolding collapsed. There was a wild scramble for cover under fuselages and half-folded wings. Smoke filled the air, permeated by sirens, claxons, and screaming.

Outside, the bow Phalanx immediately swung through ninety degrees in an attempt to acquire the last missile in the air, a Stinger that had been fired from almost directly off the bow. The horizontal blizzard of Phalanx projectiles reached the missile just as it made an abrupt vertical juke to follow a cloud of exploding jet fuel. The slugs nipped the missile's tail, shearing it off and sending the rest of the missile into an uncontrolled cartwheel. It broke into pieces from the centrifugal force, and in that condition almost accomplished the

job for which one of the AT-4s had been intended: Although
the seeker head arched a hundred feet into the air and vaulted
Jefferson entirely, and the explosive warhead skimmed past
the bridge by four feet and spent its explosion in the water,
the center section of the missile whirled directly into the
island, shearing off antennas and destroying radar masts.

In less than thirty seconds, the USS *Thomas Jefferson* was
transformed from one of the most potent weapons in the
world to a smoking, flaming hulk.

1520 local (−8 GMT)
Headquarters, PLA Air Force
Hong Kong Garrison

Tombstone knew the entire enterprise was hopeless, of
course. Even if he and Lobo managed to escape all the way
from the prison complex—not guaranteed, to say the least—
what then? After all, they were being held somewhere in
Communist China; for all he knew, just outside Beijing. It
wasn't as if a Caucasian man and woman could wander
around unnoticed.

Still, they had to try. Tombstone Magruder was not going
to end up like his father, dying in some POW hellhole. And
he knew Lobo was with him on that decision.

He already knew that this was not a prison of the sort
familiar to Americans, nor even a POW camp like the one
he'd heard described by Vietnam vets. It was more like a
dungeon. Still, he was surprised to find that the short corridor
outside the cell was not itself guarded. He glanced in both
directions, and saw a door at either end. Whenever he and
Lobo were dragged in or out of their cell, they were first
blindfolded with a black hood, which Tombstone had always
assumed was part of the psychological terror. But he'd noticed that trips to the outdoor compound were made to the
right, so he now turned left.

When he reached the door, he was surprised again. It was

unlocked. He frowned; then, with Lobo right behind him, he eased the door open.

Something on the outside hurled the door open with superhuman strength, flinging Tombstone up and out. In an instant he was drenched by a rain that pounded down on his back like a million ballpeen hammers. He gasped in shock, stumbling in the same blast of wind that had grabbed the door. Only by flinging himself sideways, tightly against the wall of the prison, was he able to halt his helpless flight.

Squinting against the blasting rain and wind, he saw Lobo standing uncertainly in the doorway. He shook his head, then looked around.

Through horizontal sheets of rain he saw various buildings move in and out of sight: long, low structures for the most part, with trees arching overhead. The trees were mostly evergreens, their crowns tossing madly. Tombstone noted that most of their branches grew from the leeward side of the trunk; these trees had been shaped by weather like this. Straight ahead of him, perhaps thirty yards away, was a narrow paved road. Nothing moved along it.

Soaked to the skin, beginning to shiver, he considered the options. Wherever they were being kept, the obvious direction to go was east. Since major storms in this part of the world cycled counterclockwise, the wind would be coming from somewhere between north and east, so at least he knew what direction to head. After that . . . who knew?

He was about to beckon Lobo out of the doorway when he heard a new sound, weaving in and out of the wind: a distinctive, high-pitched whistle. Tombstone turned his head in time to see something rushing along the strip of road. For an instant the weather parted, giving him a clear view of a manta-shaped aircraft, with upturned winglets, lifting off the road. It bobbed, recovered crisply, and lofted out of sight into the slanting rain. There were red stars painted on the winglets.

The bogey. The one Tomboy had been sent to the South China Sea to investigate.

Tombstone rushed back to the doorway, and gasped with

relief when he got out of the wind and rain. "Did you see that?" he said.

Lobo nodded. "It must be the thing that shot down the Air Force jet."

Tombstone nodded. "So we're not in a regular prison. They're keeping us at an air base."

"Why would they do that?"

"Probably in hopes of preventing an attack on the base. Insurance. That would be why they let us show our faces in the compound; to let Washington know where we are."

Lobo nodded.

"The good news," Tombstone said, "is that we must be close to Hong Kong. That would be the air base the Chinese would want to protect. If we can reach the city—"

"How?"

"Find a vehicle. Or a prisoner. Or both."

She nodded.

"Let's head toward where the bogey came from. Start looking there."

She nodded again.

Together, they plunged into the storm.

1530 local (−8 GMT)
USS Jefferson

Before the chaos began, Bird Dog was in his stateroom trying to relax. He'd picked up his copy of *The Art of War*. One thing about Sun Tzu: If you were having trouble sleeping, just read *The Art of War* awhile. Trying to make sense of it numbed the brain.

At the moment, Bird Dog was plodding through the chapter on "The Nine Varieties of Ground," which was a ridiculous pastime because he was, after all, a naval aviator. No ground around, not unless you counted the ocean floor, and only the submariners cared about that. Still, he forced himself to continue. Even if he found nothing practical for himself in *The Art of War*, he had to remember that for his enemies, the book was a treasure house of information.

So. Per Sun Tzu, the nine types of real estate were: Dispersive, Frontier, Key, Communicating, Focal, Serious, Difficult, Encircled, and Death. These were rated in order of the trouble they'd cause a general during battle, starting with the army's own homeland—nice and safe—and progressing out into "death" territory—land in which the army could be trapped with virtually no chance of escape, far less victory.

Right now, if you wanted to stretch the metaphor, *Jefferson* could be said to be occupying Difficult ground: "any place where the going is hard." Sun Tzu's advice for dealing with Difficult ground? "Press on."

"Guess the navy's doing everything right, then, eh, Sun?" Bird Dog muttered, and closed the book.

At that moment, a series of jarring vibrations shivered through his rack.

1537 local (−8 GMT)
Flanker 67

This was not optimum, Tai thought angrily. The formations were ragged, the voices over the combat radio channel too tense. Not tense because of the promise of combat, though. These were brave men, and eager for blood. No, the problem was the weather. The storm. No one had counted on that. No one had expected to be fighting the Americans in near-blindness.

The PLA fighters had excellent radar, powerful enough to fry a rabbit crossing the runway; that wasn't the problem. The problem was that using radar exclusively was new to most of the pilots—certainly, using it in the middle of a storm, with visibility diminished nearly to zero, was new to them. The fact that such combat would be a first for most of the Americans, too, was of no consolation, because everyone knew the Americans trained extensively in flight simulators. And while "virtual" experience was not the equivalent of the real thing, it was better than nothing. And nothing was what the Chinese pilots were building upon.

Damn this storm.

No wonder the men were worried, even though they outnumbered the American fighters currently in the air. And even though there would be no American reinforcements in the immediate future, thanks to the ambush Mr. Blossom had arranged. From all reports, the carrier had taken damage. How bad was not yet known, but bad enough. There would be no help there. For the American pilots, even returning to their ship might be out of the question.

So from the Chinese perspective, there was good news as well as bad. Not to mention the special surprise Tai suspected would be out to help the Chinese.

Personally, Tai Ling was not worried at all. This was one battle—fought blind or not—that the Americans would never forget.

No, correct that.

This was a battle the Americans would never *survive*.

1538 local (−8 GMT)
Tomcat 306
USS **Jefferson**

"Say again?" Hot Rock heard the disbelief and tension in his own voice. The same question was echoed over the air by other BARCAP pilots.

"I say again," came the brisk response from the E-2 Hawkeye. "Fifty Flankers inbound your location, bearing 000, ETA ten minutes."

"*Fifty* Flankers," Hot Rock murmured, feeling sweat spring out along the spine of his flight suit. That was damn near a three-to-one ratio against the Vipers.

"Vipers," the E-2 said crisply, "be aware Homeplate took a hit and is red deck. Repeat, Homeplate has a red deck. There will be no backup. You are weapons free. Fire at will."

Hot Rock felt the sweat begin to trickle. *Jefferson* damaged, the fighters weapons free . . . it could only mean that the Chinese had struck the carrier, and effectively. How? By submarine? It seemed incredible.

On a more immediate note, it meant that the odds facing the BARCAP pilots were not only three to one, but unlikely to improve. No help would be rushing in. . . .

"Better hope we don't use our go-juice too quick, youngster," Two Tone said. "There's only one Texaco in the sky—and lots of planes bound to get thirsty."

"Here we go, Hot Rock," came over his headset from his new lead, Neanderthal. "Try to stay with me."

Neanderthal's Tomcat banked hard right. Hot Rock followed.

Until now they had been flying, as much as possible, in the direction of the wind. Going that way, the air was almost smooth. But come around, and life turned into a hell of buffeting and vicious vertical wind shears. Not to mention lack of visibility. The entire world was the striped, irregular gray of oily rags. And this was the *outskirts* of the storm.

Best to ignore the view entirely. Stare out there for more than a few seconds, denying the brain reliable visual reference points, and in no time you'd start to think you were on the verge of a stall, or had entered a power dive, or even that you were going backward. There was no escaping it—no one, however hot on the stick, could fly in by the seat of his pants in zero visibility.

Instead, you watched your instruments. The blips on radar, those were real. Readings from altimeter, variometer, airspeed indicator, attitude indicator—those were real. When a pilot flew instruments, he became as dependent on artificial sensors as was any RIO.

"Picking up the bogeys now," Two Tone said. "Yep. I'd call that a shitload of Flankers."

"Phoenixes," came over the radio.

"Phoenix ready," Two Tone said. "Got us a nice juicy Flanker all picked out, Rocker."

"Roger," Hot Rock said, switching the weapons selector switch to the appropriate setting.

A moment later, the order came: "Fire when ready."

As with the helicopter, Hot Rock didn't allow himself to think: He toggled the switch and made the Fox call. The upward bounce of the Tomcat when the missile's weight dropped away was barely noticeable in the general tumult.

He watched the missile's progress on radar, knowing that the pilot of the targeted Chinese plane was doing the same thing. For all the Phoenix's weaknesses, Hot Rock was glad the PLA didn't have anything like the big radar-guided killer.

"Miss," Two Tone said. "That's a miss." Meanwhile, over the headphones came whoops from a handful of more fortunate Vipers. Sounded like three or four had successfully taken out a Flanker.

Three or four . . . out of fifty.

The Vipers hurtled northwest into the claws of the wind, intending to engage the Chinese as far as possible from *Jefferson*. Meanwhile the Flankers, with the wind quartering on their tails, intended to do just the opposite. Hot Rock and Two Tone began assigning missile tags to incoming blips.

"Hang tough, amigo," Two Tone said. "Don't leave your lead for anything this time."

"What do you mean, 'this time'?"

"Just thinking of that helo you shot down. Some people might have questioned that if I hadn't backed your story, you know? So this time stick with your lead, stay in position. Don't do anything fancy on your own. That's what I'm suggesting."

"But I—you—"

"Heads up, Rock. Here come the bad guys."

1538 local (−8 GMT)
USS Jefferson

Beaman struggled into his OBA, or oxygen breathing apparatus, and mustered with the rest of his damage control party. Hosemen, investigators, and on-scene leader—they fell into their assigned positions automatically.

"Beaman," the team leader said. "Get going. Cut around the forward end of it—see how big it is."

Beaman nodded. As the primary investigator, his first task was to figure out where the edges of the fire were so that Damage Control Central, or DCC, could order smoke and fire boundaries set. First they would try to contain the fire, keep it from spreading, contain the smoke in the damaged area with heavy curtains hung from the hatches. Then while essential systems were being rerouted through the multiple system redundancies that existed on every Navy ship, the fire party would start nibbling at the edges, forcing flames and heat back into a smaller and smaller area until they could finally extinguish it.

At least, that was the plan. Reality always threw some monkey wrenches into the mix.

"You, Jones—get down to the first deck, see if the overhead's starting to buckle. We stop it from moving down first, people. You know why."

Beaman nodded. He did indeed. Starting three decks below the hangar bay, the aircraft carrier was honeycombed with ammunition lockers. Sure, they were equipped with sprinklers, watertight doors, Halon systems, everything the carrier could bring to bear in the way of fire control. But three decks wasn't all that far away, not if this was a class D fire, a metal-burning conflagration. Given a little time, the fire could eat through steel deck plates like they were hot tortillas.

"It might have missed the hangar queen," Beaman said. "They were moving her forward last time I saw." The hangar queen, an aircraft that was virtually impossible to ever get flying again but served as a valuable source of parts, had been spotted directly ahead of them.

Even two hundred feet away from the fire, Beaman could feel the waves of heat rolling over him. The fire billowed and roared, battered the overhead, and reached out for them with tentacles of sparks.

"Get moving. Be safe," the team leader said. He gave Beaman a swat on the rear as Beaman and his designated messenger broke off from the pack. "We're right behind you."

As they neared the edge of the fire, the hosemen behind Beaman arced a stream of fog into the air, showering it around him from a safe distance away. It wasn't particularly useful for actually extinguishing the fire, but that wasn't the point just yet. The mist cooled the air off to a temperature that his fire-fighting ensemble could withstand.

Never step where you can't see. Beaman edged out just a bit from the fire, out to the edge of the cloaking smoke that roiled like a snake in the air. The banshee scream of the fire was louder now, reducing the voice of the team leader on his communications handset to a harsh whisper.

The rest of the damage control party was out of sight now as Beaman and his messenger moved around the far wall of the inferno. No secondary explosions yet, and it looked like—two more steps—yes, by God, one break. He could see the hangar queen safely out of the way. Safe for now, at least. Another five minutes and the gutted hulk of the queen would simply be more fuel in the fire. And then they would have a problem—once the aircraft's metal ignited, there would be damned little chance of extinguishing the blaze.

Beaman backed off a bit until the noise was at a tolerable level. He toggled the transmit switch and screamed, "Hangar queen's clear. Checking the far side now." He slipped the walkie-talkie into a pocket on his fire fighting suit and motioned to the messenger to follow him. If he lost communications completely, his messenger would be his only link with the team leader.

Back close to it now, as close as he dared. The air inside his ensemble scorched the delicate lining of his noise, rasped against the back of his throat as he sucked down heaving breaths. Sweat cascaded down his face, his neck, his entire body, trickling down to soak his dungarees and seep into his boots. Another few steps, another one step—Beaman struggled against the blackness crowding in on his vision, knowing on some level that he was too close, too damned close, that he had to—

He felt someone jerk him back by his elbows. He stumbled and fell awkwardly onto the deck. Heat from the steel plates blistered through the fire retardant gear. He could feel the skin along his leg where he landed starting to stick to the fabric. Beaman let out a scream, then shoved himself up and away from the deck, drawing on reserves of energy he wouldn't have guess that he had.

"Too close!" Beaman could make out the words that the investigator mouthed, unable to hear over the noise.

Too close. Too damned close. Beaman shook his head, clearing away the fog that threatened to consume his consciousness. Get himself killed, pass out or something, and he'd put the whole team at risk trying to come after him.

He nodded to let the messenger know he understood, then motioned them forward. They resumed their achingly slow progress around the fire, inching forward in the near-complete darkness.

Another two steps, and Beaman felt the heat start to decrease drastically. Was it possible—yes, by God. Through the veil of partially combusted missile fuel, burning bits of debris, he could see the open hangar bay doors. Outside, the gale raged, the wind blowing parallel to the length of the ship, sucking the smoke outside and creating a draft on the entire hangar bay.

But how could they contain the fire already raging inside? If only there were some way to channel the force of the storm into the hangar bay, let Mother Nature's rain dowse the flames, cool the inferno to a point that the man-made fire fighting systems had a chance to beat it out?

Could they push it overboard? Sure, if they were up on the flight deck with yellow gear and Tilly, the flight deck crane that was used to hoist burning aircraft over the side. But down here?

Wait. It just might be possible—he stepped back farther from the flames, felt the air inside his suit start to cool slightly. He lifted the walkie-talkie to his masked face and started shouting.

"He wants to *what*?" Batman roared.

"Turn abeam to the wind, Admiral," Coyote said. "Open the hangar bay doors on both sides. According to DCC, it might just work."

"What idiot is down in Damage Control Central?" Batman snapped. "This is lunacy—the last thing we need is to feed more oxygen in to the fire. All that's going to do is spread it and gut this air craft carrier like a—like a—" Batman spluttered to a stop, and Coyote leaped into the silence.

"I think it will work, Admiral. Frankly, with fires topside and in the hangar bay, it's our only chance. We can fight one, maybe both for a while. But not much longer if we have any chance of ever using the flight deck again. It's going to buckle—and that will be the least of it." He pointed at the damage control schematic of the ship. "Another five minutes, and it's going to get to the catapults. Then you can kiss that flight deck good-bye for good."

Batman was silent for a moment. Then he said, "What about the men on the deck? We've lost internal communications with Repair Eight. The wind shifts and it'll foul their plan of attack completely."

"Messengers," Coyote said. "In the end, it'll help them, too. They're going to have to push that flaming mass of metal over the side one way or another, and right now they're working at cross angles to the wind. We turn, we give them a tail wind."

"Dangerous."

"It always is."

Batman stared down at the flight deck, watching the co-ordinated chaos that represented one of the finest fire fighting actions he'd ever seen anywhere, in training films, in drills, in actual videotapes of disasters. The missiles that had hit the flight deck had come in at a low angle. One had plowed through four helos parked aft, another had taken out two E-2 Hawkeyes parked next to the island. He shuddered as he studied that particular hit. Another twenty feet and the missile would have snapped the tower right off the ship.

Finally, Batman said, "Do it. But don't kill anyone in the process."

"Okay, stand by," the team leader shouted. "Hosemen, get over to the other side and get the windward hangar door open. It'll take them about two minutes to get us abeam of the wind." The team leader looked over at Beaman. "I hope to hell you're right about this. DCC thinks you are."

Beaman tried to speak, but all he could manage was a hoarse croak. Pain rattled down his throat as scorched tissue protested. The corpsman leaned over him and pressed a canteen of water into his hand. "Drink a little more—you're headed down to sick bay, man."

Beaman struggled to his feet and tried to shove the corpsman away. He took another slug of water in, rolled it around in his mouth and let it seep into the damaged tissue. Finally, he felt the tightness in his throat start to ease up. "Not yet," he whispered. "I have to see if it works."

The corpsman grabbed him by the arm and tried to pull him over toward a transport litter. "Going down to triage *now.*"

The team leader stepped between the two of them, breaking the corpsman's hold on Beaman's arm. "Not yet. He earned this." A hard, shuddering, grating vibration ran up through the soles of their feet, and all three turned to stare at the hangar bay doors slowing inching back along their tracks. The world outside was solid gray, and sheets of rain were already pelting the remaining gear inside the hangar bay. Water slashed across the vastness of the hangar bay, flashing into steam as it hit the still raging fire. The howl of the fire competed with the hiss of steam and the keening of the wind through the four-foot gap in the beam of the ship.

"More. All the way," the team leader said into his walkie-talkie.

Beaman broke away from the rest of them and walked unsteadily toward the massive, three-story metal doors. He heard a shouted curse, then the corpsman joined him, steadying him by holding one elbow as they moved as quickly as they could across the open bay. They fell in side by side along the line of men and women straining to move the massive bulk of the hangar doors.

Beaman found a handhold and felt a moment of despair at that massive inertia with which the steel doors resisted the best efforts of the team. The doors inched back achingly slow, grinding and squealing inch by inch over the greased tracks upon which they rode.

Then something gave. Almost imperceptibly, the doors picked up speed, increasing the thin slit window open to the weather outside.

The difference was noticeable almost immediately. The wind picked up, battering at the flames, driving them out of the open doors on the opposite side of the hangar. The fire licked hungrily at the edge of the deck above and the low catwalk that surrounded the flight deck. Beaman saw a canister life raft sway unsteadily as the flames reach it. First one support line gave way, then the second. The canister tumbled down into the fire, and as the plastic seal around it gave way, it gouted forth the eerie shape of an automatically inflating life raft. It seemed to float for a moment on top of the burning hot air, tossed upside down by the draft, and then the tough plastic vaporized in the flames. Beaman saw one small fragment spiraling in the updraft before the wind forced it out the other side of the ship.

"It's working," the team leader shouted. "Come on now— put your back into it!" Each person redoubled his efforts, pushing muscle and sinew past the point of pain, welding their flesh with that of the ship they sought to save.

"I see it," Beaman shouted. "Grissom, I see the boundary of it." He dropped his hold on the door, now sliding easily along its track, and raced forward to the fire. He stopped just twenty feet away, the hard pounding rain and wind almost driving him forward into the inferno involuntarily. He turned back to the team leader. "We need some shoring timbers, then some flat sheets of metal. And yellow gear."

"You think it will work?" Grissom asked.

Beaman nodded. "The wind is driving the smoke away from us, the rain's acting like a fogger, and we got fresh air coming in. Come on, we got to get it off the deck *now*."

Within moments, the damage control team had a makeshift tractor rigged on the front of the yellow gear. "I got it," Beaman said and stepped forward to take the driver's seat.

"No way." This time, the corpsman locked his arm around Beaman's neck and pulled him back. Beaman felt pain flash in his upper arm, then looked up at the corpsman. The man's features were fuzzy—and there was something about a fire, some reason Beaman had to stay awake, had to, had to get to the— With the urgency beating his brain, Beaman slid to the deck, unconscious.

The corpsman held up the empty syringe. "Morphine. It'll do it every time," he said aloud.

But no one was listening.

"That's the last of them," Batman said, his voice heavy with relief. Tilly the crane had just unceremoniously released the last burning aircraft over the open water, her steel cable almost at a forty-five degree angle in the gale force winds. "How the hell they pulled this off, I'll never understand. Get the chief engineer down there. I want to know how bad the deck is."

"He's on his way, Admiral," Coyote answered. "We've lost two Hawkeyes and four helos, along with the Tomcat."

"Then let the small boys know they're going to have to pick up the slack in SAR," Batman said. "The Hawkeyes have enough crews on board to do a hot crew swap."

"If we can launch," Coyote said.

Batman stared at him, cold fire shining in his eyes. "Those people didn't just beat that fire for me not to be able to launch aircraft. You tell the chief engineer it's a question of when and how—not if. One way or another, I want metal in the air in fifteen minutes."

1537 local (−8 GMT)
Prison compound

Pushed along by the giant hand of the wind at their backs, Tombstone and Lobo needed only a minute to find the beginning of the runway. It was marked by a circular turning area and a taxiway extending to the south. Without a word, Tombstone turned in that direction. His entire body felt bruised by the wind and rain; he was grateful that the ground was covered in some kind of crushed black rock rather than slick grass or, worse, mud. As it was he had to lean to the left at almost a thirty-degree angle to keep his balance, and his feet gouged sideways ruts in the rock with every step. He tried to keep the AK-47 protected by his body.

An enormous darkness loomed through the rain ahead. Tombstone found some bushes and crept along beside them, hunched over, until he was able to see that the dark shape was a mountain black and craggy. And at its base were several pairs of enormous sliding doors of what looked like galvanized metal. They were inset beneath a stony shelf in the side of the mountain, fronted by a tarmac apron that led to the taxiway. Hangars. Hangars, hidden from aerial surveillance by the mountain and a fringe of desperate-looking trees.

The hangar doors were all closed. How well-guarded were they? What would happen if he crept up for a little peak at—

He started when a hand tugged at his sleeve. He glanced back at Lobo, who pointed to the east. A pair of headlights was brightening the storm.

Lying flat on his belly beside the bushes with Lobo just behind him, Tombstone watched as a big dark sedan—not a military-style vehicle—approached the hangars. Its horn blasted once, and one of the hangar doors slid open. Bright light poured through the aperture, giving Tombstone a view of what lay within. His heart gave a rapid stutter.

CUAVs. Not like the manta. These were smaller, double-arrowhead-shaped. Like the one that had attacked him in Maryland.

And even in the narrow space he could see, there were dozens of them, stored on tall racks like private boats in a fancy dry dock. Dozens of them, waiting to go.

The sedan pulled just inside the hangar and stopped. An armed guard appeared from somewhere, and opened the back door. Another guard moved into view, escorting a third man. The third man was considerably taller than the others, and dressed in civilian attire. The guards hustled him into the backseat of the sedan. For an instant, just before the door slammed closed, Tombstone had a clear view of the man's face.

It was Phillip McIntyre.

1540 local (−8 GMT)
Tomcat 306
USS Jefferson

Do your job, Hot Rock thought, over and over again, the words tumbling through his head like a mantra. *Two Tone's right. Just do your job and nobody can blame you, no matter how things turn out. Do your job, do your job . . .*

And of course, in his case, that meant protecting his lead's ass. Any actual shooting would be executed only in conjunction with Neanderthal's efforts, and at his direction; for the most part, Hot Rock was there as defender and nothing more.

The battle was surreal in the gray soup. Attention focused strictly on the video game screen of the HUD, with perhaps an occasional glance at some other instrument. This radar blip was Neanderthal; that one was a Flanker; that other one, an incoming missile. Far more Flanker blips than anything else.

Hot Rock kept his gaze focused on the instruments, and his hearing on Neanderthal's signals radioed from the lead's position ahead and below. Now and then, when so directed, Hot Rock triggered a missile. Like all the Vipers, he was carrying only two Sidewinders, because the heat-seekers became notoriously unreliable in extremely wet conditions. But he believed he might have contributed to the shooting down of a Flanker with one of his Sparrows. "Nice shot," Two Tone said over ICS, "but don't get wild now; remember your job." Hot Rock felt relieved. It was good to have someone experienced tell you what to do.

With another part of his head Hot Rock kept track of other reports flashing over the air. Splash one, splash two, splash three Flankers. Then a Mayday. One American down. Another. Mayday. Mayday. Unimaginable to bail out in these weather conditions; what hope of surviving the trip down, far less being in the water?

Don't think about that. Do your job. Fly, watch, fire. Follow the leader.

Mayday. Mayday. Mayday. Missile blips appearing unexpectedly on the radar screen, other blips disappearing. Vipers disappearing.

"The stealth bogey," Hot Rock blurted over ICS. "Two Tone, that UAV they briefed us about, it's here. It's taking people out left and—"

"Do your job, goddammit!" Two Tone snarled. "Stop trying to figure out—"

The blip appeared and vanished from his HUD almost before it registered on his eye. At the same time, Neanderthal's blip disappeared, too. There was a throbbing glow in the clouds, swiftly consumed by darkness.

"Neanderthal!" Hot Rock shouted. No response.

Then came Two Tone's cry from the backseat: "Shit, Hot Rock, get us out of here! That thing's gonna be after us next!"

But Hot Rock had noticed something. A pattern in the vanished Vipers. The UAV was cutting straight across the Americans, from east to west. Nothing fancy. Locating American aircraft and firing at them from very close range.

Hot Rock saw this, and once he did, it was his responsibility. He owned it. He had to do something about it.

"Shut up, Two Tone," he said, and banked hard to the right. Now, instead of staring *at* his HUD, he gazed *through* it. Let his eyes take in the radar information peripherally, while he searched for holes and gaps in the clouds.

And he saw it. Briefly, almost hallucinogenically, the UAV was there, swimming like a great sea creature through the sky. And Hot Rock remembered something from the briefing: Like American stealth aircraft, the UAVs had their engine exhausts located on top, where they could not be easily spotted by ground-based infrared detectors. But airborne sensors were a different matter. . . .

"Fox One!" he cried, and triggered a Sidewinder. The missile hurtled off his left wingtip, unraveling a garland of smoke behind it as it went, and curved toward the bogey. Instantly, the bogey nosed over in a maneuver so abrupt it formed almost a right angle. Hot Rock couldn't conceive of the G-forces involved . . . then realized the UAV was indifferent to G-forces. As long as its wings didn't snap off, it was fine.

And it was turning toward him. That was the next thing Hot Rock saw before a raft of fast-moving clouds swept across his sight, and the manta disappeared.

Two Tone was howling from the backseat. Hot Rock felt an unnerving moment of doubt, of fear that once again he was screwing up, but of course it was too late to back out now. The manta was after him.

His mind skipped through bits of information the red-headed woman, Tomboy, had fed to the Vipers concerning this bogey. He already knew one thing: She'd been wrong that it depended on visual targeting data. Not in this weather. It had radar, too.

But maybe it liked using sight the best. If it did . . .

That reminded him of something else: The UAV was subsonic.

The missile-lock alarm sounded in his headset at the same instant he yanked the stick to the left and slammed the throttles forward. A brilliant yellow streak ripped the darkness, passing beneath the Tomcat as it pulled into a vicious, diving left turn. Hot Rock had already tightened his belly against it, but the special darkness of blackout spiraled in from the fringes of his vision. He waited until all he could see was the center of the HUD, then eased the stick forward. The darkness receded; in comparison, the edge of the typhoon looked almost bright and cheery.

The Tomcat was diving now, afterburners throbbing, propelling the aircraft past mach one, and then mach two. Below, the gloom peeled back and he saw the ocean, a savage froth of white and gray. Back came the stick, as did the spiraling darkness. Then he eased out, a hundred feet above the water. "Two Tone!" he cried. "Check our six!"

No answer. "Two Tone!"

Nothing. He realized he'd lost his backseater to G-force blackout. He was on his own.

And he realized something else: That made him happy. Relaxed. Now, whatever he did was entirely his own responsibility. No one to blame, no one to receive blame from.

He banked to the right, then the left, looking over his shoulder. Thought he saw a discoloration dropping out of the clouds. Eased back on the throttle. Let it catch up a bit. Let it—

There was nothing on his radar screen. No one to keep an eye on his tail. He grabbed the control to manually extend the wings, and did so. From behind, the extension would be invisible. Then he waited. Waited . . .

Over the headset, a moan. "Wha . . . Hot Rock—"

"Goodnight," Hot Rock said, and simultaneously yanked back on the stick and jammed the throttles full forward. This time he actually felt the blood rush out of his head, like water swirling down a drain; the spiral of darkness closed down fast. He pushed the stick forward and grunted as he slammed up against the shoulder straps of his harness. Below him, through his clearing vision he saw the manta-shaped UAV zip through the airspace he had lately occupied.

Putting the nose over, Hot Rock dove and opened up with his cannon. The tracers cut across the UAV like bright needles, but the UAV immediately cranked to the right in one of its physics-defying maneuvers.

Hot Rock executed a more gentle turn in the same direction, and watched his radar screen. There it was. There it was! The cannon hits might not have put the UAV out of commission, but they had holed it, destroyed the integrity of its radar-deflecting slants and curves. There was its signature on his screen, bright as daylight.

"Fox One," Hot Rock said calmly to anyone who might be listening, and triggered his next-to-the-last Sparrow. The missile leaped away, boring off into the haze. On the HUD, its signal merged with the UAVs. Up ahead the clouds brightened, then dimmed, in artificial lightning.

On the HUD, both signals were gone.

Hot Rock realized something strange had happened to his

face; it had an achy, stretched feeling to it. God, what if all the high-g maneuvers had permanently damaged something? Some muscle or nerve? What if . . .

Then he realized what it was: He was grinning.

1540 local (−8 GMT)
Hanger bay
USS Jefferson

Like everyone else in the hanger bay, Jackson was expected to help battle the fires and damage the missile had done in the hanger bay. There were tons of debris to get out of the way, blackened and useless aircraft to shove into the passing waves, bodies to help move. Time passed in a sweaty, terrifying blur. *So this is war*, Jackson kept thinking. *So this is war*.

And outside, the storm just got worse and worse. All the exterior doors were wide open because of the smoke, and wind-driven rain kept blasting in, hard enough to hurt if any of the spray caught you. It also made the decking slippery and dangerous. But the most terrifying thing was the waves. You didn't expect to look out through those doors and see the crest of a wave pass by, all white and sharp on top like something with teeth. You never expected to see waves that big.

And yet despite his fear, Jackson carried on, doing whatever needed to be done. He worked alongside brothers and sisters at times, and alongside white men or brown men or yellow men at other times. Officers snapped orders, of course, but the next thing you knew, that same man or woman would be right beside you, helping lift a piece of metal off some trapped sailor.

Once he and Plane Captain Beaman were both commandeered by some firemen to help move debris out of the way of a hose. Together, they heaved against a jagged chunk of metal plating that had once been on the outside of the carrier. It seemed to weigh a ton, but they got it out of the firemen's way. Afterward, for a moment Jackson found himself staring straight into his plane captain's eyes. There was something speculative there that infuriated Jackson. He knew what it meant. He knew that Beaman didn't trust him, thought he'd screwed up Bird Dog's plane. Been incompetent, been lazy. Thought that this kind of work, hauling pieces of metal around, was probably more Jackson Ord's speed.

But then Beaman gave a slanted, tired smile and clapped Jackson on the shoulder. "Good work," he said, and turned away to do something else.

Jackson stared after him, trying hard not to be pleased. You couldn't buy his forgiveness that easily. No way.

Still, he went back to work with renewed energy.

1543 local (−8 GMT)
Prison compound

"You can't be serious," Lobo shouted in Tombstone's ear. In other circumstances, it would have been a whisper. "Why do you want to go back *there*?"

"I've got to check something out."

"What?"

"You'll see . . . if I'm right."

"What if the guards' bodies have been discovered?"

"With any luck, they'll be out in this mess searching for us."

She grinned. "Good point. Okay, Admiral—lead on."

1540 local (−8 GMT)
Fantail
USS Jefferson

Bird Dog stumbled onto the fantail for some air. Because the carrier was steaming head-on into the wind, it was actually rather dry and pleasant back here . . . if you could ignore the traces of smoke still whipping off the flight deck overhead.

Disaster. Unbelievable disaster, and he blamed himself. If only he really understood the Chinese mentality. If only he could really comprehend the thinking behind *The Art of War*, maybe he could have predicted . . . prevented . . .

Well, Sun Tzu had been the first to say it: *Know the enemy and know yourself; in a hundred battles you will never be in peril.*

Those junks. The missile attack. A beautiful illustration of using the direct and indirect forces. And Bird Dog Robinson, War College graduate, hadn't expected it.

On the other hand, whoever was planning the Chinese assault had missed out on something, too: the storm. Only Dr. George had seen that one coming. Ironically, the typhoon had probably been *Jefferson*'s salvation. Its might had scattered the junks across miles of heaving ocean, and caused the Chinese fighters to struggle in what had undoubtedly been intended to be a massacre. The Chinese had planned to fight on Frontier ground, at worst, only to find themselves on Difficult ground instead.

Know the ground, know the weather; your victory will then be total.

Okay, fine. If this was Difficult ground, then Encircled ground was next. He knew that. The weather? It sucked; he knew that, too. Okay . . . so where was his total victory?

Know the ground. . . .

Difficult, encircled, death.

In difficult ground, press on; in encircled ground, devise stratagems; in death ground, fight.

His grip tightened on the guardrail.

In encircled ground, devise stratagems.

"My God," he said, and ran back into the wounded gut of the carrier.

1543 local (−8 GMT)
Prison compound

There was no apparent activity around the door Tombstone and Lobo had used to exit the building in which they'd been imprisoned. Perhaps, Tombstone thought, their absence was still a secret.

Not that he cared much, one way or the other. Gesturing to Lobo, he moved up to the wall and along its base, circling the building. On the leeward side, the rain dropped off to a cold mist whirling off the top of the wall. Rifle ready, Tombstone hurried along the wall to the next corner, and peered around. Winced at the needle-blast of rain in his face. The storm was getting worse every second. Still, visibility remained good enough that he could see the dark sedan parked in front of the building, and the wide portico. Palm trees genuflected wildly before the wind.

Awfully pretty place for a Communist-built facility, Tombstone thought, and gestured for Lobo to follow him. They were halfway to the portico when a man in black commando-type gear stepped into view, AK-47 cradled in his arms. Without hesitation, Tombstone raised his own rifle, sighted it against the wind, and pulled the trigger. As he'd expected, the *crack* was swallowed by the howling wind. The guard took a wobbly step, then collapsed. Tombstone hurried forward, grabbed him by the collar and hauled him into some shrubbery. Then he looked at the main entrance to the building. Double doors of carved wood, with tall windows to either side.

He ran up the steps to the door and tried it.

Unlocked.

Tombstone looked at Lobo, saw the confusion in her eyes. Saw the water running down her pale face. There was nothing he could tell her, so he simply said, "Let's go."

"What exactly are we looking for?"

"Anything PLA."

"You're not just trying to ditch me, are you?"

"No. After this is all over, I intend to divorce my wife and marry you."

"Liar."

"Please, Lobo; just watch the door."

"Aye, aye, Admiral."

He pulled open the door and they entered a wide, high-ceilinged foyer of teak and white marble. Enormous potted palms seemed to support a curved staircase climbing upward. Tombstone raised his eyebrows, and Lobo nodded. She squeaked across the marble and slipped in amongst the fronds.

Faint light spilled down the stairs. Tombstone headed toward it, AK-47 half-raised. He winced at the soggy, squelching sounds he and Lobo made as they walked, but there was no helping that.

At the top of the stairs was a long hallway extending in both directions. The light came from the left, as did a voice speaking sharply. Tombstone moved in that direction. Gradually, words came clear. English words.

". . . couldn't have possibly gotten off the island. Of course not. Increase the guard around the buildings, but get a search party out right away. I suspect they will be putting as much distance between themselves and this complex as quickly as possible. Good. Keep me notified."

As the receiver clicked onto its cradle, Tombstone stepped into the room behind his AK-47 and pointed the rifle at the man standing with one hand on the telephone.

"Hello, Uncle Phillip," he said.

1550 local (−8 GMT)
Bridge
USS **Jefferson**

" 'Offer the enemy a bait to lure him,' " Bird Dog said. " 'Feign disorder and strike him.' "

"You're quoting again," Batman snarled. "I don't have time for this. In case you're not aware of it, we have a damaged aircraft carrier here, and an air battle just breaking up. We've lost a lot of planes."

"It's not just a quote," Bird Dog said, refusing to back down, refusing to be sidetracked even by the question, *Who got shot down?* This was too important, for all of them. "It's a strategy."

" 'Feign disorder' is a strategy? We don't have to *feign* that!"

Bird Dog glanced around at the carefully-turned-away faces on the bridge. "Could we continue this discussion in your conference room, sir?"

"What for? As far as I can see, there's nothing to discuss."

"Beg to differ. In fact, we ought to convene the whole group, plus one."

"And who might that be?"

"Dr. Alonzo George."

1555 local (−8 GMT)
Headquarters, PLA Air Force
Hong Kong Garrison

"Matthew," McIntyre said. His face was pale. Then it grew serene, and he leaned back in his chair. The room was a study of some kind, furnished like an old English den in dark paneling and ornate furniture. Lots of books. A computer console on the desk.

Without even looking at the rifle, he shook his head and smiled. "Good work. You truly are your father's son."

"And my uncle's nephew." Tombstone moved farther into the room. "Speaking of my uncle, I don't think he'd approve of what you're doing."

"So you've figured it out, have you?"

"Enough of it. You're behind this whole thing; the attacks on both Chinese and Americans, all of it. You're trying to push America and China into war."

"What exactly gave me away?"

"I spotted the UAVs parked in your little hangar. Then I remembered that McIntyre Engineering components figured heavily in the UAV that attacked me back in Maryland. I

can do simple arithmetic—like two-plus-two. Combine that
with the fact that you're still alive, and it's pretty clear you
must be up to something no good."

"I'm sorry about that incident in Maryland, Matthew. I
truly am."

"Because you tried to kill me, or because you didn't suc-
ceed?"

"In point of fact, *I* didn't try to kill you. One of my as-
sociates did."

"Meaning you weren't actually there. But you ordered the
hit."

"It was a necessary part of a larger plan. If it matters to
you, I was elated when I heard you'd survived . . . even
though I was hoping to lure your *uncle* here to investigate
your death."

"Uncle Thomas was going to be your hostage?"

"No offense, but his rank is higher than yours."

Tombstone shook his head. "How many people have you
got in your pocket?"

"Thousands. Politicians and military personnel on both
sides, at all levels of rank and experience. Ordinary citizens.
Businesspeople."

"Anyone on *Jefferson*?"

"Naturally. More than one, in fact."

"My God."

"You probably won't believe this," McIntyre said, "but
I'm doing all this for my country. The same as you."

"For your country," Tombstone said. "You had dozens of
Americans massacred at sea. Shot others out of the sky in
cold blood. Tried to start a war that will cost hundreds of
thousands of lives if it gets rolling. You're right. I don't
believe you."

"That's because you're taking the short-term view. That's
a common Western failing, in both business and politics, and
it's the one that's getting us beaten. It's necessary to think
long-term, to plan carefully far into the future."

"I still don't understand how you think starting a war with
China is going to benefit the United States."

McIntyre made a face. "You're deliberately missing the

point. It's not about all-out war. It's about fighting, and winning, a *localized* war, with a specific goal: The liberation of Hong Kong."

"Hong Kong *is* part of China, in case you've forgotten."

"But it doesn't *have* to be. Wasn't for most of the past century and a half. And during all that time, no matter what was happening to mainland China, Hong Kong always prospered."

"And still is."

"But it's faltering. The PRC is taking advantage of capitalism in Hong Kong, but that won't last. In the end, they won't be able to keep their hands off. In fact, that's already starting. Bit by bit, the PRC will kill the financial engine of Hong Kong, to the detriment of the rest of the world—including America."

"So what are you saying? You want the United States to conquer Hong Kong and claim it as a possession, the way the British did?"

"Exactly."

"Why not push the British to do it, then?"

"Please. China isn't Argentina. We're talking about the largest military the world has ever known—and it's getting stronger all the time. Hong Kong is a big contributor to that growth, because the PRC uses Hong Kong business to generate billions of dollars, and to get access to otherwise forbidden technology."

"Like UAVs."

"That's another reason I did all this, Matthew. What better way to draw attention to the utility and *inevitability* of combat UAVs than to spring them on the Pentagon in actual battle? How would you like for the Chinese to acquire that technology instead of us?"

"The fact that McIntyre Engineering International happens to be able to build most of the components in a UAV has nothing to do with it?"

"Obviously my company would benefit, monetarily, from American UAV construction. But America would benefit, too, and isn't that what it's all about? Democracy and capitalism working together, hand in hand?"

"Not when it comes to manipulating politics through terrorism, no."

For the first time, McIntyre's face lost its composure. "How can you not *understand*? We're talking about an initial sacrifice of a few thousand people in order to preserve *millions*!"

"Of dollars, or people?"

"Both! My god, Matt, even the PRC realizes the two are connected! If the Chinese aren't stopped *now*, they'll soon have not only the biggest military in the world, but the *best*. The best weapons, the best delivery systems, the best aircraft and ships and radar and sonar. Who will stop them then?"

"So let me get this straight: You're starting a war in order to prevent a war. Is that it?"

"That's exactly it. When it comes right down to it, the PRC will allow America to take control of Hong Kong. They won't dare fight over it too hard, for fear of destroying the very thing they need most."

1600 local (−8 GMT)
Admiral's Conference Room
USS Jefferson

"That's the craziest idea I've ever heard," Coyote said. There was a bandage on his forehead where he'd been cut by flying glass.

Before Bird Dog could respond, Batman turned to his right and said, "Dr. George? Do you agree?"

"That the idea is crazy? Depends on your ship. Looks like she took some damage, so . . ."

"*Jefferson* can be made ready."

"Well, then you'll be fine. Might get some kids in the infirmary with bad seasickness before it's over, but other than that you should be fine."

Batman nodded and turned to Lab Rat. "Your thoughts, Commander?"

"I think it's just harebrained enough to work."

"Then let's get started. COS, notify the fighters in the air what to do. I'm going to address the crew."

1602 local (−8 GMT)
Tomcat 306

"Unbelievable," came the mutter over ICS. "They want us to fly *through* the hurricane?"

"People do it all the time," Hot Rock said, watching his radar, carefully maintaining the interval with the other fighters of the air wing. Nineteen had survived the Chinese assault—better than half. Considering the original odds, that was remarkably fine. So far, all but two had even managed to get a drink from the Texaco. "Stormchasers, they're called. The trick is to fly with the wind, like we're doing now. It's a little rocky, but nothing we can't handle. And this is a typhoon, by the way. Not a hurricane."

"When did you get so smart?"

"When I stopped listening to you."

1615 local (−8 GMT)
Bridge
USS Jefferson

"More smoke," Bird Dog said. "More fire. We have to make this look real convincing."

Ten decks below them, flight deck crews were tending burning fifty-gallons drums. A little AVGAS, a bunch of plastics they'd been retaining on board—and finally, something useful from the tedious environmental recycling programs!—and a few flares were all it took to produce geysers of black, acrid smoke whipping around in the stiff wind.

It looked convincing enough to Batman, watching from the bridge: a dense spiral of black smoke and flame unwinding from *Jefferson*'s stern into the winds of the typhoon. It got torn apart quickly, true, but the stain it left on the storm was still unmistakable. And the flames should be visible for fifty miles in this darkness.

Still, he did as Bird Dog suggested, ordering the addition of more plastics and AVGAS to the bonfire. He hoped the damage control teams were heads-up and ready to go with their hoses, just in case.

"You're sure this isn't going to hurt my flight deck any more than it's already been hurt?" he asked. "Remember, at some point, we've got to get all those aircraft back onboard."

Bird Dog didn't even spare him a glance. "It won't do the non-skid much good, but it won't keep planes from cycling, either, no. I mean, once the deck's repaired. And the wind will clear off the deck fast enough once we douse the fire in the drums."

"Good." Batman turned toward Dr. George. "How long before the typhoon really grabs us? Before we're out of sight from the outside?"

George's eyes were bright. He looked pretty happy. "Oh, we're right on the edge of the outer wall right now. It should have us in no more than ten, fifteen minutes. But Admiral, don't you think you're taking a chance by not turning head-on into the wind? I realize this ship is no pushover, but you're talking about a 140-knot wind here, remember."

"Our present course is temporary," Batman said. "We'll turn as soon as we're out of sight of the Chinese. I want them to think we're really hurting."

George's eyes twinkled. "All right!"

Batman turned to the helmsman. "Steady as you go."

"Aye, sir," the helmsman said. His face looked greenish in the sickly light. Or maybe it wasn't the light.

1620 local (−8 GMT)
Flanker 67

"It's true," Tai Ling said over the radio. He had been asked to verify the reports made by various other sources, including land-based radar. He hated flying this low, just above the waves, but he had to get under the weather to see at all. And for once, the view was worth the risk. "The carrier's on fire. Looks severe. And the typhoon is catching up with it. Coming right around it. . . ."

1622 local (−8 GMT)
USS Jefferson

Gray-black.

It was as if *Jefferson* had sunk, and was now sailing through some underwater realm. And fighting it. Corkscrewing, thundering, shaking through dark depths.

Most of the windows on the bridge were simply obscured with rain. The water struck the glass like something solid, with a deafening roar. More than once, Batman had the irrational, but overpowering, feeling that a giant sea, a *tsunami*, had smashed directly into the bridge. Every now and then there would be an inexplicable gap in the rain, and Batman would see a world of horizontal strips of gray hurtling like comets through utter blackness.

He'd gotten a report that the anemometer—the wind-speed measuring device—had pegged at two hundred miles per hour.

And they hadn't even reached the eyewall yet. The part of the storm Dr. George described as "the heart of the typhoon."

Batman knew that people were watching him, glancing at him. He kept his expression calm but alert. Forced himself not to cringe when a fresh barrage of wind-powered rain crashed into the windows. To keep his knees loose and relaxed when *Jefferson* yawed like a tiny skiff in a squall.

What the hell had he agreed to here? What had he gotten them into?

1624 local (−8 GMT)
Headquarters, PLA Air Force
Hong Kong Garrison

Chin grinned. "And the other ships in the group?"

"They're converging into a tighter formation and moving northeast, Major General," the aide told him as he brought in the latest reports. "It appears they're intending to circle around the typhoon."

Chin nodded. "Their plan is obvious: to meet the carrier on the back side of the storm—assuming it makes it that far. We'll be ready for them."

"But shouldn't we attack the escort ships *now*, before they regroup with the carrier?"

"Before the carrier reappears, yes. But not yet. This is working to our advantage after all. Let the storm do some work for us first. Let it batter the ships and tire their crews. Meanwhile, our men will rest. Only when the time is right will we strike—and when the carrier finally reappears, there will be no escort ships left to protect it.

"Then"—He popped a closed fist against his open palm— "then, we finish the job."

1625 local (−8 GMT)
McIntyre Estate
Hong Kong SAR

"So what are you planning to do with me, Matthew?" McIntyre asked. "Shoot me?"

Tombstone shook his head. "Have my partner place a shore-to-ship telephone call. Get us a little help out here."

"What kind of help?"

"A SEAL team. With explosives."

He watched McIntyre's face tighten, but felt no pleasure in it. He'd grown up loving this man like a father.

"But first," Tombstone went on, "*you're* going to make a

little call. Whoever's responsible for prepping and launching all those UAVs, you're going to call him and tell him to forget the launch."

He saw the color fade from McIntyre's handsome face. "I can't—"

"Sure you can. There's the phone right there on your desk. Just dial and talk.

"You look nervous, Uncle," Tombstone said, leaning back in the comfortable chair. "Sun's about to come up. Hope you aren't a vampire or something."

"I'm fine," McIntyre said, but glanced toward the phone.

"What's the matter?" Tombstone demanded. "Need reassurance about current events? Need to let someone know to launch the UAVs? What?"

"Nothing, nothing. . . ."

"Good. Then you won't mind devoting your attention to a little plan of mine."

"Plan?"

"Oh, you'll love it. And it will only cost you nine-tenths of your personal fortune."

1626 local (−8 GMT)
TFCC
USS Jefferson

"Batman?"

Batman's jaw dropped. Even over the static online, Tombstone's voice was recognizable. "Are you okay, Stony?"

"Depends on what you mean by fine, because that's exactly what I wanted to talk to you about. Any chance you've got a spare SEAL team around?"

"You bet. I don't know if you've checked the weather lately, but they're sure not out on the deck doing calisthenics." *Not that there's much deck there.* Batman refrained from mentioning any of the other disasters Jefferson was facing.

"I could use them right now. I need a lift home for me and a friend."

"A friend?" Batman felt the beginning of a smile start across his face. If Stony meant what he thought he meant, then that was the only piece of decent news Batman had heard in the last couple of days.

"Yeah. Pilot by the name of Lobo needs a lift, too."

Hot damn! Lobo was alive. "Hold on, Stony. Where are you?"

As Tombstone started filling him in, Batman began issuing his own set of orders. A few moments later, the commander of the SEAL team, Lieutenant Commander Brandon Sykes, was standing tall in front of him. "Hold on, Tombstone. I'm going to put you on the speakerphone."

After listening for a few moments, the SEAL officer started nodding. "Yes, sir. No problem with that. Easy to do. See you in about an hour."

After Batman punched the telephone off, he turned back to the SEAL officer. "I assume you know what the weather's like. It's not going to be pretty."

The SEAL officer regarded him with the grim smile. "It never is, sir. I figure we go in, extract our two people, then do some damage to McIntyre's facility. Getting back's going to be the problem—we may have to find somewhere to lay low until this blows over."

Batman nodded. "I can find a helo to get you in, but it's going to be risky."

"You get us anywhere near the coast, and we'll make it."

1628 local (−8 GMT)
McIntyre Estate
Hong Kong SAR

Tombstone replaced the receiver, never taking his eyes off McIntyre. "You mind serving as my hostage for about an hour, Uncle Philip? No, I don't think you do. After all, we're like family, aren't we?"

"Tombstone, as I told you, I never meant to—"

Tombstone crossed the room in three strides. "Never meant what, Uncle Philip?" He grabbed McIntyre by the hair and yanked him up. "Come on. I've got to collect the rest of my team, and you're going to make sure that everything goes smoothly."

"Like you said, we're family." McIntyre's voice was finally taking on an edge of fear. "For the sake of your father, your uncle—Tombstone, don't do this. There's a place for you in my organization. Have you ever wanted to be rich? Rich beyond your wildest dreams? I can make that happen, Stony. You know I can."

Tombstone's grip on McIntyre's hair tightened. "I'm already richer than you'll ever be, Uncle Philip. My wife, my friends, my career—there's nothing you can offer me."

"I could give you command of your own private squadron," McIntyre said persuasively. "Think of it, Stony. What future have you got left in the Navy now? A series of desk jobs, that's all. Join me, and you'll command the most advanced fighting aircraft in the world. And fly every day if you want. I'll even get that Pitts shipped over here if you want."

Tombstone pulled him close and locked his forearm across McIntyre's windpipe. He squeezed until he felt the men start to sag against him. "I've already got my own squadron, asshole. It's called the United States Navy."

Flight deck, USS **Jefferson**

Sykes fought his way across the flight deck to the CH-46 helicopter waiting there. While he had managed to sound fairly confident in Admiral Wayne's office, he was now beginning to realize the true insanity of his plan.

Take off in this weather? What was I thinking? There's no way, not a chance in hell.

"Sir? If you'll get your men on board, we'll get going."

Sykes stared in awe at the cool, confident pilot who turned around to look at him.

"You really think you can do this?" Sikes asked, choking slightly as the wind drove rain down his throat.

The pilot shrugged. "Only one way to find out, isn't there? Now if you and the rest of the gentleman will strap in, we'll find out."

Ten minutes later, Sykes, along with most of his crew, was puking violently. They were airborne—at least he thought they were. They weren't in the water at least. But it would be hard to characterized the wildy gyrating motion of the helicopter as controlled flight.

"Sir? You see anything that looks familiar?" The pilot's voice came over the ICS. "Because according to the GPS, we're there."

Sykes unstrapped, dropped to his hands and knees, and crawled forward to the cockpit. Bracing himself between the two seats, he rose unsteadily to his feet. "There," he managed to say, before another wave of nausea swept over him. "That clearing spot."

The pilot nodded agreement. "That's what I thought. Strap back in, sir. This might be a little rough."

Rough. Just before he threw up again, Sykes wondered how the helo pilot would have characterized the last ten minutes.

USS **Jefferson**

Batman watched as the helicopter pitched violently, then let the wind sweep it away from the flight deck. Up foward, Tomcats and Hornets were already turning, but the normal noise and vibration associated with flight ops was completely indistinguishable from the sound and fury of the storm.

"I hope to God that pilot knows what he's doing," Batman muttered to himself. "Hang on, Stony. We're coming for you."

McIntyre's Compound

The walls around the compound blocked the wind only slightly. The helo smacked down onto ground so hard it felt like a fixed wing aircraft trapping on the deck of the carrier. The SEALs were thrown violently forward against their restraining harnesses. The wind caught the tail of the helicopter and spun it in a circle.

Before the last motion dampened out, Sykes was up and moving, his men crowding up behind him. They were green, stumbling slightly, but as they'd all learned during BUDS training, the mind could overcome almost any perceived physical limitation. The last time he remembered feeling like this was during hell week.

"Come on," Sykes said, pleased to note that his voice sounded almost steady. "We've got a job to do."

Sykes led the charge into the mansion, as his men fanned out to secure his ingress route. As soon as they saw him, Tombstone and a female pilot with ragged shorn hair stepped out to meet them.

"Good to see you," the admiral said, his voice flat. "Now let's get the hell out of here."

Sykes whispered into his microphone, recalling the rest of his men. Within seconds, they had formed up again.

"Admiral? I'm not sure we can make it back to the carrier," Sykes said. "This place is relatively defensible—maybe we should hole up and wait for the weather to pass."

The admiral fixed him with a steely glare. "You got in—we can get out." He took the other officer by the elbow, his grip surprisingly light. "What about it, Lobo?"

The other pilot was shivering violently. "Let me talk to that helo jockey. If he won't fly us out of here, I will."

They ran back out to the helo, fighting the wind and the rain, and Sykes was almost glad to be back inside the metal fuselage. At least it was dry. "The admiral would like to return to the carrier," he said formally.

The pilot nodded. "Why not? Can't be any worse than the ride in, now, can it?"

Five minutes later, Sykes knew the pilot had lied. The

noise from the explosion that destroyed the McIntyre compound was lost in the storm.

1650 local (−8 GMT)
Bridge
USS Jefferson

"Yep, this is it," Dr. George said. "Welcome to the eye of the storm."

Batman stared in awe through the starboard windows. The ship was still very unsteady under his feet, plunging and twisting through seas that rose as high as the flight deck on all sides; but the seas were noticeably less regular and aligned than they had been before. Their shape and direction was now chaotic and aimless, so that in some places several seas converged into a single mountainous one; while in another location they canceled one another out, creating a smooth flat area that soon heaved up again.

Everything else in the outside world had changed, too. The eyewall of the typhoon was a black wall shot through with the silvery filigree of disintegrating mist; it curved out of sight to either side, vanishing into gray-white haze. Straight up, it curved in overhead to form an open-topped dome. Sunlight fell through the hole. Alien sunlight, warm and gauzy and surreal, strained through a high layer of haze.

And high up in that haze, circling fighters. The Vipers, running on fumes, waiting in the eye of the storm.

"This is really weird," someone said.

Batman clutched his concentration back to himself and turned to Coyote. "Get crews to work on that flight deck," he said. "Now. We have to have at least one cat operational in time to get our birds into the air before this storm runs us ashore. Is that understood?"

"Aye aye, sir." Coyote wheeled away.

Dr. George was still staring out the window, face enraptured. "I've never seen the eye from this angle before," he said. He pointed toward the sun. "I'm always up there, in a storm-chaser."

"I wish that's where I was right now," Batman said with feeling.

1633 local (−8 GMT)
Flanker 67

Tai Ling was tired of circling around in the brutal conditions. Although the forward half of the typhoon had crashed ashore hours ago, to begin the process of its own disintegration, the rear wall remained intact, the air behind it as viciously windy and rough as always. But in this vicinity was where the American fleet had gathered to await the—possible—emergence of its flagship, the carrier *Jefferson*; so here the massed squadrons of PLA fighters and attack aircraft would also wait. The majority of the fighters were staying high, of course, completely out of sight of the ships below. Low-flying spotter planes would alert the squadron when the carrier finally limped out of the—

Tai started as his radar-lock alarm went off. His screen, fogged as it was with false images, abruptly showed several clear blips. Then more and more. Instantly Tai registered the signatures of SM-1 missiles, SAMs carried on American guided missile destroyers and frigates.

Tai and the rest of the squadron pilots went into defensive mode, dumping radar-confusion chaff and flying erratic routes. The usual techniques, but far more effective than usual in these weather conditions, where radar images were already degraded by air temperature gradations and electrical activity.

Not one missile found a victim. Tai watched the one intended for him hurtle past, a fast-moving yellow blur in the clouds.

"Regroup and start down," he said over the radio. "I guess we can assume the carrier is about to show up." His heart pounded with expectation. To think, he was about to contribute to the first sinking of an American aircraft carrier since the end of the Second World War. A proud day indeed. The first day of a new era in the South China Sea.

The massed squadrons found one another again in the clouds, and began to move downward through the layers of cloud and rain. Tai had to fight to keep from staring through the canopy, watching for the American battle group to reappear.

His alarm went off again. He searched his radar screen. Nothing but trash images, and the stronger blips of his nearest squadron partners. Then—

Out of the darkness and rain-battered air, a Tomcat thundered past him in afterburner. Tai jerked hard to the left by reflex, turning his tail to the Tomcat's jet wash. The storm caught his wing, started to flip him into a barrel roll before he corrected.

Tomcats! How the hell—? He realized they were trapped an instant before his missile lock alarm went off again.

1638 local (+8 GMT)
TFCC
USS Jefferson

Batman leaned forward in his leatherette chair, his hands clamped down on the armrests. "It worked," he breathed, hardly daring to say the words out loud for fear of jinxing the entire evolution. "Of all the damned foolish ballsy plans that ever stood a snowball's chance in hell of working—dear God, it worked."

The predatory cries of American pilots ravaging the gaggle of Chinese fighters rang out over tactical. Fox calls, target calls, the occasional frantic plea for a wingman, it all blended into the cacophony of combat. The same words, the same phrases that Batman had heard too many times before in too many parts of the world. He closed his eyes and followed the progress of the battle, picturing the manuevering, the tail chases that ended in perfect firing position, the hard terror that flashed through a pilot as he saw the impossibly bright fire of a missile careening toward him—it flooded him, the sense that he was airborne with them, fighting the war again as a pilot instead of a chair-bound admiral. He heard the exultant splash calls, the constant sequence of American voices, no fighter voice disappearing from the babble without warning, and knew it was coming.

"Admiral?"

Batman opened his eyes and saw the TAO staring at him. A grin started across Batman's face. "Tell them, permission denied."

Just then, the call came across tactical. "Homeplate, this is Viper lead. We got four left—looks like they're turning tail and heading back to the mainland. Request permission to follow them inside the twelve-mile limit and finish this off."

Batman heard the hot blood of battle singing in the pilot's voice. He looked over at the TAO, who was just starting to frame the obvious question.

"Because I've been there before. You heard me. Call them back," Batman said.

TWELVE

Friday, 8 August

1930 local (−8 GMT)
Hanger bay

Jackson would be almost relieved when night arrived. At least he couldn't see the ocean sweeping past the open doors. The seas just kept getting taller; now, the biggest ones completely blocked the doorway as they rushed past. You could hear them hissing, too; avalanches of water.

On the other hand, darkness did not bring rest, at least not for long. Except for brief breaks, everyone kept going, doing what needed to be done. Lots of welding up above, where the missile had come through the side and whalloped the overhead. This was a life-and-death matter, and they all knew it.

Finally, after the majority of the heaviest moving and cleaning was finished, Jackson headed for the plane now assigned to Bird Dog, to see if anything had happened to it. To make *absolutely* sure that nothing he was responsible for was wrong with it.

He was halfway across the bay, waiting for two men to cross in front of him bearing a section of fractured catwalk, when he saw Orell Blessing stroll out from under the wing of Bird Dog's plane. Orell glanced both ways, but casually, as if expecting to find a friend, then meandered off toward his parked tractor. He appeared to be whistling. He hadn't seen Jackson.

Jackson stood where he was for a long minute, thinking. Then he headed toward the plane.

"What exactly are you saying?" Beaman asked. He was standing near the disassembled tail wing of an F-14 that had been damaged by falling metal.

"I'm saying I didn't mess up Bird Dog's plane, or anybody else's," Franklin said in a low voice. "I'm saying Orell Blessing did it. And I can prove it."

Beaman tapped the heavy wrench against his palm. "Now, why would Orell Blessing want to sabotage Bird Dog's plane?"

"I don't know. I'm just saying I can prove it."

"How?"

"Well, just a little while ago I saw him walking away from Bird Dog's new plane. So I went over and started checking it out. Hydraulic lines on the nose gear strut had been cut. First time you put some extra pressure on it—like in a landing—and *pop*."

Beaman was looking grim now. "Nobody screws with my plane, Franklin, so you can bet your ass I'll check this out. But what you say still doesn't prove *Orell* did anything. Nothing personal, Franklin, but how do I know *you* didn't do it just so you could put the blame on someone else?"

Franklin clenched his jaw. It wasn't a completely unfair question. " 'Cause like I said, I can prove it."

"And like *I* said—how?"

"Well, I already set it up. I made sure Orell saw me checkin' out the plane, and replacing that cut hydraulic line. I didn't let on I was thinking anything suspicious. So Orell will think he needs to cut that line again. And that's when you can catch him."

2145 local (−8 GMT)
Flight Deck
USS Jefferson

Beaman stepped out onto the hangar deck and almost fell over. The wind was simply unbelievable, a solid hand pushing him toward the bow of the carrier. And the rain—although he was wearing a complete slicker outfit, the water somehow slashed him to the skin, even blowing up under the pant legs. He felt like he was breathing underwater.

But he wasn't alone up here. Other men were moving around, clinging to lifelines and carrying flashlights and tool boxes. Defying death to keep the carrier intact. True heros, as far as Beaman was concerned.

He moved carefully across the nonskid, his body pressed down in what resembled a wrestler's posture. A nice, stable position. Slipped past the island to the area where several planes were being stored on deck, their fuselages bobbing to the hammering blows of the wind.

And he saw a small, blurred glow bobbing around the deck at waist level.

Flashlight. Nothing wrong with that, not when we're not in the middle of flight ops. During flight operations, the personnel directing the movement of aircraft on the deck carried lighted wands, and all other extraneous sources of light were verboten.

Still, Beaman felt a rill of vindication run through him. This weather, no one was supposed to be out on the flight deck alone. No one. Beaman pointedly ignored the fact that he was on the flight deck alone in violation of all standing orders. What the air boss would do to him if he caught Beaman—just one more possibility to be ignored.

A single flashlight bobbing around, that meant one man. One man meant trouble.

Just like I do.

Beaman watched the light flick out. He waited, certainty chasing the cold chill out of his bones. Another brief flick of light.

Forward refueling station. He knows the deck, but not well enough to be certain. Doesn't want the light on all the time, not in case someone's watching. Beaman's own flashlight was clenched in his hand, his forefinger resting on the push switch.

If it's him, he's almost here. Beaman traced out the man's movements in his mind, running the time and distance problem as accurately as any RIO ever did in the backseat of a Tomcat. *Just about now—wait for him to touch it—*

There. The whiney scrap of an avionics compartment hinge resisting opening.

Beaman darted forward, grabbed the dark figure poised next to his bird, and thumbed the flashlight on. The other man howled, jerked back, and started to run. As he turned, his foot caught in the loop of an extra tie-down chain that encircled the aircraft. The man stumbled, went down on one knee, and Beaman tackled him.

"I knew it was you. I knew it." Beaman slammed Orell Blessing in the side of his face with the flashlight. "You trying to kill people—you trying to kill our people! In *my bird.*"

"No, I wasn't—I wasn't doing anything," Blessing howled, his voice pulled out of his throat by the gale force winds. "Nothing."

"Right. What's those wire snips doing in your hand, then?"

Blessing stared down at the tool he held as though the hand belonged to a stranger. "Maybe a lot of things," he said, confidence seeping back into his voice. "You got some ideas, but you can't prove a damned thing."

Beaman dragged him to his feet and punched Blessing in the gut. He lofted the other sailor, now groggy, over his shoulder and walked the ten steps to the side of the ship. He flung Blessing down on the nonskid then shoved the other man forward until he was hanging·over the end of the flight deck. Beaman kept a firm grip on Blessing's ankles. "Tell me the truth. You tell me now—or else." By way of illustrating "or else," Beaman loosened his grip on Blessing's ankles for a moment. The wind tore at the prone sailor, pulling him further out over the sea.

Blessing howled. "Oh god pull me up pull me up pull me up oh god you can't—"

Beaman cut him off. "Tell me."

"He had it coming, I was just going to—nobody was supposed to die. Slow them up, that's all he said. I was just supposed to—" The wind surged again, drowning out the babbled confession.

Beaman stared down at the chaotic ocean, surging and pounding against the side of the ship. He knew what would happen next. Captain's Mast, followed by referral to a courts-martial. Blessing would be transferred ashore for it, get some fancy lawyer. Get some brig time, maybe. All those excuses about how he was an abused child, how he hadn't really meant to kill anyone—reality at a trial was far different that the reality that every man and woman faced on the flight deck every day.

Reality was dead pilots. Reality was the wind and the sea and the typhoon and aircraft getting shot down and ordnance on the wings. Reality was paying for mistakes.

Beaman turned loose of Blessing's ankles, giving God one last chance to intervene. "You can get up now."

Blessing started to scuttled back onto the nonskid, hunching his back to draw his head back from the sea. His hands flailed, searching for something to hold on to. The fingers of his right hand grazed the rain-slick edge of the flight deck, tried to clamp down around it as Blessing reared back.

The wind gusted again, catching his exposed torso like a sail. Blessing howled, surged momentarily upright and off balance, then cartwheeled out and away from the flight deck.

Beaman watched him go, counted to ten, then turned on his flashlight and ran like hell to the Handler's office located just inside the island. He burst into it and shouted, "Saw a light in the water. MAN OVERBOARD."

The search was called off after an hour, fifty-five minutes longer than anyone figured a person could survive in the typhoon-lashed waters.

2200 local (−8 GMT)
Sick Bay
USS Jefferson

Bird Dog paced in the passageway outside of Sick Bay, fighting down the fear surging through him. Okay, maybe not fear. He was a fighter pilot, after all, one with well over a hundred traps onboard the carrier. Maybe half of those at night. A combat veteran—hell, he had the medals to prove it.

So what was the big deal about talking to Lobo? Just stopping by, one pilot to another, to make sure she was okay. No big deal. Happened all the time. Had nothing to do with direct and indirect battles, none of that crap. Just a straight-out friendly professional courtesy call that he'd—

Crap, it wasn't working. The thought of seeing her again was worse than fighting off G-force gray out, worse than tanking at night in the middle of a storm. Worse than facing down the Chinese again, worse than—

Wait a minute. Good ol' Sun had bailed him out before—maybe it'd work with the chicks, too.

Indirect. That'd done it with the carrier. He paced for a moment longer, puzzling out his approach. Dangerous ground, indirect—finally, he had it. He pushed open the door and stepped into sick bay.

Lobo was curled up on her side in a hospital bed facing away from him. The rails on the sides of the bed were up. A thin cotton bedspread in hospital dingy white was pulled up to her neck. He could see the outline of her body underneath it and saw the shallow, regular breathing change as she came out of a light doze. She twisted slightly, groaned, then shoved herself up into a sitting position.

"Hey," Bird Dog said. He looked around for a chair. Some ancient prohibition against sitting on the side of a hospital bed rattled around in his mind, momentarily displacing his well-thought-out indirect approach. "Hey," he started again.

Lobo's eyes blazed brilliantly in her pale face. Traces of grime clung to one edge of her jaw and her hair was a tattered, spiky mess. She tried to speak but started coughing.

Bird Dog glanced around helplessly and started to leave to get a doctor. This coughing—hell, she wasn't going to die, was she?

In between spasms, Lobo managed to point at the pitcher of water by her bed. When Bird Dog didn't move, she fixed him with a steely glare. Bird Dog almost knocked the pitcher over scrambling for it.

Finally, he managed to get a glass of water poured into a plastic cup. He handed it to her, then kept his hand over hers to still the trembling in her fingers.

Lobo sipped slowly, grimacing as each mouthful slid down. Finally, when she'd finished half of the water, she moved their hands over the table and loosened her grip on the cup.

"You'd make a rotten RIO," she said, her voice hoarse and slightly slurred. "Can't even figure out refueling."

"I see too good to be a RIO," Bird Dog said.

"Yeah, well. Sometime seeing's not enough, you know?" She laid back against the pillows. "So'd you just stop by to gloat? You want to know if they did it to me again?"

"Christ, no, I just—" Suddenly, his indirect plan was in shambles. How the hell could you sneak up on someone who was always on the attack? She never slowed down enough to be lured into the quiet, sincere discussion he'd had planned, to listen to the few lines of poetry he'd dredged up from ancient English classes.

"I love you," he said finally. "I came down to see you."

Lobo stared at him, the shock deepening her pallor. "This would never work," she said finally. She started shaking her head, winced as some new pain made itself known. "Never in a million years—pilots don't get involved with pilots."

"Pilot this." He leaned over and poised his lips above hers. "Just once." He moved in slowly, feeling the fear turn into anticipation. Their lips met. Electricity arced between them, fusing their flesh together. For long moments, neither pulled away.

Lobo finally gasped and pulled back. Bird Dog blinked, opened his eyes, and found her hands wrapped around the back of his neck.

"Not fair," she said. "What the hell's gotten into you?"

Bird Dog felt a lazy smile of sheer joy spreading across his face. "Let me tell you what my old friend Sunny would say about this."

THIRTEEN
Friday, 8 August

Ambassador T'ing sprinkled a tiny amount of sugar across the surface of the tea, then watched contemplatively as it sank below the surface. Sarah Wexler decided he must be tracking each atom, timing the exact moment at which it either dissolved completely or sank to the bottom of the cup. She found herself staring, wondering if she would ever be able to understand how T'ing saw a cup of tea.

Or, for that matter, how he saw the currents of power and interest that flowed so chaotically between his country and hers. Was there any possibility that America could truly understand China? Or, for that matter, that China could understand the U.S.?

"As I said—a serious misunderstanding," T'ing said finally.

Wexler snorted. "A lot of people dead over a misunderstanding."

T'ing gave her a reproachful look. "Serious, I said. As I've said before, Sarah, you must learn to pay attention to the nuances involved."

Sarah? Now just when did we get on a first name basis? Over the last several years, she thought she'd come to a better understanding of both T'ing and his masters at home than she'd had during the Spratly Islands conflict. She'd even understood what he'd meant when he'd said it was a "serious misunderstanding." In such circumlocutions are the deals of diplomacy often worked, and she fancied herself more than a little familiar with what China was likely to do in a given situation.

False pride, she'd learned over the last several weeks. Thinking she understood them—it wasn't a mistake she'd make again. She wondered if T'ing had the same misgivings, dealing with her.

And now first names. A mark of respect? A peace gesture? Or simply a reminder that much of her relationship with him would be wrapped in inscrutable layers of meanings?

She saw quiet amusement in his eyes, and realized that he'd achieved whatever he'd expected to by using her first name, perhaps no more than to throw her temporarily off balance.

Then another possibility occurred to her. Perhaps it was more in the line of a compliment—not using the name alone, but using it and acknowledging that she would take note that he'd done so.

Yes, that was it. She lifted her chin slightly, then gave the smallest of nods. T'ing returned it.

"And one that will end well," he continued. "Out of the storm comes cleansing. Those unreliable elements in our Special Administrative Region have been pruned, the balance of the people's government resolved." He lifted his spoon carefully from the paper-thin cup and laid it on the small saucer to his side. He raised the cup, inclined it slightly toward her. "To a deepening spirit of harmony and cooperation between us, madam."

"And between our nations, Su," she said, slipping his first name into the conversation as though she'd been using it forever.

"And that will appear likely as well." T'ing took a small, appreciative sip of his tea. "Your Mr. McIntyre—we are pleased that he has been restored to you. Such a terrible thing, to be kidnapped by gangsters." He sighed.

"Indeed." Wexler tried to keep the doubt out of her voice. Phillip McIntyre's story agreed far too closely with China's official party line for her taste. Kidnapped—she watched two grains of sugar collide in her own cup before continuing. "Perhaps some day we will round up the rest of the perpetrators."

"Perhaps." T'ing glanced up at her, his eyes narrowing slightly. "For McIntyre to pledge so much of his fortune in humanitarian aid for Hong Kong—well, we are humbly pleased. Repairing the damage from the typhoon will take decades."

"Indeed." Wexler sensed another layer of meaning behind that statement as well, and filed it away for later examination. The orange blossom scent of the tea was relaxing her.

"And we've all learned a valuable lesson, have we not?" T'ing continued, his voice markedly more hearty. "Particularly on how to welcome back parts of our country as they return to the fold."

"What do you mean?" Wexler said, then immediately regretted the question. With T'ing, one did not ask outright. She saw the faint disappointment in his eyes.

"Nothing specifically," he said. "I was speaking in general terms." His eyes held hers across the cup. "Of opportunities."

Taiwan. A cold shot of adrenaline flooded her system. *He's warning me—Taiwan.*

"As you said, opportunities," she answered. "Opportunities to avoid more 'serious misunderstandings', perhaps?"

T'ing looked at her with new respect. "Perhaps."

GLOSSARY

0-3 level The third deck above the main deck. Designations for decks above the main deck (also known as the damage control deck) begin with zero, e.g. O-3. The zero is pronounced as "oh" in conversation. Decks below the main deck do not have the initial zero, and are numbered down from the main deck, e.g. deck 11 is below deck 3. Deck 07 is above deck 03.

1MC: The general announcing system on a ship or submarine. Every ship has many different interior communications systems, most of them linking parts of the ship for a specific purpose. Most operate off sound-powered phones. The circuit designators consist of a number followed by two letters that indicate the specific purpose of the circuit. 2AS, for instance, might be an antisubmarine warfare circuit that connects the sonar supervisor, the USW watch officer, and the sailor at the torpedo launched.

Air Boss: A senior commander or captain assigned to the aircraft carrier, in charge of flight operations. The "boss" is assisted by the mini-boss in Pri-Fly, located in the tower onboard the carrier. The air boss is always in the tower during flight operations, overseeing the launch and recovery cycles, declaring a green deck, and monitoring the safe approach of aircraft to the carrier.

Air Wing: Composed of the aircraft squadrons assigned to the battle group. The individual squadron commanding officers report to the air wing commander, who reports to the admiral.

airdale: Slang for an officer or enlisted person in the aviation fields. Includes pilots, NFOs, aviation intelligence officers and maintenance officer and the enlisted technicians who support aviation. The antithesis of an airdale is a "shoe."

Akula: Late-model Russian-built attack nuclear submarine, an SSN. Fast, deadly, and deep diving.

ALR-67: Detects, analyzes and evaluates electromagnetic signals, emits a warning signal if the parameters are compatible with an immediate threat to the aircraft, e.g. seeker head on an anti-air missile. Can also detect an enemy radar in either a search or a targeting mode.

altitude: Is safety. With enough airspace under the wings, a pilot can solve any problem.

AMRAAM: Advanced Medium Range Anti Air Missile.

angels: Thousands of feet over ground. Angels twenty is 20,000 feet. Cherubs indicates hundreds of feet, e.g. cherubs five = five hundred feet.

ASW: Antisubmarine Warfare, recently renamed Undersea Warfare. For some reason.

avionics: Black boxes and systems that comprise an aircraft's combat systems.

AW: Aviation antisubmarine warfare technician, the enlisted specialist flying in an S-3, P-3 or helo USW aircraft. As this book goes to press, there is discussion of renaming the specialty.

AWACS: An aircraft entirely too good for the Air Force, the Advanced Warning Aviation Control System. Long-range command and control and electronic intercept bird with superb capabilities.

AWG-9: Pronounced "awg nine," the primary search and fire control radar on a Tomcat.

backseater: Also known as the GIB, the guy in back. Non-pilot aviator available in several flavors: BN (bombardier/navigator), RIO (radar intercept operator), and TACCO (Tactical Control Officer) among others. Usually wear glasses and are smart.

Bear: Russian maritime patrol aircraft, the equivalent in rough terms of a US P-3. Variants have primary missions in command and control, submarine hunting, and electronic intercepts. Big, slow, good targets.

bitch box: One interior communications system on a ship. So named because it's normally used to bitch at another watch station.

blue on blue: Fratricide. US forces are normally indicated in blue on tactical displays, and this terms refers to an attack on a friendly by another friendly.

blue water Navy: Outside the unrefueled range of the air wing. When a carrier enters blue water ops, aircraft must get on board, e.g. land, and cannot divert to land if the pilot gets the shakes.

boomer: Slang for a ballistic missile submarine.

BOQ: Bachelor Officer Quarters—a Motel Six for single officers or those traveling without family. The Air Force also has VOQ, Visiting Officer Quarters.

buster: As fast as you can, i.e. bust yer ass getting here.

CAG: Carrier Air Group Commander, normally a senior Navy Captain aviator. Technically, an obsolete term, since the air wing rather than an air group is now deployed on the carrier. However, everyone thought CAW sounded stupid, so CAG was retained as slang for the Carrier Air Wing Commander.

CAP: Combat Air Patrol, a mission executed by fighters to protect the carrier and battle group from enemy air and missiles.

Carrier Battle Group: A combination of ships, air wing, and submarines assigned under the command of a one-star admiral.

Carrier Battle Group 14: The battle group normally embarked on Jefferson.

CBG: *See* Carrier Battle Group.

CDC: Combat Direction Center—modernly, replaced CIC, or Combat Information Center, as the heart of a ship. All sensor information is fed into CDC and the battle is coordinated by a tactical action officer on watch there.

CG: Abbreviation for a cruiser

Chief: The backbone of the navy. E-7, 8, and 9 enlisted

paygrades, known as chief, senior chief, and master chief. The transition from petty officer ranks to the chief's mess is a major event in a sailor's career. Onboard ship, the chiefs have separate eating and berthing facilities. Chiefs wear khakis, as opposed to dungarees for the less senior enlisted ratings.

Chief of Staff: Not to be confused with a chief, the COS in a battle group staff is normally a senior navy captain who acts as the admiral's XO and deputy.

CIA: Christians in Action. The civilian agency charged with intelligence operations outside the continental United States.

CIWS: Close In Weapons System, pronounced "see-whiz." Gattling gun with built-in radar that tracks and fires on inbound missiles. If you have to use it, you're dead.

COD: *See* C-2 Greyhound.

collar count: Traditional method of determining the winner of a disagreement. A survey is taken of the opponents' collar devices. The senior person wins. Always.

Commodore: Formerly the junior-most admiral rank, now used to designate a senior navy captain in charge of a bunch of like units. A destroyer commodore commands several destroyers, a sea control commodore the S-3 squadrons on that coast. Contrast with CAG, who owns a number of dissimilar units, e.g. a couple of Tomcat squadrons, some Hornets, and some E-2s and helos.

compartment: Navy talk for a room on a ship.

Condition Two: One step down from General Quarters, which is Condition One. Condition Five is tied up at the pier in a friendly country.

crypto: Short for some variation of cryptological, the magic set of codes that makes a circuit impossible for anyone else to understand.

C-2 Greyhound: Also known as the COD, Carrier Onboard Delivery. The COD carries cargo and passengers from shore to ship. It is capable of carrier landings. Sometimes assigned directly to the air wing, it also operates in coordination with CVBGs from a shore squadron.

CV, CVN: Abbreviation for an aircraft carrier, conventional and nuclear.

CVIC: Carrier Intelligence Center. Located down the passageway (the hall) from the flag spaces.

data link, the LINK: The secure circuit that links all units in a battle group or in an area. Targets and contacts are transmitted over the LINK to all ships. The data is processed by the ship designated as Net Control, and common contacts are correlated. The system also transmits data from each ship and aircraft's weapons systems, e.g. a missile firing. All services use the LINK.

desk jockey: Nonflyer, one who drives a computer instead of an aircraft.

DESRON: Destroyer Commander.

DICASS: An active sonobuoy.

dick stepping: Something to be avoided. While anatomically impossible in today's gender-integrated services, in an amazing display of good sense, it has been decided that women do this as well.

DDG: Guided missile destroyer.

Doppler: Acoustic phenomena caused by relative motion between a sound source and a receiver that results in an apparent change in frequency of the sound. The classic example is a train going past and the decrease in pitch of its whistle. When a submarine changes its course or speed in relation to a sonobuoy, the event shows up as a change in the frequency of the sound source.

Double nuts: Zero zero on the tail of an aircraft.

E-2 Hawkeye: Command and control and surveillance aircraft. Turboprop rather than jet, and unarmed. Smaller version of an AWACS, in practical terms, but carrier-based.

ELF: Extremely Low Frequency, a method of communicating with submarines at sea. Signals are transmitted via a miles-long antenna and are the only way of reaching a deep submerged submarine.

Envelope: What you're supposed to fly inside of if you want to take all the fun out of naval aviation.

EWs: Electronic warfare technicians, the enlisted sailors that man the gear that detects, analyzes and displays electro-magnetic signals. Highly classified stuff.

F/A-18 Hornets: The inadequate, fuel-hungry intended replacement for the aging but still kick-your-ass potent Tomcat. Flown by Marines and Navy.

Familygram: Short messages from submarine sailors' families to their deployed sailors. Often the only contact with the outside world that a submarine sailor on deployment has.

FF/FFG: Abbreviation for a fast frigate (no, there aren't slow frigates) and a guided missile fast frigate.

Flag officer: In the navy and coast guard, an admiral. In the other services, a general.

Flag passageway: The portion of the aircraft carrier which houses the admiral's staff working spaces. Includes the flag mess and the admiral's cabin. Normally separated from the rest of the ship by heavy plastic curtains, and designated by blue tile on the deck instead of white.

Flight quarters: A condition set onboard a ship preparing to launch or recover aircraft. All unnecessary person are required to stay inside the skin of the ship and remain clear of the flight deck area.

Flight suit: The highest form of navy couture. The perfect choice of apparel for any occasion—indeed, the only uniform an aviator ought to be required to own.

FOD: Stands for Foreign Object Damage, but the term is used to indicate any loose gear that could cause damage to an aircraft. During flight operations, aircraft generate a tremendous amount of air flowing across the deck. Loose objects—including people and nuts and bolts—can be sucked into the intake and discharged through the outlet from the jet engine. FOD damages the jet's impellers and doesn't do much for the people sucked in, either. FOD walkdown is conducted at least once a day onboard an aircraft carrier. Everyone not otherwise engaged stands shoulder to shoulder on the flight deck and slowly walks from one end of the flight deck to the other, searching for FOD.

Fox: Tactical shorthand for a missile firing. Fox one indicates a heatseeking missile, Fox two an infrared missile, and Fox three a radar guided missile.

GCI: Ground Control Intercept, a procedure used in the Soviet air forces. Primary control for vectoring the aircraft in on enemy targets and other fighters is vested in a guy on the ground, rather than in the cockpit where it belongs.

GIB: *See* backseater.

GMT: Greenwich Mean Time.

green shirts: *See* Shirts.

Handler: Officer located on the flight-deck level responsible for ensuring that aircraft are correctly positioned, "spotted," on the flight deck. Coordinates the movements of aircraft with yellow gear (small tractors that tow aircraft and other related gear) from maintenance areas to catapults and from the flight deck to the hangar bar via the elevators. Speaks frequently with the air boss. *See also* bitch box.

HARMS: Anti-radiation missiles that home in on radar sites.

Homeplate: Tactical call sign for *Jefferson*.

Hot: In reference to a sonobuoy, holding enemy contact.

Huffer: Yellow gear located on the flight deck that generates compressed air to start jet engines. Most Navy aircraft do not need a huffer to start engines, but it can be used in emergencies or for maintenance.

Hunter: Call sign for the S-3 squadron embarked on the *Jefferson*.

ICS: Interior Communications System. The private link between a pilot and a RIO, or the telephone system internal to a ship.

Inchopped: Navy talk for a ship entering a defined area of water, e.g. inchopped the Med.

IR: Infrared, a method of missile homing.

isothermal: A layer of water that has a constant temperature with increasing depth. Located below the thermocline, where increase in depth correlates to decrease in temperature. In the isothermal layer, the primary factor affecting the speed of sound in water is the increase in pressure with depth.

JBD: Jet Blast Deflector. Panels that pop up from the flight deck to block the exhaust emited by aircraft.

USS *Jefferson*: The star nuclear aircraft carrier in the US navy.

leading petty officer: The senior petty officer in a work-center, division, or department, responsible to the leading chief petty officer for the performance of the rest of the group.

LINK: *See* data link.

lofargram: Low Frequency Analyzing and Recording display. Consists of lines arrayed by frequency on the horizontal axis and time on the vertical axis. Displays sound signals in the water in a graphic fashion for analysis by ASW technicians.

long green table: A formal inquiry board. It's better to be judged by six than carried by six.

machinists mate: enlisted technician that runs and repairs most engineering equipment onboard a ship. Abbreviated as "MM" e.g. MM1 Sailor is a Petty Officer First Class Machinists Mate.

MDI: Mess Decks Intelligence. The heartbeat of the rumor mill inboard onboard a ship and the definitive source for all information.

MEZ: Missile Engagement Zone. Any hostile contacts that make it into the MEZ are engaged only with missiles. Friendly aircraft must stay clear in order to avoid a blue on blue engagement, i.e. fratricide.

MiG: A production line of aircraft manufactured by Mikoyan in Russia. MiG fighters are owned by many nations around the world.

Murphy, law of: The factor most often not considered sufficiently in military planning. If something can go wrong, it will. Naval corollary: Shit happens.

national assets: Surveillance and reconnaisance resources of the most sensitive nature, e.g. satellites.

NATOPS: The bible for operating a particular aircraft. *See* Envelopes.

NFO: Naval Flight Officer.

nobrainer: Used to signify an evolution or decision that should require absolutely no significant intellectual capabilities beyond that of a paramecium.

Nomex: Fire-resistant fabric used to make "shirts." *See* Shirts.

NSA: National Security Agency. Primarily responsible for evaluating electronic intercepts and sensitive intelligence.

OOD: Officer of the Day, in charge of the safe handling and maneuvering of the ship. Supervises the conning officer and other underway watchstanders. Ashore, the OOD may be responsible for a shore station after normal working hours.

Operations specialist: Formerly radar operators, back in the old days. Enlisted technician who operates combat detection, tracking, and engagement systems, except for sonar. Abbreviated OS.

OTH: Over the horizon, usually used to refer to shooting something you can't see. Targeting can be provided by virtually any other military platforms, including aircraft, satellites, or ground forces, or can be based on latitude and longitude.

P-3's: Shore-based anti-submarine warfare and surface surveillance long-range aircraft. The closest you can get to being in the air force while still being in the navy.

Phoenix: Long-range anti-air missile carried by US fighters.

Pipeline: Navy term used to describe a series of training commands, schools, or necessary education for a particular speciality. The fighter pipeline, for example, includes Basic Flight then fighter training at the RAG (Replacement Air Group), a training squadron.

Punching out: Ejecting from an aircraft.

purple shirts: *See* Shirts.

PXO: Prospective Executive Officer—the officer ordered into a command as the relief for the currect XO. In most squadrons, the XO eventually "fleets up" to become the commanding officer of the squadron, an excellent system that maintains continuity within an operational command—and a system the surface navy does not use.

rack: A bed. A rack-monster is a sailor who sports pillow burns and spends entirely too much time asleep while his or her shipmates are working.

red shirts: *See* Shirts.

RHIP: Rank Hath Its Privileges. *See* collar count

RIO: Radar Intercept Officer. *See* NFO.

RTB: Return to base.

S-3: Command and control aircraft sold to the navy as an anti-submarine aircraft. Good at that, too. Within the last several years, redesignated as "sea control" aircraft, with individual squadrons referred to as torpedo-bombers. Ah, the search for a mission goes on. But still a damned fine aircraft.

SAM: Surface to air missile, e.g. the Standard missile fired by most cruisers. Also indicates a land-based site.

SAR: Sea-Air Rescue.

SCIF: Specially Compartmented Information. Onboard a carrier, used to designated the highly classified compartment immediately next to TFCC.

Seawolf: Newest version of Navy fast attack submarine.

SERE: Survival, Evasion, Rescue, Escape; required school in pipeline for aviators.

Shirts: Color-coded Nomex pullovers use by flight deck and aviation personnel for rapid identification of a sailor's job. Green: maintenance technicians. Brown: plane captains. White: safety and medical. Red: ordnance. Purple: Fuel. Yellow: flight-deck supervisors and handlers.

Shoe: A black shoe, slang for a surface sailor or officer. Modernly, hard to say since the day that brown shoes were authorized for wear by black shoes. No one knows why. Wing envy is the best guess.

Sidewinder: Anti-air missile carried by US fighters.

Sierra: A subsurface contact.

sonobuoys: Acoustic listening devices dropped in the water by ASW or USW aircraft.

Sparrow: Anti-air missile carried by US fighters.

Spetznaz: The Russian version of SEALS, although the term encompasses a number of different specialties.

spooks: Slang for intelligence officers and enlisted sailors working in highly classified areas.

SUBLANT: Administrative command of all Atlantic submarine forces. On the west coast, SUBPAC.

sweet: When used in reference to a sonobuoy, indicates that the buoy is functioning properly, although not necessarily holding any contacts.

TACCO: Tactical Control Officer: the NFO in an S-3.

Tactical circuit: A term used in these books that encompasses a wide range of actual circuits used onboard a carrier. There are a variety of C&R circuits (coordination and reporting) and occasionally for simplicity sake and to avoid classified material, I just use the word tactical.

tanked, tanker: Navy aircraft have the ability to refuel from a tanker, either Air Force or Navy, while airborne. One of the most terrifying routine evolutions a pilot performs.

TFCC: Tactical Flag Command Center. A compartment in flag spaces from which the CVBG admiral controls the battle. Located immediately forward of the carrier's CDC.

Tombstone: Nickname given to Magruder.

Tomcat: The F-14 fighter operated by the seaborne military forces.

Top Gun: Advanced fighter training command.

Undersea Warfare Commander: In a CVBG, normally the DESRON embarked on the carrier. Formerly called the ASW commander.

VDL: Video Downlink. Transmission of targeting data from an aircraft to a submarine with OTH capabilities.

VF-95: Fighter squadron assigned to Airwing 14, normally embarked on USS *Jefferson*. The first two letters of a squadron designation reflect the type of aircraft flown. VF = fighters. VFA = Hornets. VS = S-3, etc.

Victor: Aging Russian fast attack submarines, still a potent threat.

VS-29: S-3 squadron assigned to Airwing 14, embarked on USS *Jefferson*.

VX-1: Test pilot squadron that develops envelopes after Pax River evaluates aerodynamic characteristics of new aircraft. *See* Envelope.

White shirt: *See* Shirts.

Wilco: Short for Will Comply. Used only by the aviator in command of the mission.

Winchester: In aviation slang, out of weapons. A winchester aircraft must normally RTB.

XO: Executive officer, the second in command.

yellow shirt: *See* Shirts.